ALSO BY ALICE ADAMS

Careless Love

Families and Survivors

Listening to Billie

Beautiful Girl (stories)

Rich Rewards

To See You Again (stories)

Superior Women

Return Trips (stories)

SECOND
CHANCES

SECOND CHANCES

A NOVEL BY

Alice Adams

ALFRED · A · KNOPF

NEW YORK 1988

THIS IS A BORZOI BOOK
PUBLISHED BY ALFRED A. KNOPF, INC.

Copyright © 1988 by Alice Adams
All rights reserved under International and Pan-American Copyright Conventions.
Published in the United States by Alfred A. Knopf, Inc., New York,
and simultaneously in Canada by Random House of Canada Limited, Toronto.
Distributed by Random House, Inc., New York.

Library of Congress Cataloging-in-Publication Data
Adams, Alice, [date]
Second chances.
I. Title.
PS3551.D324S44   1988   813'.54   87-35295
ISBN 0-394-56824-9

Manufactured in the United States of America
First Edition

for
Dorothy Funk Clark
Judith Clark Adams
and Timothy J. Adams

with much love

SECOND
CHANCES

1 Often January brings a strange false spring to much of northern California. Meadows and hillside are a violent, promising green, the landscape fairly undulates with green. And the air is pale and blue, deceptively soft, as though in fact there were to be no more winter, never any more rains, or cold.

On such a day, actually New Year's Day of 1985, two people, a man and a woman, can be seen to walk quite unsteadily across a field, on the outskirts of a town called San Sebastian, which is south of San Francisco and some miles inland from the Pacific Ocean. Both these walkers, in their long heavy coats, are very tall, and their wobbly gait suggests too much to drink, or possibly some extreme of passion (they could be weak with lust); however, they are in fact neither drunk nor lovers, but simply rather old. And they both have arthritis. Very old friends. And the ground beneath them is very wet indeed.

They are Dudley Venable and Edward Crane, and they are discussing another old friend, Celeste Timberlake, who is recently widowed, her husband, Charles, having died "after a long illness" at the end of the preceding November. And Celeste is acting very odd—or so her close friends see it.

"Celeste keeps reinventing her life," Edward pontificates, between difficult puffs of breath. "She keeps imagining alternatives. She lives in the past, which is *such* a mistake." He begins to cough as cautiously he and Dudley pick their way across the treacherous ground.

And with considerably more assurance (they are better at talk) they continue this highly pleasurable discussion of Celeste who—at her age, and with Charles just dead!—has taken on, apparently, a suitor, a beau. So far unseen by any of Celeste's close friends, he lives in San Francisco. And what could be described as Celeste's "silliness" in terms of Bill is what startles her friends; she who was always the soul and voice of propriety is now acting very—well, foolishly.

Regarding Edward with some anxiety—Dudley is a kind woman, and younger by some five years than he is—she continues his thought. "Well, yes, of course she does do that, she does live in the past, and reinvents. Or is it a question of finding new parts for herself? Still an actress, sort of? So very much the wife of Charles Timberlake when she was that, and now, God knows. This new person. It does seem a kind of acting out."

"I think it's more the same temperament that led her to act in the first place," Edward manages to say.

"Well, that's true."

Dudley and Edward are by now aware of sounding rather alike as they talk. Both from Boston, originally, they have been friends "forever." What they see less is that to others they even look somewhat alike. Thin but not fragile, strong-boned people, both given to hiking, tennis and summer swims, their skins are similar: now finely wrinkled but "out here in California" (both these transplanted New Englanders still say that) they maintain a constant light tan. But bald Edward, aware of Dudley's short thick gray hair, sees only that, and does not see himself in her at all. And Dudley, once herself a semi-alcoholic, is sure that Edward, with his longtime companion, still drinks too much; it shows in the ruddy color of his nose, his sometimes tremulous hands. Thank God she doesn't look like that, thinks Dudley. To anyone else, however, they could pass for brother and sister.

"In any case," sums up Edward as, by unspoken mutual agreement, they stop for a moment to rest. "In any case it is quite odd, this business of Bill. Somehow the last thing one would have expected."

"Very odd," Dudley agrees, aware that this is a thing she often says, and especially to Edward. "All those years with Charles she was so perfectly his wife."

"Only nineteen years of it, though," reminds Edward, who has lived with his friend Freddy for almost thirty. "And not exactly a girl when they got married."

"Still," says Dudley, "I think those were great years for her. Her favorite role, maybe? The wife of Charles Timberlake? You know she was crazy about him."

"A charming guy, who was not?" murmurs Edward, suddenly sad and feeling, just as suddenly, quite cold. "We all miss him. Dudley, are you cold?"

"Yes, I am."

"How about trying that new place for coffee? It's right down there."

"Would they be open? That would be wonderful, I could use some."

Warmed and cheered and invigorated by the very idea of coffee, Dudley and Edward walk on more quickly now, headed for semi-civilization, for one of the narrow white back roads that wind between the foothill mountains and the sea, that encircle their town. On one of these roads, they have heard, a new "old-fashioned" diner has just been opened.

It is in fact colder now as midafternoon becomes late; it is not only thoughts of Charles and of death that have made Edward feel the chill. Strange clouds, of some shade between dark gray and midnight blue, stretch across the sky like torn rags, and the sky itself has changed from soft blue to some odd non-color, intensely clear and cold, a shining blank.

Dudley, as she much too often does (and she chides herself), is thinking of sex. She is wondering: when Celeste goes off to San Francisco to spend time with this man (Dudley believes his name is Bill), whom she talks about in large, vague but impressive terms—just what do Celeste and this Bill do? (Assuming that Celeste does in fact spend time in San Francisco with someone named Bill.) And, for that matter, what did Celeste and Charles actually do, along those lines, married as they were in their middle fifties? Just oral sex? Dudley has heard this recommended as a possible course for the old.

Sexual habits are something that you don't know ever, really, about your good friends—or perhaps nowadays some people do know? They tell each other, and talk about these things?

Dudley only knows (with certainty) what she and her husband, Sam Venable, do in that way, and she smiles to herself, what could be described as a brave, sad smile. Her prayers and incantations, not to mention certain magic potions (commercially scented, and yet authentically magical), certain chemicals, "controlled substances," whatever: she'll try anything. The point is, they still sometimes do it, she and Sam. Not too often, and not always with total success, but still, still, they keep doing it.

Another thing you don't know about your close friends, generally, is what they *have*, in a medical sense. (This was so much the case with poor sick Charles, so proudly concealing his illness, with of course the adoring contrivance of Celeste.) Dudley continues this monologue in her own mind, Edward being clearly too winded still for conversation. But at their ages, hers and Edward's, and Sam's, and at Celeste's age (she is older than Dudley)—at all those ages health is quite naturally a prime concern. And they all have something: Dudley has high blood pressure, as well as arthritis, for which she refuses pills, relying instead on exercise and calming thoughts (when she can manage calming thoughts). Sam's pressure is even higher, his cholesterol count not good, and he is overweight. But what do Celeste and, for that matter, Edward have? Freddy is younger; he must be forty-something.

Dudley does not know what Edward has, nor why he coughs like that and has so little breath. And as for Celeste, the oldest of them all, no one has the faintest idea about the state of her health. A positive thinker, Celeste always says that she feels "simply wonderful," and God knows she looks and moves quite wonderfully, with her heavy silver-white hair, her huge brown-black eyes, so dark and brilliant, luminous. Her perfectly erect, small vigorous body.

At that moment Dudley is struck by a new thought that she is unable not to communicate to Edward. "Have you noticed how prudish we are about diseases, all of us?" she asks him. "Especially, uh, cancer? It's sort of the way we were about sex, a long time ago. Something not quite to be mentioned, something very much involving our bodies. Causing a lot of secret speculation."

By way of response Edward frowns, so that Dudley worries again about his cough: could she have said precisely the wrong thing? *Can* Edward have—?

Almost instantly, though, he reassures her. "Well, if you feel the same positive terror that I do every time I go for an examination, I don't mind telling you. Well, really, it's no wonder that we're prudish. I can't tell you the relief, just last week . . ."

But he looks very glum, and Dudley decides that she has indeed said a wrong thing; besides, she and Edward have never in their fifty-odd years of friendship had a talk about sex. How could they? No more than they could discuss cancer.

In motion again, walking along, they have slowed their pace considerably as the land slopes gently upward. They must crest a small hill before descending, finding the road. A small hill but by this time quite difficult to achieve, so that, once on top, "Ah!" they simultaneously say, with relief: a minor triumph.

Most immediately in their view now are their own houses, and those of their closest friends. Nestled among the nearest hills they can see the bright white narrow Victorian that Freddy and Edward share.

The big wooden house, once termed "contemporary," belonging to Dudley and Sam is hard to see, unless, as these two do, you know its exact location. It has weathered to a silver now that merges with the silvery landscape, as was intended by Sam, a painter.

Always most visible is the house that Celeste and Charles Timberlake fell romantically in love with, on first sight—to some of their friends, quite inexplicably: an ocher stucco, Italian-style small mansion, with balconies and turrets, vaulted windows—and a flying flag, which Charles explained as being obscurely Basque in origin. "And very likely, with all the recent ETA terrorism, its obscurity is just as well," Charles in the months before his death was heard to remark. A retired newsman, once a European *Time-Life* bureau chief, Charles "kept up," in a way that most of his elderly friends, and his wife, did not.

In the other direction, that of the small town of San Sebastian itself, they can just see a small house inhabited by a woman called Polly Blake, a close friend, and in her way a heroine among them all: a mysteriously admirable, if most eccentric woman, with her rattling old bikes, her crazy headscarves, and her rumored large trust fund.

Farther into the distance lies the town, a farming crossroads: a Safeway, a 7-Eleven, a dime store (these particular people still use that term), and three hardware stores, all specializing in various farm

supplies. The bulk of the town's population, mostly very poor Mexicans or Portuguese, live in small, bright-painted, mostly peeling one-
story houses near the center of town. A few have straggled westward,
out toward the coast, and these last are the poorest of all, the desperate, the almost forgotten.

Eastward, between the town and the central valley, Highway 101,
there are several quite prosperous farms, herds of cattle and sheep.
Thriving orchards, and acres of corn and alfalfa.

But Dudley and Edward from their green hilltop can see neither
the town nor the farms and the cottages of the poor. All they can see
is more green, brightly flowing across the gentle hills. They see spring,
in which they believe.

Just before starting downward on a well-worn, firmer path to the
highway, and to the alleged warm diner, their two glances for a moment lock. Affection, concern and a certain wry wit with regard to
each other are equally present in their look. It is possible that Edward
is more amused by Dudley than she by him. He was quite taken by
her notion of prudery as applied first to sex, and then to the truly
unmentionable disease—though at the time of its voicing a variety of
private anxieties (sexual, rather than concerned with disease, except
that these days the two are so linked, so horribly) was all that kept
him from a proper response.

Dudley does find Edward amusing, but she really likes him for
quite other, more complicated reasons, perhaps the strongest being
the sheer longevity of their connection; she revels in the range of
their frame of reference. No need ever to go back and explain anything to Edward; he was probably *there*.

Edward, even, was the first person to (almost) reconcile her to her
name, which especially as a young girl Dudley felt as a mockery: she
was so tall then, so skinny and generally sad; she did indeed resemble
quite strongly her rich Uncle Dudley, whose name she bore, with ill
grace. But, "I think Dudley has considerable style, as names go," said
nearsighted, bookish Edward, at the summer camp to which the two
of them, awkward adolescents from rich but "progressive" families,
had been sent. In Vermont, "about a thousand years ago." At night
they would retreat from the campfire into the shadows, the oldest
and youngest campers there, those two, while everyone else sat
around singing all those horrible songs with great vigor. Dudley then

began to like Edward very much. He is much nicer than the other boys, she thought; and the ones who call him a sissy are really jerks.

Later on in her life, Sam's deep-Southern (Louisiana) voice further redeemed her name, making it very beautiful, if multisyllabic.

"And then there is Sara," continues Edward, somewhat later, over hot and exceptionally flavorful coffee.

For along with her love affair with "this Bill," if love affair is what it is, at this time Celeste had proposed to more or less adopt a young woman named Sara, actually her goddaughter, and the true daughter of Celeste's own oldest friend, a woman named Emma, from northern California, where Celeste is also from, somewhere north of here. Emma died; they are vague about just when that was—some time before Charles's death, they think. Celeste always took the functions of a godmother very seriously; she was always very close to Sara until some sort of trouble arose between Sara and Charles, and Celeste (had she a choice?) took the side of Charles. And Sara, who used to visit long ago, is generally acknowledged to be difficult; she even spent time in a jail, in Mexico, during the sixties.

"We are now to see Celeste in her role as mother," Edward goes on. "She is as you say 'acting out' indeed, all over the place."

"She surely is," agrees Dudley. "But maybe it's all just a form of keeping busy, so as not to brood about Charles?"

"Well, yes, of course, Dud darling. The point is, though, the odd forms of her busyness. Some people just do needlepoint."

Dudley laughs. "Well, yes. But I think really we should all just admire Celeste. You know we always do, *au fond.*" The good coffee has caused her slightly lowered spirits to soar, suddenly: after years of striving to calm these swings of mood Dudley had concluded that she might as well enjoy them. Or that is her conclusion during upward phases. "Worrying over Celeste won't help her at all—nor us, for that matter. And just think how absolutely furious she'd be if she knew," Dudley continues excitedly. "She'd feel so condescended to."

"That's surely true," Edward speculates. "That's really one of the things we all really enjoy the most, though, isn't it? This worried clucking over our friends. The implication being that our own lives are exceptionally well run. We're terrific. They're, uh, fucking up."

Dudley laughs. Edward says words like "fuck" so very infrequently that they have a sort of comic force, coming from him. "You're absolutely right," she tells him. "So wonderful the way we mask our condescension as concern. We do it all the time, don't we?"

"Of course."

Like the coffee, the diner has turned out to be a welcome surprise. If either Dudley or Edward or both spent more time in San Francisco, which they do not, they would find its pattern familiar: lots of pale polished wood, bright brass fittings, and many dark red clay pots filled with enormous ferns. As it is, they think all this extraordinary, an unusual and interesting and attractive use of fairly simple materials.

And the young man who brought them their coffee, making offers of cinnamon toast (crumpets? bagels? croissants?), could also be viewed as a recent San Francisco type, with his soft brown beard, sad yellow-brown eyes, and gentle voice: a post-hippie, probably, mellowed out and mildly depressed. To both Dudley and Edward he seems quite remarkably nice: Edward also hopes that Freddy will not meet this person, and he resolves to insure that this will not happen—but how? oh dear, in this small town, just how?

Thinking in that unhappy way of Freddy, and in order to avoid even unhappier thoughts, Edward renews his lecture on Celeste. "The point is" (this is a phrase frequently employed by Edward, especially in conversations with Dudley)—"the point is that we seem to know less than nothing about this Bill. An importer, antiques, but just what on earth does that mean? Greek pottery? Iranian rugs?"

"Maybe something quite contraband. Maybe heroin? Cocaine?" Dudley means to be helpful.

"Darling, you're such a romantic. I'm sure this Bill is not of an age for drugs."

"Oh dear heaven, do you have to be young for that too?" Dudley laughs, with a rather stagy, quite false despair: actually she and Sam quite often smoke dope on Sunday mornings; it is one of their happiest rituals. Dope, sex, long naps and then an enormous, slightly exotic breakfast, pasta or something similarly non-breakfastlike, long after noon. Partly to change the subject, for naturally she tells no one of this practice (but now she wonders if Edward could possibly, somehow, *know*; and do he and Freddy, conceivably—?), briskly she says to Edward, "I do wonder what Sara's like now."

"Well, she must be thirty-something, mustn't she?"

Dudley, in many ways given to vagueness, has almost always a quite startling accuracy in regard to dates. "No, of course not. She's closer to forty—in fact she is forty, or she will be in April. I remember the day she was born. In 1945. It was when I met Sam." She blushes, aware of the blush and feeling very silly about it.

"Odd that none of us ever met this Emma, Sara always coming alone to visit," Edward muses. "Even small hints that there was no Emma, that Sara was the result of what we used to call an indiscretion."

"I don't believe that for a minute," Dudley tells him. "It's just Celeste making dramas. Besides, she used to read me letters from Emma—she wouldn't go so far as to make them up. It's just her revising things again, as you say. Not to mention her somewhat proprietary nature." She sniffs. "Besides, I did meet her once, in 1951."

Catching her intensity, although uncertain as to its cause, a little cruelly Edward carries on: "Well, it is strange, still. So much talk about this Emma, whom I at least never saw. And now this Bill, whom very likely we are never to meet at all."

"Well, it's a little late for you to meet Emma, she's dead, and probably we'll all be forced to meet Bill, and we won't like him at all. Honestly, Edward, you're sometimes as bad as Celeste is. Making mysteries when really it's all so simple. Celeste is just terribly lonely, and has taken up in some way with a man in San Francisco named Bill. And Sara's had nothing but trouble all her life, all that time in the Mexican jail, and God knows what else happened to her lately— Celeste invites her to come and stay." She repeats, "It's all terribly simple, really. You'll see how it is."

At that moment, perhaps fortunately, the attractive bearded young man again appears at their booth, announcing himself. "I'm David," he tells them. "In case you'd like anything else. More coffee?"

Both Dudley and Edward smile with surprise and genuine pleasure. As with the diner's décor, this custom, a waiter's proclaiming his name in a friendly way, is quite new to them (though of course very current and sometimes extremely annoying to many people elsewhere, at that time).

What a very nice boy, they both think. And Dudley, not really given to such meddling, generally, further thinks: He should be introduced to Sara. They must be about the same age, they might get along. Otherwise she could be very lonely here, with just us, and we're all so old for her.

Leaving the diner a little later, after not much further conversation—the walk has tired them both, indeed much more than either would admit—Dudley and Edward continue along the narrow white highway whose other, eastward direction is Salinas. They are heading westward, toward the coast, where an almost setting sun now blazes, blindingly. After a short walk they reach another, narrower highway, and there, at that crossroads, they separate. As always, with some ceremony.

They kiss *and* shake hands; they both say, "Goodbye, see you soon. Stay well."

2   "Oh, it feels like being on a ship!" This is what almost everyone says, with an air of wonderment and pleasure, on first coming into Sam and Dudley's house. Sam and Dudley are too polite and too tired to explain the obvious, that their house has the feeling of a boat because there's so much wood, the walls and high vaulted ceiling, everywhere wood. Bare wood, never waxed or polished but sometimes scrubbed, so that by now, some fifty years after the house was built, the effect is mellow, soft and rich. It is indeed like an old, extremely well built boat. A thirties yacht, perhaps.

Some people of course come to see that for themselves. "It's all the wood," they say. "Remember wooden boats?"

Polly Blake changed the formula a little by saying that to her it looked like a church, when Dudley and Sam first moved in. But then Polly is thought to be religious, possibly, in some curious, entirely private way of her own, and even Dudley and Sam, agnostics, can see the aptness of the association. Their house has the look of a New England church.

And they had been living in New England, in Maine, before moving out to California. There too, first married, they had fallen in love with a house—or, rather, recognized it as their own. They recognized its small compactness (so manageable) and the much larger barn for Sam's studio, with the enclosed connecting passageway for the months of deep snow, all perfect for their needs. Also, it was so far from everything in those pre-thruway days that no one else wanted it; it went very cheap, and the low mortgage payments left Dudley and Sam with a little money for time in New York, or Boston. All in all a good time for them, frequent fun. However, that house and that life had seemingly outlived their function; as they did not quite say to each other, the long, severe winters became more than they could cope with. It was time for a change. And so they came to California, first spending time in San Francisco, where they had fun, but decided it was not their city. And then they found the house in San Sebastian.

They made very few changes in all this wooden space with which they had fallen in love. No real remodeling. What little money they had left after buying it they spent on a big studio, mostly glass, for Sam, adjacent but not (this time) connected to the house. Dudley, a journalist-writer, works at a big desk in the living room, where she is frequently interrupted by Sam, who has just thought of some small thing to say to her. Believing him to be in serious trouble with his own work (he does only charcoal drawings these days, and not many of those; no large oils for years), Dudley for the most part is "nice" about these breaks in her own concentration; occasionally, however, uncontrollably she does snap out, "For Christ's sake, I didn't need to hear that right now!"

It depends, she has come to understand, very much on how her own work is going: the better she is doing, the more equable she is able to be with Sam. Still, she very much wishes she had a room of her own.

Sam's old paintings, all those not sold or currently housed in some gallery, are stored out there in his studio; there are none in the living room or anywhere else in the house, not a single "Sam Venable" on display, as there were none in Maine, this being one of Sam's somewhat eccentric principles.

In the living room there are, for decoration, only the very wide picture windows, with their peaceful view of green and gently sloping hills—quite a contrast to Sam's paintings, had there been any: his canvases tended to violence, jarring slashes of color and line.

There is, just now, far beyond the windows and above where the sea would be (had their view included the Pacific), a delicately peach winter sunset, an opalescent glow.

If what could be said to bother Dudley most, in a practical way, in her daily life is her lack of privacy for work, what most bothers Sam is their distance from the ocean, the ten or so miles, over hills. "*Crazy*," he laments. "To come all this distance and still be inland. We could be out on a bluff somewhere, overlooking rocks and crashing waves." However, he has more or less refused to look in a serious way for a seaside house. Nor does he like to drive over to the coast for a hike—one of Dudley's favorite things to do—on just such a romantic, craggy bluff as he likes to describe.

Dudley believes that men are more irrational than women are: what do they want?

However, both Sam and Dudley continue on the whole to be fond of their house, as they are generally content with their life in San Sebastian. Their friendship with Celeste has continued and deepened, and while Charles was alive he too was very much their friend; Dudley especially took to Charles, a most attractive man.

And it was Dudley who, a year or so after they had moved in, wrote to her closest, oldest friend, Edward Crane, and said that he must come out there; she and Edward had always half jokingly said that they would retire together. And, quite coincidentally, about that time Freddy was offered a teaching job in San Francisco. And so there they all were, plus Polly Blake, who was (or perhaps she was not, not at all?) one of the reasons for Charles and Celeste settling there in the first place.

No longer drinking (or hardly ever drinking), Dudley and Sam still have what they think of as their cocktail hour; what is actually drunk varies from time to time, their current favorite being a mixture of clam and tomato juice. Sometimes during these hours they talk, at others they both leaf through magazines, reading bits aloud to each other; it is Sam who is more apt to read, seemingly unable to remember that Dudley dislikes being read to. At other times (at worst, in Dudley's view) she talks, and Sam looks both at her and at his magazine, unseeingly. A man of exceptional, extreme politeness, generally, Sam is possibly then at his very rudest, and so Dudley refrains from complaint.

At the moment, though, Dudley is talking and Sam is listening in an interested, quite alert way.

"It's curious how rarely Edward mentions Freddy these days" was her opening salvo. "Really, in the couple of hours we spent together, I don't think once."

Sam laughs. A green-eyed, white-haired, considerably overweight man, he is still very handsome. And very confident. "You talk a lot about me?" he asks.

"Well, no, actually not. Or I don't think I do. You'd have to ask Edward." Dudley laughs. "I must at least have said your name."

Sam makes an assenting sound.

"Not that any of us do. Talk about Freddy, I mean. And I guess it is sort of embarrassing to poor old Edward, these days. All those years in the closet and then there's his lover out carrying placards. Heading Harvey Milk parades." Dudley sighs, mostly out of sympathy for Edward but also for Freddy, of whom she is fond. And she admires his recent stand.

"Poor old Edward." Sam's chuckle is affectionate; he too is very fond of Edward, and of Freddy.

Their voices, Sam's and Dudley's, both in tone and accent present extraordinary contrasts. Being so used to each other, to years of private conversations, this is not something of which they are conscious, but another person hearing them would be aware of an odd antiphony. Dudley's voice is both higher and softer, a sweet voice, really, more so than her somewhat weathered exterior would suggest. She sounds considerably younger than she is, and so Bostonian—still. Whereas Sam's voice is closer to what his appearance would suggest, the deep, raspy voice of a very large, aging man. His deep-Southern accent is as slow and courtly as Dudley's is pure Yankee.

"Oh dear," now quite suddenly says Dudley. "I'm doing exactly what I accused both Edward and me of doing this afternoon. I'm sounding so smug, I'm taking such pleasure in worrying over Edward."

"I think you're what Catholics call scrupulous." Indulgent Sam.

"Well, that can't be the worst thing to be." In a pleased way Dudley bridles; she likes this sort of teasing attention from Sam. And then, with a certain bravado, she tells him, "He and I were worrying over Celeste, naturally."

Sam's answering sound is wholly ambiguous.

"More of the same about 'Bill.'" Dudley telegraphs, meaning: None of us can understand what's going on, if anything. Who is this Bill?

"I guess we'll meet him sometime." Sam's voice is even vaguer than his words.

"Or maybe not? Maybe there isn't any Bill? Edward and I both thought of that."

Sam laughs at her. "You do make mysteries sometimes."

"Oh, that's just what I accused Edward of doing."

We are getting along better than usual, is one of the things that Dudley is thinking as they talk. We're in a good phase, she thinks. But is any phase, ever, final? She bears scars still from some of their worst old times, from horrifying words voiced violently between them, ugly drunken scenes. Dudley sometimes recalls all that with genuine fear, which is not exactly to say that she chooses to dwell on an ugly past (as Sam might say if he knew how often she thinks about all that); it is simply hard for her to believe that they are home free, as it were, that they have finally settled into a peaceful old age, as people are supposed to do. (Sam probably believes that they have. Of a happier disposition, generally, than Dudley is, he does not tend to "borrow trouble"; he even forgets that things ever have been bad.)

Neither Dudley nor Sam is drawn to explicit conversations about the nature of their "relationship" (a word that neither of them would ever use); their temperaments, though quite unlike, their early training and the fact of their generation all conspire to prevent confrontations—and just as well, either of them might easily say. Dudley would never, even now, for example, ask Sam: Well, were you and So-and-So ever actually lovers?—although she would surely have been interested in a true response. But, temperament and habit aside, several sound reasons argue against such a question. First, Sam would be genuinely shocked. And, second, if he did in fact have affairs with any of the women they both knew (which was highly possible, during or just previous to one of their many impassioned, horrendous separations), Sam would still say that he had not, his code being Southern-chivalric, at least in part.

Even, sometimes, with her own particular black self-torturing logic, Dudley has imagined that Sam and Celeste were lovers, in the old days, in New York. Well, why not? It was certainly impossible to deduce anything from their later relationship; Celeste treated Sam with the same friendly flirtatiousness that she used with all the men she liked. And Sam with Celeste was affectionately courtly.

Some time ago Dudley even considered or fantasized having an affair with Charles Timberlake, husband of Celeste, as a sort of rounding out of (possibly imagined) sexual connections. Also, more to the point, Charles was extremely attractive, though perhaps a shade too attractive? Lean dark elegant Charles, with his famously jutting eyebrows, was surely an antithesis to Sam, who tended to be messy, given to ragged sweaters, shabby tweed and baggy flannel. But nothing came of that plan, that fantasy—well, of course not, and how ridiculous, really, to have thought of it at all.

"Just when is Sara coming, actually?" Sam now asks. A slight surprise; Sam is apt to wait and more or less see what happens.

"Oh, well, that's another thing, Celeste's so vague about it all." Dudley finds herself a little breathless, and conscious of an oddity that she has observed before: these non-alcoholic cocktails still can make her a little drunk. "I think maybe she doesn't know when Sara's coming. Sara will simply arrive. You know how young people are." Dudley refers to Sam's four daughters by two earlier marriages. All four, no longer children, closer to middle age (and all four, curiously, lawyers), still tend to arrive inconveniently, to be vague as to plans.

"But Sara's not all that young," says Sam. Meaning, no doubt, that he *knows* his own girls are too old to behave as they do.

At just that moment, as Sam and Dudley regard each other for an instant, slightly unwelcome thoughts on both their faces, into their silence the phone begins to ring. As always, too loudly. Jarring.

Sam says, "I'll get it," and he lumbers toward the hall, just catching it on the third loud ring. "Oh, hello, honey. Well, honey, how've you been?"

Celeste. Sam calls her honey because she says she hates it, or so Sam says; Dudley believes that it is really because he likes her so much. As he speaks, Dudley hears the familiar teasing in his voice, the old affection—although he says very little beyond "Yes," "Yes," and, once or twice, "Oh, really?"

Looking out into what is now pure blackness, beyond the glass, Dudley thinks that she should go in to baste her chicken; she can just catch its garlicky aroma. But phone calls are rather like visits, she reflects; they make you less lonely, even when you are two people, who in theory should never feel alone. And then she has a fearsome thought, the most impermissible thought of all. She thinks, Oh, what will I do if Sam should die before I do? She prays, she murmurs (to no one), "Oh, please, couldn't we just go together, please? Don't let Sam leave me again."

Because, in their worst times, that is what Sam always did: he left her. In the middle of a quarrel, he would rush to the door, rush out into the night and away, away for days, weeks, months. And this leaving came to be Dudley's greatest fear—although when they spoke of it Sam claimed it was the sensible thing to do: "Why stick around to get hit? You can look pretty dangerous when you're angry, lady." He did not always leave when they fought; more often he stuck around for his own share of shouting, accusations. But those quick and total departures haunted Dudley. As sometimes, these days, she is haunted by fear of his death.

Returning from the phone all smiles and affability (this is an effect that Celeste often has, on many people), Sam announces the news: "Well, some of your mysteries seem about to be cleared up. Sara is getting here next month. In early February. And Celeste is giving a Valentine's dinner for her. Why Valentine's I've no idea."

"Oh, you know Celeste. She likes holidays. Celebrations."

"Sure, but why Valentine's? Anyway, she said that the person you refer to as 'this Bill' will be there too."

Startled, Dudley nevertheless at that moment remembers, again, her chicken. And gets up and starts toward the kitchen.

Sam follows her, still talking. "So you see? We do get to meet him, after all."

Bending down to the oven, breathing in steam along with the heavy aroma of herbs, the rosemary and lemon along with the garlic, Dudley just gets out "He might always be somehow not able to come."

Sam again makes an ambiguous sound. He has begun to put some dinner things on the round oak kitchen table, where they always eat when they are alone—stainless-steel cutlery, very bright and plain, and bright cotton napkins, unironed. And the room itself is large and bright and rather plain: gently weathered bare wood on walls and shelves and counters. Wide windows. It could all have been calculated (possibly unconsciously) to look as little as possible like the houses in which Dudley and Sam grew up: her parents' narrow Georgian, with its lavender leaded windows, rooms filled with mahogany and cut glass and heavy silver; Sam's family's drab Victorian country farmhouse, up the river from New Orleans, bayou land.

Standing up, Dudley is aware that sudden shifts in position are harder for her these days; in her back something suddenly hurts. But as usual she manages to speak banteringly. "I'll make you a small bet," she says to Sam. " 'Bill' somehow won't show up. There'll be something about a business trip. A suddenly dead relative, or something. So there'll be just us."

"And Sara," Sam reminds her.

"Well, Sara's one of us, isn't she?"

"Well, I suppose she must be. She's probably Celeste's heir, in fact." Saying that, Sam grins with what Dudley recognizes as his look of provocation. "Unless there really is a Bill, this person you seem to think Celeste's made up. A real Bill, whom Celeste has it in mind to marry?"

So that Dudley remembers. One day, not long after Charles died, Dudley and Celeste ran into each other at the local post office—a common enough occurrence in small San Sebastian. They stood there in line together, wanting stamps; Celeste had a letter to be registered. "I always register letters to my lawyer," she distractedly whispered to Dudley, in her way. (As though anyone in town would care about or understand her dealings with her lawyers, Dudley not very kindly thought.) And then, pushing at some vagrant strand of hair, her eyes raised to meet Dudley's eyes, Celeste, still in a whisper, said to Dudley, "Of course now everything will go to you and Sam. And Sara. So be sure to outlive me, darling Dudley."

An impossible statement to respond to. Dudley made a sound of embarrassment, confusion. Denial. She changed the subject to the weather, the lovely fall that they just then were having. How long could it last?

* * *

But now all that she did not report back to Sam comes vividly to Dudley's mind, and in a horrified way she thinks, Have I been denying the existence of this Bill because I want to inherit from Celeste? To get half, of whatever? An intolerable thought, at which she frowns—she makes a small involuntary sound, an *oh*, which in her connotes extreme embarrassment, self-censure.

Sam so often reads Dudley's mind (or they so often seem to have thought of precisely the same thing at the exact same moment, as must be true of many people, long together) that Dudley sometimes takes steps to avoid just this process of thought transference, or whatever. Not wanting Sam to know that she has even considered inheriting from Celeste, she says to him, "We really know so little about Celeste, when it comes right down to it." She has thought and quite possibly said just this before, surely to Edward, who speaks her language, and maybe also to Sam. However, no matter.

"You mean, who her people were?" This is said teasingly: Sam teasing Dudley's Boston past, where certainly one would have known. But the same could surely be said of Louisiana.

"Oh Sam." Dudley's standard response to teasing. "I suppose I do mean that. But she's as mysterious in her way as this Bill. But tell me more about the party. Edward and Freddy?"

"Yes, she said she was just going to call them. But I think she plans some really big old bash. Maybe sort of like the last one." At this he gives Dudley a look that is not exactly of accusation but rather a reminder that at the last big party of Celeste's, while Charles was still alive, Dudley drank, drank much too much, and was up to some sort of mischief (Sam has never actually said this, but Dudley can read him) with a fellow down from Marin, guy name of Brooks Burgess. A damn silly name, in Sam's view.

Partly to forestall any conversation about that party (a topic they must have exhausted: actually Sam drank too much too, and he told a perfectly nice woman that she was a harridan, and spoiled rotten, to boot), Dudley goes on even more about Celeste.

"Whatever is happening with this Bill is fairly crazy," she tells Sam. "He takes her to these incredibly expensive places, I'm a little afraid that's part of his charm for her. Assuming always that there really is a Bill, whom she actually sees. But do you know? Sometimes when we're talking on the phone, you know, the way we always do, she tells me that she has to get off, Bill might call. Or even that she can't come out for tea, she's expecting a call. She waits for his calls! At her age. Talk about acting girlish."

"Well, after all, poor girl" is Sam's more kindly, if somewhat inconclusive comment.

As Dudley thinks: How awful—could I possibly be like that, ever, again?

3   Freddy, whose real name is Fernando Fuentes, comes from Mexico City, originally. A small, dark man, compact and tightly built, with regular, tidy features, in his early youth he could have been described as pretty. And he was so described, by some of Edward's less kindly friends. "That pretty little boy of Edward's." To Edward he was and is, simply (or not simply at all) quite beautiful. Long ago, soon after first meeting Freddy, Edward to Dudley wrote somewhat plaintively (to Dudley, very movingly): "Freddy is so beautiful that people tend to accord our connection less dignity than it deserves."

Edward has also had occasion to think of Auden's lines: "Mortal, guilty, but to me, / The entirely beautiful."

Just now, having spoken to Celeste and returning from the phone, Edward sees Freddy in the lamplight, at the far end of their tufted brown sofa, and he is struck by the dark perfection of that face—as far too often Edward is struck, he thinks, by Freddy's beauty; he is thus kept vulnerable. Also, in the linen-shaded lamplight, Freddy looks much closer to forty, or even thirty-five, than to the fifty that he almost is.

For a variety of reasons Edward says none of this to Freddy; instead he announces, "Well, at last we get to meet the mysterious Bill. Celeste's Bill. Whom Dudley will not believe actually exists."

"Dear Dudley" is Freddy's only comment. The friendship between Freddy and Dudley is warm, but at certain times a little strained—possibly because, first passionately in love with Edward, Freddy experienced a dark, Latin jealousy of all Edward's friends. But for the most part he and Dudley get along quite well these days.

"A Valentine's dinner, of all things," Edward continues. "Can you imagine?" As he thinks: Why in God's name do we have to sound so silly with each other? Two intelligent men, who in their ways care a lot about each other, but we go on and on like aging queens. Especially me. And he further thinks: We avoid all major issues. Can we no longer afford them?

The issue just now being avoided is that of the night before, which was New Year's Eve, and which Freddy spent in San Francisco. At a meeting to discuss the possible closing of gay bathhouses. The meeting went unmentioned in this morning's paper, Edward was half-gratified to note; after such events in which Freddy (Fernando to those friends: no one here in San Sebastian calls him Fernando except, puzzlingly, Polly Blake), Freddy-Fernando, is increasingly involved, Edward often imagines a huge and appallingly clear news photograph: Freddy embracing another man, or some boy.

On the other hand, poor Freddy was no doubt disappointed at the lack of publicity for his cause—in which, after all, basically Edward also believes.

Edward has no idea whether he is more terrified of Freddy's being with another man in a sexual way or of Freddy's dying of AIDS: he fears that the two terrors are almost equal, in his mind. Since he and Freddy no longer make love (they simply stopped, gradually, some time ago, for no specific reason—and again, something never discussed between them), Edward does not think of the possibility of AIDS for himself.

Last night Freddy came home at an eminently sensible hour, though; Edward heard his car and then Freddy himself shortly after midnight. That would mean that he must have left San Francisco at about ten-thirty. Edward, lying awake despite resolutions to the contrary, considered getting up, saying Happy New Year, even suggesting champagne. But he did not, mainly not wanting to admit that he was awake, that he was in fact waiting up. Still, Edward now observes that Freddy looks rather tired.

But suddenly (and why?—why just then?) with an enormous effort Edward does manage to ask, "It went all right, last night?"

Visibly surprised at the question, Freddy, after a short look at Edward, turns a little away and frowns. "Actually not too great," he says.

Gratified in ways that he does not choose to examine just now, Edward comments, "Oh? That's too bad."

"Well, as you can imagine it's terribly complicated." As always, Freddy's whole body is eloquent; his tight shoulders suggest concentration as his small, elegant hands gesture complexity, discouragement. (He is somewhat like Celeste in this, Edward has observed; once an actress, in a rather minor way, Celeste still makes statements with her gestures.)

Freddy shifts on the sofa, so that once more he faces Edward fully as his posture announces an intention to confide. "It's so complicated," he repeats, with more emphasis. "And confused. You know, you'd probably agree, that closing the baths is not really a homophobic move. And even if it does only a little good, it might be worth it."

Cautiously: "That's very possible," says Edward.

"We have to face it, that kind of sex these days is suicidal." Freddy has averted his face from Edward's for a moment, but now he comes back. "There's a lot of pretty violent and simplistic thinking going on," he says. "Some of which includes the rather odd notion that AIDS was invented by Jerry Falwell. Not to mention our wonderful President and some of his old cronies."

Still cautious, Edward laughs.

"But to make it more complicated," Freddy continues, "there's the obvious fact that closing the baths may not do any good at all. Guys who're really into that sort of thing." A wry smile. "The suicidal promiscuous types will go right on doing their thing. As one says. And then there're the civil libertarians who say it'll very likely do more harm than good. You can get lost in all this. You know, the best lacking all conviction."

"Well, as you say, it is difficult. And complicated," Edward agrees. He is experiencing a surge of pure happiness, though, from the sheer fact of their conversation. They talk quite a lot, of course, but so often it is simply concerned with practicalities: what to have for dinner, what needs fixing around the house. Or fairly silly gossip. Slightly malicious bitch talk.

Edward has imaginary conversations about serious matters with Freddy. About poetry, for instance. As a very young man, he published one small book of verse—not distinguished, in his own view.

Since then he has tried, and tried, to write more, better poems. On moving to San Sebastian, since Freddy was to teach in San Francisco, Edward in a burst of practicality went out and got his real-estate license; real estate seemed something he could do in a part-time way, and still write. However, these days he accomplishes very little along either line, few finished poems, and possibly even fewer houses sold. (Charles used to tease Edward about being a one-man anti-growth movement for San Sebastian.)

Nor, come to think of it, does Freddy talk to Edward much about his teaching job—at which Edward assumes he is bored.

Over the past few years, the years of Freddy's emergence as an outspoken gay activist, there have been, though, some stiff arguments between the two of them about being "out," as Freddy would put it. Edward thinks of this as simply coming to terms with one's sexual orientation, but Freddy points out that that is not quite the same thing; according to Freddy, it is characteristic of Edward only to think of his own private life.

Most of these arguments, then, have been neither pleasant nor conclusive. "But I've always accepted being queer," Edward has said, deliberately choosing that word—and not quite speaking the truth. "I have never pretended otherwise. I just don't choose to wave flags."

And Freddy has countered, "With the Religious Right still around, and fag-bashing on Polk Street, and all over, not to mention AIDS, maybe it's time to wave some flags." Freddy scowling, very heated.

Freddy now sounds, though, as if all that had been somehow resolved, as if Edward were in fact "out." (Edward himself is unable to hear that phrase without recalling his mother's use of it—to signify Boston girls who had made their début. And sometimes, ludicrously, along with the words there comes a mad vision of himself in pink tulle, a small drag princess, at a coming-out party in Beverly Farms, his parents' country place. He is not entirely sure that Freddy would think this was very funny. And so he has never told him.)

Some time ago, someone even older than Edward now is (Who—when? Was it Charles? Celeste? Edward can't remember: *does* he have Alzheimer's?)—someone said that in old age it takes less to make you miserable, but also much less to make you happy. He now considers the truth of that remark, as he finds himself so extremely pleased at the tone and the turn of this dialogue with Freddy. He chooses, however, to ascribe his pleasure to another cause.

"You must admit," he joyously admonishes Freddy, "that our room looks better and better. You could say it's aging well. Even coming into its own."

At which Freddy smiles, agreeing.

For although their house and all its contents are owned in common, Edward can and does credit himself with its décor. And he is right about their house, and especially this living room, which is warm and comfortable and very beautiful. Mainly, everything there looks as if it has been there forever: the velvet sofa, dark red leather chairs, the "good" Oriental rugs, brown Calvin linen draperies. The walls of books, shelves of records and tapes. The chastely framed line drawings, which, closely inspected, turn out to be very good indeed: a small but exquisite Picasso, a male nude; more nudes by Seurat (very early Seurat). A Paul Wonner still life. An oil (more nudes) by Theophilus Brown.

Edward and Freddy, from this narrow, high Victorian house, have much the same view as that of Dudley and Sam from their architecturally so dissimilar house: hills, now in almost total darkness, only a couple of lights from distant houses visible. But they can see lights both from Celeste's and from Dudley and Sam's. Polly Blake's house is too far away, too close to the village, for her friends to see her lights.

"You're absolutely right, this is a perfect room." Freddy smiles his pleasure at the room, his appreciation of it. And returns to their more familiar mode of conversation, or one of their modes. "Sara coming to live with Celeste will make quite a difference in our social life, such as it is," he says, and gives a small laugh.

In fact, their social life consists of a curiously formal exchange of dinners, lunch parties—quite ritualized as to their order, as to who owes whom. On rare occasions, people from San Francisco and environs have been imported by one host or hostess or another, but this has generally led to trouble, and is regarded as a risk.

"I guess Sara will be there at Valentine's, along with Bill?" now asks Freddy.

"So Celeste says."

"And Polly?" Freddy asks. For reasons that none of the others have quite worked out, not even Edward, Freddy and old Polly Blake are markedly close friends. True pals. The fact that they both speak Spanish is not quite an explanation, it is felt, since they do not always speak it with each other. Polly, somewhat mysteriously, speaks an exceptionally fluent Castilian; and Freddy, the professor of Spanish and Portuguese, speaks a variety of dialects, mostly South American.

"I guess. I'm afraid it'll be another huge bash." But, saying this, Edward still smiles, in a private way: he has his own memory of the last big party given by Celeste. His last tiny love affair, his one and only act of infidelity to Freddy, and he has always wondered if somehow Freddy knew.

"Well, you must admit, the last was rather fun." Freddy says this with a certain innocence, however; or maybe he had some good time on his own?

"I wonder if this Bill will really show up" is what Freddy says next.

"Funny, that's almost exactly what Dudley said. She thinks he won't."

"Well, Dudley's not all bad, I never said she was. She just talks so much. And this Bill of Celeste's is probably some tearing old queen. Importer, my eye."

Edward laughs. He is uneasy, though, at this return to their more usual tone. However, "What an idea," he contributes.

"You must admit, quite plausible? It's a little hard to see our dear Celeste as anyone's sex object, don't you think? And heaven knows she does at least look rich." Freddy then adds, "But what isn't plausible, these days."

"Oh, right."

And then Freddy asks, "It is true—isn't it?—that Sara's Celeste's only heir, or heiress, whatever?"

"Well, I think so. What with Charles not having any children either. But I think somehow Dudley and Sam would come into it too. Assuming always that there's something to come into." Descended from lines of New England bankers on both sides, Edward is almost involuntarily knowledgeable about such things, as though such information came along with his genes.

Freddy laughs. "Suppose she marries this Bill? She's surely acting like a woman in love. Getting her hair done every week in Watson-ville—I get that information courtesy of Polly, who thinks it's funny. All these new clothes. She even giggles. But her marriage would really throw everything out of kilter, wouldn't it?"

Edward looks at him oddly. "Again, that's just what Dudley said. You two must be in tune, somehow. But I do agree, anything's possible. Given Celeste's addiction to fantasy. And really, I think she misses Charles so much that it's made her dizzy."

He smiles, and after the smallest hesitation asks Freddy: "Speaking of dizzy, shouldn't we have some champagne? After all, it is New Year's Day."

"But why not? As you always say, it is the perfect apéritif." Freddy's tone is teasing but very affectionate.

"Heavens, do I always say that?"

"No, but you used to. It's something you taught me."

Their eyes lock: a small moment of great affection.

And as Freddy goes off toward the kitchen for the wine, Edward even thinks, I will tell him about my coming-out dream, my pink tulle nightmare. He will laugh, and we'll both drink just a little too much wine.

And it will have been a good evening together, after all.

4 Polly Blake's house is much smaller and closer to the town of San Sebastian than the other houses of this particular group of friends. Her house in fact looks very much like the poorer houses of her neighbors: a square, vine-covered stucco box, with a falling-down trellis on one side, an even more dilapidated garage where Polly keeps her succession of bikes: Polly does not drive, and her bikes are always fallen apart or stolen, she doing little to prevent either fate.

Inside, the ceiling of her living room is low, and the hardwood floors uneven, but the rugs, if somewhat threadbare, are handwoven and beautiful—a few from the Yucatán, most from Spain. And the exposed wood of what furniture there is, a desk, a table, a couple of chairs, is walnut, old and highly, very lovingly polished. Another large rug covers what serves as Polly's sofa, which is also her bed. On this rug, this bed, there are usually at least two or three of Polly's five quite variously handsome cats. All former strays, now sleek with love and good food, and vitamins. Two tabbies, female; a big black tom; a fat brown female, vaguely Burmese; and an orange kitten, the newest addition.

An eccentric house, then, for a woman whom Celeste believes to have come from much more money, originally, than any of them did. But this is simply a theory of Celeste's, possibly a story she has invented to try to explain Polly Blake.

And some explanation for Polly would seem to be needed: of them all, these close, rather homogenous people, least is known about Polly. She is friendly enough, a "warm" person, who speaks very openly about everything except herself. Why doesn't she drive, for example?

And when and where did she learn such perfect Spanish? She never mentions having lived in Spain—or, for that matter, Mexico or South America. Has she ever been married, had lovers? Is she "gay"? And if she did have money, as Celeste believes, what in fact has she done with it all?

The only thing known for sure is that Polly had cancer, of a terrible, usually fatal sort: pancreatic. And she survived. (This information was given by Polly to Celeste as a form of present, a true gift, recognized and received by Celeste as such—a kind of palliative to Celeste's own cancer phobia, which has always been severe, her darkest nightmare. She suffers chronically, acutely from this fear.)

The several unknowns, then, about Polly's life, about which her friends still sometimes speculate (and Polly, highly intuitive, is aware of those speculations; they amuse her)—everything would be made quite clear if anyone knew about the two years, 1947 and 1948, that Polly spent in Spain as a border-crosser, a smuggler for the Loyalist underground—and as the part-time lover of Charles Timberlake. None of which Polly is about to tell anyone, obviously. Celeste knows that Polly met Charles when Charles lived in Paris with his second wife, rich Jane, but Celeste has been told, by Charles, that Polly and Jane were college friends. And Freddy certainly knows that Polly has traveled and spent some time in Spain, but he has no notion what she was doing there.

None of them can imagine their tall, bony, very eccentric and half-bald old friend, Polly, as a strong, good-looking (not beautiful but very striking), shy, almost silent young woman. With heavy dark hair and pale skin, and remarkably wide, intense pale blue-gray eyes.

There is much to be said against a violent sensual experience that arrives somewhat late in life, especially if it be one's first: the sex itself is taken much too seriously, is perceived as a cataclysm, and is thought to be love. All this happened to Polly in her late thirties, as she fell in love with clever, good-looking, manipulative Charles Timberlake. Polly made a hero of him, for a while. And, more disastrously, she made the (unhappily fairly common) mistake of believing that Charles felt and reacted to everything that happened between them exactly as she did.

They met at one of those crowded, frantically festive post–World War II parties in New York to celebrate someone's return from the wars, as it was then somewhat ironically put. The someone in this case was Charles Timberlake himself; he had been in Paris during the war as a news-bureau chief, and was now going back to Paris to work for UNESCO. A leftward move, this was viewed as, and thus the presence of Polly, whose small inheritance (Celeste was wrong on that score) allowed her to work, barely paid, for a small left-literary magazine.

But why Charles, why Charles for Polly, who had never "been with" anyone before? And why that particular drab November afternoon? Impossible to work it out; Polly never could, and neither, for that matter, could Charles, the surprised and somewhat reluctant recipient of a major passion, a total dedication, the only form of true love that literary-radical Polly could conceive of.

Charles was only to be in New York for a week on that visit, his wife and children having stayed in Paris. (Jane, the wife, actually had gone to Vassar, as Polly had, but just enough earlier, four years, so that they had not in fact known each other.) Charles counted himself lucky indeed to have met this dark, deep-breasted young woman—if slightly overintense for his taste—with the extraordinary eyes, and the nice big uptown apartment in the East Eighties. Alone. Polly then, as always, lived alone, sleeping in an uncomfortable single bed— a high, spooled bed, from Maine.

From the beginning, the ferocity of Polly's response to him was startling to Charles. A skillful, highly experimental lover, he was used to more difficult, if not genuinely passive women, hard-to-please beauties, semi-frigid débutante hysterics, or pitifully nervous secretaries. Whereas with Polly—making love to her was like falling off a cliff, Charles sometimes thought. Falling into a thrillingly dangerous void. He was at the same time horrified and deeply flattered to learn that he was the first.

It was Polly's idea, of course, that she come along to Paris. Charles had said that he was married, being in his way an honest man, and when Polly proposed Paris he reminded her that seeing each other there would present certain problems. However, he also felt himself compelled to show enthusiasm: how marvelous of her to come to Paris, he could not wait to see her there. (He had to say all this; it was the level on which they spoke.) He was very grateful to discover that his divorcing Jane did not seem to be among Polly's expectations.

And so Polly came to Paris, and through some college friend she even achieved a borrowed apartment, not far from the Trocadero. Not far from UNESCO.

Charles did not—at no point did he—actually suggest the driver job for Polly: transporting certain outlawed Loyalists back into Franco's Spain, across the just opened but heavily guarded border. He did not, he would not have mentioned all that simply to get Polly out of Paris. Although later it may have struck both of them that Charles did precisely that.

At the time it seemed quite accidental. Charles simply described a man who had been in his office that afternoon, Juan Salido, a refugee from the Generalissimo. Poor, desperately poor, saturnine, embittered but perpetually hopeful Juan, with one leg gone, and a cough. Juan was why Charles was late in coming to Polly that afternoon, which may have led Charles somewhat to overdo this sympathetic description. "The poor man," he had said, and sighed. "He'd give his life or what's left of it for a couple of days in Madrid."

And almost immediately Polly responded, "Well, why don't I drive him there? He could hide in the trunk of my car. I've been wanting to go to Spain." And Polly's pale eyes flashed as she thought this out. Aroused, her eyes flashed like opals, Charles had thought, and had said to her: pale fire opals. But this did not seem the moment for repeating that remark.

Instead he said, "But, my darling girl, it would be dangerous. I really couldn't let you—"

"I'll be all right. I'm a terrific driver." And she added—seriously, passionately—"I love you, Charles."

Along with the use of the friend's apartment Polly had the use of a large American car, a sky-blue Nash Ambassador, with bulbously swollen sides. And an ample trunk. It was soon decided, though, that the trunk was dangerous: so obvious, in terms of search, as well as extremely uncomfortable for an already sick and miserable man. The three of them discussed all this: eager Polly; worried Charles (had he somehow outsmarted himself? Was the plan a little too good, too advantageous for himself?); and sad Juan, who was actually about the same age as Charles, in his late thirties, but looking and no doubt feeling at least ten years older.

The experience of driving Juan—and then Paco, Enrique, Andrés, Carlos, until she began to forget the names—of being stopped and each time successfully passing herself off as an upper-class young American, an innocently lost tourist (asking questions in a certain panicked "female" way was a great ploy, Polly soon discovered), but being always so entirely frightened that she developed colitis, as well as mysterious joltings in the region of her heart—all that made Polly come to think of "love" in quite a new way. And sex: there too her views underwent radical change.

She began to feel that the deep, intensifying multiple spasms that she experienced as she received Charles's member, his hand or his tongue were simply not world-shaking, as previously she had seriously felt that they were: they were simply body-shaking. They had mostly to do with friction, healthy tissues rubbing against each other. Friction and her own romantic preconceptions. She began to recognize that in bed with Charles she did not have mystical experiences, just sexual ones.

Which is not to say that Polly began to dislike either Charles or sex itself. She continued for some time to see Charles, and they continued to make love; and she continued for many, many years with what would surely be counted an active sexual life. However, driving down from San Sebastián (Spain) to Burgos, observing the beautiful changes from mountains to plains, with Juan huddled, blanket-wrapped, coughing, on the narrow back seat, she began to realize that she was more concerned with Juan (or Enrique, or Pablo, none of whom she ever made love to, ever, nor even thought of with "love," in that sense) than she was with Charles. Whatever was meant by "in love," and she suspected, au fond, very little, she was no longer in love with Charles. Nor did she ever after that in her life imagine herself "in love."

Some men quite liked this attitude in Polly, her enthusiastic acceptance of sex as a considerable pleasure, her lack of emotional concomitants. It was how they believed that they themselves reacted.

More often, however, the men involved with Polly accused her of coldness: no matter what it was that they themselves felt, they wanted her to be—or felt that she should be—giddily, vulnerably, even demandingly "in love."

Handsome, fairly spoiled Charles was of course the first member of the latter group.

"I think you don't love me anymore," he began to complain. Intending a light, ironic tone, he instead conveyed high seriousness, sincerity—no doubt because he was indeed quite serious, and troubled by this new Polly.

This was a post-Paris conversation, in New York, at Polly's new apartment, above a liquor store in the then unfashionable East Thirties. A turgidly, killingly hot July afternoon: Charles had not gone out to Long Island (Sag Harbor, before that became fashionable) with Jane, just in order to spend some time with Polly; he was therefore less than pleased when just after making love Polly got up to shower, to start dressing, and announced that she had an appointment. Charles knew his Polly; he knew that the appointment was more apt to be political, or connected with good works, than amorous. But still.

"But I told you you'd have to go. You didn't believe me." Her gentle, firmly confident voice.

"You don't love me," sweating Charles repeated. "Or not as you used to."

This was of course acute, and so "Well, maybe not," confessed honest Polly. "But mightn't that be just as well?"

And that was more or less the end of Charles and Polly as lovers. They sometimes met at parties, at fund-raisers for Henry Wallace, whom they both supported; at Spanish refugee fund-raisers, the sort of social-political party mix that fairly often occurred in the generally good-hearted, victory-celebrating, getting-rich late forties.

During the Cold War days, starting in the early fifties, Polly's meetings with friends were necessarily much more guarded. Never even close, herself, to being a C.P. member, she knew quite a few people who had been, years back, and who now were seriously endangered. Her lovers of this time included a physicist who had opted out of the Manhattan Project, a blacklisted screenwriter. A Soviet defector, a Hungarian psychoanalyst.

Whereas Charles's life took an increasingly safe and "social" direction. Later he was never sure that he had been told that eccentric Polly had moved to California, after a serious illness: ". . . lost all her hair—but that's frightful, I must get in touch with her" had been his reaction, except that he did not get in touch with her, being by then too preoccupied with Celeste—or if not with Celeste yet, with someone, with someone not bald.

And when Charles and Celeste themselves moved to San Sebastian, where Polly was, the coincidence of Charles and Polly's having known each other before was explained as just that, a coincidence, which of course it was. And their connection was explained as having been through Jane, handy Vassar Jane, Charles's second wife.

Thus Celeste was allowed her assumptions, and Charles took on his final role, or roles, in Polly's life: first as the adored and adoring husband of a friend, and then as the terribly ill, soon-to-be-dying friend, to whom Polly behaved with infinite, unsparing kindness, even performing certain nurse chores (well, bedpans), between nurses, that Celeste could not quite bring herself to do.

"Darling Polly, how good you are," Celeste would tearfully say. "It's just that—well, since I've so much loved him, in that way, you know—"

"Of course, I really don't mind," Polly told her.

Once, startlingly, when Polly was administering to his needs, alone with Charles in the hospital, he suddenly spoke to her, saying, as before, "But, Polly, you don't love me anymore."

"But, Charles. Yes, I do."

He smiled. "But not in the old way."

"Well, not quite, Charles." Smiling back.

After Charles died, it was hard for Polly to believe that that exchange had actually taken place, and certainly she spoke of it to no one, ever, for no one in San Sebastian (California) ever had a hint of Polly and Charles as lovers, which would have struck them all as quite preposterous.

And now, in her almost old age, Polly has yet another clandestine occupation, unknown to her friends and to the world at large. Clandestine, infrequent, and sometimes quite frightening.

It goes like this. First, as though she were being observed, with extreme caution, from a hidden compartment (a narrow oblong slot) behind the creaking bottom drawer of her desk, she extracts a large package of hundred-dollar bills. Not counting them out, she subtracts a considerable sheaf from the pile, puts the rest back into hiding, then wrapping the sheaf in foil.

Polly then envelops herself in heavy sweaters, a sheepskin coat, some thick scarves; carrying the folded bag, pushing it into the pocket of her coat, she goes outside, out into the cold, the densely fogged and starless night—not locking the door behind her. From the falling-down garage she brings out her latest bike. (Always bought second-hand, they are probably "hot," as Polly likes to put it to herself. Neither Celeste nor the rest of the local friends would find this funny.)

And then she is off, down the rutted, familiar, quite precarious road (although this is not really the dangerous part, a broken head or a collarbone or an ankle being all that is risked, at this point, in Polly's view). She is headed toward the town.

But I know it's silly, Polly sometimes remarks, inwardly, of these nocturnal forays. I know it's silly and probably doesn't do much real good or so little considering the general terribleness of life for most people, and I know it's fairly dangerous, some scared farmer might assume I'm a thief and shoot me. A shrink might say I'm trying to recapture Spain, all that danger. A repetition, I think they call it. I know all that really better than anyone. But it's what I like to do, or not actually the doing of it, I don't like the actual fact but I like to think about it, and if it does even the slightest good—well, so much the better.

Having said all that to whatever fantasized person, the person who had just told her that she was being silly, or that what she did was totally, entirely useless (it is sometimes her friend Freddy, or Edward or Dudley or Sam; it used to be Charles, quite often, but it was never, curiously, Celeste)—having said or verbalized all that, Polly has arrived at her destination: a small (about the size of her own house), overpopulated, crumbling stucco cottage, with a rich, thick garden, great flares of flowers, fanned-out leaves, and a large dog that is chained (she hopes) in its packing-crate house. A steel fence. A house that Polly has scouted out on several innocent-looking daylight excursions. A house in which there lives a Portuguese family, the Pessoas, whose apricot trees were devastated by a freakishly violent winter storm. And whose land is on the verge of being taken over by a major conglomerate in Salinas. (Polly has spent the weekend in various forms of research, getting all this clear and accurate.)

It would not do simply to throw the package into the yard, in a random way; a dog could carry it off, a sudden rain could camouflage the foil with mud. Once about a year ago, by mistake, a defective throw, Polly did just that; she watched the money land some feet from the door of the González family (a tubercular child, a medfly-ruined crop) on soft grass. Failing to convince herself that it would be all right there, that they would soon come out and find it, Polly then had to scale the fence, not high but difficult, with no footholds. She kept slipping, falling back, in the wet black night, and she was so frightened, her heart and every other muscle strained to capacity.

After that night she spent two full days in bed with an actual fever, shaking from panic.

Now, though, at the crisis moment she is not afraid. And she makes a perfect pitch. The money package hits the Pessoases' front door with a loud, resounding thud, and Polly hurries back to her bike, which she has hidden behind a conveniently spreading mulberry tree. As she hides herself, she can hear the front door being opened behind her. And a blast of exclamations, at first quite fearful: is this thing a weapon, a bomb? But mostly they sound surprised. In another moment they will note the innocent, slightly tattered, domestic-looking foil; they will dare to open it and will find the money. The several thousand dollars that at least will serve to cheer them for a while.

One of the things that Polly counts on entirely is families not telling each other about these strange events, cash money thrown into their lives in the dark of night. And in this assumption she is very likely correct: she knows these proud poor people, their superstitiousness, their iron clannishness. Their eternal suspicions. To tell anyone outside would jinx their luck, they would reason—"outside" meaning anyone not living in their house, in their immediate family. If they told about it, the person who threw it on their doorstep—no doubt by mistake, they might think—that person would come back and try to claim it.

That at least is Polly's reasoning, her reconstruction of reactions to her clandestine presents.

* * *

Remounted on her bike, Polly pedals as long and as hard as she can, remounting her hill. Then she gets off and pushes the bike along, avoiding the ruts as best she can. The fierce damp cold has penetrated the layers of clothes she wears, despite her exertions. She looks forward to her house, to warmth. To her cats.

Dumping the bike on the floor of her garage, with no energy left to pick it up and prop it, properly, she approaches her own door. And she hears, from within, the first ring of her telephone, and she thinks, almost saying the name aloud, Oh! Celeste.

5 Celeste is possessed of a small and perfectly proportioned body, on long thin perfect legs. Large hands and feet, about which she once was sensitive. First coming to New York, in the early thirties (after the demise of her first and only pre-Charles marriage, to a man named Bix Finnerty), Celeste worked briefly as a dancer; she was (very briefly) what was called a chorus girl, a phase of her life that she never talks about. But she has retained a dancer's walk: a tall stride, rather aggressive.

Her nose too is imperious, high-bridged, impressive. Once, after a love affair whose ending coincided with her fortieth birthday, Celeste considered having her nose made shorter and smaller. "I'm tired of having such an impressive nose," she wrote to her California best friend, Emma (mother of Sara). And Emma, still in San Francisco, involved in labor strikes, wrote back, "For God's sake, forget the size of your nose. The world is much uglier and larger than your nose." And so Celeste did forget it, almost for good.

As a very young woman, back in the days of Bix, Celeste had fine silky pale red hair, and fine white skin. Dark, dark large eyes. Shy-looking, even frightened eyes, despite such beauty. "Doe eyes," Bix Finnerty used to say, as did quite a few others, later in her life.

What Celeste was most clearly to remember from that on-the-whole-dismal first marriage, which took place when she was only eighteen, was a curious trick that Bix played on her—and on his mother.

Having left her family on the farm, near Sacramento (that farm, along with the chorus and a couple of other minor autobiographical facts, went unmentioned, ever, by Celeste), Celeste took the train to Oakland, and then the ferry to San Francisco, where she was to be met by Bix's mother, Mrs. Finnerty, Bix being at work selling shoes at that particular hour. Almost immediately Celeste spotted a woman of about her own height, but round, a jolly type with the red plastic cherries on her hat that her son had described. But why was she looking up into the air, as if for someone tall? Celeste went up to this woman anyway, who was indeed Mrs. Finnerty, who greeted her effusively and giggling with pleasure—she adored this only son. She very soon apprised her new almost daughter-in-law of the wonderful prank: what Bix had written to his mother was "She's tall and blonde and terribly beautiful, of course."

"But of course I knew right away it was you," laughingly lied Mrs. Finnerty. "The terribly beautiful part. I'd have known you anywhere."

For an instant, then, there at the Ferry Building, Celeste considered going right back to Sacramento, even back to the farm, and taking up that life again; but she did not. Although "in love" with Bix, she did not think this funny at all. It struck her as very mean to them both, to herself and to Mrs. Finnerty. Also, she was more or less aware of the wish contained within the "joke"; Bix wanted a tall blonde wife. Small wiry Bix, whose hair was a brighter red even than her own.

The only person to whom Celeste ever described this scene of her windblown, apprehensive young self in search for red plastic cherries on a hat was her early best friend, Emma, when the two of them were "office girls," after Celeste's divorce and before her move to New York. "Once I caught on, I thought, Oh, then he really doesn't like me," Celeste said to Emma, back then.

"I think men are better at what they call love than liking," Emma told her. "But, Celeste, you are terribly beautiful, really."

"Oh, I suppose." Meaning: Yes, I guess so, but what good does that do me? Meaning: So far, being beautiful has only brought Bix Finnerty in and out of my life.

Celeste's eyes indeed seemed to gain in intensity, in depth, as she aged. They became more passionate, or more passion showed in her eyes. "In truth they are the very mirrors of your soul," said bantering Charles Timberlake, in his cups, early on in their love affair.

Celeste's voice too is passionate, a vibrant alto, even as she now only says, "But, Polly, child, I worry about you." There are almost tears in her voice.

From the white plastic receiver at Celeste's left ear come Polly's breathy sounds of reassurance: ". . . just for air, it gets so stuffy in this house, you mustn't fuss. I wasn't out long."

Celeste is sitting upright, legs crossed before her. A semi-lotus, on a bed that another might have sprawled across. It is in fact just where Charles did often sprawl, and that is one of the visions at this moment foremost in Celeste's mind: tall lean lanky Charles all sprawled, all those long fine bones gone limp. Celeste fights off that picture.

An expanse of fine gray linen with borders of heavy lace is pulled taut across the bed, evidence of no one sprawling.

Celeste tries to laugh, and succeeds in a sound that is just a little unreal. "Oh, I know it's selfish, my wanting you home," she says to Polly. "But I like your being so near. I like everyone around me, you and Dudley and Sam and dear Edward. And Freddy. I guess I really want all of you home all the time available to me." And she laughs again, this time with somewhat more success.

"But tell me about Edward and Freddy," she demands. "Do you think they're still getting along? You don't notice any new, uh, tensions? I couldn't bear it if they got a divorce." A small, perfunctory laugh. "I can't bear it when friends divorce—or, for that matter, when they die."

A pause, during which she listens somewhat perfunctorily as Polly reassures her about Freddy and Edward, the permanence of their connection.

Celeste's various despairs are genuine enough, but so is her odd, very clear wish to prolong this conversation, despite her definite sense that Polly is tired and would like to get off the phone and into bed— with a good book, probably. And, despite all Celeste's intended and unintended conversational gambits, Polly does manage to get off the phone quite soon, with kindly affectionate good-nights, but still leaving Celeste all alone, and leaving her waiting.

*　*　*

What Bill quite clearly said was "I'll call you New Year's Night." Which is surely now, tonight?

Why does he so often not do precisely what he said he would do? Why does he seem to forget what he so clearly said?

Or, for that matter, why did he in the first place follow her out of that antique shop on Jackson Square (*he* followed Celeste, an old woman), out to her car, and insist on having her card before handing her into the Jag? He seemed very excited, almost "high." And then all those flowers, that lovely mass of spring flowers, and the invitation to dinner? It can't have been the sheer coincidence of their having met earlier that day in the horrible, dingy IRS office (where Bill seemed to work) where they did not talk; he only passed her along to someone else. But, "Fated," they both said of it, laughing to each other, that afternoon in the store.

Why then the long, romantic and extremely expensive dinners, the great interest in everything she said about Charles? About Sara? And then between those dinners the broken dates, the waiting for calls? Is this what it's like, an "involvement" with a handsome, younger man?

Celeste knows the answers to none of this, and is fairly sure that she never will.

In the meantime she does have friends, and what are friends for, if not an occasional phone call?

Dudley (so gratifying!) answers on the first ring.

"Darling Dudley!" Celeste exclaims. "Happy Happy New Year! It doesn't really seem like New Year's, does it? Well, actually I'm fine, barring the usual aches and pains that we all find so boring. I am somewhat apprehensive about Sara, though. I mean, I've been so selfish. Frankly I've only thought about how much I need her here, or I think I do, and now I really wonder if she'll enjoy herself. Find things to do."

This conversation—or, rather, this monologue of Celeste's, with small polite but warm murmurs from Dudley—all this talk is a considerable success. Dudley reassures Celeste that Sara will love being in San Sebastian: walks, all that. And after all if she gets restless there is always San Francisco, so near. And Dudley is reassuring too about Edward and Freddy, describing her morning walk with Edward, during which he seemed perfectly fine. Not worried and assuredly not sick.

"I know you worry about his cough," puts in Celeste, a little sharply; she is generally opposed to a scrutiny of symptoms and especially to talk about those symptoms, in one's self or one's friends.

"Oh, I do," Dudley admits contritely. "I can't help it. You know, you read so much, one simply does, all this in the papers about coughs and lungs."

"I never read those articles," Celeste tells her, now enjoying this part of the conversation. Feeling in charge. "What earthly good? You never learn anything useful. Doctors change their minds every couple of years about almost everything. Don't eat salt, do eat salt, don't exercise. Do. Next they'll be saying that everyone really should take up smoking."

As she continues, though, in this silly vein, Celeste's enjoyment lessens; she is increasingly aware of having said all this before, quite possibly too often. She is talking to hear herself talk, as her father used to say. And so she stops.

But Dudley—oh, bless her!—continues. "Speaking of walks," she interjects, "as we just were. This morning Edward and I went to that new diner sort of place for coffee. It's quite attractive. And a quite adorably bearded young man waited on us there. David, he told us his name." Dudley laughs. "I could see that Edward was quite taken with him. I'm afraid Freddy would be even more so. But I don't think he's, uh, gay."

Celeste has spent considerably more time in restaurants than Dudley has, in San Francisco. With Bill. "So annoying, this new friendly way with names, don't you think? I don't care bugger-all what their names are, as dear Charles might say."

Dudley, however, is struck with a new idea, or an idea new to her conversations with Celeste. "Have you noticed," Dudley asks, "how we seem to impute much stronger sexual feelings to homosexuals than we do to each other? We really do."

"Oh, do we?" vaguely asks Celeste, who has begun to think again of her anticipated call: perhaps she is overdoing this keeping busy of her phone? He might give up?

"Well, I do think so," Dudley tells her. "Even old Edward, honestly. Do you think it's a sort of outgroup thing, like white people all hung up on the sexual prowess of blacks? I remember girls at college who were convinced that going out with Jews would get them instantly pregnant. Or was that Catholics?"

"Well, maybe." So ironic: now Celeste can hardly get Dudley off the phone. And all this about sex, really the last subject one would choose, although she has an impression that Dudley thinks about sex considerably, more than one would expect in a woman of her age. "Well," Celeste attempts. "You're so good to chat with me like this. Letting me keep you away from dear Sam all this time."

"Dear Sam and I have been chatting for almost forty years, dear Celeste. We can stand an occasional break."

"Well, darling, of course you can. I guess I just wanted reassurance about Sara, and you know how I get about parties. I worry."

"But, Celeste, your last big party was terrific. Lord, it must be ten years ago, is that possible? With all those attractive people."

Dudley would clearly like to reminisce in detail about that party, when all Celeste can remember of it is that everything was yellow, the yellow-gold night, and the dress she wore. Was that the night that Dudley, uh, drank too much—something to do with Brooks Burgess? She can't remember, and in any case does not want to discuss it now. "I might just have a small dinner, after all," she tells Dudley. "You and Sam, Edward and Freddy. Sara and me. And, uh, Bill."

"You could have Polly, make it eight." Helpful Dudley.

"Of course Polly would make it eight. But then suppose someone can't come, or something. . . ." Celeste hears her own voice trail off unconvincingly. "Well, of course I'll probably invite Polly, after all. You know I always do."

"Besides, Polly's used to being odd, so to speak." Dudley meant: When Charles was alive, we were often seven at dinner.

This unspoken remark is afflicting to Celeste, though; she feels it cruelly, yet she cannot bring herself to blame Dudley, who did not even utter it, actually. But, *Charles*, cries out Celeste, within her heart.

Sensitive Dudley, however, seems to have heard her own unvoiced remark; her tone is much gentler, is infinitely affectionate as she tells Celeste, "In any case your parties are always fabulous, dearest Celeste. You know that. Sam and I always so look forward—"

"Well, you're dear to say so. And now I do believe I should say good night. Good night, and sleep well, dear Dudley."

"Oh! the same to you. And much love, Celeste."

This note of great affection is natural to all these people. To the occasional outsider, invited into their midst (no one could just wander there), it might have a sound of exaggeration, even of extremity, but to them, this group of almost very old people, it is both genuine and sustaining. What they say to each other is true, and real: they feel great affection for each other. One could call it love. And particularly at partings. Any parting, even the end of a phone conversation. They all need blessings, reassurance. The old have that need in common with small children, seemingly.

And, though indeed reassured, Celeste observes that it is still too early, really, to go to bed. And so she stalks about her room, a caged lioness, sniffing at shadows.

The tall, handsome Biedermeier bureau, with its tiny linen runner, holds many (seven or eight, at least) large, heavy silver-framed likenesses of Charles. Of Charles and Celeste together, but mostly just Charles. Attractive Charles, an American classic, with his sad-boyish, sincere blue eyes, his clear wide brow and those eyebrows. His nose is a shade too small for true handsomeness, but his chin is deeply cleft.

Celeste herself never photographed well at all—interestingly, age has made her more photogenic. Then, in those pictures, her eyes and nose both seemed somewhat too large, and her expression tended, in pictures, to be severe. When she did smile, the smile looked reluctant, forced.

Celeste does not just now look at any of those pictures.

Instead, pausing momentarily, she inspects a small carved desk, hers since childhood, and the only piece of furniture from that distant time. The desk was in fact brought out across the plains by her grandparents from Vermont, in post–gold rush days. Long ago Celeste had some trouble wresting it from her brothers, when both parents died in the flu epidemic of 1918. Finally, "It's the only thing I want, I need to have it," she told them, over the objections of a sister-in-law, who predicted, "You travel all the time. It'll break." "It won't." Celeste got the desk, and she did travel and move a lot, and the small desk remained intact, always perfectly polished. A lovely piece, which always seemed part of Celeste, an essential.

Now, though, it is piled with letters, so many, though neatly stacked. All something to do with Charles. And inside are more letters, and old photographs, snapshots from everywhere. For a long time now, Celeste has meant to go through them all: suppose she died and some interested person (Sara? Dudley? Edward? Those three first come to mind, as survivors)—suppose someone found all these pictures, these letters. "Well, how extremely interesting." (She can hear this in Dudley's voice, those loud implacable accents of the East Coast rich.) "Celeste seems to have grown up on some sort of *farm*, not terribly far from here, up in the Valley. And her first husband was a shoe salesman, can you imagine? With her big feet? Explains quite a lot, don't you think?"

She has got to go through and get rid of most of that stuff, but is this the moment? She is very tired but she knows that she won't be able to go to sleep. Not yet.

But—no. No, no.

She cannot go through letters and pictures now, any more than she can make any more long-drawn-out phone calls. She is *waiting for Bill to call.* And my God, thinks Celeste, to be doing that—*at my age.*

Sitting down abruptly on her bed, she even smiles a little to herself at this truly frightful irony, that she should spend her old age waiting for a handsome man (looking very much like a younger Charles, is the truth of it)—for a much younger man to call. She, who as a young woman never waited for anyone, never for a minute. Well, thinks Celeste, with a small involuntary lift of her chin, I never had to. Then.

At that very moment, though, the phone begins to ring. Her heart jolted, Celeste breathes deeply, for peace; she allows three rings before she answers. "Hello?"

At the other end is silence, but it is the whirring silence that signifies long distance, and signifies, to Celeste, not Bill.

"Hello?" she says again. To nothing.

After a minute or two she hangs up; she is shivering, although she is now less cold than she is tired, most terribly tired. Perversely, though, she begins again to walk about, to stalk.

From their bedroom she walks through her dressing room, through what was Charles's study (more photographs, chronicling Charles's long, highly public career: studies of Charles with important people, Roosevelt, Einstein, de Gaulle. But none of course of Charles with former wives). Celeste stalks on through the dining room and into the guest room, slated now for Sara.

Very quickly she passes through all these rooms, all unseeingly. And then back to her own room. Their room.

Outside, the night is very cold. And dark, and still. All the winds have died.

Celeste thinks, New Year's Day. She thinks, 1985.

And then with no warning at all a great scream comes up from her throat. A small woman, old and thin and most elegantly erect, in a dark blue, heavy silk robe. She stands there in her beautiful bedroom, stands screaming. One syllable: CHARLES!

She screams, and screams.

THE PAST

6   Dudley, at that time Spaulding, née Frothingham, and Celeste, then Finnerty, became friends in a very gradual way, beginning
sometime in the early forties, in New York. And their friendship was
unusual in having its origins at cocktail parties, at a time when at
parties young women were not supposed to talk to each other at all,
not ever. Received opinion then held that women in the presence of
men became instant enemies, as wholly dedicated to rivalries with
each other as they were to pleasing men.

But Dudley and Celeste kept meeting at upper East Side parties,
during those lavish wartime years of fashionable complaints over ra-
tioning, restrictions. They seemed to be on all the same guest lists,
those two; and, for whatever reasons, they were drawn to each other
in the way that those destined to be permanent friends sometimes
are. And they did talk, breaking the rule.

One source of mutual attraction may have been sheer opposite-
ness: red-haired California Celeste; and tall, very Bostonian Dudley,
with her thick short curly dark hair, and sea-blue eyes. Her Back Bay
voice.

Dudley's first husband, Hammond Spaulding, was killed soon after the outbreak of the war, not in combat but in a frightful (partly
because so avoidable) training accident at Camp Lejeune, North Car-
olina: a defective cannon backfired, killing Hammond, a marine lieu-
tenant, just out of Yale. That "incident" was hardly mentioned in
the newspapers (only the *Yale Alumni Magazine* made much of it) in
those days of unadulterated marine heroics.

Dudley remained in shock, or nearly, for almost a year, shock darkly tinged with rage.

And then she picked up and went down to New York; she got a receptionist job with some friends of her father's, a job she did not much like, but still a job, on lower Park Avenue. And she began to go out.

Meeting Celeste, Dudley thought Celeste was the most beautiful woman she had ever seen, with her pale red hair, pale skin, her impressive sculptured nose and her huge dark, dark eyes. Celeste, coming into parties, would have been conspicuous even had she not learned that trick of the momentary pause just at her entrance. But she had learned that trick, and she almost always wore black—although one of her most successful dresses of that time was a green so dark that it too looked black, a fine green silk. She was highly visible.

She looked very shy, though, almost frightened, and Dudley, observing her, began to suspect that the pause at the entrance to parties was as much for retrenchment, for self-assurance, as for display.

"That's the most beautiful dress." Dudley to Celeste, in a floral powder room, on East Seventy-second Street, just off Park.

"I like it too, thank you." Wide-eyed Celeste. "But I think I wear it too often."

"Oh, no, I don't think so. You're a friend of the Bradfords?"

"I must be, they keep inviting me here." Celeste's edgy laugh. "Actually I think they're mostly grateful. I found this place for them."

Dudley: "I'd imagine they are." Her own edgy laugh. "In this day. However did you?"

"Well, that's what I do now. Apartments." Shy dark eyes, now somewhat evasive.

"Oh." Unasked, Dudley volunteers, "I'm a sort of receptionist. Apartments sound better, I must say. You'd be out and around."

"Oh, not really. Or maybe too much out and around. I should try staying home."

They both laugh.

Another powder room, this one boldly striped French wallpaper, on lower Fifth Avenue.

Celeste: "Oh dear. I have on the dress again. I seem to always, when I run into you."

"No, actually you don't. Last week you had on that black, with the ruffles. At the Ameses'. How's the apartment business?"

"Slow." Again powdering her nose, Celeste then remarks, half to Dudley, "Oh, if only I had somewhat less nose, you know?" A look from the huge black-brown eyes.

Wanting to say, But you're so beautiful, your nose is beautiful, Dudley did not say that (although she may have conveyed that message to highly intuitive Celeste). She only observed, "We all seem to think we have something wrong, have you noticed?"

Celeste, thoughtfully: "Yes, women do. I don't think men worry in just that way, do you?"

"No, they don't seem to." Hammond Spaulding was a confidently handsome young man, generally untroubled. (And uninteresting, Dudley has almost admitted to herself.)

"My husband worried that he was small. Not tall, I mean." Celeste hurries over this, then asks, "You're not married either?"

"No. I was, but he died," and now Dudley too hurries. "It seems like years ago by now." She adds, "Thank God."

At still another party, this time near Gramercy Park, at a corner of the buffet table the two young women, Dudley and Celeste, exchange information as to where they live: Celeste, on Park Avenue, near Eighty-ninth. "It's tiny, really minute, but so quiet, and all my own." And Dudley: "Mine's pretty far uptown, near the end of the A train line. It's called Isham Park. A funny sort of enclave. Some professor friends of a Socialist aunt of mine were there. Oddly enough I have more space than I need, and it's so cheap I can't afford to leave."

"You must make up for it with cab fare." Quick practical Celeste.

"Oh, I do."

Tacitly acknowledging whatever affinity has drawn them into so much conversation, they further exchange phone numbers, along with proper names. They mention meeting for lunch, maybe some Saturday, at one or the other's apartment. Maybe.

* * *

Not quite luckily, the day that Celeste is to come up to Dudley's apartment for lunch is the day after the night that Dudley and Sam Venable first met—and spent the night together, which was not a usual occurrence in those days.

Quantities of bourbon, much love and no sleep have produced in Dudley a high, emptied trance-like state. Very slowly, before the arrival of Celeste, she straightened up her apartment; fortunately she had had it all cleaned the day before, for Sam, her "blind date." And she and Sam really did not make much of a mess, only their two glasses and two sheets, which, with a slight blush at their condition, Dudley thrust into the hamper before remaking the bed. Two coffee cups and saucers, which she washes along with the glasses. Sam had a downtown appointment at ten this morning, in some ways a stroke of luck. But dear God, how drunk they got! What quantities of booze.

Having done all the cleaning in slow motion, Dudley commenced the peeling and cutting up of fruit for salad, reflecting that fruit salad is really the last thing she would choose to have today. She would really like—oh, she would love!—a strong, spicy Bloody Mary, and then maybe a piece of cheese. But from observation she has gathered that Celeste does not drink.

But mostly she is longing to hear from Sam—she is dying to hear from him. She cannot wait for more of Sam. Although for much of the evening they were so drunk that she is not entirely sure just who he is.

Sam Venable. A good-looking, not very tall painter, from somewhere in the South. Who works in advertising, which he hates. A dark man, with slant green eyes.

Isham Park indeed is, or was, a small, rather pleasant space of grass and trees, up above the clamor and dirt of upper Broadway. A park surrounded by a modest group of two- or three-story apartment buildings. Where Dudley lives.

Where now, coming up through the trees, beautifully picking her way in what must be very high heels, Celeste arrives. Celeste in pale gray, something soft, a long fringed scarf. To Dudley, watching, Celeste is a vast surprise, although expected; she simply looks so unlikely in that place.

Nimble Celeste, slightly hurrying, no pauses for any audience, soon disappears into the building's entrance as, up above, Dudley has the odd thought that it must be difficult to be so extremely beautiful. Many people would dislike you just for that, your beauty; they might even assume you were stupid, or mean, and certainly that you were self-centered, a narcissist.

And Dudley further thinks: This is the worst hangover and at the same time the best one I have ever had. My head could go anywhere. It could fly!

Celeste, greeted and made welcome, then announces, "What I'd really like—for some reason I was thinking of it walking across your park, which I must say is charming—what I'd love would be a Bloody Mary, but without the vodka. Is that called Bloodless?"

"I'm afraid it's called a Virgin Mary." *Wonderful*, Dudley is thinking. She can have her Virgin and I'll just slosh some vodka into mine.

But just at that instant the telephone in the front hall rings, and Dudley runs for it.

Sam's laughing voice. "I just had to check on you. Are you *real*? In my mind you feel like some woman I made up."

Gesturing to Celeste: Please, go in, sit down—Dudley's throat constricts. "Very real," she manages to say. "How are you?"

She hears his laugh.

Sam says, "I'm fine. The most peculiar hangover of my long mostly hungover life."

"Oh, me too."

"What I really need—well, mostly I need to see you. Tonight? The other thing I think I need is a Bloody Mary. I wish we could—"

"Oh, so do I! In fact a friend is here for lunch, and we're just—"

"Oh." He has understood. "Well, then. But he won't hang around? I'll get to see you later?" His voice has gone stiff, as though rebuked.

"*She*." Dudley laughs, a little hysterically, from sheer nerves. "In fact a beautiful woman named Celeste. And yes, tonight, I want to see you—"

Confidence restored, Sam too laughs. "Baby, I can't wait. I really can't."

But actually I was supposed to have dinner with an old friend, Edward Crane, Dudley does not say. Instead, "Shall I meet you down there again?" she asks.

"No, I want to come up to you."

Disjointedly, they say goodbye to each other. If voices can be said to cling, theirs do—they longingly cling to each other.

"Well," says Dudley, now back in her living room. To Celeste, her beautiful guest.

Something in her face, her voice, in her whole demeanor, has made Celeste laugh. She laughs, and she echoes Dudley's "Well."

Which allows and even encourages Dudley to explain. "I went out with a new man last night. One of the lawyers I work for knew him, and decided to fix us up. God knows why."

"You liked him." Celeste is highly serious now.

"Oh, yes. But we drank so much. Oh *dear*."

"Well, a drink now should help you. And do put the tiniest splash of vodka in mine. I'm sort of celebrating too. My really closest friend had a baby yesterday, out in California. What's your friend's name?"

"Sam Venable."

Celeste frowns, concentrating. "I think I met him somewhere, maybe. Once. A painter, Southern, good-looking? Sort of rumpled? Green eyes?"

This description of Sam is a thrust to Dudley's heart, as is the fact that Celeste has met him "somewhere." (A fact that Celeste seems later to forget, and Sam never to admit, giving rise to Dudley's fantasies: *had* they actually known each other, and if so how well?)

In any case, that day was both the day that Dudley and Sam Venable met and the day that Sara was born. And on that day Celeste became for better or worse quite closely involved with Dudley and Sam. For the first years of that love affair's unsteady and at times calamitous progress, Celeste was to hear a lot about it. She was to be the sole witness of their City Hall marriage, some ten years later. And Dudley was always to have a particular, slightly odd regard for Sara, whom she did not actually meet until the fifties. But Dudley always remembered hearing of her birth, on that particular day.

Now the two women, new friends, simply toast each other with their drinks, along with the absent Sam and the infant Sara.

"It's very brave of Emma, really, I think," Celeste tells Dudley. "Having a child all alone. Brave or nuts, I'm not sure."

"Probably both?" Dudley is thinking that if Sam should leave her, would she want a child? But then instantly she dismisses this half-formed thought. She does not even want children; at twenty-five she is already much too old, she thinks. (Although on that day much of her mind could be a sixteen-year-old's.)

She asks Celeste, "There's no chance of their getting married?" as she wonders: Do I want to marry Sam Venable? And what a crazy speculation that is! To be thinking of children, marriage, after one single night in bed with a handsome, drunk man.

"His wife has some sort of stranglehold on him, I gather," Celeste explains, of Emma, her California friend. "You know, generally they do. Especially when the husbands involved are prone to affairs with young women. But I must say, I do feel very aunt-like toward this baby Sara."

"Oh, that's so nice!"

"Well, it's surely easier than being a mother."

They smile at each other.

One of Dudley's several strict rules of life is that engagements of any sort whatsoever once made are never to be broken. In her view this is both moral and pragmatic; it saves on indecision. However, today, as she talks in a pleasant, if slightly keyed-up way while she serves their lunch, she is also thinking that it is very important that she see Sam tonight—she *must*. It is not simply that she wants to see him— oh, violently! There is also an emblematic significance: to see him the night after their meeting is crucial.

And so, both because she already likes Celeste very much, and also because she senses Celeste as a person of authority, in all ways a definite person (Dudley's sense of herself is often somewhat amorphous), she asks her, "This is probably a silly question, but tell me, do you ever break dates? I mean, if something you'd much rather do comes up?"

Celeste laughs. "Well, almost never." She then adds, "You were supposed to see someone tonight, and now—"

"Exactly. I was supposed to have dinner with an oldest friend—not even a beau, I mean. In fact, I think he's, uh, queer."

"I always seem to like those men too," Celeste comments. "And they *love* me. But they make me feel good. They're fun, most of them."

"Actually Edward's the only one I know, but I've known him so long. And he's so sensitive. Oh dear."

One of the pleasantest features of Dudley's apartment is its outlook onto trees, the oaks and maples of Isham Park, just now all feathered out in soft pale green. Which is where Celeste's gaze is directed as Dudley observes her profile.

It is very severe, that profile. Celeste's nose determines her whole expression, and it is such a strong, high-boned, authoritative nose. Dudley considers that nose, and hopes it does not mean that Celeste is going to scold her.

"Such a divine view" is what Celeste first says, turning back to Dudley. "Such lovely trees." And then in a very serious way she asks, "Suppose you simply told your friend what happened? Just said that you'd met someone you think you really care a lot about." She smiles. "I have a sort of motto. Well, actually a lot of them. But this one goes: When in doubt, tell the truth."

"Well, that's right," agrees Dudley. "In a way I do that too, and it works." But even as she is saying this she is thinking, But no, it would never do with Edward. For one thing we never discuss our love affairs with each other, we don't even mention the fact that we have them. I suppose because Edward can't, or he feels that he can't. And maybe he really doesn't. Oh dear, poor Edward.

At that instant, though, from down the hall the phone again rings, and Dudley goes to answer.

And it is Edward, sounding terrible. "Sweetie, I am so sorry to do this to you, but I woke up with the most frightful cold, which I simply could not bring myself to inflict on you. I feel dreadful."

Having reassured Edward, as she walks back to Celeste in the living room Dudley is aware of a strange elation, a sense that she has been especially blessed. She has even, from somewhere, been given a sign.

* * *

Years later, wildly drunk, insanely raging, Dudley shrieks at Sam: "Even Celeste, you said you'd never met her, but she had met you, she said she had. You lie, you've lied to me from the start!"

"You crazy drunk bitch—"

But all that is later, and is happily unforeseen.

Now making coffee in her kitchen, though light-headed, nearly breathless, Dudley still makes plans: as soon as Celeste goes, she will walk down the hill to the butcher and buy a really great steak. A chateaubriand? Just a perfectly simple steak dinner. Last night they barely ate, they just drank and drank. Tonight, lots of food, and maybe no drinks at all? But that would seem censorious, Dudley decides, by which she means that she is afraid Sam won't like rules.

Perhaps (after all, they are grown-ups, supposedly civilized) one Scotch before dinner, and a nice split of Beaujolais with the steak? A sober evening, all around. Lots of food. Moderate drink. Love.

In the meantime, there is still her new friend Celeste to talk to. Celeste, with her delicate wildflower look, her air at once fragile and hardy. She is like some cross between a flower and a faun, Dudley thinks, and of course does not say. Something rare and wild.

And although she is glad of the presence of Celeste, just then, it would not do to talk about Sam—thinks carefully brought up Dudley. And so, serving coffee, she asks, "Please tell me more about Emma, your friend."

Half-laughing, Celeste very affectionately describes Emma, her impetuous, impractical and danger-courting friend. And as she listens Dudley thinks of her own danger-prone friend, Polly Blake, with her nutty small-magazine jobs, her leftist intensity, her mania for good works and her absolutely veiled (if indeed it exists) private life.

In fact, as Celeste, in her rather clipped and very discreet way, describes Emma's clandestine love affair with the labor organizer in San Francisco, Dudley not for the first time thinks that Polly could very well be involved *right now* in just such an impossible liaison. There have been certain signs with Polly: last-minute changes of plans, always with profuse apologies from Polly: "Dud, I'm so sorry,

I just can't tonight. Something, work—" (Polly evidently cannot bring herself to invent a lie.) Plus strong, if indefinable changes in Polly's voice, in the expression of those amazing pale eyes.

Yes, Dudley thinks, yes, of course Polly must be having an affair with someone who is married. (But she does not think, she would never think, for Polly, of famously charming, famous Charles Timberlake.)

The steak, rubbed with garlic and oil, lies on the kitchen table, achieving, perhaps surpassing, room temperature. Potatoes are in the oven, baking, baked. The salad is crisping in the refrigerator. And Dudley is bathed and dressed, all lotioned, scented, brushed and powdered.

And where is Sam?

Seven-fifteen, and he was due at seven. He could have come early, even, were he truly ravenous to see her, as he said. Not able to wait, as she was not.

Overprepared, far too ready, Dudley walks in short rapid spurts from here to there in her apartment, senselessly pausing at one place or another. And wondering: Suppose Sam was killed on the way, fallen under a subway, or even murderously attacked in Isham Park? Or suppose he has decided to go back to whoever he was seeing before they met? Will he phone and say he's really sorry? Or will he just not show up?

And oh, how she would love, how she needs a drink at this moment! If he doesn't come, quite possibly Dudley will do what she has never done before, so far: drink alone, get drunk and cry, all by herself, as her parents always say the Boston Irish are prone to do.

Of course he will come, though, a more sensible part of her mind informs Dudley; twenty minutes is really not late at all—unless you are the person waiting for someone you are anxious about, or crazy about, or something. But oh, how a drink would help. *Right now.*

And even if Sam does come, after all this she will still need a drink, Dudley now believes.

But at the sound of the doorbell, a shrill missile going to her heart, Dudley just manages not to run toward the door, and reminds herself that it is to be a sober evening. Lots of food, little drink.

And there is Sam, huge Sam, with his red-brown curls and his green-eyed grin, Sam gasping, "Oh, beautiful! Oh, my brand-new Dudley! Here, I've got to put this down." And before they can anywhere nearly embrace he deposits on the floor what has been his encumbrance, his burden: a magnum of Mumm's. All chilled, all ready to drink.

7   Dudley looks awful, even slightly preposterous, thinks Edward, her oldest and in many ways closest friend. Her dark hair, a few years back just threaded very lightly here and there with gray (and gray hair, or white, would be most becoming to Dudley, Edward believes, would add both distinction and softness)—in any case, that hair is now blonde. Not movie-star blonde, or hooker blonde, but streaky, as though it had happened in the sun and were natural. The effect is neither distinguishing (God knows not that) nor softening. The truth is, it makes her look old, considerably older than she is; which is to say, also older than Edward is.

Dudley is telling him, though, that she feels terrific. So happy, such a relief, at last to be shed of Sam, after all these years. Ten years.

"The point is that Sam is an alcoholic," says Dudley very firmly. "Purely and simply. A classic. Personality changes. Awful morning depressions that only another drink can possibly cure. God, when I think of the Bloody Marys we've consumed, whole days of Bloodys. Bloody days. Not to mention all the champagne Sundays. At first— well, Christ, for years, it seemed so charming. You know, drinks when you're not supposed to be drinking at all. Well, Edward, imagine. Our parents?"

Edward forces himself to smile, although he knows that Dudley is so caught up, so carried away by what he deeply hopes will not become a total confession that she is quite unaware of his relative inattention. At this particular moment he does not truly care about

Dudley and Sam, or even, frankly (he might as well admit it to himself), does he care about Dudley, his dearest oldest friend.

For Edward is thinking with a difficult-to-bear mixture of passion and anxiety about a very young, an extremely beautiful person with a lovely name: Fernando Fuentes, with whom he is to have dinner, later on.

But, along with the smile that he forces, Edward manages to say, about their parents, "Oh, you're quite right there. 'Disapprove' would be the wildest understatement."

Dudley laughs a little too loudly. "I guess what I really have to find out, though, is why I went along with it, all that drinking. For so long. And I have to admit, I have pretty alcoholic tendencies too. I must have. I mean, a lot of women would have left the first time Sam passed out on them, not to mention getting really ugly, quarrelsome. Celeste would never in a million years stick around for anything like that."

"How is Celeste?"

"Oh, beautiful. Successful. Just slightly remote." A forced laugh from Dudley. "Of course her remoteness makes me a little envious, sometimes. Remote people don't get into trouble the way we do."

"Oh, I don't know," says Edward, whose sense of himself in fact includes a certain remoteness—and he knows that he is headed for some form of trouble, probably, with Fernando Fuentes.

But Dudley in her total self-absorption continues: "I'd really rather be like Polly. She seems to pay no attention to her love affairs. Men come and go in her life, and it doesn't matter much to her. Her mind is always entirely somewhere else. She's like a man, in a way."

"Like some men," Edward murmurs.

"Oh well, dear Edward, I didn't mean all men, of course not. Even terrible Sam is more sentimental than Polly is, actually, about love." And (most alarmingly, to Edward) her blue eyes fill.

"You're certainly right about Celeste looking wonderful," he improvises (too quickly?). "Her own sense of who she is seems so much more strongly, uh, developed. She knows who she is. For one thing I do think getting out of real estate and into decorating has been on the whole very good."

"You're right, she's become very secure. Very absorbed in her work. If she's having love affairs, she never mentions them. She always seems to be with, uh—"

"Homosexuals," Edward rather dryly supplies. "Yes, she does have a seeming closetful of queer escorts." He is thinking, I must not introduce Fernando, ever, to Celeste; she would gobble him up. And next he thinks, But this is crazy, what am I thinking of? Introduce Fernando to anyone indeed. I may never see him again after tonight. Unless I am most incredibly careful. Or most fabulously lucky. (In a general way Edward does not consider himself a lucky person.)

It is getting on toward late afternoon, teatime, but Dudley and Edward are drinking instant coffee, in her tired-looking, cluttered living room, which in Edward's view has not been improved by the addition of several large canvases by Sam. The new Abstract Impressionism, Edward guesses it would be called—all jagged lines and jarring colors.

He looks out instead to the reliable trees of Isham Park, just now, in late November, quite bare and gray, but most beautifully articulated, like line drawings—Edward's favorite form of visual art. Intricate twigs against a rosy sunset sky.

At this moment, for several reasons Edward would like to ask Dudley about her work, her "journalism"—and he is aware of setting off the word, of the semi-condescension of which sensitive Dudley has more than once accused him. It would be polite now to ask, and also it would serve to change the subject.

However, so embarrassing! He cannot, at this moment he absolutely cannot, recall the name of the magazine for which Dudley now works. Which proves, of course, that all her allegations are correct: it is not simply that she is touchy; he is in fact condescending. He only remembers that she was enthusiastic—at least at first—about her new job, but he finds it impossible now to mention her "work" without the name of the journal.

Another truth, half recognized by Edward, is that his own work, his writing, has recently not gone very well at all. His last book of verse was published precisely ten years ago, a fact that he very much dislikes facing, but there it is. Edward, at thirty, was hailed everywhere as "promising," even "brilliantly promising." Since then there have been five poems in *Poetry*—and one each in *The New Yorker*, the *Yale Review*, and *Shenandoah*. All excellent publications (all sev-

eral cuts above the magazine on which Dudley now works, Edward
is sure of that); still, eight poems in ten years is not exactly promising,
much less brilliant. Not to mention the still-unearned doctorate (the
unfinished thesis on Forster). The repeated sections of freshman
comp. Not what anyone would call a distinguished career, so far. He
is not in any position to behave in a superior way to Dudley, nor to
forget the name of her magazine.

Dudley sighs. "I really should move from this place. It's the scene
of too much, mostly bad." And then, alarmingly, her eyes again fill,
as her gaze shifts toward the canvases. "What I'll miss about him
most, curiously enough," she tells Edward, her unwilling, less than
half attentive audience, "the big lack for me will be Sam's talent. My
sense of it, when I'm with him. He's quite simply a genius, I know
that. But Christ, he's so crazy."

"I'd think twice about giving up this place, though," counsels
Edward. "You know how hard they are to come by, and especially
bargains like this one. People are paying the earth. Why, I know a
young man, more or less the friend of a friend—or, rather, the stu-
dent of a friend—doing graduate work down at NYU, and he's paying
I think he told me something outrageous for a walk-up on Bleecker
Street. Of course I've never seen it, but still." (Dear heaven, does he
have to go on and on about Fernando, in this lunatic way? Perhaps
he does, decides Edward.)

At that moment, though, Dudley bursts into tears: loudly, miserably, horribly. A woman in her thirties, just standing there and sob-
bing like an adolescent, or a child.

His heart racing less in sympathy than in true personal anguish,
Edward is transfixed.

And after a long and entirely awful moment Dudley raises her
face, all reddened, haggard, *old*. And she tells him, "Edward, dear
Edward, would you please just go? We're not helping each other at
all. And, Edward, I'm so *sorry*."

Of course Edward has given far too much thought, energetic searchingly imaginative thought, to the choice of what is, he hopes, his only
first dinner with Freddy, Fernando Fuentes, whom he met and began
talking to in a Morningside Heights bookstore. He did not pick Fer-

nando up. And although he tries to tell himself that there are many, many good restaurants in New York, his obsession persists.

Nothing too grand, too intimidating. On the other hand, a reasonable elegance. *Not* the Village, where Fernando lives. Nothing even slightly, faintly camp, and heaven knows not one of the special haunts of certain people. (A tricky problem, that: such things are so sensitive, subject to such very quick change.) And ideally a place where Edward himself is known, but there again, not too known: an overly familiar waiter of a certain sort could give precisely the wrong impression.

Settling at last on the Café des Artistes, on West Sixty-seventh, Edward calls and makes the reservations. Yet still he wonders: would, after all, the Plaza have been better? Or should he have stretched a point, and gone down to the Lafayette, or the Brevoort?

However, once seated at his really quite ideal corner table, and greeted by an elderly, most dignified and respectful waiter, Edward feels that his choice has been exactly right. The window boxes overflow with fresh, eager-looking chrysanthemums, all white; they impart a light tart scent of fall, hinting at longer nights, warm rooms. More darkness.

And the dining rooms are busy at that hour. Every table seems taken, but the bustle is dignified. No disorganized running around. No mistakes.

But dear God, what an old fart I'm becoming, I sound like my *father*, Edward chides himself. I simply must not talk in this vein to Fernando, he'll think I'm ancient. I wonder if anyone ever calls him Freddy? Sounds rather sweet.

And just where is the little bastard, anyway?

He is just crossing the room, led by Edward's waiter. Fernando (Freddy?) dark and shy, taking everything in with darting, slightly scared small glances. Fernando, who is indeed perfectly beautiful. Breathtaking.

Edward stands to greet his guest, and in a manly way they shake hands. They tell the waiter that they will have martinis. Very dry.

"Such a nice restaurant. I have not come to here before," Fernando volunteers politely.

"I'm glad you like it. I come here fairly often. It is attractive, and actually the food is quite good." Bored, in fact appalled by the sheer triviality of what he is saying, Edward trails off.

But Fernando seems not bored; quite eagerly he takes up where Edward left off. "Oh, so hard to find places agreeable in this city. In the Village, where I think to have told you that I live, so few that are sympathetic. But of course I am accustomed only to Mexico City." A modest laugh, as Edward considers all sorts of quite inadmissible questions, in addition to the very basic question, the all-important and entirely forbidden one. In addition to *that*, Edward also wonders, what social class? What, for instance, does Fernando's father do? Not that it matters, but it is so hard to "place" a person from Mexico City. Still, the extreme good manners must be a sign of something?

"With restaurants it is as it is with people," Fernando continues, and then he very modestly laughs, as though apologizing for having said so much.

"In a general way you don't much care for New Yorkers?" Edward ventures as at that moment the perfect martinis arrive.

Daintily Fernando sips at his. "Oh, so very good," he says, as though this were the first drink of his life. His virgin drink, as it were. And then another sip, and a smile as he says, "I do not so much care for the women of New York."

Oh, marvelous ambiguity! To which Edward's lively, overstimulated mind gives instant full play. Does Fernando mean, as opposed to other women, possibly Mexican, whom he does like, possibly quite a lot? Pretty dark young girls? Or is the implication a preference for men?

As neutrally as he can manage, Edward agrees. "They can be difficult. Many women are extremely difficult."

"Impossible!" Fernando's laugh just then is a small surprise as he widens his liquid eyes to look at Edward. Complicity? Is that one of the things to be read in his look? Dare Edward hope—?

"Well, I suppose we must decide what to eat" is all that Edward dares just then. But how stuffy he sounds, to himself. How Bostonian. How *old*. "Or maybe another drink?" he daringly suggests.

"I will be daring if you also," Fernando sparklingly offers, eyes alight, small white teeth just visible in his smile.

During those second drinks, though, Edward and Fernando again find themselves discussing women. This is possibly in part because of the somewhat festive Friday-night atmosphere in that restaurant, at that hour. Lots of women, all around. He and Fernando are, as far as Edward can see, the only couple of men alone in the place. There seem to be very dressed up women everywhere, in their furs and small hats and pearls. But no other men without women. (Maybe just as well?)

"In fact, I had a rather difficult time of it this afternoon with a woman friend," Edward hears himself saying. "Tears, all that."

Fernando makes a sound that is probably sympathetic, but is there also a quick cold flash of disbelief across that extremely *bien élevé* (however you say that in Spanish) face?

Quite suddenly, then, for whatever reason or combination of reasons, including Fernando's possible reaction, his own hopes and his second drink, Edward decides that what he is saying is quite as ridiculous as it is false. And he decides that whatever is to happen with this boy they must not, *must not* begin or even waste preliminary time with total lies. "The tears were over a fight she'd had with her lover, who drinks too much," Edward tells Fernando, with a slight, wry smile. "Actually she's someone I'm extremely fond of." Speaking only the truth, he plunges ahead. "In fact, I do find that women can be quite wonderful friends. I wonder if you also feel that."

"Oh, I too! I like them so much. For friendship." Fervent Fernando, who then laughs as he admits, "And I do admire their clothes."

They continue their laughing together for some moments, although Edward feels himself closer to tears of sheer joy: is it possible, at last? But the waiter just then interrupts—though deferentially, most discreetly, asking what they might care to eat.

Which they manage to order.

Still elated (dangerously so? Is he taking too much for granted?), over the smoked salmon Edward begins to talk about his work: his early writing, his current teaching job. And he soon realizes that he is talking in a way that he has not talked before, not even to Dudley, whom he often considers his favorite friend. "In many ways I like teaching very much," he tells Fernando. "Sometimes I think almost too much, it's too easily ego-inflating, do you know what I mean? But the worst is that it takes the same sort of energy that writing does. I wonder if I should teach, really, or if I should get into some entirely other, entirely non-literary job. And write." Edward has never said any of this before; he has barely allowed himself to think it.

Fernando's eyes, so marvelously flashingly changeable, now are solemn, serious and intent as he says, "I think it is what you must do. To write again. To do anything that is necessary for that."

"Oh, I do so enjoy talking to you," bursts from Edward.

"I too, I too enjoy. So much." Soft, luminous eyes.

"Fernando—"

"My friends, my certain friends call me Freddy. I should so much like that you—"

1 9 6 5

8   "If it weren't for being so worried about my darling Sara, I think I might be at last quite terribly happy," says Celeste to Polly Blake. In the absence of Dudley, now married to Sam and moved out to California, Polly has become Celeste's closest friend. (However, Polly too is considering a move to California.) "Why must there always be one fatal flaw, though? One ugly fly in one's nicest ointment?"

"God's way, I suppose," contributes Polly.

This conversation takes place in Celeste's large bedroom, in her very pleasant new East Sixties apartment, during the short and very hurried week in April that precedes her marriage to Charles Timberlake. Celeste is indeed almost dizzily happy, "in love." "So ridiculous, in fact quite ludicrous at my advanced age to be so madly in love," she has more than once said to Polly, who quite probably agrees.

She is happy except for the fact that Sara, now twenty years old, is apparently lost. Somewhere in Mexico, where she was traveling with an unspecified, never described or, God forbid, not named group of friends, Berkeley classmates.

In addition to so much conversation, Celeste and Polly are also engaged in sorting out Celeste's clothes, from her very full but perfectly organized closet—or, rather, that is Celeste's occupation: Polly would never help or give advice in that area. "You know that basically I don't give a shit what anyone wears, especially me," she has said, the *shit* earning a distressed "Must you?" from Celeste, to which Polly has answered, "Yes, I must."

Meticulous Celeste is going through the cavernous sections of that closet: blouses, suits and coats, dresses, night things, furs. Choosing what to keep for her new life with Charles Timberlake. What to give away. And then the giveaways themselves must be sorted out: some for friends, some for some reliable secondhand store. St. Vincent de Paul.

They are to travel a great, great deal, she and Charles. And as Charles keeps insisting, with an indulgent smile in Celeste's direction, they must travel light. Actually she knows very well that he loves all her luxuriousness, all her fancy silks and cashmeres; nevertheless, both to please him and to satisfy her own innately orderly instincts, she is getting rid of a lot, a task that she has to admit to herself she enjoys. Throwing things away, getting rid of surplus stuff is cleansing; she is sure that it is good for the soul.

And, as she has just said to Polly, if it weren't for this awful, seemingly bottomless worry over Sara—whose mother, Emma, died the year before, so cruelly, of cancer—if it weren't for that, Celeste would be perfectly happy. But no one even knows *where* in Mexico; they simply took off, a group of kids. Being constituted as she is, a woman of will, Celeste determines not to think about Sara, about whom for the moment she can do absolutely nothing. Don't worry unless there is something active you can do, has been one of Celeste's more helpful personal mottoes.

If only Polly or any of her friends wore the same size 4 that Celeste wears—this wish has been repeatedly in her mind as she fingers the discards. But so far she has managed not to say this to Polly, who would snort in some awful way. However, at the sight and then the touch of a gray silk organza coat, very sheer, Florentine, impossible to pack, almost involuntarily Celeste cries out, "Oh, if only you could wear this!" Already she feels that she misses the coat, in which she has looked, she is quite aware, spectacular.

Polly laughs—the dreaded snort. "Wrapped around my old bald head? Or just over fat old naked me?" She laughs again, seemingly enjoying this imagined picture of herself. (But how can she, really?)

Since her cancer surgery two years ago (her recovery has been astounding, an amazement to her doctors) and her subsequent baldness, Polly has been given to this awful form of humor, so distressing to her friends, and especially to Celeste, who now murmurs, "Oh, Polly."

At which Polly laughs, or snorts again.

A long time ago (Celeste is quite sure of this) Charles and Polly had some sort of love affair: Celeste has simply, infallibly deduced this. And neither of them, neither Charles nor Polly, knows that Celeste does know. Which makes it all the more interesting for Celeste to watch. Not upsetting, really on the whole not upsetting. They were such very different people then, Charles and Polly. They were not her adored almost husband and her almost (after Dudley, now that Emma is gone) dearest friend. (In fact, both Emma and Polly were mortally ill at the same time, diagnosed within weeks of each other, so that Celeste was flying back and forth, from coast to coast, trying to care for her friends. And then Emma died, and Polly, against every prognosis, got well.)

But Polly's "relationship" with Charles must have taken place when he was married to Jane, Celeste (correctly) believes, when he was in Paris. Probably, they actually saw very little of each other— and how perfectly inappropriate, how entirely unsuitable a match! Warm handsome sociable Charles, who is nearly a clotheshorse (more like an Edwardian dandy, actually), with his silly jokes, little songs that he hums, his flirtatious ways. And serious, heavy Polly.

Although certainly Polly was very beautiful at one time, with those pale, brilliant burning eyes, and her heavy hair, and great huge breasts. Well, she still has the eyes, and the breasts, although of course large breasts are not nearly as attractive in an older woman, as Polly now is.

These are Celeste's thoughts concerning Charles and Polly in the daylight hours, possibly when she is with one or the other of them; at those sunny moments she will have these somewhat disbelieving, these less than kind thoughts. However, at lonelier hours, at night, she cries out against this atrocious—this almost obscene—historical fact: the love affair between Charles Timberlake and Polly Blake. *How could they?* she inwardly screams, as though she herself had been present at the time, in Paris—the location, she imagines, of their love.

She has even had to ask herself, Is the love affair with Charles what truly draws her most to Polly? Otherwise it is surely an odd-looking friendship. But if that is true, thinks Celeste, how perverse and horrible. I am then a sort of voyeuse, oh *dear*.

"Well, anyway," Celeste now says to Polly, with her customary briskness, as she holds up a rose-colored taffeta New Look skirt (Lord, almost twenty years old), "Anyway, no one alive could have any use for this old thing."

"Incredibly enough I remember having one made in Paris that was quite a lot like that" is Polly's startling response.

"Did you, darling Pol? So odd, I often forget that you were there at all."

"Well, actually I didn't spend much time in Paris," Polly tells her as she has before. "I was traveling a lot. Ah, youth. But I just for some reason needed a party skirt. Oh, 'needed,' " she snorts.

"Well, you certainly don't have to be so apologetic about it," Celeste almost snaps. (*Why* must Polly keep insisting that she really wasn't there, was not really in Paris?) "All young women need things for parties. Don't be such an old puritan, Pol."

"Well, you needn't be so cross. Such a dictator, Celeste."

But what on earth has happened, suddenly? Polly and Celeste, so fond of each other, really, are quarreling, or nearly. In the yellow April sunshine from Celeste's long open window, in the attractive room, now all festively strewn with pretty clothes, soft fabrics—in the midst of all this attractiveness a quarrel has erupted. It is present in their eyes, Celeste's and Polly's, as for an instant they simply stare at each other, glittering brown-black into pale blue.

Suppose I said it? Celeste now wonders. Suppose all vulgarly like a fishwife I said to Polly: I know you had an affair with Charles, whom you don't—you could never deserve. You were never beautiful enough for Charles. But I *know*. You can't pretend any longer.

Celeste shivers at the very thought of saying such a thing, such *things*. And for an instant she closes her eyes to cancel the thoughts. Opening them after an instant, she says to Polly, "I'm sorry, darling. I am being snappish today, I know. Do you think it's pre-bridal tension, even at my age?"

"Well, that would be quite legitimate, I think."

"The truth is," lies Celeste, "I'm just so worried over Sara. In some way she's more like my daughter, you know? Especially now that Emma's gone. I suppose it has to do with not having children, don't you think?"

"I guess." Enigmatic Polly, so solemn. Polly who never in a million years would have done for Charles, at any age.

Sara and her lover, a thin, towheaded boy named Alex, were picked up for buying dope in Puerto Vallarta, and that is where they are now, in jail: a single room with no floor, just smooth, unevenly worn-down dirt. No windows, no air. A toilet hole for men on one side of the room, for women on the other. People take turns shielding each other while they defecate, and then they give up on privacy, usually.

One couple, a girl from Florida and a very young Mexican boy, about sixteen, make a point of humping into each other in a corner of the room as a few people watch, idly clapping to the rhythm of their fuck. The girl, whose hair is long and blonde but now all heavily dirty, darkened, tangled, cries out as though in climax, but Sara for one does not believe her. Sara does not believe that she is at all enjoying what she does.

Sara and Alex themselves sit chastely and angrily some feet apart, and Alex, whose beauty has been so frightening, so powerful a force to Sara—Alex now looks greasy and fat; he looks like everyone else in the room. He looks like Sara. Except that this is probably how she has always looked to him: a dark fat girl whom he happened to fall into bed with, stoned. A girl who kept hanging around after that and who finally said, "Why don't we go down to Mexico during spring break? I know a place near Vallarta where we could score some really good stuff." And handsome, evasive Alex, with his wild white-blond curls, unkempt beard, strong nose and clear sea-green eyes, Alex said, "Yes. Well, okay. Why not?"

Sara's birthday check from her Aunt Celeste covered the cost of the two round-trip tickets, and they found a cheap hotel out near the tiny, corny airport. The town was fairly corny too, but sometimes extremely pretty: a pink plaster wall all overgrown with falling purple flowers, with heavy, sexy blossoms. They walked a lot, Alex and Sara. They crossed the bridge where to one side women were spreading their laundry out over the rocks to dry in the sun, and where on the other side the river came down from the hills. Where rich Americans have large fancy houses. A whole colony of them. Gringo Gulch— Alex had somehow come by that name. So disgusting.

But everything was fine, everything going really well between them: a lot of sex, early-morning sex and siesta sex and then long stoned hours of sex at night. And, in between, all those long beach hours, sun and swimming. "You should stick to bikinis, Sara," Alex even told her. "You look really good."

Their habitual political controversy abated too: Alex stopped describing the Socialist state of Sara's dreams in terms of horror, he stopped telling her how she would hate the actuality of Socialism. And Sara did not mention Vietnam, not once.

Everything was fine, until the morning that began with margaritas at the appointed hour, at the bar of the Oceana Hotel, with its louvered view of the sea, its seedy American drunks. The day began there and ended in jail—all clearly Sara's fault, she having made the contact, all the arrangements.

Once we are out of here Alex will never speak to me again, Sara now thinks, in jail. Well, fuck him, I won't care. And she knows that for the rest of her life this room will inhabit her mind: the slick dirt floor, here and there worn down to paths, long indentations and holes like basins of dirt. The dim, never varying day or night light. The smells, and the huddled prison population: a legless man with furious, malevolent eyes; skinny ragged women, some with children. Americans, Mexicans, a couple of German kids. The boy and the Florida girl, there fucking. All of that in her mind forever. Becoming her mind. Her unconscious.

In Venice, where Celeste and Charles are spending a week, a part of their glamorous, amazing, beautiful (oh, wonderful!) honeymoon, at American Express Celeste receives a letter from Sara, which she instantly (or almost instantly) decides not to read to Charles.

The end of May: Venice is still all raw with rain, and gray and cold. On the Piazza San Marco, plank walks have been erected to keep all the tourists clear of the water lying there. Lines of tourists: the practical Germans and English who thought to bring raincoats; wet, shivering American kids in their trusting jeans, "hippies," long-haired boys and girls with flowers in their hair, even here in Venice, out in the rain. And Charles and Celeste, in their new London-purchased Burberrys. Small, perfectly erect Celeste, taut-faced, her smile a stretch of skin. And loose, comfortably ambling Charles, securely handsome—Charles, who, if bothered by anything relating to his honeymoon, does not look bothered.

In any case, returning from American Express, alone, as she makes her way over small arched bridges, through narrow stone passages that open out onto miraculous squares, stones, tracery, Celeste thinks of the just read letter, now well hidden in her passport case. She thinks of the letter even as almost despite herself her whole soul responds to the beauty, to the sensual complexity of Venice. (Overstimulated, she thinks, not smiling. Wryly thinking: The irony.)

"I am living with a group of friends here in Berkeley now," Sara has written. "We are a commune, in the truest sense of that word. We are working together against the war."

Reading, Celeste for a moment thought, What war? But then quickly remembered Vietnam. Of course Vietnam, where Charles believes that "we" are performing a sad but necessary duty. "What we are doing may at times involve violence," Sara's letter continued (so curiously sounding like Charles, whom she has never met). "But whatever happens, Celeste, I want you to know how much I have always appreciated your unfailing generosity to me, and your wonderful love and support when mother was sick. I want you to know that I love you, Celeste. Sara. P.S.—Mexico was awful. It is a beautiful country, with beautiful people, but the man I was with and I did not get along well at all. Basically we have political views that are totally opposed. In fact, I think he is trying to get into the army."

A strangely stilted letter, Celeste is thinking as she approaches their hotel: the Fenice; they have the most wonderful penthouse suite. It is as though Sara's whole commune, solemnly, all together had written this letter.

But it is certainly not a letter to read or even to mention to Charles, who at this moment is no doubt lounging in his bath. It is already established between them that Celeste is the early riser; especially in foreign cities, she can barely contain her morning eagerness, her passion to be out, to walk around and to see.

Charles is in his bath, in their bedroom. Naked Charles. Hidden. Forbidden.

They sleep in marvelous silks, the two of them, between clean crisp linen sheets. They kiss affectionate good-nights, not quite turned toward each other, their bodies not in contact. They murmur temperate endearments.

Lying awake at night, Celeste wonders: Is this, then, the end of my sexual life? Did she "fall in love" and marry for these nights? And in that case, what about all the passionate kissings and heavy breathing, the heartfelt (she supposed they were) sighs, in the months and weeks before this marriage—Charles's kissings and sighs?

Well, she supposes that this is it. After all, she is fifty-five, though her body seems to believe itself some other age; it stays thin and smooth, and it demands, it *wants*. Sometimes aching with wanting.

Their wedding was in San Francisco, less because Celeste's dearest friends Dudley and Sam live out there now (nor because Celeste, after all, began her life as a Californian) than because Charles adores that city. "I've always wanted a wedding breakfast at the Palace," Charles confided to Celeste, in his laughing, bantering way. Celeste would have been happy with a wedding breakfast almost anywhere at all, with Charles.

However, it was finally Celeste who made all the fairly complex arrangements: the suite at the Huntington (Charles's favorite hotel), wedding breakfast at the Palace. Dinner at Trader Vic's. And before that the federal judge in his Montgomery Street office.

"But what will we do all day, between breakfast and dinner?" Celeste had half laughingly, half shyly inquired.

"My darling, wait and see." Suggestive, sexy Charles.

At the wedding breakfast, then, in the huge vaulted green dining room of the Palace, there were Dudley and Sam—very thin and healthy-looking, both of them; Dudley had written that they had pretty much stopped drinking. And Dudley's old friend Edward, now living out here too, and whom Celeste had always rather liked. And Edward's young friend, Freddy something.

But why Edward and Freddy at all, at Celeste's wedding to Charles? Celeste herself wondered this, later on, and she concluded that she had simply needed to swell her own ranks, as it were, there having been so many friends of Charles's, from all his prior visits to San Francisco: the slightly overdressed people. (Overdressed to the very practiced eye of Celeste, but perhaps that is how San Franciscans are, these days?) All very prosperous people, up from Atherton, Hillsborough, Woodside, or down from Ross and Kentfield. All Charles's friends. Now here.

There was no real time or place to talk to Dudley, for which Celeste had longed; she yearned to ask Dudley, How are you now, really? Are you and Sam really happy—really getting along all right? But they could only press their cheeks together, almost meaninglessly, and Celeste could only observe that Dudley was perhaps a little too thin. Her neck looked strained, and her eyes.

Sam did not look thin, or strained, but neither did he look particularly happy. And Edward was as elegantly trim, as punctilious, almost pompous, and going bald, as ever; and his young friend, Freddy, was very dark and handsome—perhaps a shade too handsome? They all talked a lot about the new place where they were living. San Sebastian. "I think I've talked Polly into coming out here," Dudley whispered to Celeste.

"Oh, how very nice for you—for all of you."

"San Sebastian. Well, I sure like the name," Charles informed them all. "I have some fond and exciting memories of the one in Spain. From the war." Nostalgic Charles.

What they did between breakfast and dinner, Celeste and Charles, was to drive across the Golden Gate Bridge for lunch, in Sausalito. They sat out on a wooden deck, above the churning oily water of the bay, before a misty view of the pretty pastel city, San Francisco. They threw scraps of bread to a gnarled old sea gull perched on one of the rope-bound pilings that lined the deck, in the gentle April California sunshine.

And handsome Charles talked to his bride, Celeste, about their honeymoon. Where they would go.

Especially he talked about Venice. "What with one thing and another, I never got there until after the war," Charles told her, his sincere blue eyes taking on the particular light that any mention of that war—what Celeste has come to think of as Charles's war—seems to bring.

"Curiously enough I first saw Venice from a boxcar," says Charles, with his famously attractive smile. "In the summer of '47. I'd been up in Salzburg, checking out the festival and a seminar that Harvard was running in Schloss Leopoldskron, Max Reinhardt's old digs. Anyway, our train crossed the border at Innsbruck, and headed down toward Venice. A very hot, misty afternoon, I can see it now. Then at Mestre the train simply stopped, and we were all herded into these boxcars. So right for 1947, right? As the train crossed the causeway, we all peered out. We were standing, of course, holding on and craning our necks, and all over the lagoon there was this incredible rosy light. A pink dusk. And then that magical city, rising up from sea fog. I can't wait to take you there, my lovely Celeste. To see you there."

Smiling, widening her dark eyes in his direction, against the sun, behind those eyes Celeste is wondering, is asking: Will you make love to me there? Is that what you mean by seeing me in Venice?

And how about this afternoon? she wonders. Later on, will we take a nap, for love?

But they do not.

The war, that war, Celeste very soon and increasingly comes to understand, was for Charles his own heroic time, his prime time. Charles was too old for active service; also, a prep-school football injury had left him deaf in one ear. However, participate he did: as a correspondent he was vividly everywhere. Following Montgomery across the desert, with Ike all over Europe. And not only did the exotic glamour of those places arouse Charles's susceptible heart, he was thrilled by the cause itself, Celeste, listening, realized: the Allies were right in some absolute way and Hitler was wrong, in a sense that nothing would ever be quite so right and wrong again, and Charles was not a man at home with ambiguity.

And he now believed in "police actions." Korea. Vietnam.

Celeste will neither show Charles the letter from Sara nor mention it, ever.

From Harry's Bar, that day at noon they take the speedboat to Torcello, crossing the May-blue choppy lagoon, past small fishing boats and little islands with single houses, a dock, down near the edge of the water. With sometimes a shrine.

And arrived at the actual, ancient island, Torcello, the boat that carries eager Celeste and proud Charles and the other tourists to whom Celeste, at least, has paid no attention whatsoever—the heavy dark boat with all its polished wood heads up a narrow canal. Past old, old peeling red plaster houses, with spiky flowers and an occasional bandy-legged, decrepit cat.

And Celeste falls in love, in love with Torcello. She might stay there forever, she thinks, like a nun, in one of those houses. She would grow more flowers, and have more and younger cats, but no one would come to disturb her. No more tantalizing proximity of Charles, with his false male scents, and the strong, passive sculpture of his body. She could just live there in Torcello, perhaps sometimes sending for books, magazines from the mainland. From Venice, to which she would never return. She would never emerge from her island.

Charles's warm, practiced fingers barely graze her naked neck, just then—causing Celeste to shudder, mildly. He asks her, "Whatever are you thinking, my serious darling?"

Aware of her own enormous dark eyes, now turned fully on Charles, "I was thinking that this is the most perfect honeymoon possible," Celeste tells him. "It's divine."

9 Tawny yellow is the color of fall in northern California: the wrinkled, rounded hills near the sea are crouched there, leonine; on either side of the coastal highway yellowed cornstalks straggle up- ward from the fields. And near Half Moon Bay, just below the town of San Sebastian, the yellow becomes bright orange, in hundreds and hundreds of pumpkins, lying all carelessly across the fields in late October.

Much of this spectrum of color is visible from the small enclosed deck that Celeste and Charles (her design, actually) have had built just off their bedroom, where on sunny days they often have breakfast as they observe the view: the hills, fields, and the somnolent, bland blue sea.

At the moment, they are discussing a projected party, theirs, with a somewhat odd raison d'être: it is to be a coming-out party, of sorts, for Edward, who has been operated on for an intestinal polyp, "not benign," as the doctors delicately phrased it, but they also said that "they got it all"; Edward is all right now. (Edward, somewhat to the surprise of Charles and Celeste, found the idea hilarious: "Really? my coming out? I can hardly believe it." Amid gales of most un-Edward- like laughter.)

"Yes, it is somewhat macabre, as a reason for a party," Charles agrees, as though Celeste, whose idea the party was, had used that word. "However, however. I like it. I assume you'd do the same for me, my darling."

"Charles!" Celeste feels genuine shock waves through her narrow chest; it is her first instant of imagining an illness, possibly mortal, of

Charles's. And she thinks: I could not bear it. But in the next instant she amends this, thinking: After all, I may have to.

In the meantime she waits for Charles to laugh, to make the terrible thing he has just said an innocent joke.

But Charles does not laugh. He frowns. "My darling, please don't be quite so, so sensitive."

"Oh, Charles." Celeste hears her own small hopeless voice, not quite controlled.

The air of this day is not clear, although on the deck where they now linger over cooling coffee there is a little sunshine; below them, across the hills and closer to the sea, the morning fog remains—gray and thick, inimical. However, what Celeste next says is "How beautiful all this is. I think this place will always seem utterly magical to me."

And now Charles does laugh. He likes to feel himself in a somewhat paternal role with Celeste, and indeed with most women. He always has, like many men of his generation. He is happiest when women are being just a little silly. (A considerable problem with Polly, in the old days, for Polly was never even for an instant silly. Charles these days manages, though, never really to think of Polly as a former lover, since Celeste must never know, and he is aware that Celeste, despite her silliness, is frequently able to read his mind. So he simply does not think of Polly in that way.) "Such a romantic," he now says, smiling, to Celeste, his wife.

Which allows her to become quite brisk—an adult. "Well, now about our party," she says. "I do think it's a good idea, even if Edward keeps saying he hates all the fuss and attention. It'll be a way of congratulating him."

"And cheering up ourselves," offers Charles.

More shock waves assault Celeste, but she manages a silly laugh as she says, "As though we were ever depressed. In our beautiful house."

The house—most of the remodeling of which was grandly, if somewhat vaguely planned by Charles—was supervised minutely by Celeste and carried out by a talented local contractor. It is loosely Mediterranean in style: a sprawling, ocher-colored stucco villa, red-tiled roof—its wings spread across the top of a hill. The house's center, the focus of those clustered wings, is a glassed-in courtyard—the "atrium," in Charles's parlance. Heated by strong overhead lamps, yet still open to the view of hills and (sometimes) the sea, this space is filled or nearly filled with enormous plants—exotics, their names known only to Celeste—all glossily thriving, with thick heavy slick green leaves. And giant ferns, with leaves of a lighter, lacier green. "The damn place looks more like a rain forest than a house," well-traveled Charles has more than once been heard to remark. "Sometimes I think my angelic Celeste prefers plants to human beings."

Well, the truth is that I do, Celeste does not say. I adore my plants, every leaf and frond and tiniest flower of them all, and I adore my handsome Charles, and I love my friends. I love Dudley and Polly, and sometimes Sam, and sometimes Edward and Freddy, and that's about the end of it—as brilliant Charles has pointed out.

And how sad that Charles never got around to writing his book about the war, his war. What a terrible waste. But surely even now it is not too late?

Basically indifferent to people or not, Celeste gives superior parties; they are beautiful, exciting, generous, memorable parties. And behind all the wonder of flowers and candles, silver and linen and crystal, the always exceptional foods and wines—behind all these voluptuous effects lies the steel efficiency of Celeste.

"Oh, why am I such a perfectionist? What does it matter?" she sometimes cries out, to no one. Knowing, though, that her very efficiency, the apparent ease with which she "brings things off," is a quality much valued by Charles, who in small matters is somewhat careless. Who tends to be vague.

And so the meticulously planned party indeed takes place, and everything is as beautiful as at all parties given by Celeste, by Celeste and Charles. Even the weather seems to yield to the will of Celeste, which is no surprise to her. Having planned a fairly elaborate cold buffet, seafood platter, everything beautiful and cold, Celeste is rewarded with exceptionally warm weather: one of those rare end-of-October nights that can occur in northern California, much more like full summer than autumn. And the weather seemed to increase the air of festivity, of heightened celebration.

Which was exactly what Celeste had in mind.

Her perfectionism of course extends to her dress, her wonderful "looks," or perhaps that is where it all begins. On the night of the party she is in palest yellow silk, of which she says, deflecting compliments, "Oh, but it's so old, actually. Charles bought it for me on our honeymoon, in Venice. Ten years ago, can you believe it?" And for an instant she widens her eyes quite boldly, before she smiles.

Dudley, who has just praised the dress—". . . and in this room, in this wonderful yellow weather, Celeste, it's perfect"—Dudley, though tall and thin, with her beautiful proud carriage, still does not look especially well. Dudley is not at her best in evening clothes, Celeste decides, privately thinking that the "interesting" batik caftan might be much better on a smaller, younger person. And she further laments the fact that Dudley waited so late in life before stopping smoking—as though giving up the one thing, drink, were all she could manage. Admirable of course only last year for Dudley to stop smoking, at what must have been her mid-fifties; still, the damage to her skin was done already: Dudley, despite her brilliant azure eyes, looks withered, looks older than she is. At which Celeste catches herself with a start. We are all older than we look, than we *feel*, she hears, from some rude interior voice. We are older than middle-aged. We are almost *old*, we're a party tonight of nearly old people. We are the sort of people I used to look at and wonder why they even bothered getting so dressed up.

But these thoughts are so new and at first so ludicrous that Celeste lets out a small laugh.

So that Polly, standing near her, asks why: "Whatever struck you so funny, Celeste?"

"Oh, nothing really funny. I was just thinking how *old* we all are."

Strangely, though almost bald, Polly herself does not look old—or not very old. Scorning wigs, instead she wraps her proudly molded skull in scarves, tonight a very fine, very soft white linen, faintly threaded in pale blue. With her strong, clear lightly weathered skin

(Polly is always off on her bike somewhere) and her violently bright pale blue eyes, Polly in her way looks better than anyone—her own highly original and somewhat peculiar way. She looks younger and better than I do, is what Celeste now thinks, observing Polly. And I work so hard at these vestiges of beauty. (But really I do that for Charles. For myself I don't care so much—or do I?)

"It's lucky you think old age is so funny, dear Celeste," says Polly. "Many don't." But she smiles, mitigating what has been gruff.

"Well, I simply don't think old age is funny at all." This has come from Dudley, now moving closer to stand between her two friends. She has laughed a little as she said this, even as she adds, "I hate it, I really do."

The three women stand there together for a moment, each smiling a private smile, each with thoughts of her own.

Until Celeste, considerably the smallest of the three, reaches suddenly to touch first Dudley's shoulder and then Polly's, abruptly, and in a rushing way she says, "Oh, why don't we spend more time together? Just we three."

"Do you mean, Celeste, spend more time together while we're still around to do so?" Ironic Polly.

"Oh, no, I just mean that I love you two, and there's always something else that one of us has to do. Like now. I have to go and be a hostess. Charles's friends."

A somewhat odd line of reasoning has indeed led Celeste to invite many of the group whom she thinks of as Charles's old friends, the couples from Woodside and Atherton, from Ross and Kentfield, many of whom were at their wedding. Aside from the fact that in a social way she "owes" these people, Celeste has thought it out in the following way. If the party is to be, in spirit, a coming out for Edward, a celebration of triumph over mortal illness, the effect will be both stronger and more subtle if the party is not limited to Edward's intimates—and besides who would those intimates be? Young poets, with whom he is known to correspond? His old professors, of whom the same is known? His recent doctors?

If most of the guests do not even know what they are celebrating, so much the better. Celeste has tried without success to explain this to Charles. "If they all follow my intentions without having even been told to do so, it will be all the more effective," Celeste has said.

"It sounds very much like witchcraft" was Charles's comment. "Some propitiatory rite that you've made up."

"Oh, Charles."

Encouraged, he carries it further. "If you really wanted to get into exorcism, as it were, why didn't you invite some contingent of fagolas down from the city? Some pretty boys for Edward?"

"Oh, Charles," Celeste repeats, more severely. Sometimes she does not think Charles is funny at all. "I love Edward very much," she now reminds Charles. "And he could have died. It all could have metastasized. We have to celebrate his being well."

And so the party is not announced as having anything to do with Edward, nor his illness—not to Charles's friends, that is; Celeste more or less whispered her intent to Dudley and Sam, to Polly. And to Freddy. To Edward she flatly said, "It's your coming-out party. So you simply have to come. It won't be strenuous, I promise. You can leave whenever you want."

"Darling, dear Celeste, do you know that 'coming out' has a somewhat new meaning, these days?"

"Oh, Edward, of course I know that. Who doesn't?"

Charles doesn't, is one of the things that Edward thinks. And very possibly not Celeste either.

At his actual party, though, Edward is one of its least lighthearted guests. He is sad, a sadness caused not primarily by his recent surgery, that whole trauma (although the episode did leave him feeling older, weaker and more frightened; he sometimes dreams of those horrible hospital nights, the bright lights and noise from the corridor, himself in pain).

But far worse than all that for Edward, and lodged in the forefront of Edward's mind is Freddy, the new Freddy with whom he lives. Whom he loves, in a seemingly permanent way.

Did Gay Liberation and Freddy's midlife crisis have to coincide so precisely? This is how Edward states the main source of his own unhappiness to himself. For Freddy, who became forty the previous

June, had (not coincidentally) spent a great deal of the summer at a beach just south of San Francisco, a beach known for nudity and known too for being gay (and oh Christ, how Edward loathes and despises that word, in its current application). After years of discretion and relative monogamy (only a few quick encounters in Freddy's case, which Edward could suspect with some certainty but also pretend to ignore; Edward himself was faithful, absolutely), Freddy, at forty, decided that he should "come out." To do otherwise was to be hypocritical, if not downright reactionary, retrogressive. Freddy also began to feel that only gay men were truly sympathetic, and only gay restaurants permissible. Easy enough to find lots of both in San Francisco, in the seventies. But sometimes a great bore for Edward, who yearned for a good old-fashioned dinner out, in a straight place like Jack's, or Sam's.

And gay beaches.

Freddy's idea, at least at first, seemed to be that Edward should come along; he encouraged a view of the two of them as sexual adventurers on a quite equal footing: loving friends who could also, if fleetingly, love others. However, Edward's first exposure to that beach was a nightmare, and his second worse: lying there all stripped in the cold June California fog, his pale, scaly sixty-year-old flesh, with his paunch and his graying, thinning body hair. Edward felt his very sex shriveled down to snail size, a small cold gray slug between his ropy old legs: incompetent, entirely undesirable. As, somewhere near him, tautly muscled, small brown Freddy, who seemed destined by nature for nude beaches, cavorted and laughed with new friends, themselves all athletically lithe and firm and warm, eager-blooded. The genuinely gay, those already "out." All in all a most horrible summer for Edward, one from which he has in no wise recovered. (Indeed his cancer surgery seemed at times a continuation of that nightmare—having to do, as initially it did, with formerly erotic areas of his body.)

He still has nightmares of those nude-beach afternoons, in which he is either there alone with Freddy, or else Freddy is there, and hardly alone, and he is not. All equally horrible, and a persistent vision—even now, in this strange warm October. He might be going mad, thinks Edward, forcing himself off in the direction of the bar for another drink. Or maybe it is really a Valium that he needs. Or a shot of Demerol, the hospital's sole blessing.

*   *   *

It seems, though, that there really is some madness prevalent that night, at the overheated, crowded but beautiful party. It is as though Celeste's ideas about age and exorcism had become actualized, made manifest. As though everyone present had been infected with Celeste's earlier notion of the lateness of all their lives, their being past middle age. Of the propitiation of lurking disease.

By midnight these unconscious rites have taken the form, in some of the assembled guests, of an unaccustomed, heated sexual urge. The mouths of many people, mouths that for years have just not met, in dry, cool, "social" kisses—those mouths now part to each other, wetly, avidly, searchingly, in darkened corners of terraces, in small barely candlelit rooms.

Dudley, coming from the downstairs powder room, finds herself accosted, quite stopped in her tracks—"Say, Dudley, I've been looking all over for you"—by one of Charles's Ross retiree friends, a man whom she has always half secretly liked. Brooks Burgess. Sam has joked that Brooks has a crush on Dudley—very funny, Sam seems to think this is. They now come upon each other in that small darkened passageway, Dudley and Brooks Burgess, and they fall upon each other like randy adolescents, kissing and groping. They remain upright, more or less, prep-school kids at the door of the dorm at curfew time. In some exhilarated corner of her mind Dudley thinks of this, remembers—as the genital area of Brooks Burgess thrusts against her, and Dudley comes, and comes.

Half an hour or so later Edward, also leaving what has been designated as the men's room, has a similarly (for him) unusual and happy encounter: thank God he was not successful in persuading Freddy to come along home! This meeting is with a young man all in white whom Edward at first takes to be one of the waiters, as that man's strong and very firm hands make his intentions absolutely clear. Edward first thinks, No, this is wrong, it's condescending to have sex with working-class people, remember poor Forster. And he next thinks, For God's sake, it's Russell Carter's nephew, out from Princeton. And really why does that make it any better, morally? He next laughs to himself in sheer pleasure, and follows the young man (who is neither a waiter nor Russell Carter's nephew but a local boy gate-crashing, just for fun). This young man has apparently worked out a more private destination for the two of them. Edward goes along, he stops thinking at all. He enjoys, enjoys.

Unaware of course of what her guests are up to, in any detail, Celeste moves from group to group like a small yellow bird, the center of her party, the very source of all its mysterious energy.

In a way that she herself would be hard put to define, Celeste is a "believer," just in what would be difficult to say. Charles has been heard to describe her as a transcendentalist: "Celeste finds imma-nence everywhere." Which is not entirely wrong. "Religious" and "spiritual" are words also applied to Celeste occasionally, both of which she firmly rejects, the one as being too rigid, too circumscribed for the vagaries of her instincts. The other, spiritual, these days sounds more than a little vulgar, smacking as it does of cults and born-agains.

What Celeste clearly does believe in, and count on, though, is the strength of her own will—even its magical powers. When Polly was sickest, tube-sustained, dead-white, at the end of her strength, in her terrible hospital cubicle, at her bedside Celeste would sit and whisper, with all her own strength, her eyes and her voice both passionately intense, "You have to get well. You can't die. You have to decide not to die. Polly, you have to get well. We love you. Decide. Now. Decide to get well."

Later on, when Polly was in fact well, she would joke that Celeste had cured her. But she half believed it, and Celeste was quite sure that she had. She had simply forced Polly to live.

On this party night, though, Celeste's powers seem not to extend to Charles. Perhaps he is overly conscious of her witchcraft by now, and thus is immune. Or it could be that severe and secret worries render him impervious to all her warm yellow magic.

One of Charles's worries has in several ways to do with Sara, who seems more or less adopted by Celeste, since her mother, Emma, died—ominously close to the time when Celeste and Charles were married. (And why did Emma have to die? Lung cancer, very bad, but no worse than pancreatic, surely: couldn't Celeste have managed to save her, as she managed to save Polly? Can Celeste save him? Charles wonders.)

Charles and Sara have always quarreled, on each occasion of their meeting—mostly over the war in Vietnam and Sara's "pacifist" activities. Her *actions,* as she insists on terming them. Sara is a strident, pig-headed young woman, no doubt of that. However, in recent years, the early seventies, Charles himself has been so deeply rocked by the Watergate disclosures (one of his few remaining certainties is the fact that Ike never had much use for Nixon: Ike, whom Charles knew pretty well, and liked a lot)—Charles has been so upset that he has come to question almost everything in public life. Vietnam was of course not only Nixon's war; still, when Sara ran on about Nixon and Kissinger (she seemed to hate them both with true vehemence; "callous killers" she called them both), some loud inner voice has cried out to Charles that she could be right.

But he and Sara have such a history of rancor that now when it seems important to make friends with her, he has no idea how to go about it. Should he simply write to her, and if so what to say? If he changed his will now, leaving something substantial to Sara but still the bulk to Celeste, should he tell Sara that?

And how could he make that change without alarming Celeste, since their lawyer is a longtime personal friend? Celeste would know, and then she would also know of his fears.

Charles is convinced that Celeste will live forever, refusing always to die. Or maybe quite suddenly, almost whimsically, she will simply decide that it is time for her to go. An actress, stepping off stage. In any case he is sure that she will be in charge of her death.

Whereas he, Charles, may well not be in charge at all. And at the thought of his own mortality Charles is seized by a great wave of anxiety, deep in his chest, almost suffocating.

He will have to talk to Polly. There are certain symptoms that she may have had. He would simply like to know. To know everything that she knows, before he goes to any doctors.

Charles's mind, in many ways excellent, is highly compartmentalized; most conveniently for himself, he is able to keep certain aspects of his life and even of his memory quite separate from each other. Thus, these days, in his dealings with a large, quite eccentric woman named Polly Blake, who is almost bald, and a conqueror of cancer, he sees her as the sum of just those and only those qualities: eccentric, fat and bald. Someone who beat out cancer. He does not connect her to the other Polly Blake who used to be so madly (embarrassingly, when you came right down to it) in love with him. The Polly Blake who in bed used to be so, so violent. So—abandoned. For a time he believed her to be a nymphomaniac, but then he read somewhere that nymphos almost never have actual orgasms, and Polly certainly did. Lord! like a torpedo going off, half the time.

And so it is not that strange young woman, that former Polly Blake, whom he now approaches as he sees her standing alone, among plants, in the floodlit atrium. Big Polly, her head in one of those scarves she always wears. The friend of Celeste.

"Well, Charlie. Hello there."

Charlie. No one calls him that, and Charles recalls that Polly did not call him that either—before, in the period of which he never thinks. And so perhaps "Charlie" is her way of making him into someone new? In that case he decides to forgive her.

But Polly never misses a thing. "Such a benign smile," she tells him. "What can I have done to deserve it?"

"Nothing at all, my dear. It's just such a lovely, lovely night."

"Yes, Celeste's lovely party. As she herself would say, it's divine." Polly sniffs at something in the air. "But then Celeste is divine."

Charles scans her face for irony, finds none. So that his second thought is a question. Can she mean that Celeste is too good for him? Very likely she does mean that, but at the moment he has no time for such female foolishness. "Oh, right. Absolutely" is what he says.

"Now everyone will love her even more than we already do." Polly focuses those pale, oversized eyes of hers on his face. "Celeste is passionately greedy in that way, isn't she? Never enough love, or approval. She's famished."

This strikes Charles as vaguely, slightly insulting to himself, and surely not a topic he wishes to pursue. In fact, why are they discussing Celeste at all? This is not quite what one does, in Charles's view, not at all what one does. And perhaps this whole notion of talking to Polly, of asking her certain things was wrong.

Just then, though, a quick, familiar pain somewhere around the area of his stomach makes Charles gasp. He clutches at that region of his person, lets out an "Oh!"

Polly is instantly at his side, one arm pressed around his body. How strong she is!

"Charles, ah, my old darling," Polly murmurs, so softly that later Charles is not entirely sure that she said that. Eventually he comes to believe that she did not.

"Honey, come on. You're drunk as hell." Sam to Dudley, whom he encounters emerging from a bathroom. She has not done a very good job of fixing up her face—Lord knows how it looked before she even tried.

"I most certainly am not drunk. Just because you—just because you happen to think."

"Baby, come on. I'll take you home."

Dudley stiffens away from him. "I'm not at all sure," she says.

"Honey, it's time to go home. The party's over."

"But we haven't even danced."

"Neither has anyone else." Sam has begun to laugh. "It wasn't a dance, remember?"

"Well, in that case." Dudley then allows herself to be led away.

An hour or so later the party is truly, entirely over, all the guests and all the help have gone, the house restored to cleanliness and order—except for the stray hidden Scotch-tinged glass of melted ice, the cigarette stub pushed into a potted rhododendron.

Perhaps looking for just those unlovely remains, Celeste still prowls about, in her yellow silk. Moving fast, looking everywhere.

Suddenly arrested by a sound, a household creak, she stops, hears the shuffle of footsteps. In an instant of alarm she imagines some barefoot intruder, lurking, waiting for her. But then of course a door opens, and it is Charles. Charles, in his handsomest dark red satin robe, just emerging from the study, which is actually his bedroom now. For years that room has been where he sleeps, alone.

And even though it is Charles and not some scary stranger, Celeste is still a little frightened: Charles goes to bed early, generally, and he goes instantly to sleep. Passing his room, she can always hear him snoring. He never gets up in the night. Never stalks around.

Going over to him and receiving a gentle, dry connubial kiss, Celeste asks, "Charles darling, are you all right?"

"Oh, yes, of course I am. But I heard you walking around, and I wanted to tell you something."

With no idea what to expect, Celeste looks up at him.

What Charles says, after the briefest but still the strangest little pause, is "I just wanted you to know that you're the most beautiful woman I've ever, ah, known. By a long shot the most beautiful, my dear Celeste."

THE PRESENT

10 Somewhere in the hills that lie between San Sebastian and the coast there exists a strange tribe of wild goats, very shy. The tribe is small: nine goats. Dudley, who has been observing these creatures whenever she can, always counts them, and there are always nine, and only nine, as though at the birth of each kid a grandfather goat keels over, dead. Or do the other goats kill him, in some esoteric ritual of goats? Dudley is intensely curious about the habits of these animals but she has managed to find out next to nothing. She can't find them in any books, and no one she knows has ever seen them. Walks with Edward or with Celeste invariably take place on days when the goats have chosen to be invisible. And Sam won't take those walks with her at all. He does not even believe in her goats.

They are especially beautiful goats, in Dudley's view. Their horns are large and very white, gracefully curved, like shells, and their hair is fairly long, some interesting pale color. Possibly it is silky—of course she has never seen them that close at hand, much less ever touched. And the goats seem to have some curious fifth or sixth sense about field glasses: whenever Dudley remembers to bring hers along, the good strong glasses inherited from her father, a noted Boston bird-watcher of his day, she either fails to see the goats at all or she catches only a glimpse of one of them: horns just protruding from above a rock, a tail just disappearing over the crest of a hill.

Her relation to these goats is intensely personal, Dudley feels. They are emblematic of some important area of her life, her consciousness—just what, or which, she is not at all sure. And in a practical way she worries about them: do they get enough to eat? Could someone ever possibly take a non-benign interest in them, with a view to capture—or, much more unthinkably, slaughter?

Voicing any of these goat thoughts to Sam invariably turns out to be an error; still, at times, under special circumstances, she does so. As on a rainy Sunday morning, near noon, when they are still in bed.

Not thinking at all, Dudley then says to Sam, "I do wonder about my goats. Do you think they get cold in this weather?"

And Sam begins to laugh. He starts to say something, and is then prevented by the laughter that shakes his throat, erupting from deep in his chest. So that Dudley laughs too. And as they look at each other it gets much worse, more impossible to stop laughing. So *silly*.

"Wet goats," Sam manages at last to say—at which basically not very funny phrase they start in again, laughing, in their tousled, floral-sheeted bed, now redolent of sea smells, stained with love. In an ashtray on Sam's nightstand are the sucked-down ends of two joints. Dirty roaches. And each of their nightstands holds an empty, high fluted champagne glass. Somewhere, quite possibly under the bed, is an empty split.

"Oh dear, how very dissolute we look" is Dudley's comment, a little later.

"Who cares? Who can see us? But Christ, I'm absolutely starving. What's for breakfast?"

"Breakfast. My God, let's have lunch." Sitting up, Dudley smooths her nightgown, her prettiest blue silk put on last night in hopes of just this occasion, this happy stoned morning with Sam, whom today she truly loves.

"I'd like a few pounds of pasta with lots of garlic and scallions and some cheese, and maybe a steak," Sam tells her.

"Well, lucky you. We just happen to have all that stuff. Even steaks in the freezer."

"And another split of champagne, don't you think?"

"What I think is, why not?"

Dining as she so elegantly does with Bill, in San Francisco restaurants, Celeste nevertheless spends a great deal of time alone in those restaurants. With elaborate apologies both as he leaves and upon his usually delayed return, Bill goes off to make phone calls. Sometimes, if the phone is in sight, Celeste can watch him there, talking, gesticulating. Often looking in her direction and blowing kisses. Or quite often he just goes to the men's room. At least that is where Celeste supposes he must be when he is out of sight.

It seems to her now that these absences have become both longer and more frequent in the course of her dinners with Bill. This present evening, this dinner in a brand-new restaurant, all smoke-tinted mirrors, brown leather banquettes and bright brass, everywhere brass as bright and white as gold—this evening makes their seventh dinner. (Celeste keeps count.) And Bill has been away for—well, for quite some time. Having finished her dessert—pears in cointreau, divine—Celeste is sipping at her fresh-brewed decaff, which from time to time a solicitous waiter replenishes.

And she is thinking: Is it possible that Bill is, uh, gay—or, as Charles would have put it, a bloody queer (although this was just a sort of joke, with Charles; actually he became very fond of Edward, and of Freddy too). That would explain a great deal. Bill at this very moment could be at the bar, which is out of sight, as the telephones are. He could be meeting someone.

It could also explain the fact that although Bill says a great many romantic things to Celeste, how beautiful she is, all that, he has no interest whatsoever in, uh, touching her.

But Celeste, in most ways a realist, a practical woman, has faced the fact that a much younger man who has for whatever reasons some sort of crush on a quite old woman, such a man might still not be interested in that woman in that way. A non-gay man, that is. Celeste does not really believe in the current mythology, fantastic sex between just such a pair.

Undoubtedly Dudley has various fantasies about Celeste and Bill; Celeste is quite sure of that. Dudley thinks in those sexual terms, she is given to speculations along those lines, whereas Celeste does not even allow herself to think about Dudley and Sam, or for that matter about anyone, in that way.

And suddenly Celeste comes up with what seems a very good idea: she will tell Dudley that Bill is gay. And then, when Bill comes down for the party, and stays over, as Celeste hopes and believes that he will, everything will be readily explained. No one will think it odd that they don't sleep together.

And she can also tell Sara that, and Polly. And Edward—or will Edward somehow know? Do they sense these things about each other, gay people?

All of these thoughts and plans are quite abruptly interrupted, though, by the return of Bill. Handsome Bill, in his perfect dark suit. Bill bending in his funny half-mocking way to kiss her hand. "Darling Celeste, whatever have you done to deserve such a rude old bastard?" He laughs and slides in beside her, continuing to talk, to explain. "The truth is, I got hung up on the phone, no way to get off. Business stuff. Oh, Lord, why didn't you make me something sensible like a poet?" He laughs again.

Celeste just manages a laugh of her own, though she has felt the smallest chill of estrangement. As though Bill for even the tiniest moment was not quite sure who she is. As though Bill, who is always so warmly interested in Celeste, in certain ways, who has encouraged her to talk about herself as no one ever has before (assuredly not Charles, who preferred the silent, listening Celeste, as most men did, in her experience)—as though that Bill had been exchanged for another person, who is talking to himself.

"But where on earth were we?" Bill now asks of someone, possibly Celeste. "I think I was telling you about Deauville, was I not?"

"I think so." Deauville, where Bill's parents often took him, long ago, was actually a couple of dinners back, but Celeste doesn't really care. She likes to hear about this glamorous childhood of Bill's, just as for the most part she used to enjoy Charles's wartime stories. And when Bill insists, as he sometimes does, that she in turn tell him about how and where she grew up, she is deeply pleased by his interest. "It's very important that you tell me all about yourself. I want you to be as open as you can with me. I want you to learn to be open," Bill has said. No one else has ever asked such questions of her. But at the same time that she is pleased, Celeste is made somewhat uncomfortable—no doubt her own fault: she is not an open person.

First meeting Bill, all those long-short months ago, Celeste was struck—indeed quite stricken—by his really remarkable resemblance to Charles: the high clear brow and those same wonderfully jutting eyebrows, the blue eyes and the nice small nose. (Their mouths are quite different, though; Bill's is much smaller, a tighter mouth.) The more she sees of Bill, however, while the likeness still is there it has certainly diminished. For one thing Bill is so much younger even than Charles when they first met, she and Charles. Very possibly Bill looks like a younger Charles? It occurs to Celeste to ask Polly that when Bill comes down for the party; for, after all, Polly knew Charles first.

"Obviously the trouble with such a perfect childhood, or one trouble, is that it quite ill-equips you for life," says Bill, with what Celeste has come to recognize as his small frown of sincere self-revelation. (He frowns in this way quite a lot.) "You're not comfortable in what turn out to be reality spaces. Nothing could quite come up to those beautiful old days. The beach, and sneaking around to peek into the casinos, the gaming rooms at night. Oh, I can so easily imagine you there, my lovely Celeste. I can even see you! And how good you are to let me run on and on like this. I tell you things—I feel so free with you, so comfortable sharing space. Do you think it's possible that in another life—?" He quickly laughs, turning this into a joke. And just now he looks most unlike Charles, this Bill, with his restless, brilliant animation. Charles was almost always serious, and often preoccupied.

"I had no friends at all in Berkeley," Bill says next, quite as though they had been discussing Berkeley. However, they have talked about Berkeley, at times, so this does not seem to Celeste an unreasonable transition. Bill was in Berkeley during the sixties; he was working for a news service, he has said. And Celeste has told him that her almost daughter, Sara, was there. But of course Bill did not know any students. "Nor I must admit did I want to, although I'm sure your Sara is charming."

As Bill talks on about Berkeley, his isolation there, those terrible years, Celeste's own sense of isolation returns. I really can't hear him, she thinks; he is trying to talk to me, to tell me something, and I can't hear. How lonely and isolated all people are, though, basically.

And then something quite new and startling comes to Celeste's mind, really something crazy. She thinks: Suppose we were married? Suppose—well, why not? Bill could just live in my house. We'd be company for each other, and I would leave him everything when I die. He could do whatever he wanted.

Gulping at his coffee, Bill next says, "Now please, don't let me go on like this about myself. Tell me about being a little girl, in the Valley. Will you have a brandy? No? But first, one instant. I'll be back in the tiniest flash."

A question that Celeste has put to herself more than once is: Just what does Bill see in me? Or, an alternate version: What does Bill *want* of me? The obvious answers being: Money. A house in the country.

Now, though, for the first time Celeste asks this of herself: What do I want of Bill? And the amswer comes quite easily: Companionship. I want to be less lonely.

And so why should they not marry? Marriage would serve both— all their purposes quite well.

Why not?

11 In the twenty years since she left Berkeley, Sara has lived in approximately as many places—and one of her invariable, by now unconsciously compelling rituals is a fairly long perusal of each new phone book. With more pleasure and interest than she quite admits to herself, she opens each new book, from the very thin, say, in Wheeler, Vermont, to the big thick fats in Pittsburgh or Cleveland. And, at the moment, the very fattest of all: Manhattan.

This fugitive existence has been at times, in fact for several very long periods, exactly that; although Sara herself has not been the fugitive, not "wanted," she has been shielding, somehow covering, a wanted person. For two years in Cincinnati (of all places, Sara sometimes thought) she lived in a basement apartment on Adams Hill, ostensibly alone, but actually Clyde was there too, in hiding, total hiding. Sara worked, as she usually did, as a temporary secretary, moving from office to office, scrupulously avoiding making friends (rather hard on her, a basically curious, gregarious person). She bought food at various groceries, never establishing herself as a person who shopped for two, not daring even a mythic absent husband. Black Clyde, who had killed one of the three policemen who were coming after him (very likely trying to kill him—they would have killed him, Clyde thought, and so did Sara) during a disturbance at a peace demonstration in San Francisco. Big black gay Clyde, whom no jury would ever credit with having acted in self-defense. (Clyde of course knew that very well, as did Sara.)

Seven months of Boise, Idaho, at times very cold, with Daryl, from Georgia, whom Sara's poor judgment allowed her to fall in love with, against all her rules.

Six months in Bishop, California—alone, resting up, which after those strenuous months with Daryl seemed a treat, and even deserved, but which involved more visits with Charles and Celeste.

A year in Memphis—crazy! What on earth was she doing in Memphis, with all those good old boys and girls, and their music, and their churches?

Five months in San Diego.

Et cetera.

It is very suspect, this non-way of life that she has quite deliberately chosen; God knows no one made her do it. She was asked; certain organizations would contact her, but always tentatively, saying, "Are you sure that you really want to take on ———? She [he] can be really difficult?" Clyde, Daryl. Joe, Dick, Luther, Grover, Betsey and some names she no longer remembers, although they belong to people with whom she lived quite intimately, took care of, worked and usually cooked for, discussed basic issues with, endlessly—oh, those labyrinthine, evasive but stubbornly persistent, always present basic issues!

People whom she has laughed and quarreled with, sometimes made love with, sometimes truly loved.

It is very suspect; what kind of gratification does she get out of all this semi-dangerous, often arduous, often downright unpleasant taking care? Sara has asked herself this hard, not pleasant question, has too often been asked it by others—including some supposed well-wishers: "open" people, friends. And she has come up with nothing. Surely no explanation so trite as a lack of children of her own would suffice, Sara tells herself; she is not even especially fond of children, and on the two occasions when she found herself pregnant, all the circumstances (including the fathers, who were surely a part of those circumstances) made bearing those children quite unthinkable, and the two abortions (especially the first, without anesthetic, in Seattle, in 1967) seemed necessary ordeals. Possibly even punishments that she deserved.

To Sara it has rather seemed that she has done whatever she has because whatever it was was there, something to be done, like Ever-

est, to be climbed. If someone did not hide and succor those movement fugitives, they would be arrested, and so certain people like Sara
took on that role. It was simply what she did, as another person might
dance, or do accounting.

Was it also some form of competition with Emma, her politically
correct but most non-maternal mother? Sara has wondered that too.

Even, Sara has felt, her body has had its part in the shape of her
destiny: she has always been a large dark person, with big soft breasts,
big thighs and legs, broad shoulders and heavy black-brown hair. A
couple of men who have loved her have found her beautiful: sculp-
tural, statuesque—"So generous, your body, it is like you." Those are
the words of love and praise she sometimes heard. But then all women
have some sort of hoard of love words, don't they? Sara very much
hoped so, for even the most impoverished. She surely did not see
herself as a beautiful woman. Just a very strong one, a woman built
for a life that required great strength.

In any case, leafing through phone books in any new city or town,
she looks for familiar names: the names of the people she has cared
for, or known in that life. And she looks despite her knowledge that
most or all of those people, those still at semi-liberty, even if they
surfaced would not be likely to have a phone in their own names.

New York is almost the only city to which Sara has not been, not
once, in those years since Berkeley. And she is only here now, in this
oversized, vast upper Fifth Avenue apartment, by a fluke: the place
belongs to the parents of Nancy, and after Nancy quite carelessly
surfaced (she was got off charges by the parental lawyer, her parents
being good old checkbook radicals), she got in touch with Sara. The
family's "second home" is in Bermuda, and so when a long vacation
was contemplated, grateful Nancy, who is a nice young woman, despite where she comes from—good Nancy asked Sara if she wouldn't
like a week of privacy and some rest. Which perfectly coincided with
Sara's California plans. A place to get herself together, peacefully,
before the big move: the new life in California with Celeste. The

interval between taking care and whatever it is that she does next.
Or the interval of taking care of Celeste, after Charles.

Also, Sara has just risen from two months of flu in Ithaca, New
York—but apparently not quite risen: every time she gets up, it seems
to knock her down again. Illogically, perhaps, when Nancy's offer
came along, Sara felt that the apartment would be large, warm and
quite safe (if anything is safe, these days)—as if Nancy's proffered
rooms would be therapeutic.

Sara now contemplates enormous windows, and beyond them Central Park, lashed with February rains, unceasingly. Trees billowed and
bent with wind and rain. Rain, and the wild shades of green in the
trees, the thin yielding leaves: that is what Sara looks at from her
unwontedly luxurious spaces—the depths of leather and velvet, heavy
folds of linen, palest wool carpets.

If she closes her eyes—as Sara at intervals does, for long, medi-
tative stretches—she notices that the sound of rain on glass is like
that of thrown sand; and she wonders about desert storms, sand-
storms, and tents, and refugee camps. Would this be the sound that
they too hear, are now hearing, in Africa?

However, Sara has disciplined herself (or tried to, very hard) not
to spend time worrying about conditions that she herself is not immediately addressing; since she is not at the moment actively working
on aid to African famines, African refugees from everywhere, and not
doing one damn thing (now) about the hungry, the cold and wet
street population of New York, she will not (non-constructively, sen-
timentally) brood about them. You do not do anyone any good by
just crying over them, is one of her firmest tenets.

And so she opens her eyes, sees rain now pouring in long sheets
down the window before her, no longer even sounding like sand. No
longer connecting Sara to deserts and windstorms, or to plague- and
famine-ridden multitudes.

She picks up the phone book again with, as always, the same
pleasurable expectation that a heavy novel by a favorite author might
arouse, and she starts on her list of names—all memorized, all sum-

moned up at random, varying according to mood and to the vagaries of remembrance. In a sense there is no list.

One of the names that appeared from time to time, thinly threaded to all the other names, is that of Alex Crispian, the once-lover, then furious prison companion of Sara's in Mexico. Green-eyed Alex, so tall, so extremely thin, with that huge tangled mass of white-blond curls, that scraggly reddish-blond beard. Alex who after Mexico, all that horror and quarreling, went off to wherever he came from (it turned out that no one, not even Sara, his lover, was ever quite sure), and no one heard from him again, least of all Sara.

And now there he is in the Manhattan phone book, at an address quite unfamiliar to Sara, but then most of New York is unfamiliar to her. She knows no one here. Except Alex, as things turn out. And even after so much time she experiences a certain excitement at his proximity, at the possibility of Alex, a person with an address, and a phone number that could be called.

She remembers, though, all their quarrels over Vietnam; sometimes Alex threatened to go, or to let himself be drafted. Suppose he did that, suppose now he is permanently, hopelessly damaged in some way, a Vietnam vet? Alex in prison was certainly enraged, but boyishly so; he was still a kid to whom something bad had accidentally happened. And all Sara's fault, as he saw it then.

Does Sara really want to risk it now, a grown-up, damaged and possibly still angry Alex?

She wishes the rain would let up. She very much needs some air, exercise, a change of scene. And at the same time she does not really feel well enough to go out. She continues to leaf through the phone book, searching out names quite at random.

To judge by appearances, an hour or so later, Alex is neither damaged nor visibly enraged. Nor is he down-and-out. He is only very wet, the rain not having let up for an instant—but he is laughing in apology for his condition. Handing his dripping raincoat to Sara, he props his wetter umbrella in the stand, in the marble foyer of her temporary quarters, which have turned out to be familiar to Alex. Over the phone, being given her address, he told her that some friends of his lived upstairs in this same building—or maybe down, he can't quite remember. People he knew some time back.

"New York is a smaller town than you'd think," he said. "The apple within the apple."

Now divested of encumbrances, he says to Sara, "You look so good! Just the same."

Knowing herself to look not the same at all (well, hardly, after twenty years—and not especially good: the siege of flu has left her looking older, Sara thinks, and visibly tired), Sara is mildly annoyed by this *politesse*. Does he believe women have to be told that they look good, that they haven't changed?

"Would you really like tea?" she asks, since that has been her offer, over the phone. "There's wine, there's some Scotch—"

A bright flashed smile. "Then there must be Perrier," he says.

Alex himself does not look much the same: he looks (so irritating) considerably better. His rain-wet, well-brushed hair is still a shade too long, but, as he must know, it is very attractive, a darker blond than before, waves rather than tangled curls. And the scraggly beard is gone. The few pounds that he had put on have made him look stronger, more in control, more at peace. His tweed coat is a little shabby, but still a very good tweed; his gray flannels bag at the knees— attractively.

So minutely observing this new grown-up Alex, Sara thinks, *Shit*, he looks great. He always will, no matter what happens to him.

Now, relieved of not having even the small task of making tea, Sara understands that she is more than flustered (that quaint word being the one that comes). She is more upset than she should be, much. In the kitchen, simply coping with ice, Perrier, she assures herself that she is simply feeling the effects of flu, she is not up to much.

And why, then, did she even ask him over for tea? But that question instantly answers itself as she recalls: I didn't actually ask him, he invited himself. He said he had an appointment in this neighborhood. (This neighborhood? With Nixon? With Mrs. Onassis?) An appointment at five-twenty, could he possibly come up? He'd like to see her. And so Sara had said tea.

Returning to the living room, the room termed the library by Nancy's parents, with her tray of Perrier, ice, glasses, wedges of lemon (it turned out to be more trouble than she had thought, after all), Sara observes how perfectly in keeping with this room Alex has proved to be—and she wishes she had changed her clothes. And she chides herself: *Changed clothes?* And for what purpose, exactly? However, there is Alex, clearly at home in that heavy aura of expensiveness (but from what is called old money: old books, embossed in gold, leather-bound. Old money). He has made her feel shy, in her old denim skirt, her silly faded T-shirt (A WOMAN NEEDS A MAN LIKE A MONKEY NEEDS A MUSHROOM, fortunately hard to read). And she hates herself for that shyness.

"Well, you're not exactly the Vietnam vet I thought I might see," she blurts out, defiantly, even before setting the tray down.

Alex laughs, a warm light sound that Sara remembers, but does he also, very slightly, blush?

"I didn't go," he tells her. "I don't think I ever really meant to. I was just a silly kid, sounding off." He seems then to wince at this memory of himself. "Besides," he adds, "I was getting a lot of static from my parents that I didn't tell you about. How could I? They wanted me to go to Vietnam. You see? You look shocked."

"I guess I am, a little." Oh, poor Alex, is what Sara just prevents herself from saying.

"But now tell me what you've been doing," Alex commands her. "I really want to know."

At which they both laugh, acknowledging the sheer impossibility of bridging twenty years.

But Sara tries. "I've moved around a lot," she tells him. "Different jobs. Different people. Nothing very conclusive. But now I'm going out to California." Wryly: "A fresh start." And she explains a little about Celeste, and the death of Charles. San Sebastian. "But what about you?"

Poor Alex blushes again as he tells her, "I have a feeling that you didn't know much about me at all, in Berkeley. I mean, where I came from, anything like that. Well, I guess in a way none of us did, it wasn't what we were talking about. We barely knew each other's last names."

Sara laughs, suddenly liking him a lot. Suddenly feeling him as a trusted, interested old friend. "I guess I just thought you were 'Eastern,' " she says. "I guess from New York."

"Well, it's a little more complicated than that." His look at her then is very intent, and worried. "I didn't know how to say it to you. How to say, 'Look, Sara, by the way, my dad is really rich. And he's also CIA.' Because that's how it was. Is."

He has so perfectly imitated a Berkeley sixties voice (his own) that Sara laughs, even as she says, "But how come I didn't know any of this? I mean, no hints?"

He too laughs. "I can be very cagey. It's an inherited trait." And then he continues: "I don't mean the CIA is how my father made his money. You know, the other way around. He's just the kind of guy they used to recruit back then. A rich boy, from old money. Princeton. For what he is, he's an okay person, really. Sort of idealistic. Of course we still fight a lot."

Alex is more or less between jobs, Sara gathers. He describes himself as a free-lance editor, naming magazines; he also says that from time to time he has taught at community colleges. He does not say that he lives on money from home, which may well be the case. He is studying Spanish. When he gets it together ("as we used to say"), he plans to go to Nicaragua.

Sara finds much of this, his job trouble, fairly familiar. Theirs is not exactly a work-oriented generation, she has thought. She files his Nicaragua plan in her mind for future conversations, noting as she does so that she must have decided that they are friends now, he and she.

And for the moment she is most interested in what she did not know before: his family. Money, the CIA. "I still can't quite believe it," she repeats. "And if you'd told me I would have been sympathetic, I think. Your arguments with your father. I could have identified with that, all my fights with Charles."

"But I was really intimidated by you," he tells her. "You and your friends. I remember when you told me your mother wasn't married, plus being a Trotskyist—I didn't even know what it was until I got up the nerve to ask someone."

"*You* were intimidated," Sara gets out weakly, feeling herself to be in some area past irony, even past laughing. "I thought you were the sun-god."

"Well, you see? If you'd known I had money too, it would have spoiled everything. But I did feel cheap when you paid for that trip to Mexico. I think that's one of the reasons I acted like such a shit. A guilty shit."

They laugh quite amiably. And then, quite as though she were alone, Sara closes her eyes, and hears the rain, and whine of wind.

What has been entirely left out of the story of Alex's life is any hint of the personal: no friends have appeared, much less any lovers, girlfriends. Maybe even a wife or two, why not? Most rich and handsome men have married at least once or twice by forty, Sara thinks. But then so of course have most women, most women at forty.

In the abrupt way that she recognizes as rude but can no longer control, Sara asks him, "What about girls, though? Women. You didn't mention at all—"

At this Alex blushes, but he gives a sober, even rational (for a while) romantic history. "I got married just out of school. Blonde beautiful Cecelia. Now she's a tap dancer, a teacher, in Tenafly, New Jersey. Where she's from. We lasted a year. I don't know why. Why we lasted or why we broke up either. Then, just women, a sort of line of them. Some lasting longer than others. It got sort of frantic. Meeting people, drinking, getting high. Doing some coke, a couple of other drugs. Someone's bed. All faster and faster. I began to think, If I could just spend some time alone. Get off. Maybe, even in some religious way, I could find a retreat. I've got a friend, a guy I grew up with, who's an Episcopal priest. I thought he could help." He laughs. "You see? I'm desperate." He has looked away from Sara in the course of all this; now he turns back to her, and in a resolute way he says, "I think I just don't want anything close with anyone, you know?"

"That's pretty much how I feel, though for sort of different reasons," Sara says—to reassure him? Maybe, she decides. But what she says to him is true: for almost a year now she has felt herself as an asexual person, and she has wondered, Is this how it is to be forty? Is this for good? What's all this I hear about geriatric sex: does that come later?

"Oh Jesus," Alex suddenly cries out. "Do you know it's after six-thirty? Holy shit."

"You missed your five-twenty," unnecessarily Sara comments. "Something important?"

Alex starts to laugh. "Just my shrink. Honestly. I've never done this before, missed an hour. It's sort of funny. But she might not think so."

"You could send me the money instead."

"One fifty? I'll have to pay her anyway, the stingy bitch."

"Is that what it is these days? Good God. Well, direct your check to some shelter."

"That's the price for us rich," Alex tells her. "And of course I send money to shelters. But couldn't we go out to dinner? First let me make two phone calls. I have to let her know I'm not dead."

Digesting the information that Alex, so tired of women, of "relationships," would still choose to go to a woman psychiatrist, Sara asks him, "Do I have to change?"

"Not unless you want to." He hesitates. "But maybe. Well, yes."

"I don't know," Alex ponders, somewhat later in the restaurant. His attention is now directed to Sara's immediate future. "I don't know," he repeats. "What I'm not really clear about is how you feel about Celeste. I mean beyond gratitude, old loyalty. All that."

"But all that's quite a lot."

"Oh, of course. I just meant in terms of getting along with her. The day-to-day rub. Small conversations. You know."

Sara laughs. "Not to mention basic issues."

"Oh, right, those crucial basic issues. But honestly, Sara, for all you know she could be really right wing. Lots of people are these days."

"Well, I know she's too snobbish to have gone for Nixon. I'm sure of that. Also she'd hate a scandal. Publicity. Which pretty much cuts out Ronnie-babe too. But of course I have thought, and worried."

"You really don't know her very well," Alex unhelpfully sums it up.

"That's true, I don't."

But who, as far as that goes, who do I know very well? Including you, dear beautiful Alexander. Sara asks herself this, and then smiles at an odd new thought, appearing not quite for the first time in her mind. Men are much more at ease when you've made it clear you don't want them, is what she thinks. So odd, and really quite a change.

Previously, in the old sexual mythology, men were always eager and women the ones who had to be lulled into ease. A theory sometimes employed to get someone, some woman into bed, a lulled woman being an unsuspicious one, in theory.

But that is not what she is doing with Alex; this is not the lull before a seduction, it really is not. Sara even wonders how much longer she can sit up in this restaurant. She feels very, very weak.

The restaurant itself is very pleasant, a good choice on Alex's part: a converted brownstone, up in the East Eighties, more or less around the corner from Sara's borrowed digs. Alex and Sara have a small room entirely to themselves, all dark and severely paneled. Old wood that gleams in the candlelight, from their pale blue linen table.

We are always in the most romantic places in the most non-romantic circumstances, is one of the things that Sara has thought, from time to time.

But the food is very, very good, the first that she has been able to taste for some time, the flu having deadened all her senses. But still she thinks, When I was in love with Alex, and maybe he with me, in his way, we spent all our time in dirty coffeehouses, and made love on broken boardinghouse beds—or sometimes, a big treat, we would go to some seedy motel down on University, smoke dope and drink awful wine and ravage each other's bodies, endlessly. And we ended up in jail, in Mexico, hating each other—as we watched that other couple, the dirty Florida blonde and the Mexican boy, humping, humping. Filthy, empty-eyed.

Whereas now, nowhere near in love, we bask in glamorously suggestive privacy and, both almost middle-aged people, we discuss the new directions our lives are taking.

"Well, I really hope it works out for you," Alex tells her, with his instant, still very boyish smile. "I might even come out to check up on you."

"You would?"

"Well, sure." But Alex's laugh is uncomfortable, as though he in some way still wonders why she called him, just what she was up to. For surely she, a woman, must be up to something?

Feeling his unease, and just then liking him very much, despite all his trouble (or because of it? She wouldn't put that past herself), Sara speculates aloud: "I wonder whether extreme beauty isn't really harder on men than it is on women. Oh, poor Alex!" But has she, despite herself, sounded unpleasant. She intended an idle remark— she thinks.

And Alex, though blushing, bears up fairly well. "Just knock it off, Sara, will you? Aren't we old friends?"

Considerably later, lying in her oversized bed, very much alone, exhausted, sleepless and nervously irritated, Sara castigates herself for what may well have sounded like rudeness. Why tease Alex in that way, about his good looks, which he really can't help? Alex, a vulnerable, confused but essentially decent person.

Why put him off with dumb jokes, when actually—actually, Sara tells herself, you long for Alex to be here with you now. And he could be, he could easily have come home, come to bed, if you had been even slightly nicer. If you had been the kind, humane woman you always pretend to be. Whereas in truth you are a total, an absolute crude jerk, and no one will ever love you or even like you again. Not ever. You are the fat forty-year-old person whom you have always scorned and dreaded. The fat white middle-class middle-aged woman. The enemy is you.

She is more or less used to these bouts of self-laceration, and they do not keep her awake for very long.

12 What Celeste first thinks—or, rather, what she feels—
on seeing Sara is an impulse to turn and run. Sara, just off her plane
and emerging from the flight tunnel in the San Francisco airport.
Celeste would like to pretend not to be there, or not to have seen
Sara.

Dark, tall, heavy-looking Sara, who is fortyish (that is perhaps the
biggest surprise) but still unmistakably herself, in an awful sheepskin
coat, a denim skirt and some big old boots, all pale and scuffed. Her
hair is long and bedraggled, worn in no discernible style.

Why have I done this? Celeste cries out, within herself. And, almost at the same time: Whatever will Bill think when he meets her?
Her third thought is, by contrast, a pious one: Thank God Charles
isn't here to see her.

"Darling Sara, how wonderful! But you must be exhausted" is
what Celeste actually cries out, aloud.

They embrace. Sara smells of shampoo, and some sharp rather
lemony astringent. Nice smells, really. A nice surprise.

"Well, I am sort of exhausted," Sara says, in a voice so familiar
that Celeste experiences a rush of affection, despite how Sara looks.
If she could just keep her eyes closed, could simply smell and hear
Sara, it would be all right, she quite nuttily thinks, and she smiles a
little bleakly to herself. Since Charles's death, Celeste has felt that
she is sentenced to private jokes.

"This thing is pretty heavy, though," Sara continues, shifting the
bulging, strapped and patched brown knapsack on her shoulder.

"It's immense," marvels Celeste, as though admiring strength. "I wonder they let you on the plane."

"Well, you have to get on carrying it as though there were no possible question, you have every right to have it with you," instructs Sara, quite as though Celeste would ever travel with such a burden.

By this time they are walking together along the broad corridor to the terminal—and an odd couple they must make, thinks Celeste. She in her little black Valentino, trimmed with the red silk braid, an old suit but still a Valentino. And Sara in those, those clothes. "We'll pick up your luggage downstairs," Celeste chatters, imagining God knows what sort of trunk, probably something with a rope around it. And she thinks again, How fortunate I didn't ask Bill to come along, or anyone else, for that matter.

Although Dudley offered and seemed genuinely to want to come. "You may need help," Dudley somewhat ambiguously said: could she have somehow foreseen how Sara would look? Did she mean that sort of help, support? But no, more likely she was thinking of luggage. Carrying things.

"This *is* my luggage," Sara tells Celeste. "This is it. Funny how traveling light can turn out to be so heavy."

"Well—" is all that Celeste can manage to say. Trotting alongside big Sara is taking all her breath, although she herself generally walks quite fast. "Well," she repeats. "How wonderful that we don't have to go down and wait for luggage. And so often they lose it," she babbles. "Impossible!"

She must stop talking, she truly must or she will faint. And so Celeste concentrates on looking at the crowds, all those others hurrying toward or past them, or just slopping along in the same direction that she and Sara are moving. And how terrible most people do look, these days, in airports! Celeste, though of course not actually traveling, is dressed quite as she used to believe that everyone should dress for trips: something dark, for practicality. And in those days a hat and gloves.

And how handsome all the men looked then in their hats. Celeste now sighs (a considerable expense of breath) at the sudden vivid picture with which she is assailed: Grand Central Station, the main concourse on a summer evening. All that elegant marble space, all the gilt, and those wonderful-looking men with their summer tans from weekends, in their linen or seersucker jackets, or dark blazers, their rep striped ties, and their hats!—those wonderful panamas, or dark straws with madras bands. When was the last time I saw a handsome man in a hat? she wonders. Even dear Charles had stopped wearing hats, except for his funny old Irish tweed caps for the country. Would Bill wear a hat if she went to Brooks and found him a wonderful one? Celeste very much doubts it; he just wouldn't. Bill is too young for hats.

"... so cold in New York," Sara seems at that moment to be saying. "And rainstorms. From this place I was staying in, the one I told you about, I could watch the storms in Central Park. Really violent."

"It sounded like such a nice place."

"Well." Sara can be seen to scowl. "I have to admit it was comfortable. Physically. Chock full of creature comforts. Christ, I was choking on comfort. Warmth and bath salts. But mostly I hated it there."

At which Celeste's strong but aging heart sinks, as at her first sight of Sara, and she wonders how Sara will feel about her house, this time. All the warmth and bath salts. "But in a way you enjoyed being in New York?" she asks hopefully.

"No, I didn't. I hated it." Defiant Sara. Always defiant—she hasn't changed at all.

"Well, darling," Celeste attempts, "I do hope California will be an improvement. This time."

A grin. "It'd almost have to be. But remember, Celeste, this is where I come from. I've been here before."

By now they have passed through the main lobby—or lobbies, so confusing. They have reached the parking area. And then, although she has carefully recorded it in her mind, Celeste cannot—she cannot for the life of her remember where the car is. Letters and numbers tumble about in her mind, a hopeless jumble: B one six H G L M N O P. Six—six seven eight nine. Oh, dear God!

However, so that nothing will show, she carefully controls her face; Sara must not begin by thinking she is dotty. (But no one even gets to be dotty these days, they call it Alzheimer's, a person not knowing where her car is.) Still. Celeste leads the way, toward rows and rows of bright shiny cars that are not her car. Then, when she can, breathing better, in a casual way she remarks, "My goodness, I could have sworn I left it exactly here." (She may have sounded silly but surely not senile, not sick. Not exhibiting the panic that she actually at this moment feels.)

Surprisingly, she is rescued by Sara. Sara saying, "I do this all the time. Whenever I have a car. I write down the number of where it is in my head, but never on paper. And then I mix it up."

Celeste looks up at her. "I'm afraid that's just what I've done."

"What you have to do is stop and close your eyes. Blank out your mind, and the right numbers will come to you, I promise."

"Like meditation." Meditation, her own sort of meditation, is a practice that Celeste has long employed, never mentioning it to anyone. Especially she did not mention it to Charles, after all the silly sixties transcendental business. Charles would have laughed.

"Yes. Like meditation," says Sara. "I've always done it."

"B. Nine." These syllables come to Celeste almost the instant her eyes are closed, and she says them aloud to Sara. "B. Nine."

"Well, look." Sara points to a big cement column on which is painted, in yellow, a very large B. "You see? We're in the right place. You really weren't lost at all. Nine must be right over there."

And, naturally, there it is, her nice small pale brown Jag. Celeste might have seen it herself. Why on earth was she so worried? Still, she has to admit that Sara was helpful.

"I'm afraid it's rather a long drive," Celeste says to Sara as at last they swing out and onto the freeway.

"Celeste, I remember. I know it's not next door."

Oh, why must she sound so gruff sometimes? It is frightening to Celeste, the very idea of gruffness. Having such a tone right in her house, for what she had thought might be forever. However, Celeste tells herself, Sara is not always gruff, not solely rude and gruff. And besides, she herself, Celeste, should be more tolerant of differences. (Polly tells her this often, as though Polly were not a mass of prejudices of her own.) Young people simply speak differently, these days.

She will take the long way to San Sebastian, Celeste then decides: over the hills to the coast, and then down. Instead of the freeway route, through ugly, boring San Jose.

* * *

"Oh God, it's so beautiful! How could I ever forget how incredible? That yellow!" Sara cries out, at the sight of a field of mustard: only mustard, but its thick bright color is spread across a billowing green meadow. "And look, there's the sea! Celeste, it's too much, I never saw anything so marvelous."

There are tears in her voice, Celeste is sure that she hears tears. Very moved, Celeste nevertheless controls her own voice as she says, "Yes, it is nice, isn't it?"

"*Nice.* God, Celeste, you're really spoiled." But Sara has laughed as she said that, not really scolding. Celeste only wishes that Sara would be less profane, and she decides—she determines not to mention that wish. After all, Sara is almost forty.

In some of her earliest imaginings of this meeting, her picking up Sara at the airport, Celeste had thought that they would then head into San Francisco, maybe for lunch at the Clift, or somewhere. Maybe, even, Bill would join them there?

It was Dudley, though, who talked her out of this plan. "Honestly, Celeste, you don't know how tired she may be. It's not always fun to be met and then just whisked off somewhere."

"That's quite true." And then Celeste acutely recalled Charles's habit of just such whiskings: her arrivals to meet him in Paris, or for heaven's sake Dubrovnik, she longing for just a bath and bed, but no, she would have to look perfect, as Charles always wanted and expected her to look. And then he would whisk her off for lunch.

"Besides," continued Dudley, in her brisk, Bostonian way, "you haven't seen Sara for quite a while. You hardly know what she looks like."

Prophetic, really, Dudley has turned out to be. No, Celeste had certainly not been sure how Sara would look, this time, and if she had she would not have thought for one minute of taking her to the Clift. With or without Bill.

However, recalling the conversation with Dudley has suggested an alternative plan, since it is almost lunchtime, and Sara cannot have eaten anything decent on the plane.

"You must be starving," she says to Sara. "There's a new place in town that a couple of friends of mine have been raving about. They had lunch there recently, I think. You remember Dudley Venable, and Sam? And Edward Crane? Well, you'll see them all again soon—in fact I'm giving a little dinner, the week after next. Valentine's Day. I know it's terribly silly, and Valentine's is certainly not the point of it. I just thought—"

Glancing over at Sara, Celeste observes an expression of puzzlement, perhaps annoyance? What has been wrong? Does Sara hate the very idea of a party in her honor—hate Valentines? And why is she, Celeste, talking now about the dinner anyway—what was she talking about before? She is lost!

"I am sort of hungry," Sara after a pause remarks. "The stuff they hand out on planes. Incredible. Pure shit."

Back in focus, Celeste registers shock: did Sara have to say that word? However, she manages only to say, "Well, do let's try this new place that Dudley and Edward seem to have liked so much."

The San Sebastian Bar and Grill. That is the name of the place, which, without much trouble, Celeste manages to find, where she stops and parks. It looks very much like several San Francisco restaurants that she has seen recently with Bill: a window of ferns, bright brass, white napkins, mirrors. Much more San Francisco than San Sebastian in spirit, is one of Celeste's reactions; it even strikes her as just slightly presumptuous. And then recognizes that that was a Charles reaction, not at all her own. Why should she care what anyone calls his restaurant? In fact, she does not care, could not care less, as Edward might say. (But she must stop this miming of other people, of men. It is not a good sign.)

As they enter, Celeste opening the door for Sara and Sara then stalking ahead, at first they see no one around, neither customers nor waiters. No help. Murmuring that they might as well sit down, someone will come, and she for one is exhausted, Celeste leads them to a table by a window, near a broad recessed bank of giant, exuberant ferns.

Quickly, though, Celeste begins to feel that Sara is reacting very badly to this place. She observes the stiffness with which Sara adjusts to the booth. (Celeste has been reading about body language, so interesting, so unconsciously revealing, especially in people whose bodies are entirely untrained. And she thinks of her own very rigorous training, the disciplines of dancing, those early years in New York.)

And Sara is frowning, but then Sara seems to frown a lot. Celeste has already noted these frowns; there must be a deep line between her eyebrows.

Minutes later, though, an attractive (despite his beard) young man appears soundlessly before them. So nice-looking, and now Celeste thinks she remembers Dudley mentioning such a person, or was it Edward? Dudley, she decides; it was Dudley, who still has such an eye for handsomeness in men, really more than Edward does. This person looks to be about Sara's age, although he is clearly in much better shape than Sara is. A young person who takes care of himself: clear smooth skin, barely tan, a soft beard and sad yellow-brown eyes.

"Hi, I'm David," he tells them familiarly, and Celeste begins to like him slightly less. She knows this to be the current custom; still, they don't actually have to introduce themselves.

"Is that so?" Sara interrupts both the musings of Celeste and anything else that "David" might have had to say. So rudely! So loud.

"Well, yes, that's my name," the poor fellow almost stammers.

"Is it really." Glaring, terrible Sara.

"Well, we're very hungry, both of us." Celeste feels that she must break up this highly unpleasant exchange. And so mysterious: doesn't Sara know that that is how waiters talk these days? Maybe she never goes to restaurants. "Could you tell us what you have?" Celeste asks David.

The young man, who now uncomfortably blushes, begins to reel off names of dishes. Vegetables, pastas. Cheeses, salads, omelettes.

"Oh, California purism," Sara snarls.

"Well, uh, yes. You could put it like that. We are vegetarians."

Anxiety and a strong desire to get it all over with and to leave have combined to deafen Celeste to the list of foods. She orders the last thing she is sure she heard on the list, or almost sure: a cheese omelette. Sara orders the same.

"I gathered you didn't like him." Celeste hears her own dry voice, dry and very stiff. It is, she fears, a way that she often sounds.

Sara sighs. "I don't seem to like many people these days" is her comment. "And he did seem such a type. I hate friendly people."

Oh *dear,* is the strongest inner complaint that Celeste allows herself as, later that afternoon, she lies at last across her own bed. Their bed, hers and Charles's. The large window faces west, faces just now into what may be a wonderful sunset; these late-winter or early-spring skies are often amazing, rare luminescent colors. But Celeste is quite simply much too tired to look, and she lies there with her eyes closed. And tries hard not to think of Sara.

Mantra. Mantra. Mantra. She repeats and repeats this word, rhythmically, meaninglessly. Again and again. Because (this is one of her secrets) the word "mantra" is her mantra. Celeste enjoys the small private joke of this.

But it doesn't work. Or not quite. Sara, who is presumably asleep, or resting in the guest room down the hall, still forcibly intrudes.

After the entire failure of their lunch (Sara's unabating rudeness, then her silence), Celeste had to fight off sheer despair as they drove home together. Toward Celeste's house. She will hate it, Celeste was thinking. Probably she always has, every time she visited. And what is worse, she will say so, loud and clear. ·

She was thinking all this as they rounded the last curve in the pale green hills.

But, "Celeste, it's so beautiful! I never thought—Celeste, your house is just like you!" was Sara's exclamation. "That yellow, I forgot how wonderful!" and there seemed to be actual tears in her eyes.

"It's rather Florentine, actually," Celeste, very moved, informed her guest.

How strange she is, Celeste now thinks, in the privacy of her room, behind her closed eyes. How contradictory. How very like her mother. She sounds like Emma. Even the smells of Emma. Soap and astringent. Lemon.

But everything will be fine, Celeste assures herself before returning to her mantras. It will all be fine, she says firmly to herself, before sleep.

13 In February, shortly after the arrival of Sara at Celeste's, the wind and cold, the winter rains returned to San Sebastian, and the two events, Sara and winter, were not unconnected in the minds of certain friends of Celeste's, at that time. In a practical sense, it was the weather that kept everyone close to home for those weeks— not entirely at home; they all went out for normal shopping errands, including certain essential visits to their doctors, lawyers, accountants. But by tacit mutual agreement it was established that any real social contact was in abeyance.

Thus no one really saw Sara for a while, and though it seemed eminently reasonable that they should not, still it was also felt as slightly odd.

Dudley especially thought it strange, although she knew better, knew it was actually not strange at all. Of course, she said to herself, given Celeste's very high regard for formality even among her closest friends, Celeste would not simply come by with Sara along. She would not just call up and say, "Sara and I have an errand in the village. If we came by about five, would you give us a cup of tea?"

No, Celeste would not do that; she would want some ceremony attached to their first visit—or, rather, revisit—with Sara. After all, Dudley had met both Sara and her mother, Emma, years ago in New York.

A skinny, tall, very dark and extremely defiant child, with her small pretty yellow-haired mother—that was Sara then. Their total dissimilarity to each other, physically, suggested that not looking like Emma was Sara's first act of rebellion—along with other, darker possibilities.

This was during the bad period when Dudley and Sam were "not seeing" each other, times when Dudley was aware of very little outside her own pain. Horrible: at those times, perversely, her ravaged mind remembered only the best of Sam: Sam's voice, his face, his jokes. His body, Sam in bed. Not the swollen-faced drunk, the stranger who hated her and whom she hated back (she too being pretty drunk, usually). The Sam whom she had told to leave her life. Recalling only the good Sam, and unable not to think of him, desperate Dudley had had her hair streaked blonde, a great unsuccess. (In an effort to be a woman Sam had never even met? She was never sure.) She continued, mostly, to drink too much, she sometimes fell into bed with other men, too often (oh Christ, the ultimate sordid humiliation) weeping in bed with strangers. She had hardly dared mention his name, Sam's name, not even to Celeste.

It was during one of those frightful times (dear God, to have had more than one of them, and still survived) that Celeste called and asked Dudley to come and meet her friend from California, Emma. And Emma's young daughter, Sara. Sara, whose birth Dudley so clearly remembered, since it occurred the day she met Sam. In 1945.

Though, really, she was in no mood for either an old friend or a child. Or even Celeste, who surely meant well, intending distraction. (She must have known or had some idea how Dudley felt.) But still.

Now remembering mostly the pain of that time (how vivid it is, remains), all that pain over Sam (people are quite wrong to say you can't remember pain, Dudley thinks), Dudley now can recall very little of Emma beyond that California shock of straw-colored hair, and a surprisingly deep gruff voice from such a small woman. And a sense that Emma was somewhat subdued by being with Celeste. (Celeste sometimes had that effect, probably unintended.) And that Emma was afraid of her daughter, somehow guilty toward her daughter, perhaps for providing her with no father? Dudley remembers that Sara made a terrible scene about something. What to wear? Where to go? And that she, Dudley, felt a strange sympathy for the child. How enviable to be able to say, as Sara did say to her mother, "I absolutely will not go. There is no way you can make me."

Something like that is what Dudley should have said to Sam, she thought then; she should have said, No, no, you can't drink that much, you can't keep drunkenly rushing out of my house as though you hated me, you can't say the things that you do say when you're drunk. What she did say, under those circumstances, and always in her crisp New England voice, was "I simply don't want to see you again." Instead of a passionate, childish tantrum. Like Sara's.

Now, with the bad, unexpected weather, which is linked to Sara (in Dudley's mind, at least), during a short respite from the rain Dudley watches stray sea gulls wheel and soar, as though seeking to lose themselves in clouds. Silently, standing still and alone in the big wooden room, their bedroom, she watches until the rain starts again. A heavy, punitive gray downpour, bleak, imprisoning.

Later that afternoon over tea with Sam, she tells him, "I can honestly see why people move to Florida, or Arizona. The older you are, the worse bad weather seems. Have you noticed?"

"Not yet. Maybe next year, though." Sam smiles, referring to an old joke: the fact that Dudley is almost precisely one year older than he is.

But his smile is a surface smile, involving only the automatic muscles of his mouth, and Dudley sees the sadness in his eyes. And she knows its focus, its source, which is his present inability to work, to paint. That is what aging means to Sam: not painting. Which is not a fit subject for jokes. Dudley has even caught herself pretending similar problems; she has not yet told Sam, for instance, about a recent offer from a travel magazine that would like to send her to Ireland.

"Poor Sara, though, coming out to visit in this weather," she brightly essays. "Or, rather, poor Celeste, all cooped up with her."

"Celeste must like her, though?"

"Well, but it's been such a distant liking. It's quite another thing to have someone under your roof." Can this conversation be of any interest to Sam, though, possibly? It seems to Dudley familiar; they have had this same talk before—but on the whole even talking redundantly seems preferable to not talking at all.

"She's going to change our lives quite a lot," Sam suddenly pronounces. Sam, who rarely pronounces, who is rarely portentous.

A thrill of sheer interest seizes Dudley; of course, he must be right. "Whatever do you mean?" she asks him.

He retreats—of course he retreats, how like him! "Well, I probably don't really know what I mean," he tells her. "And very likely I'm wrong." Saying this, Sam sounds much more like himself: mildly ironic, vaguely self-deprecatory. Evasive.

"You must have an idea, though?" Dudley pursues, somewhat aggressive.

"No, I was just talking to hear myself." His familiar bad-boy grin is nevertheless of some cheer to Dudley, and she thinks, as she sometimes does, How *fond* we are of each other, after all. No wonder we're still together, *malgré tout*. (At other times, she still is capable of thinking, Oh, how could I not have left him for good, long ago?)

To Sam she says, "One thing I do wonder, though. Have we said this before? I do wonder what Sara will do out here. Visiting Celeste isn't exactly a full-time occupation."

"Maybe she's a painter." Sam, heavily ironic. "Almost everyone seems to be these days. If they're not writers. Her form of self-expression—God forbid any self should go unexpressed."

"I suppose she actually could be." Dudley had not thought of an artistic endeavor for Sara, but what Sam has said is quite true, of course; it is what everyone seems to be doing—or, if not, feeling guilty about creative lacks. And she thinks, Oh dear, suppose she is a painter. Suppose she's a good one, quite successful; we might not have heard of her—how awful that would be for Sam. "More likely a writer, don't you think?" she asks him.

"Who knows?" Sam gets up to kick at the small fire that sputters in the grate. "Wet wood," he mutters, but his kick has been effective; the flames enlarge, reaching higher and higher up into the chimney, and other logs farther back catch on, joining the conflagration.

"You're incredible with fires, you really are," Dudley praises him as she stretches long legs, now in velvet pants and slippers, her evening garb. And then, musingly, "How narrow of us, though, to assume anything 'artistic' for Sara. I do think there's so much pressure on people these days to do that sort of thing. How hard it must be on women who simply want to marry and have a lot of children."

"I'm sure you're right." But Sam has gone vague again. This conversation, like so many, does not engage him. An essentially practical man, he is made slightly uncomfortable by theoretical talk.

And so Dudley, who is writing an article for a new women's magazine, called *Women*, on just this issue, the social pressures mitigating against the domestic woman, decides (again) not to mention this to Sam. For one thing he might quite reasonably question her ability to deal with such women: childless Dudley, always scribbling away. She rather questions it herself, but she knows that she has a certain knack for empathy.

"Maybe she's some sort of spy," Dudley now lightly, idly speculates. "Gathering information on the habits of the old."

"Good God, who'd care."

"Well, people rather seem to, these days. We're almost a fashionable minority, younger people are a little afraid we'll try to take over, the way blacks and women are feared. They wouldn't put it past us to live forever, and what on earth would they do with all of us then?"

"Myself, I'm just afraid the President will live forever."

"Well, exactly," Dudley tells him. "Anyway, there've been a lot of articles about us. The over-sixty, getting-into-seventies group, I mean."

"Oh, your ladies' magazines."

"Well, if you read them you'd know a little more about the world," Dudley gently chides, not adding that those very magazines to which Sam condescends have in large part supported them both, over the past ten years of his non-work. "But I doubt that anyone would want to spy on us. Not even the IRS."

"Maybe Sara has a secret lover stashed away out here, and they plan to settle down. In Celeste's house."

Dudley laughs. "How romantic," but at that moment the phone rings, and she goes to get it.

Sam hears her say, "That's great. In fact, we're just having tea." He can tell from her voice that she is talking to Celeste. "Come on by," he hears Dudley say. "We'd love to see you. And Sara."

Returned to Sam, she remarks, "How odd. Just what I would have sworn she wouldn't do."

"She could be desperate. I'll get some more wood."

"I'll make fresh tea."

* * *

"Did this Sara ever have children?" Freddy asks this seemingly irrelevant question of Edward on a Saturday morning as they laze over their traditional large, late breakfast, a meal once invariably preceded by love. Today it is relatively early, nine o'clock, and Edward, not Freddy, has done the cooking. Thus cod cakes (frozen), beans and bacon, instead of the wilder, spicier Mexican treats that Freddy once provided.

However, Sara has suddenly become such an obsessive topic in this small household that no question about her seems irrelevant. "Not that I know of," now says Edward. "But she could have had several without our knowing. Without even Celeste's knowing."

"True enough." Freddy pours out coffee for them both, in oversized blue pottery cups, at their pretty blue checkered-clothed table. Glassed-in from the rain. All around their cozy porch, winds lash at cypresses, they batter the eucalyptus; rains dash against the glass noisily, threateningly.

"It's interesting that none of these women in our lives seem to have had any children." Edward has not quite thought of this before. "Not Dudley, not Celeste or Polly. Not a mother in the bunch. Do you think that's why we like them?"

"Maybe more why they like us. We're child substitutes." But Freddy laughs.

And Edward thinks, How wonderful for a change not to be discussing AIDS, or some aspect of that horror. At least Sara is a sort of diversion for us all.

"Didn't any of them ever want to have children, do you know?" Freddy now asks. "In my country—" and in a helpless way he shrugs, with the gesture implying the hundreds and thousands of babies born each year in Mexico; as Freddy sees it, born into a relentless wave of poverty, hunger, illness.

"I don't really know. It's not the sort of thing that women tell one," Edward muses. "Even Dudley has never discussed it, as long as I've known her."

"You mean, it's not fag-hag conversation?" Freddy in his social-political involvements has picked up a lot of argot that Edward could very well do without, as he does not say to Freddy. The use of the word "poke," for instance, inflicts true pain on Edward.

Choosing to ignore that particular sally of Freddy's, Edward continues, "In Dudley's case, whatever her feelings were, I'd say there just never was an appropriate time for her to have kids. Her first husband died so early on. I mean, they could have but it's surely just as well they did not. And then with Sam, things were so very turbulent, for such a long time. All that booze. And his kids. Already those four daughters."

"And Polly's never been married." Ironic Freddy then becomes serious. "She'd never let that stop her if she wanted to, though. If she wanted kids. With her it must have been a principled decision."

"It could well have been that for Dudley." Edward defends his own true favorite among all women. "One would prefer to think so, wouldn't one?"

"One surely would," Freddy says, smiling.

"Even Celeste." To Celeste too Edward is loyal, a staunch admirer. "With her first husband nothing worked out—he simply dumped her, is the way I hear it from Dudley. Celeste never mentions him at all. And then when she met her true love, Charles, it was quite a bit too late."

"I still wonder about Polly, though." Polly is Freddy's favorite person, inexplicably to many, including Edward, who has had to admit some jealousy to himself. But it must be something other than her fluent Spanish that draws them together? "I can so easily imagine her braving everything, even back there in the forties or fifties, to have the child of the man she loved. As Sara's mother must have, as a matter of fact."

"You do romanticize her." Edward has spoken more dryly than he meant to.

"She's a romantic woman." As he says this, Freddy's eyes enlarge—such intense dark eyes. But then everything about him abruptly changes, eyes, mouth, his voice, as he says, "But how about us, darling old Edward? What do you think, shouldn't we adopt a kid?"

"You can't be serious." This new gay, liberated Freddy is often a person whom Edward is not at all sure that he knows.

"It's a little tricky sometimes, but it is now an option for gay men. Think what we could do for some dear handsome little boy. The trouble we could save him."

He is not serious—thank God. "Why not some adorable little girl?" asks Edward. "So much more of a challenge for both of us."

Freddy laughs. "Well, you're right there." And then he says, "Why don't we just not read the paper at all today?"

"We always say that, especially on Saturdays."

"Actually it seems less bad to me on Saturdays than on other days. It's so much shorter. Besides, someone might have died."

And there they are, Edward thinks. Back to AIDS. Even over-familiar complaints about the *Chronicle* seem preferable, and so he announces, "It's such an appalling paper that degrees of appalling-ness hardly seem to matter. If someone we know has died, you will simply have to tell me about it. I'm going to see if Dudley's game for a nice rain walk."

Freddy's estimate of Polly has at least an intuitive correctness; he is right, that is, in believing that (probably) she would have had a child by a man she loved, had she wanted to. Alone. By Charles, for in-stance: if she had become pregnant while they were lovers, she might—well, she would have, she knows, put up a fight for that child. (In which case Charles and Celeste could have never married, could they? At some point Polly would have had to say to Celeste, "But he's the father of my child." Wouldn't she? Instead of pretending that she barely knew Charles, and thus did not mind tending him in intimate ways as he lay there, dying.)

But Polly did not become pregnant by Charles; she was only preg-nant once, and then in her early forties, the early fifties of the cen-tury. By a man whom, except in bed, she did not care much about. As it turned out, though, he cared a great deal about Polly, a very great deal: he wanted them to marry and have the child.

"But, aside from everything else, I'm too old to have a child. Especially a first child."

"But I love you." The man was a surgeon, quite illogical in mat-ters outside his immediate expertise.

"But, my dear, I don't love you" was Polly's counter. "We would not be good parents together."

"You're unfair, you want to kill our child."

Reasonable Polly saw the logic of this; in a sense she was being unfair in refusing to bear a child that was also his. However, as in subsequent arguments, she pointed out with varying degrees of tact and gentleness (not always Polly's strongest suits) that it was she who would bear it, she who would be ultimately responsible, no matter what he said or believed or promised.

And so, an abortion.

For whatever deep-rooted reasons of her own, quite possibly including some guilt toward "the father," Polly decided to undergo one of the cheap abortions that poor women had in those days: she went to an Atlantic City chiropractors' clinic, with two hundred and fifty dollars, in cash.

This is not an event that Polly ever thinks of. And she would certainly have supported, as she does, women's rights to legal, funded abortions even without such horrible personal knowledge of the alternative.

This strange, prolonged wet spring has been for Polly an exceptional time: as she herself might put it (and she did so put it in a burst of confidence to Freddy, her only confidant: they trust each other), she has taken a lover. A considerably younger, though bald, nice man. ("I quite like bald men, don't you? No? Well, for me I guess it's reassuring, it seems to even things out.") A dark Spaniard, named Victor Lozano, who works in the local garage.

Victor grew up among the poor, in San Sebastian, in the terrible thirties, his family having come from Spain some ten years earlier to work the vineyards of the San Joachim Valley. Generations of passionate proud anarchists, Polly has gathered. Cataláns. He and Polly first became friends on the basis of language; she addressed him formally, always in the purest Castilian, as she biked around the town on her rattling, failing bike. In her tattered jeans, her own bald head concealed in a red bandanna.

At some point Polly asked Victor if he knew anyone who could fix bikes, and Victor replied that he could, of course he could. He could and also did fix her refrigerator; he fixed, one by one, all the things that broke in her house. At some point, recognizing a mechanical skill that amounted to genius, Polly thought, How sad that he did not become a doctor; later she decided that he was probably better off as he was—he would never have made it in the medical establishment. Only, he was still fairly poor. He was married and had four or five children—at no time did they talk about any of those people.

In fact, they had very little personal conversation until the day, a couple of weeks ago, when Victor arrived to fix Polly's radio and found her in bed, taking aspirin, fending off (she hoped) a cold. And practical Victor simply joined her there. He attended to her long-weary, long-unloved body with the same gentle care that Polly had seen him lavish on old machines.

And he in turn seemed very pleased by her. "The greatest woman, the most beautiful for fuck," he told her. (For reasons of his own, Victor always spoke English in bed: perhaps believing that that was what Polly expected?) "I knew it would be so," he said to her.

What would happen after that? was one of Polly's concerns, that first time with Victor. Would he want to see her a lot? Or, worse, see her never again? Either would be in its way intolerable.

It soon became clear that Victor chose to see her on Thursday nights. In fact, on each and every Thursday night. And when they saw each other in the village he was as friendly, as courtly as ever. And as slightly distant. Victor, a very formal man.

Thursdays have obviously some special significance, then: his one night out? Or, less likely, his wife's night out? Polly chose not to inquire. She took what she could of Victor, and gave him as much as he would allow her to. Theirs was not a guilty connection, for either of them; they both felt and expressed the most tremendous affection for each other.

(Still, it would have been more than a little hard to explain to Celeste, or to Dudley, both of whom would insistently have referred to Polly's "lover." But Polly had less than no desire to explain.)

Before Victor, in her hazy, infrequent thoughts about a possible late-life love—or "a little sex in my life," as Polly would have been more apt to put it—one worry or deterrent to those thoughts was the very fact of her baldness. But Victor touches her bare head with the same gentle tenderness felt on all her bare skin, everywhere. Her whole exposed old self. As she touches him.

And no one knows, except Freddy, who knows that Polly has "someone" but not that it is Victor.

Forced in upon themselves by the wretched, inimical weather, Celeste and Sara are not doing terribly well—as Celeste might have put it, had she been able to discuss the subject. Unused to each other in every conceivable intimate way, most of their daily encounters have been fraught with trouble.

Sara thinks: At least it's a large house. Suppose we were sharing a bath? The time she takes!

And Celeste thinks: At least we have a maid. At least there is silent, industrious Margarita making our meals, washing up. Although actually Sara is considerably tidier than one might have thought, given her general appearance. And one night Sara insisted on making dinner, a great surprise: just pork chops, simple enough, but very, very good.

What they say to each other, perhaps once or twice too often, is "How nice that we both like to read." And they add, "Especially in this weather."

The telephone, curiously, seems to present the most nearly insurmountable problem, trouble lying in the fact that there are two and only two instruments in all that large and sprawling house. This eccentricity is due to an idea of Charles's that there should be only one telephone in a house, and that in the living room. (What he really liked, Celeste has admitted to herself, with disloyal twinges, what Charles cared about was an audience for his own calls. All their friends knew that there was only one phone, and so, in the midst of a dinner party, when a call came for Charles from the White House—this actually happened; Celeste enjoyed telling Sara—what could he do but take it, right there before them all?)

After Charles died, Celeste had a phone installed in her bedroom. However, now that Sara is here, Celeste reflects that she should—oh, indeed she should, as she meant to—have had several new instruments installed before Sara arrived. Along with a few other things that she surely meant to do but did not quite get around to.

It is especially bad when she, Celeste, has an urgent phone call to make, one that must not be overheard, as is so at present. (Unbeknownst to Celeste, Sara has just the same problem.) Talking to Bill in the idle way that they do, in range of Sara's long censorious ears, has been bad enough, along with some friendly, innocent chats with Dudley and with Edward, although these chats sound much less innocent and far sillier when overheard. But the call that Celeste most wants to make demands absolute, strict privacy. It's a matter of life and death, Celeste inwardly murmurs: I have got at least to call Polly.

At last: Sara is audibly, splashily bathing in the guest bathroom, which is nearer the front of the house than it should be.

With just-not-shaking hands, her gaze fixed on the beautifully massed clouds beyond her gray-linen-framed window, Celeste dials Polly's familiar number—and gets it wrong: a small child answers, shrieks, "No, no we got no Polly!" More shrieks, and shrill unchildish laughter.

Quite unnerved, Celeste still tries again, dialing very, very slowly. This time she gets it right, she gets Polly. Polly who at some point in her life is known to have had some training as a nurse. Plus Polly's own intimate experience with major illness; in Celeste's view that is what most counts.

"Well," Polly begins, having heard what Celeste has reported. "Well, the color of the blood is very important. Indicative of where it is. Where whatever is bleeding is, if you follow me. The darker it is, the higher up."

"Oh."

"But look, Celeste. There're five or six first-rate hospitals in San Francisco. A couple of hundred of good doctors, probably. I don't like them either, but this is nothing for you to fuck around with."

"Do you have to use that word?"

"Yes, sometimes I do. I repeat, this is not something for you to fuck around with by yourself. I just don't know very much. I don't keep up. And I think it's to my credit that I know how little I know. Look, Celeste—"

Celeste sighs deeply, a sigh that is infinitely tired. "I'm just too old for all that. Young doctors, new treatments, hospitals, new machines. Oh, I'd just rather—I'd rather be sick."

"You'd rather die, are you saying?"

Celeste's laugh is light and almost convincing. "Darling Polly, don't be so melodramatic. Please. I could live for years and years. I'm in terrifically good shape, actually."

A pause. "Sure you are. Except for this bleeding you're great. And it could be nothing. But, Celeste, you've got to find out."

"Oh, darling Polly, I will. I promise."

Later that same day, during Celeste's own bath, which Sara well knows will take at least half an hour, at that time she makes her own phone call. Collect, to Alex in New York. (He has tactfully suggested this arrangement to avoid any possible questions from Celeste about the phone bill; Sara has gathered that money is not among his problems, but she still feels an occasional spurt of guilt over the length of their conversations. Which Celeste would certainly notice.)

"Well, things could be worse, I guess," Sara now tells him. "But this filthy weather isn't helping any. California! I'm beginning to feel like I carry some plague around with me, everywhere I go it rains. And Celeste is—well, she's a very positive thinker. She tries so hard. And she's got something going with some guy, some 'Bill' up in San Francisco. Honestly, she waits for his calls like someone in junior high, and then she just giggles a lot. But she means well, I guess. And I like her friends pretty well, I always have. Dudley, she's the sort of old but very sexy Boston type. Married to the painter Sam Venable. Remember him? And a great woman named Polly, everyone's sort of afraid of her, they can't get a handle on her. And a nice gay couple, two guys. It's interesting, really. Watching to see what they make of me, for example."

Alex tells her, "My parents are off in St. Martin. Their idea of what to do in the winter. Retirement is very hard on the rich."

"This dumb thing has happened, though," Sara next says. "There's this stupid guy, in fact he's a waiter—nothing against waiters of course but he's the kind who tells you what his name is. So goddam friendly. Hi, I'm David. And everywhere I go I seem to run into him, and this is a very small town. The worst of it is everyone else seems to think he's 'cute'—they use that word. Celeste would like to fix us up, I think. *Jesus.*"

Alex laughs. "It sounds very Californian out there. Oddly enough." And then he tells her, "Guess what, my shrink set me free. Enough already, she said."

"Well, that's good, I guess?"

"I think so. Anyway, it leaves a lot more time and energy for more interesting areas than my psyche. Like Spanish, which is really beginning to come together for me. I'm reading Neruda—fantastic."

"You can give readings in Nicaragua."

"Don't kid, I just might."

This is more or less the tone of most of their conversations, which take place with increasing frequency. Alex and Sara, long distance.

14 Dudley and Edward, inveterate old walkers, share a New England commitment to hardiness. In the course of that long, wet, unanticipated season, they take not one but several long rain walks, not always as much for the pleasure of the walk itself (impossible not to get wet, not to feel the penetrating cold, the winds) as for the ensuant sense of virtue, even of moral rectitude. As both Sam and Freddy, though separately, have remarked, they have tended to come home terribly (most annoyingly) pleased with themselves.

On certain other days, though, some sudden shifted view can make it all more than worthwhile, in fact breathtaking, memorable: the wind-pulled skies, and shifting, kaleidoscopic formations of clouds.

As now. They stand on a hilltop, its deep thick green grasses all flattened by winds, even the gray outcroppings of rock lying low, as though worn down by the elements. A moment of clearing: a massive parting of gray clouds to blue skies, the sun. And from where they stand, on that broad smooth flat height, Dudley and Edward can see everything. In the distance, flat and shining, lies the sea, and before the sea, stretching, reaching far out into the water are long green fingers of land, curving to estuaries, descending down to beaches. An enormous view, so much green land, black water, so much gray sky, with its sunny burst of blue.

To Edward it looks like the Algarve, in Portugal, before (he remembers) the Germans came and ruined it all, with their greedy developments, terrible apartment buildings, condominiums. He is thinking fondly and sadly of a now distant trip to Spain and Portugal that he and Freddy took, soon after first meeting.

Dudley thinks that it looks like the coast of Ireland, where she has never been; but all that green, that must be more or less how Ireland looks, mustn't it? She hopes that she and Sam will make that trip; her magazine still wants her to do it, but she vaguely feels that they will not, that for some reason or other Sam will refuse to go.

However, instead of mentioning these associations, Dudley and Edward continue their already begun conversation, which concerns Celeste and her party. Celeste and Sara. Celeste and "Bill."

"It is rather scaring, actually," Edward remarks. "The extent and the strength of the fantasy involved."

Dudley ventures, "But it won't necessarily fall apart, do you think? Celeste has the most enormous powers of will."

"Well, that's quite true. But I don't think even Celeste can will herself back to being a young mother. With, as she puts it, a 'beau.' "

Dudley laughs, just barely. "I don't think it's entirely motherhood that she wants with Sara. In a way she just wants to like her, and maybe somehow to help her. Of course it's a way of having Emma back too."

Edward sniffs, from the cold rather than in contempt. " 'Wanting to like' has always a rather ominous ring, wouldn't you say?"

"Oh, would I. It's what Sam's girls all said about me, the new Yankee mom. 'We'd like to like Dudley,' they said, more or less in chorus. But with Celeste and Sara—well, I do think there's more good will involved, I mean it's not just *will*. Sam's daughters really didn't want to like me at all. Of course not."

While they have had this short exchange, the skies have closed again; now everything is gray, and the folded clouds threaten rain.

Edward coughs.

"You do see a doctor sometimes?" Dudley asks him.

A curt laugh. "The irony of it all. Our doctor, Freddy's and mine, has just died of AIDS. But yes, we're checking out a new one." Another laugh. "Not saying so to each other, we're looking for one who's not, uh, gay."

"Lord, Edward."

"Indeed. Well, time to start back?"

They turn back, heading into light rain.

"I just can't say that I like Sara very much," confides Dudley, the next to speak. Out of habit, and for comfort, she walks very close to Edward, in the scent of his damp tweed. "She's so, so abrupt."

Celeste did indeed bring Sara to Dudley and Sam's house for tea, that day: Sara, now a large and silent young woman who for the most part simply stared at them, or so it had seemed to Dudley. When spoken to, she answered rather curtly. She had lived in a great many places, she told them. None for long. No significant jobs. And then, with somewhat more feeling: Yes, she was genuinely tired of living like that. She liked it here. (This last had, to Dudley, a sound of defiance: I like it here even if you don't like me to be here, was what Dudley heard.)

And the call on Edward and Freddy was quite similar in effect, at least.

"She stares so," Edward now remarks to Dudley. "With those quite feral black eyes. If only she'd pick up a little lash-batting from Celeste."

Dudley giggles. "Oh, maybe she will!" And then, "Darling Edward, whatever in the world would I do without you?"

Edward frowns, a disclaimer, and he tries to take up their talk. "What we are saying—aren't we?—is that we're worried about Celeste. Isn't that about it?"

"Well, yes." Dudley hurries along beside him. "But since you put it like that, should we, really? Sometimes worry seems a form of condescension toward a friend, you know? 'Poor So-and-So, she just can't cope.' Whereas the truth of it is that Celeste copes better than anyone, ever." She adds, "Sam hates it unspeakably when I worry over him. It makes him think he must be dying."

"So does Freddy. But the point is, I think that Celeste has not, as one says, seemed quite herself. Since Charles died. And this 'Bill.' You must admit that it's odd that none of us, still, have met him."

"Sara did tell me something very strange about him." Dudley has in fact been wondering whether or not to tell Edward this strange thing that Sara said, one morning when Dudley phoned Celeste and got Sara instead, and they made a sort of conversation—soon getting around to Bill. That is where Celeste was, having lunch in San Francisco with Bill.

Now, in the gathering, thickening rain, she decides that she will tell Edward what Sara said—what Sara said that Celeste had said to her. "Sara told me that Celeste told her that Bill is, uh, gay."

"Strange," murmurs Edward, through rain.

"Well, supposedly we all get to meet Bill next week, at the party."

"You think he won't show up?"

"How you do read my mind," marvels Dudley.

In from the rain, in her own house, even before her awareness of warmth and dryness, Dudley senses the absence of Sam. How she feels it, always, his not being there. And she feels too, quite loonily, after almost forty years of Sam, the familiar clutch of fear: where has he gone off to, and will he come back to her, ever? These days, though, it is less the old primitive fear of abandonment than a new one: that Sam has died. Well, men in their middle sixties, her own age as well as Sam's, do die; they are simply found dead somewhere, sometimes. Given out.

Stripping off wet clothes and hanging them up to dry, turning on her bath, into which she pours an exuberant amount of bath salts, carnation scented, Dudley tries to remember. Did Sam say he was going somewhere? *Is* she losing her memory?

In the tub, however, in the fragrant steam, all slithery and soaped, Dudley tries not to think so much of Sam as of her own body, and, not unconnectedly, of Brooks Burgess, whom she has not seen since their encounter (so sexy! so promising) at the crazy drunken all-yellow party that Celeste and Charles gave in—dear heaven—1975. Ten years back. When she was only fifty-five—itself a laughable phrase, like "only forty." And the worst one could charitably say (the worst Brooks Burgess could legitimately say, or think) is that she looks a little scrawny. Too emphatically tendoned, somewhat. Dry-skinned. Too white. But no flab, no (whatever is that new word?) no cellulite.

And Brooks will, presumably, be at Celeste's party. Her Valentine's party, next week.

They have not seen each other during all that time; with Brooks up in Marin County they were not likely just to run into each other, and also, sadly and more to the point, for most of those years his wife was very sick, and then dying. Brooks was engaged in her care and comforting, up until a couple of years ago, when she died. And so presumably Brooks is all right now? Is, more or less, "over it"?

But I would never get over Sam, is what Dudley next thinks. After all, I never have. And in the succeeding instant she remembers in a flash (and how could she have forgotten for several hours?) that Sam was going up to the city, to San Francisco, with some new slides. Oh, poor old Sam, and how could she forget?

She hurries out of the tub, dries, powders and scents herself and takes time over her clothes, choosing things that Sam especially likes. Gray silk and a silver necklace he once gave her. And, like a fifties magazine wife, she is in the kitchen fussing over drinks and dinner when Sam arrives. Except that the drinks are their old tomato and clam juice, with lemon.

Sam looks awful—so bad that Dudley instead of asking how things went begins to babble on her own. "Darling, such a rainy day for your drive! But Edward and I were terribly brave and took our walk anyway. Actually it was quite beautiful, though. Those moments of clearing. The most extraordinary light."

So used to Sam's face, Dudley can still be surprised by changes, by new or perhaps simply deepened lines, a slackening of flesh, of tone. He gets no exercise; she has sometimes briskly, imperiously thought that he should take up something. However, at other times she sees that it is of course not that simple: age and life itself have lined Sam's face. Nothing to do with lack of exercise, or fat.

"Every time I go up to the city, I'm glad we don't live there, gladder and gladder" is what Sam says.

Which Dudley understands to mean: No luck, no interested gallery.

"It's getting so much worse, so fast," Sam goes on. "But I guess most cities are. High rises and dirt. Crowds, panhandlers. But the very visible new poor. That's something I hadn't quite seen. Lines of middle-class-looking people at St. Anthony's Dining Room. I drove by there, not exactly on purpose but there I was. And there they were."

Dudley shudders. As always, listening to Sam, she has seen what he has just described: a long line of formerly doing-all-right people, with anxious, apologetic smiles, embarrassed small laughs. People feeling in the wrong, simply being there, where they are. Standing in the rain, the wind and cold.

"It's horrible," she says. "Terrifying."

"It sure is."

The moment between them then contains such sadness, such vast regret for everything in the world gone wrong. For themselves gone wrong, old and exposed to frightful weather, interior weather. An unbearable moment, which Dudley must break, she thinks, and so she says what she had not meant at all to say to Sam. She asks him, "How would you feel about going to Ireland? The magazine wants me to, they'd pay—"

Sam frowns and, as though she had not spoken, he says, into space, "Fucking galleries."

15   Polly, having walked the uphill miles from her house to Celeste's, in a gusty, cold, directionless rain, arrives at the Valentine's party wet and disheveled, and late. She waits for what seems a long moment at the door, and then is simultaneously greeted by three small maids, who divest her of her outer garments. Did it really take all three of them? Polly feels not quite in focus, not quite all there. But before her, against the background of crowd, noise, party mess, is impeccable Celeste, in ice-blue silk. Celeste, saying to Polly, with her most sinuous, social smile, "And this is Bill."

As she introduces: Charles.

For there before Polly is Charles, reincarnate. But not Celeste's Charles, not the elderly man who died, but Polly's Charles: a just-graying, fiftyish man, immensely tall and thin, a narrow face, small nose, with the famous flaring eyebrows. Charles, bending now to shake her hand, saying that he is glad to meet her.

Celeste laughs a little meanly—triumphantly? "Quite a resemblance, isn't there?" She is clinging to Bill's arm.

"Yes," says Polly. "Quite."

"You still look cold," says Bill. "Come on in, get comfortable." And in that instant of his speaking he is not at all Charles; he is in fact so unlike Charles that Polly wonders at the power of that first delusion, that summoned presence of Charles, her Charles. The life within this frame, this skin, whatever its animating force, is quite other than whatever animated Charles, so that Polly is violently aware of the sheer strength of human difference.

This Bill is constantly in motion, gesturing, shifting expressions, whereas Charles tended to be—well, rather passive. "Charles's face always makes me think of what Forster said about Walter Scott," Dudley once said, in her musing, slightly musty schoolgirl way. "A landscape that cries out for passion, or something like that. And no passion there." Well put, Mr. Forster, was Polly's thought.

Celeste now leans forward to whisper, so that Polly breathes in light sweet French scent. ". . . getting married," Celeste murmurs to Polly's ear. "Or I think we are. At least I've asked him. Don't you think I'm brave?"

"Brave. Yes, you're very brave," Polly tells her. And stark raving, out of your bloody mind, she does not also say.

Bill, who has either not heard or pretended not to hear Celeste, now says to Polly, "I do hope we get a chance to talk sometime. Celeste has said all these great things about you. I really want to get to know you."

"I hope so too," Polly tells him. She is already longing, miserably, to be away. Even back out in the rain.

Looking around the room (which is not, thank God, decorated with Valentines), she sees a corner with a chair, where surely she could sit down? Surely, after such pounding blows to what passes for her sense of reality, these days?

Celeste and Bill are now off, swept back into the party, and Polly goes over to her corner, out of the fray. She sits down and closes her eyes, and she lets the sounds and the smells of the party wash over her. She feels weak, almost drowned. But she knows that it is necessary to make an effort of some sort. In order to force herself to concentrate she tries making a list of worrying topics, starting, as is her habit, with the worst, the darkest of her thoughts. She thinks, If Celeste is even considering a marriage, she must be all right? The blood she was worried about was minor, innocent?

Then, scurrying off from that issue, the health of Celeste, she next wonders: Could this young man, this Bill, be what was once called an adventurer, just after Celeste's possessions? She chides herself for this thought instantly, though: as if things were all that would draw anyone to Celeste, her beautiful, strong, superior Celeste.

And lastly she thinks, Oh Christ, a wedding. How many fucking parties am I supposed to survive?

But slowly digesting this series of powerful notions, as she might the courses of an overrich meal, Polly begins to relax a little. She feels overfed, quite stuffed with new information, new ideas. Her very body sags with spent energy, the weight of absorption.

A little later, however, a much simpler thought comes to her. She thinks, Well, of course. It is marriage much more than the actual Charles that Celeste has missed; along those lines old Charles was probably not much to mourn. It's the marriage that she feels the lack of, and what could be more logical, more perfectly Celeste-like (so practical, so efficient) than to do it again? To go out and find a brand-new Charles. This Bill could even be an actor, impersonating Charles. A new edition, as it were. After all, Polly thinks, we've got an actor in the White House. Impersonating a President.

Dudley too has reeled from this whispered announcement from Celeste, which she also was given on arrival. But the effect on Dudley has been quite curious, once those odd words ("I'm getting married") were absorbed. Dudley has been thrown into a kind of mania. Overexcited, she can't stop talking, chattering. And all her chatter is a substitute for talking to Celeste, she knows that—a very poor substitute for the deep, long conversation for which she yearns. A conversation that is absolutely out of the question now. But even if she could have this talk with Celeste, Dudley reflects, most of the questions that she would like to ask are inadmissible.

She would like to ask, and she will! *Why didn't you tell me?* I had no idea that things were so serious with you and this Bill. And I couldn't quite hear when you said what he did. Did you say doctor, or actor? Or was that some kind of joke? And how incredibly he does look like Charles! At least you could have warned us all about that, Celeste.

Even these more or less conventional questions and responses, then, are not to take place for the moment, despite close friendship, true intimacy. And how much more forbidden are the deeper questions plaguing Dudley's overheated brain. The sexual questions. The life-and-death questions. The prurient, the essential.

* * *

The weather that night has for once not conformed to the wishes of Celeste, who would surely not have chosen such a storm, such lashing gales, wild rains, such violent gusts of wind each time the door is opened, as repeatedly it is. People keep arriving late, from everywhere. Delayed by weather, saying, "Well, you would not believe the Bayshore. An absolute flood. I thought we'd never get here."

Brooks Burgess and his group from Ross, the farthest away, have been especially late. Passionately observed by Dudley, they enter at last, five people—all shedding wet slickers, Burberrys, dark wet furs smelling of animals. All shed onto the strong dark dry arms of the maids. (Dudley, watching so intently, sees no flicker on those impassive Indian-Spanish-Mexican faces, but how can that be, Dudley wonders. Such wetness, so heavy.)

And although she is standing some distance from them, from that new wet group, Dudley could almost believe herself among them, so clearly does she see and feel the vibrations as Celeste breathes her secret to a chosen one of them, a beautiful dark young woman— someone's daughter, probably. Dudley feels it as that young woman in her turn reels, as she tries to hide her shock, as she murmurs, "Oh, wonderful."

And Dudley can hear Celeste as with an out-of-character trilling laugh she tells this daughter (possibly of Brooks Burgess?)—as Celeste says, "In a year, if I'm still alive."

Chilling! Those words have shivered through Dudley, who quite suddenly, acutely longs to be with Sam, to be with him alone. Sam, who is perversely nowhere to be seen.

Only, there is Brooks Burgess, to whom she had so girlishly looked forward, until this moment of actually seeing him.

Brooks is approaching her now, all purposeful, with an expression that Dudley in one quick instant dislikes. He looks so, so exactly what he is, she thinks: an elderly investment counselor, a senior money man, all slicked steel hair and narrow mercantile eyes. And even though his general look is very sad, and he has visibly aged, Dudley still is hardened toward him.

However, she chimes into his hearty "How great to see you! Much too long" with her own "Marvelous! You haven't changed!" And she wonders, Is there any way to speak politely without quite so many total lies?

Standing there together, separated for a moment from the party, Dudley and Brooks regard each other with looks that are almost hostile—is each of them, then, so much less than the other expected? Or has that extraordinary announcement of Celeste's thrown everything off balance, unhinged the whole atmosphere of this party, a sort of greenhouse effect? Wondering all this, Dudley concludes that any explanation at all might do; the important thing is they not remain alone, isolated in this way, for very long, he and she, who have less than nothing to say to each other.

And how adolescent this all is, Dudley next thinks, this quick descent from lust, from sexiness to enmity. And, as she has before, she wonders if old age is indeed, in its way, to be a repetition of adolescence. And she thinks, Oh *dear*, I cannot go through all that again.

Oh, where is Edward? Just now when she needs him, where is he? For it is to Edward, and to Edward alone, that she could voice such a probably preposterous notion.

Edward, though, is across the room, she can see him. In an almost cloistered corner he is talking to Sara. And there (oh dear!) not far from them is Freddy, who is talking to the young man from the diner whom Sara so much dislikes. That David—and how very odd indeed of Celeste to invite him. Celeste's fantasy of "fixing up" David with Sara persists.

"Well, how've you been?" Brooks Burgess asks her.

But just at that moment they are saved from each other by, of all people, *Sam*, unruly, unreliable, most inefficient non-businesslike Sam, arriving so punctually in response to Dudley's need of him. "Darling, you remember Brooks Burgess?" (She can hear a small tremor in her own voice.)

"Oh, of course. How've you been?"

The two exchange hearty handshakes.

Sam in fact has been watching Dudley for some time; deliberately he positioned himself so that he could see her perfectly, whereas to her he remained invisible. (He knows himself to be good at this: I am an artist of camouflage, he has said to himself.) She was hidden by the corpulent bright madras body of some old pal of Charles's from Woodside, a former Stanford football great. A conveniently huge man.

Sam could watch, then, the greeting and the ensuing scene between Dudley and Brooks Burgess. A scene of which Dudley has dreamed for years, Sam knows: since that party, which must now be ten years back, the golden harvest moon party, the sultry sexy party at which everyone seemed to have taken some sort of erotic energy pill, Sam thought, some sexual spike in the punch. And since then all Dudley's sexual fantasies have had Brooks Burgess's name on them. Impossible to say how Sam knows this: surely not from anything said by Dudley. He simply knows, and he is always right, about Dudley.

Observing Dudley, Sam is also as acutely observant of himself, and he inwardly remarks: Twenty years ago, or thirty—and good Lord, I've spent most of my life with this woman, this crazy foreign Bostonian, this Dudley—in those days I would have been watching her hot and sick with jealous blood, my whole body poisoned, enflamed, and very likely I would have made some god-awful scene about this, big shouting, schoolboy words thrown out like garbage. Not hitting anyone, at least I never hit, but a lot of ugly noise, and then lurching out. With or without Dudley. Blind crazy drunk.

And now, he thinks, now I am old and sober, and instead of jealousy I feel the most excruciating tender compassion for my wife, who is also old and sober and sometimes very silly. And I hardly know which emotion is the more difficult to bear.

He sees then, from her gestures and her posture, that Dudley is no longer interested, not in any way, in Brooks Burgess. But there the two of them are, in a social trap of their own making: they are standing alone, they have to talk for a while. It's enough to make Sam laugh a little, which he manages not to do: invisible people don't laugh; it's one of the rules of camouflage.

He sees that Dudley would very much like him to come to her rescue, even though she cannot see him, and after a few more minutes, which he has to admit he enjoys, Sam does just that: he goes over to where Dudley stands with that Brooks Burgess.

And when Dudley says "Darling, you remember Brooks Burgess?" that fellow soon takes himself off. He is not all bad, Sam judges; he knew when to go.

Brilliant-eyed, as though she couldn't wait to speak, Dudley asks him, "But what do you think?" She holds his arm as she whispers. "Celeste," she breathes. "Getting married!"

"I think it won't happen," Sam tells her. Until the words appeared he had not known that that was his thought.

"Oh, Sam, how can you say that? What do you mean, it won't happen?"

He does not know what he means, nor does he want to explain, not even to try. And this is a familiar stance of his, quite enraging to Dudley, he knows that. But he can't, he can't help it. "I could be wrong," he temporizes.

"You're never wrong, that's what's so irritating. Oh Sam! But where did she find him, do you know? So amazing, the resemblance to Charles."

"I think she said they met at the IRS," says Sam in a deliberate, factual way.

"The IRS? Darling, what an awful joke. You're losing your hearing. I can't believe Celeste would have said that. I thought he was an importer."

"You mean, even if it were true Celeste wouldn't say it?"

They both laugh at the accuracy of this: impossible to imagine Celeste ever saying, Actually I met him at the IRS.

"But actually," Sam tells Dudley, "they don't look so much alike, this Bill and Charles. It's more like someone just wearing Charles's clothes."

"Darling, whatever do you mean?" (She is always asking him this, Dudley knows—hopeless, he hates explanations.)

"Just what I said. Don't ask me to explain."

"But Sam."

However, at that moment, some beautiful woman from somewhere, someone they both know, arrives with flurries of kisses and greetings for them both, thus occupying Dudley, so that Sam doesn't even have to pretend to explain what he means.

This is a familiar sense, for Sam: that of having said everything quite clearly but in such a way that no one, not even Dudley, could understand. And to Sam his own meanings are always so clear. Obvious, even. This Bill (will they always call him "this Bill"?)—this person, Bill, does not really look much like old Charles. They are merely about the same size, with faces shaped the same. All of the more important aspects of impression are very unlike, though; it's that simple. Annoying to be asked.

More pressing and far more severe just now than that annoyance, though, is a dizziness, quite physical, concrete, that Sam at this instant experiences. The party seems so hot, all those candles, they seem to emit more heat than light. He feels swollen with heat. If he took one bite of Celeste's quite predictably elaborate buffet, he would burst, an obscene display of guts all over Celeste's too lovely house.

He feels drunk. Drunk and sick, after one long glass of club soda.

Dudley will think he just doesn't like the party if he tells her that he is going home—as Sam now sees that he must, and soon. Well, better for her to think that. She can deal with Sam-the-bad-sport much better than she can with sick Sam, he knows. Or maybe she is right, and it is not real, what he feels. He is not sick, only bored.

Reconnecting with Dudley—not easy: the rooms are so full of silk- or satin-straining flesh, with a few thin wraiths in black, like dead trees; getting through them all has been like traversing some horrible surreal forest, for Sam—he tells her that he has a headache. Nothing serious, and clearly having to do with an ugly note that afternoon from his former dealer. He doesn't really feel like being at a party, okay? Edward and Freddy can drop her off later, on their way home.

He will not seek out Celeste. He will simply, quickly, get out as soon as possible. Before he is sick, or sicker. Before he bursts.

And he almost makes it. Just at the final door, however, coming out of the powder room is Bill, and since they have barely met, some conversation seems required.

"Oh, you're off?" from Bill.

"Yes, unfortunately a headache. But I couldn't seem to find Celeste. Would you—? If you could—"

"Oh, sure. Don't let it make you uncomfortable. Can I get you anything though, like aspirin?" Making this vague offer, Bill smiles, so very unlike Charles.

"Oh, no. Thanks." In fact, an aspirin would have been a good idea, but Sam simply wants to get away. Right now.

"Well, I hope we get a chance to talk sometime," says Bill. "Celeste feels so close to you, you and Dudley."

"Me too! Great!" Haste fuels an insane enthusiasm in Sam—just before he rushes through the door. He is propelled by pain: a worse pain has attacked him, encircling his chest. A heart attack? No, heart-burn. Gas. He has had this before. As he runs toward his car, impeded by his pain, and his very weight, his heavy old misused body, Sam still quite consciously thinks: This Bill, who does not sound or really look like Charles, who *is* he?

Amazingly, to Edward, who is fussy in these matters, Sara looks almost beautiful tonight, at this party. It is quite as though, Edward thinks, Celeste-the-strong has willed her to be so, like a fairy godmother. "Be beautiful for my party," Celeste could have commanded. (Edward would not put that past her.) It is clearly not a matter of clothes, though; had that been the case, a discreetly expensive "wonderful" dress, Celeste's urgent, controlling hand could have been clearly implicated. But Sara is only wearing some gauzy white "import" thing, most likely from Cost Plus.

In this cheapo dress, though, tonight Sara is beautiful. And Edward in his mind ticks off the virtues that make her so, in a visual way: good skin, if a little on the dark side; a long, strong-looking neck (it could be a little thinner, but no matter). Heavy, almost straight-across dark eyebrows. And her eyes: no qualifications there, her eyes are wonderful, so large and dark, with those (naturally) heavy lashes. Really clever of her to add nothing to them, no touch of mascara, even. Another woman, aware of such beautiful eyes, would have made them up, and made too much of her eyes. Whereas Sara looks as though washing her face and her hair had been the sum of her effort.

They have of course been discussing Bill. "This Bill."

"She hadn't said a thing before about getting married," Sara has earlier told Edward—to his considerable surprise: such a step should surely have been discussed with someone? "Honestly," continues Sara, "I was as startled as anyone."

"Do you think it could have been a last-minute decision on her part?"

"Possibly."

And since that initial flurry of conversation they have managed as best they can to continue above the din of the party. But by now some taped music is issuing from loudspeakers, which is no help at all.

"God, what is this music?" asks Sara.

Older, more knowledgeable Edward laughs. "It's from way before your time, my dear. All forties classics. That hoo-ha trombone sound was very big in those days. What we're hearing at this precise moment is called 'Moonlight Serenade,' by Mr. Glenn Miller."

"It's kind of dull, don't you think? Sort of slow, repetitive?"

"Oh, indeed. But Celeste really loves this stuff. Come to think of it, so did Charles. I think she played these same tapes at a party about ten years ago, and everyone went mad. All us oldsters."

"I like this one better. What's it called?"

"This, my dear, is 'Little Brown Jug.' Played by, I think, Mr. Jimmie Lunceford."

"At least it moves along. Edward, you see that young man across the room?"

Edward hesitates. "You don't mean Freddy?"

"Of course not. David, the guy from the diner. Celeste asked him here tonight *for me,* can you imagine? She said I should see more people of my own age, and she doesn't know anyone."

Not at all wanting to go into this, Edward tries for another gambit. "It is quite remarkable," he tells Sara, "how this Bill resembles our Charles. Quite striking. Startling, really."

"I don't know. I mean, I hardly knew Charles. I probably didn't really look at him," and Sara laughs. "I was probably too busy fighting him. His politics were so, so retro, I thought. But this Bill does look like someone I used to know. A long time ago." She laughs again. "His last name was Priest, so we always referred to him as Judas."

Typical Berkeley sort of joke, thinks Edward, who has begun to feel that Sara talks too much, once she starts.

"In fact, it's a little creepy," Sara tells him. "Very unnerving. My past all crowding back," she continues, quite unaware that Edward is no longer listening.

The most observable fact about Bill—and he is most meticulously observed, by a number of people—is his excessive animation. "The man can't seem to stop," Brooks Burgess noted to a friend from Ross.

And his conversation, as with most non-stop talkers, is mostly about himself. He seems to have a curious knack, though, for relating phases of his own history to that of his audience-of-one. (Bill can be seen to shy away from groups, clearly preferring an intimate *tête-à-tête*.) He has told Freddy about a town just south of Oaxaca, in the mountains, where he, Bill, found the most extraordinary pottery, much more remarkable than anything in Oaxaca itself. He speaks feelingly to Polly about the plight of the San Francisco poor: some people he knows, he says, have a plan for "creating a space" where all those people could go for food and shelter. He announces to Dudley that he has never before felt comfortable with anyone from Boston; he feels that he and she should spend more time together, should really talk.

Watching him as best she can while maintaining and continuing her hostess chores, overhearing what she can, Celeste wills herself to believe that all this is Bill's way of ingratiating himself to her friends. He is simply very eager to please.

A darker inner voice, however, insists that there is something more than a little wrong: he does not quite look at the person he's talking to, he does not quite make sense. He must have drunk too much. And Celeste thinks, Oh dear, I never should have said that about getting married, which was really a sort of joke, a Valentine's joke. (Wasn't it? She makes this inquiry of herself and comes up with no answer.)

Others in the room, for the most part fairly heavy drinkers themselves, of an old-fashioned sort, Scotch and gin and vodka drinkers (Sara is the only white-wine consumer present)—those people have come to much the same conclusion: this Bill has drunk too much, it's made him gabby.

Dudley, who in some ways is more "in touch" than the rest, has come to another conclusion, which is that Bill must have done time in est or some similar self-realization enterprise. She thinks she can recognize the vocabulary: his "comfortable with," his "spaces." And she too believes that he must drink a great deal: he is not as comfortable in this particular space as he says he is; in fact he has begun, observably, even from a distance, to perspire.

To Sara, who has been watching Bill with possibly the coolest, clearest eyes in the room (she is also the lightest drinker present), it is obvious that he is doing a lot of coke. She knows the signs, and she is also sure (she would make book on this) that he is either getting close or perhaps has already come to the end of his stash. And so she plans to continue to watch. To see what happens. She is fairly certain that something will happen.

This party, though, by almost any definition is not a success. Except in a purely visual way: on the surface it looks quite wonderful. But in more rudimentary ways it could be described as a bust: most people ate and drank too much, and around eleven they began to start off home.

Anxiety about the weather, that seemingly unabating, lashing storm could indeed be blamed; certainly that was the given excuse as guests began to reclaim their wraps. But at another, better party the bad weather could have played quite another role: everyone could have chosen to wait it out, which as things turned out would have been the wiser choice: by midnight this storm was dead and gone.

Quite depressed, for a number of related and unrelated reasons, Sara starts toward her own rooms, her bedroom and bath. The bedroom door is open, she sees from the hall, although she knows she left it closed, and just as she has thought, *Shit,* some old drunk using my bathroom, a tall thin person comes out. A man. "Bill."

So startled that she almost screams, Sara cries, "What in hell! What do you think you're doing in my room?"

She pushes past him so that she stands in her doorframe, then turns to stare up at him.

Bill's face is very white, and sweat runs down the narrow indented cheeks as he tries to smile. "Baby, you're someone I can relate to, I can tell. The truth is, I thought you might have something for me."

"Asshole! I don't do any dope."

"Look, I'm serious." His face has entirely changed, all attempts at ingratiation vanished. "I have to connect," he tells her.

"That's your problem, creepo."

"But I don't even know this town. I've never been here—"

"Get out of here. Get lost."

Staring at him with almost the purest hatred she can remember, Sara still does not quite dare to say his name, what she believes to be his name. She does not say, Priest, you goddam Judas Priest, although those words are pounding in her brain so loudly it seems impossible he cannot hear them.

And perhaps he does, for with yet another shift in expression, a muttered "Bitch, fucking bitch," Bill turns and leaves, rushing not toward the bedroom that has been prepared for him, for his comfort, but toward the front door. Unseen by Celeste, who is helping the maids clean up in the kitchen.

He is out the door. Gone.

Celeste's tired voice shows strain. And with an uncomfortable lurch of affection for this woman whom half the time she doesn't even like—deploring her vanity, what could even be called shallowness— Sara now thinks, Oh, why couldn't you just say that you wonder why the party didn't go? Or that you really wonder what everyone thought of Bill?

Instead, sitting edgily forward on the deep white sofa, her chin at its accustomed forward angle, Celeste speaks of Charles. "We often quarreled, Charles and I," she tells Sara. "Sometimes for days at a time. But then in some very sweet way we'd make it up. And I think he kept up with a few old girlfriends—you know Charles was always just catnip to women, they were all crazy about him. He probably even saw his old girls, you know, even spent time with them when he went on his trips." She laughs shortly, sharply, and shrugs. A large shrug. "He could even have, uh, made love to them, for all I know. But still he always came back to me, and we had each other. We were always in some way in love. And then when he died I simply couldn't accept it. I kept thinking we'd had a fight, or he was off on some trip and he'd come back. The finality—I couldn't believe it. But you see how silly old people get, dear Sara?"

"How long was it before you met Bill?" Sara knows her question to be brusque, but she has said it deliberately. We might as well get right to it, is what she thinks.

But she has reckoned without the practiced evasions of Celeste.

"All the beaux I had," Celeste now ruminates, "they never took care of things, or maybe sometimes one of them might fix a radio, or something, might carry something upstairs for me. But Charles did everything. I got so spoiled! I got so I just couldn't cope with insurance forms and all that, the IRS things, all that mess."

"You really met Bill at the IRS, in San Francisco?" Sara persists, determined at last to get the whole story. "When?"

Celeste frowns, then shivers, recollecting. "Since you ask, it was last November, after Charles died. And such a terrible cold day. I had a lot of trouble parking, that awful Polk Street neighborhood. I had to walk a long way, and then at the Federal Building there were all these pickets, all kinds of people with placards. Big signs about Nicaragua, about not fighting there. Big anti-Reagan signs. But these terribly friendly people, and a lot of them quite well dressed. I was really surprised." She laughs, a small mild laugh, apparently at herself. "They thought I had come to be part of them, or else they pretended they did. 'Come on in,' they kept saying, and they'd hold out their hands. 'We can use you,' they told me. They were all singing some song I didn't know. But you know I was really tempted, in the craziest way. I thought I'd just join them, and not bother with the IRS."

It is easy for Sara to visualize that scene: the "well-dressed" (middle class, middle age) strays among the radical young, the undeterrable old activists. The middle-aged rather manic at the sheer unusualness of their action, and extending their hands to Celeste: Please come and join us, be one of us. It's fun.

"Well, sometimes I think I should have," Celeste somewhat surprisingly now says. "It was like the sixties—sometimes I even wanted to join those people, those funny kids with their banners and tambourines. But with Charles that was out of the question. But now Charles was gone, and I could have changed my whole life right there. I mean, not that it already wasn't."

But Celeste did not linger with the protesters that day, well-dressed and middle-class though they appeared. She went straight up to an office, and there was Bill. Bill Jones.

"Well, I almost fainted. People say that all the time about fainting, but I really did. At first so much like Charles. Then I thought it must be some incredibly cruel joke, some actor got up to look like Charles. But who on earth would do that to me? And it turns out that Bill actually was an actor for a while during the fifties."

During his acting days, Bill had lived in and around L.A., Celeste told Sara. Twice married, no children, at that time nothing in his life really working out. And then he began to do work in TV, mostly announcing. And he met a lot of people. Big executives in the industry, who liked him very much. (In fact, Bill told Celeste, he came within a hairsbreadth of getting the job that Reagan did so well with, with General Electric.)

Somehow the TV work led Bill into government work, although Celeste is vague as to how this connection was made. By the sixties, anyway, he was all the way out of TV and into some government agencies, their San Francisco offices. In charge of the West Coast.

"What agencies, Celeste? He must have told you?" Sara hesitates; the extreme tension that she feels will show in her voice, she knows; always voices are the total giveaway. But she has to ask, to find out. "Was it FBI?" (Shit, her voice did crack, just barely but it did.) "CIA?"

Celeste unconvincingly laughs. "Oh, they're all so alike, those letters. And I still think in terms of the nice old agencies, the war ones. NLRB, and OPA. And further back the NRA, and the CCC. WPA."

"Celeste, do you think it was CIA?"

"Well, Sara, it certainly could have been."

Sara leans back and regulates her breath. In, out. In, out. Celeste too is quiet, and she too breathes very deeply. (Is she upset, or simply very tired?) Sara at last is able to bring herself under control.

The "help" has all gone home by now. Someone left an open window, somewhere, no doubt to clear out all the lingering smoke and perfume smells, the too rich food odors; now freshly washed, cool night air drifts through all the rooms, on strong clean currents.

And the silence between the two women prolongs itself. Ostensibly resting, they sit there, each with her eyes closed, and each powerfully engaged in serious thoughts, so that an outside observer, had there been one, would have viewed them as linked in a common ritual. And in a sense perhaps they are: two women worrying, heavily. Two women trying to comprehend the ways of men.

At last it is Celeste who breaks it, laughing lightly, asking, "So sweet of Bill to go around telling everyone how he hoped to talk to them again. I really think he meant it, don't you?"

To which Sara with a frown responds, "Not me. He did not tell me that he hoped to talk to me again."

But then, as though there had been no silence between them, Celeste takes it up again. "So we met in the IRS, but we hardly talked there, he just directed me to where I was supposed to be going in the first place. But we must have registered something. *I* certainly did. Anyway, that afternoon there he was again, in an antique store in Jackson Square. You know, it did seem fated."

"I suppose it did."

And then rather surprisingly Celeste remarks, "He probably thinks I have a great deal more money than I do."

16 Those resident in San Sebastian are quite apt to forget that the sea is very near, by car. It sometimes takes a visitor, some eager newcomer, to remind them of their almost coastal situation; at other times they think of the sea because of its sporadic acts of violence: ferocious, ravaging storms, shipwrecks. Drownings, loss. On the day following Celeste's party, then, both conditions pertain: Sara, the visitor, has said all along how she wishes to see that coast. Also, the night before, during those very party hours, two fishing boats were lost in the storm, no trace as yet but a couple of ominously empty lifeboats, their vacant oarlocks rattling in the wind.

But now the weather is perfectly, innocently clear, the sky pale and soft, small fleecy clouds adrift near the unmenacing blue horizon.

The sea itself, though, some twenty or thirty feet below the flattened, grassy area where Dudley and Sara now walk, in the balmy sunlight—that sea is still violent, lashing at rocks, churning, leaping, breaking into foam. It is terrifying to look down: the two women stay respectfully back from the edge, yet are unable not to peer down for quick momentary glimpses of peril, of doom.

They have been speaking, naturally, of last night's party, and particularly of Bill, who, Sara has just informed Dudley, telephoned Celeste this morning to say that he would be away for a while. Something about a sick cousin in upstate New York.

"She was so upset," Sara emphasizes. "In that awful schoolgirl way he seems to engender. I don't mean to sound unsympathetic, really. But I'm just so tired of the way men infantilize us, so many of them. The truth is, I'm really worried about Celeste."

"Really I am too," Dudley tells her, with a small frown.

"Her upset seemed so extreme, as though he'd died, or gone off for good," Sara next says. "I got the feeling that she thinks she won't see him again. And the point is, I think she's right."

"Well, maybe she won't," supposes Dudley. "Celeste is uncanny, in some ways. She's very in touch, she has this curious sort of power. She and Sam are sort of alike in that, these extraordinary insights, and instincts."

"Do you mean, she thinks she might die?" Blunt Sara.

"Well, uh, I guess that is one of the things I mean. She might."

"Do you think she's got some specific worry, healthwise?" Sara persists in asking.

"Oh, not that I know of. But she certainly might have, and she wouldn't necessarily tell me about it. Her worry," Dudley says.

This conversation is difficult and painful, even, for Dudley, who is extremely worried over Sam—and determined not to say so. Sam is at home in bed, feeling, he says, just plain terrible. Sam who is never sick, who never stays in bed. Dudley herself is almost sick with worry, but she believes that she would only feel worse if she talked about it—current views to the contrary notwithstanding.

"I just get a feeling that she's concerned about her health," says Sara. "No special reason, and I'm not especially intuitive. Or I don't think I am."

"What you're saying," Dudley attempts, "is that all this upset seems to go beyond strong feelings over Bill."

"Exactly." Sara looks over at Dudley, and they smile at each other, beginning a friendship. "It has a lot to do with still mourning for Charles, I think."

"Oh, of course!" If Sam should die, she might behave—oh, any way at all, it now occurs to Dudley. And she remembers poor Caitlin Thomas after Dylan died, sleeping with all those people, that boy in Italy. And then writing about it all. *Leftover Life to Kill*, the saddest title ever, and exactly right.

Would she get in touch with Brooks Burgess? Well, she might even do that. And then she begins to berate herself. How can she so callously contemplate the death of Sam, her great true love, whom she hates a great deal of the time, who is only at home sick with the flu (probably)?

Sara too is preoccupied with thoughts that she has so far not chosen to communicate to Dudley, despite strong new feelings of friendship. She is thinking about "Bill Jones," who according to Celeste works at both the IRS and at a Jackson Square antique store— in itself a little odd; is an IRS person allowed to have another line of work, even if he only has "an interest" in a store? Or, is it the IRS in which he only has an interest? But he is a strange and terrible person, Sara thinks, in view of the night before.

And she is almost sure that he is the man whom she knew in Berkeley as Priest. The trouble is that she only saw that person once, and then not too clearly. Not to mention the inevitable blur of time. Twenty years.

What she remembers, though, is a night in a San Francisco restaurant. What restaurant? She has no idea, just one more North Beach joint with curtained booths, serving huge portions of okay food, for not too high prices.

Ten of them, that long past night, in a booth. All close-knit movement people, except for two: Alex, brought along by Sara; and another man who had sort of hung around them. "Priest," who was Carol's new love. "Really okay, not political at all but all right," Carol had assured them. Carol, the most politically correct of them all— and Priest, the quintessential hippie, then: the John Lennon glasses, long hair and beard. Rags and sandals. (An odd way to dress if he was not "political," is Sara's retrospective perception.) At the time he looked very much like a lot of other people, if a little more so.

(As he now looks like Charles? "Bill" the actor?)

Whose idea was it that they all turn on, once dinner was over and they sat around with coffee, all in a festive, self-congratulatory mood: there had been a huge peace march the day before, to which even the *Chronicle* gave some space. But was it Priest who brought out the joints? It could have been anyone; still, they were usually more cautious about restaurants, public places.

Full of food and wine, then, warmed with a group sense of self-approval, virtuous activity rewarded, flushed with wine and rectitude and affection for each other—they all lit up, became silently happy, in that blurry, dopey sixties way—when, suddenly, plunging and crashing into their booth were huge uniformed Nazis, black plastic hats, big nightsticks. But not Nazis, of course: the Tac Squad. Instantly familiar and recognizable to them all from rallies, protests. But why now, why when they were only smoking dope in a restaurant? Celebrating a peace march, at which they had all behaved very well?

Curtis, who was very small and black, got the worst of it. Hearing a crack, wood on bone (she can hear it still, always), Sara turned to see Curtis all bloody, dark red blood streaming down his dark black face. Curtis's hands reaching up to staunch his blood, his fingers leaking blood.

Sara began to throw up. Her stomach clenched, a fierce spasm. She retched, erupted.

"Get that woman out of here!" someone shouted. And another, "Wash her off, but bring her right back."

Alex grabbed her arm up, pulled her from the booth and headed with her not for the rest room; he jerked her along in the other direction, toward the kitchen, and then all through the kitchen, everyone staring but standing back. Out into a dark cool alley. Free. And later to the far side of a gas station where there was a rest room, where at least superficially she could wash.

The others were taken in the wagon to the North Beach Station, in Vallejo Street. Released on O.R. Probation: no more actions.

But why the Tac Squad, for a bunch of kids from Berkeley blowing joints? Why not just one cop, whom a mean waiter might have called?

After that, "Priest," or whoever he was, completely, totally disappeared, and the rumors began. Or, rather, an old rumor emerged, and was amplified. A man in the CIA, this rumor ran, was a specialist in radical-bashing. Persecution. Violent confrontations. One theory held that this agent was viewed as slightly wacko even by the CIA. Anyway, at that time Sara and her movement friends, including Carol, who was hurt and even more enraged, put it together that Priest had been CIA; clearly it was he who had somehow called in the Tac Squad to beat up Curtis. It was even suspicious that Alex and Sara got away with such relative ease; they were obviously less concerned with a dope arrest than with getting at Curtis, a known leader, a "Berkeley radical troublemaker." No one could remember Priest's going off to phone, but he would not have had to do anything so obvious; Carol remembered that since it was a Saturday night someone had thought to make reservations for a restaurant they had been told was so great, and so cheap. "Which," Carol venomously remarked, "Priest could have noticed." She always further insisted that it was he, Priest, who passed around the after-dinner joints. "He was always very well supplied." Bitter Carol. "I have to admit it, that was one of the attractions. Shit, we're lucky he didn't give us acid in our coffee. You all know about that little CIA ploy?"

These rumors over the following months became fixed ideas, a part of the gospel.

Curtis retained a long scar across his forehead. Imperfectly sewn, it never healed quite smoothly. But Curtis found a good new life for himself, in Amsterdam. Teaching.

Unlike Dudley, Sara is committed to the view that talking about trouble tends to help with its removal. You "deal with" things; you "handle them" first by verbal examination. She believes too that if you care for a friend you tell him or her what is most on your mind. And so with Dudley she makes an effort.

"I had this curious sense about Bill last night," she begins. "I really thought I'd known him before, in Berkeley. In the sixties. With another name."

"Oh, really? That's so interesting. There is something so, so bogus somehow about him," Dudley takes it up. "So too much like Charles, and at the same time not."

"Exactly. Well, when I knew him, sort of, or when I think I did, he was too much like someone else, a whole other person." And Sara goes on to tell Dudley about the night she remembers of "Bill" or Priest. With a few additions, a couple of subtractions.

As it turns out, Dudley the journalist is very knowledgeable about FBI-CIA anti-peace-protest activity, back then. And she is tremendously interested. "So marvelous," she at last comments, having asked and heard so much from Sara. "It sounds like a psychopath outdoing an essentially psychopathic process. Oh, wonderful. A most logical conclusion."

"Hoist on their own petard." Sara laughs.

"Exactly."

By now the two women like each other very much, feeling themselves almost perfectly in accord.

"And then," Sara continues, "at the end of the party I had a really
ugly scene with him. He's a cokehead, I was pretty sure about that,
and I could see he was running low. In fact out." And Sara describes
that scene to Dudley: Bill's rage, her own anger, and her fear.

Dudley asks, "You mean you think he recognized you?"

"Well, not necessarily. Probably not. He was half-drunk, and getting into withdrawal. I got the feeling he just deeply hates all women.
Which of course is not at all the same thing as being gay. Celeste
gets some things very confused."

"Oh, right," says Dudley. "Edward likes women a lot. So does
Freddy, actually."

"None of this explains what he was up to with Celeste, though,"
Sara muses.

Surprisingly, Dudley seems to have worked out this last. "I think
that was mostly Celeste. That relationship, whatever you want to call
it, was mostly her doing, and mostly in her own head, I think. She
took the initiative. You know, she was the one so struck with his
looking like Charles. She made so much of that, and then running
into him in the antique store, that same day. I really think she was
so deranged with missing Charles that she was looking for omens,
and almost anything would serve. And I'm sure he was interested in
her money—Celeste always looks richer than she is."

By now so absorbed in their conversation, Sara and Dudley have
halted in their walk, without quite knowing that they did so. In the
brisk blue sunny air they stand there on a grassy hillock, high above
the still-raging sea, the angry surf of which they are for the moment
quite oblivious.

It is Dudley who poses the next crucial question. "What do you
think this Bill Jones really does, though?" she asks, quite as though
Sara would know.

And Sara seems to, or at least she has a very definite opinion. "I
think he's still CIA. Of course he is. He was probably just monkeying
around with the files at the IRS, getting after some poor bastard. Up
to no good. I'm sure all those agencies 'cooperate' with each other.
And Celeste saw him there looking official, so what was easier than
to tell her he worked there?" She pauses, then plunges ahead. "His

antique store is probably a front for dope dealing in Central America. That's what the CIA is really into these days."

"Jesus," Dudley breathes. "You know, I'm absolutely sure you're right."

Sara for her part is exhilarated, both with new friendship and with having been proved right, or almost. Her sense of herself during much of her life has been of muddle, of misguidedness. She did the best she could, Sara has thought, but so often things did not work out, and she felt that she could and should have acted otherwise. She could have been saner, wiser, stronger, more generous.

"I must tell you a really far out theory of Sam's," now says Dudley, in the tone (recognized as such by Sara) of a new friend proffering a gift. "It sounds so crazy, but then he's so often right. Well, he thinks that the contras are somehow getting money from Iran."

"Iran? But however—"

Dudley laughs. "He won't say, and he hates it when he gives out one of his theories and then you ask him about it. But you wait, it'll turn out he's exactly right."

Sara can accept this. "Well, I certainly wouldn't put it past anyone."

"You'll see," repeats Dudley. "And then, this is a sillier idea, but it's pretty strange. He thinks that Charles and Polly had some tremendous affair, a long time ago. When Charles was in Paris."

"Polly? How amazing. But really not, when you think of it. She's such an unusual woman, she could have done almost anything. I feel that about her. But how extraordinary of Sam. What made him think that, do you know?"

"He won't ever say. I'm not sure if he *can* say, actually. He just gets certain vibrations—oh, messages, like a medium. And he hates to be asked about them."

"What's his sense of Bill, then? Has he said?" Sara has asked this a little anxiously, despite new confidence, new friendship. The fact that Bill is both a cokehead and very hostile to women does not necessarily make him a big CIA dope dealer, she knows that perfectly well. Nor can she be absolutely sure that he is or ever was Priest.

"Really not." Dudley hesitates. "He's not so well today, in fact he feels terrible. Remember, he had to leave early last night? But it's just the flu, I'm sure."

"My flu took forever to get over," Sara tells her (Sara, whose own intuition has just informed her that Sam is sicker than sick with flu, but of course she must be wrong). "But now I feel great."

"And, Sara, you do look marvelous. I hope everyone said that to you last night."

"Celeste's regime." Sara laughs. "She's got me entirely off meat. Lots of fruits and veggies. Fish and chicken. She swears we'll both live forever. Which I doubt. But at least I've taken off a few pounds. But poor Celeste, do you know that she sometimes sneaks peanut butter, just hoping she'll gain a little?"

Dudley has sometimes thought, and she now thinks again, of the similarity between the start of friendships and love affairs. There are discoveries of areas of rapport (so charming!—so seemingly unique!); the compliments; the laughing at each other's jokes; the richly insightful discussions of other friends. And then the later days, as in love, when the friend is less amusing, and you forget to tell her how great she looks, if indeed she does look great. Dudley sighs. She feels that she is almost too old for the intensity of yet another new friend— and surely too old for new love. And then her mind reverts to Sam, and she thinks, He *has* to get well.

Smiling to herself with pleasure at Dudley's compliment (and knowing it to be true: she does look well, Sara can see it for herself), she smiles too at a further memory of that crucial sixties night in North Beach. Or, rather, she recalls the ending of that night, back in Berkeley, with Alex. And it is not love so much as cleanliness, safety and warmth that Sara remembers.

At that time Alex had a room with a private bath, on Parker (the only hint from that era that he had more money than the rest of them, although the room was explained at the time as a favor from someone, some family connection). And that night, having escaped together from the Tac Squad, from that North Beach alley, after the long, jolting, uncomfortable and slightly frightening ride on the E bus, back to Berkeley, to Alex's room, then Sara took a long bath. Such a luxury, at a time in her life when the most semi-functioning, almost powerless stand-up showers were treats. She lay in the long tub, in deep hot water. Her heavy breasts floated upward, and she thought, Such a relief, floating breasts. (On principle, Sara went bra-less, so uncomfortable for a D-cup woman.) Alex came in, himself all clean and fair, and beautiful, and as she sat up he soaped her back, and then he wrapped a nice big towel around her. He seemed more aware than Sara herself of how frightened she had been, and how cold. Later in Alex's bed they probably made love—at that time they always did, given privacy and anything resembling a bed. But what Sara now most remembers, what makes her smile, is the memory of Alex's care—in Sara's life an almost unique experience: generally she has been the person taking care, the one giving baths, rubbing backs. Comforting frightened people. Coming up with clean clothes, clean towels, hot soup.

She finds these last thoughts slightly embarrassing, though. Is she sorry for herself, after all? And is that what she really wants from men, such primitive care? Well, sometimes it is, she has to admit. But surely that is what they often seem also to want? It may be all right?

The weather has begun to change again as Dudley and Sara have slowly walked along—paying little attention to either weather or scenery while they were talking, so absorbingly—on the beaten-down grass, above the turbulent sea. Dark clouds have appeared, amazingly sudden, and a strong cold wind has come up.

"There could be another storm," Dudley tells Sara, the newcomer to these parts.

Sara shivers a little, and she laughs as she says, "I never can understand California weather. It's always so, so irrational. So abrupt."

"Oh, right, that's how I've always felt. Even after all these years. The weather in New England made some sort of sense to me. Or at least I used to think so."

"Oh, that's how I felt when I was back there, I recognized the weather in New England," says Sara.

"But I think we'd better get back." Worried Dudley.

"Yes. God, it's so cold."

Almost running as they head for the car, Dudley has the sudden and absolute sense that Sam is extremely, quite possibly mortally ill. No chance of error: she knows. And she stumbles across the soggy ground in her haste to get to him. At the same time, she has the irrelevant thought, I forgot to tell Sara about the goats! I meant to and now it's too late, I can't really think about anything but Sam.

17   "It's as though a tidal wave had hit the town." This is how, in early March, Sara describes the death of Sam Venable. She is speaking to Alex, whom she has instinctively called for comfort; also everyone else around is too upset for conversation. Sam's death is still so painfully felt by them all.

Sam died on the day that Sara and Dudley took their walk, during which so much of moment was discussed—the sunny afternoon that succeeded the stormy, wind-whirled night of Celeste's least successful party. Dudley came home from that walk to find Sam in what appeared to be a deep sleep, which was in fact a coma, from which he did not emerge. A most fortunate, peaceful death, Dudley was assured, as though that were more than the very smallest comfort.

"They're all so stricken," Sara now goes on to Alex. "It's terrible for them. The reminder of their own mortality, of course. That's partly it. Sam being the first of that charmed circle of theirs to go. After Charles, I mean."

"Of course."

"Celeste has been so upset that she can't even mention it," Sara continues. "I guess Sam's dying has made her think even more about Charles."

"Well, it would."

Sara and Alex have fallen into a pattern of frequent conversations—every week or so one or the other of them calls, and Alex by now is almost familiar as Sara is with the habits and histories of the people she lives among in San Sebastian. Alex is an excellent listener—the best, Sara often thinks, of any man she has ever known.

"Besides," Sara tells him, "she's still so upset about Bill just cutting out like that. And still not another word. I'm awfully tempted to tell her what I really think of him, including the coke. And how he acted with me. But I know I shouldn't, she really couldn't handle it."

"You're probably right," Alex tells her. "But it was a very Priestlike disappearance."

"It sure was."

"Well," says Alex, "I'm still trying to find out what I can. But it's got a lot harder. They're much more closed down, you know. Signs that are hard to read."

"I'll bet."

"I'll keep at it, though."

A small silence between them ensues, until Sara takes it up again, saying, "Anyway, poor Dudley. Celeste's really been no help to her at all. Celeste can't help Dudley, she's not well enough herself."

"It's good you've turned up, then, so to speak," Alex tells her.

"I guess. It does seem oddly provident. My being here for all these events. On the other hand I think Celeste always knows what she's doing, really. I mean, she would *know* just when to ask me here."

"What I really want to know is, when can I see you?" Alex now says—as he has before, fairly often, in the course of these new-old long conversations.

"Well—" Sara, as always, hesitates. "Oh, Alex, I'd love to see you, in a way. But."

" 'But.' " He laughs. "It's complicated where you are, I know. But, Sara, it's so cheap now, fares are down to nothing, how can I afford *not* to come?" This is of course a joke, the fact that Alex has money has become something they laugh about—otherwise Sara cannot, as she puts it, "deal" with it.

"It's very complicated," is all that for the moment she says.

"I send love, then," says Alex. "Whatever I mean by that."

She laughs. "Me too. Whatever."

"Sara, do you need any, uh, money?" He has not so clearly asked her this before.

"Dear Alex, no. Unfortunately, uh, money wouldn't help."

* * *

Sara's description of the effect of Sam's death on that small group of his intimates was accurate: it was quite as catastrophic and as unexpected as a tidal wave would in fact have been. What they had all, their separate ways, believed would happen to none of them had indeed happened to Sam. Handsome green-eyed, somewhat strange, Southern Sam, now gone. Overweight, occasionally surly, more often hypercourteous Sam, entirely gone. Talented, remarkable unique Sam Venable, reduced to cold flesh, now buried in his box and becoming dust. It was as terrible, as horrendous, as it was unthinkable. And they thought about it all the time. About Sam. About dying.

In a way they all felt, and they said to each other that they felt, they had hardly known Sam. He was not an easy man to know, and they were not given enough time with him.

The comforting and the general care of Dudley have fallen to Sara, or perhaps out of lifetime habit she takes them upon herself. It was Sara who, on the evening of the funeral (to general surprise, Sam had wanted a traditional Episcopal service; "You have no idea how Southern Sam really was," Dudley told them all)—on that evening Sara called Dudley to say that she was coming over with a casserole. She'd be glad to stay overnight, if that would be helpful at all.

Well, it really would, said Dudley.

Together, at Dudley and Sam's table, now Dudley's table, Sara and Dudley ate their dinner. (The excellent food was a considerable surprise to Dudley: radical, far-out Sara, a most sophisticated cook?) And they talked, that night, almost not at all (another good surprise for Dudley, who had feared that conversation would be expected).

Only, once or twice Dudley said, "Dear Sara, it's so good of you to be here, and this dinner is wonderful." To which Sara answered, "But I'm afraid I'm not much help."

"Oh, but you are, you don't know."

Dudley looked very bad, Sara thought. At least five years older than she had on the day when they walked on the grassy space above the sea. The day Sam died. Since then Dudley's dark-blue eyes have blurred, her skin reddened and ridged, and her mouth pulled nar-rower, all tight. She looks drowned, thinks Sara.

This quiet evening, with just the two of them, was repeated, and repeated. Celeste encouraged these visits of Sara to Dudley: "I'm perfectly fine alone," she told Sara. "I *want* you to go to Dudley."

One of Sara's impulses, at first, was to insist that Dudley talk about how she felt, to bring up Sam. Death, dying. But another impulse, which at last won out, was to leave Dudley alone, to allow her to establish her own pace, her own moods for speech, or for silence.

Dudley's idea, or instinct—it was hard to tell how conscious she was of what she did, at that time—was to speak when she did speak of Sam of happy days, good times. Years when Sam was working well, selling paintings, enjoying painter friends in the Cedar Bar. The fun that Sam and Dudley used to have: "The first few drinks were always so much fun," Dudley tells Sara. "It's the tenth or the thirteenth that do you in." The trips, the romantic reconciliations after fights. But: "We were really addicted to each other, as well as to booze," Dudley also says. "When we'd break up, after some horrible fight, I'd want to die, I literally did not see how I could go on living. Talk about withdrawal symptoms. And that's just what I can't have now. I can't afford to."

Fortunately there is a great deal for Dudley to do, of a practical na-ture. Sam's four daughters, the lawyers, seem uncharacteristically united in their demands: they want Sam's paintings. If possible, his letters. Sam (so like him) left no instructions, so that what she does about his girls is up to her—and to her very New England conscience.

Thus, during the first days and weeks that succeed Sam's death, it does not even occur to Dudley to call Brooks Burgess. Nor does the thought of running amuck, Caitlin-style, cross her mind. She is entirely absorbed in "keeping busy," in trying to believe that Sam is gone. He will not be around to hear the joke she just heard, although he would like it. He won't be able to read the book she just finished, which he would appreciate. He won't eat the second fillet of salmon that out of habit Dudley just brought home. She *can't remember* his death, to a degree that seems a form of madness. Or Alzheimer's? Is that possible?

Thank God there is Sara, available for an impromptu salmon supper—for which she, Sara, devises a delicious mustard-caper sauce. Sara, for listening and for talk.

"It's really so lucky that he died" is what Celeste has said, several times. To Sara, an astonishing statement. "So fortunate," Celeste continues. "He could have been crippled or even paralyzed by a stroke. And Sam was such a vigorous, handsome, masculine man, that would have been terrible. He would have hated it! He was even spared horrible cancer, lingering for months the way poor Charles did. Such a blessing for Dudley too, although she probably doesn't know it yet, poor dear."

All perfectly true. All correct. But still.

"I can't quite make out what Celeste is really saying," Sara confides to Alex, having just repeated Celeste's version of the death of Sam. "She keeps on using the word 'lucky.' It must drive Dudley crazy, although fortunately she's so preoccupied, Dudley is, just holding herself together. I doubt if she hears very much. But Celeste, I'm sure she means something. She's signaling, and I'm not getting the message."

"She means that she wants to die," Alex tells her after a pause.

"Oh, Alex. Christ, do you really think so?"

"Yes I do. She must."

They both are silent then, long moments of long distance, until Sara says, "You must be right. She thinks the dead are lucky. She's tired of being alive. Oh—*shit*."

"I'm, after all, six years older than Sam is—was" is what Edward remarks, and repeats, and repeats, to Freddy.

"Darling Edward, I know how old you are. And now I know Sam's age quite as well." Freddy is unable to control a certain snappishness: of course it is too bad, really awful about poor Sam, whom Freddy really liked, as everyone did. But need Edward be quite so lugubrious?

What good does that do? Need he take Sam's death quite so personally? "Sam's dying does not mean that you're going to die any sooner," Freddy at last is able to formulate.

But I don't feel well, Edward decides not to say. I cough a lot, I feel weak. Hypochondriacs get sick too, you mean little Mexican prick. And even though we haven't had sex for years—for seven, exactly— I could still get AIDS. He says none of this.

"I think we need cheering up," Freddy tells him. "I think I will make a small party, a little dinner. With your favorite *huachinango*."

"*Al mojo de ajo*." Edward smiles, if thinly. A party with Mexican food is one of the last things he would choose, at this moment. But, "How nice," he gamely agrees.

"I will even make the phone calls," says Freddy, which is not exactly a sacrifice on his part; he enjoys telephoning quite as much as Edward hates it (a considerable drawback in Edward's real-estate dealings).

The results of his phoned invitations are somewhat mixed, Freddy sometime later reports back to Edward. Sara would love to come, but she is not quite sure about Celeste, who is not there at the moment. Celeste has not been terribly well this week; Sara thinks she might have gone to see a doctor.

Dudley is really sorry, but a daughter of Sam's has shown up in San Francisco, and Dudley is driving up to meet her for dinner, she'll stay over at the El Drisco. "It's really easier than having her down here," Dudley tells Freddy. "Besides she's always been rather nice, comparatively. She's the only one of them who did not want to examine Sam's will."

Polly can't come. "Have you noted how Polly is never free on Thursday nights?" Freddy asks Edward.

"It's her secret-lover night."

They both laugh, companionably.

"Well, so far only Sara for sure." Freddy frowns. "Lord, what a small circle we really are. To lose Charles, and then Sam has reduced us to almost nothing. What we need are some additions."

Freddy's small perfect cleft chin goes up, a gesture that Edward knows well—and admires; Freddy does it beautifully.

"I do hope Celeste will be able to come, after all," murmurs Edward.

* * *

Celeste does not come.

"Quite honestly I just don't feel up to it," she tells Sara. "You young people," she vaguely adds.

"Celeste, you really worry me," Sara can't help saying. "If you don't feel well—"

"Sara, my dear, I'm quite all right. Really. But frankly I've had more to deal with, as you put it, than I can, this past year. Charles, and then Sam. And then that Bill behaving so very strangely. It's as though I'd taken a stranger into the house and been robbed."

This is actually Celeste's first admission of upset over Bill. And so far, out of character, Sara has refrained from asking, or from making any comment on his total, continued absence. This unaccustomed discretion comes partly from not knowing what to say—as in fact she still does not. "It could have nothing to do with you, dear Celeste," she attempts. "He could have had to go somewhere else on business."

Celeste's laugh is light, quite unconvincing. "For the IRS? Really, Sara."

"Well, they do travel about, getting after people. But maybe he's off for more antiques. To Central America, or somewhere. I think I have to tell you, Celeste, I don't have good feelings about this Bill."

"You never liked him, I knew that."

"Celeste, it honestly isn't as simple as not liking. I told you, he reminded me a lot of someone I knew, who was really bad. And for all I know he really was that person."

"And you think he ran off when you recognized him? Sara darling, what a melodramatic imagination. I think it's his way of saying he doesn't want to get married."

"And he drinks too much, not to mention—"

"Sara, please. Enough. I really find this all very upsetting. Let's not discuss Bill further."

Arrived a little late at Edward's and Freddy's, Sara is relieved to see the pretty table set only for three.

"Well, as you can see, we're only three tonight," unnecessarily announces Edward, as after drinks he leads the way toward their small and elegant dining room. "I hope you won't mind."

"As a matter of fact I'm most pleased," responds Sara very warmly. "I had some odd instinct that you might have asked that David. I still can't get over Celeste's inviting him—for me."

A glance passes between Edward and Freddy: brief, opaque. And then Freddy tells Sara, "As a matter of fact he almost was. We thought of it—we were afraid just us would bore you. But you mean that you actually have something against our adorably friendly David?"

"Frankly he gives me the pip," announces Sara.

Dinner is a blackened redfish that smells strongly of garlic, at which Sara exclaims, "Oh, my favorite smell. I never get enough garlic."

"Well, quite possibly tonight you will" is Edward's somewhat dry comment.

"It's wonderful." Digging in, Sara smiles across to Freddy, as she thinks, How nice these men are, how enviable, in a way, with their cozy life. Together.

And next she thinks, Could I do this? Could I live like this with someone? These involuntary questions are new to Sara, she has never thought at all in those terms before. And so she further thinks, What is this, some forty-year-old softening of the head? But the image persists: a house with regular furniture, meals cooked in a kitchen. Clean bathrooms. Some permanence with another person. And, startlingly, she recognizes that that person who shares the newspaper at breakfast and sleeps next to her in the same bed every night—that person, that man is Alex.

Well. Jesus, Sara thinks. Jesus, I might have known.

"And then there's 'Bill,' " says Freddy somewhat later. His quirky eyebrows as he looks at Sara, saying this, make it a question.

Sara starts to say: What a horrible guy, I can't stand him, he's a cokehead who really hates women. And I'm almost sure he's FBI, I used to sort of know him, I think. But some out-of-character caution stops her from saying any of that, and she only says, "Yes, there's Bill."

Her tone, though, has evidently given away more than she intended. Edward and Freddy look first at each other (an enviably intimate exchange, Sara feels), and then they both laugh.

"Not, one gathers, your favorite person?" It is Edward who has said this.

And Freddy: "He is a little much. So, so friendly, I have to tell you. He made me very suspicious."

"Suspicious? Why?" False-innocent Sara.

"Just the way he was coming on to me. So interested in everything I'm doing in San Francisco. All about gay activism. And he is not a gay person, he simply is not. There's no reason for him to be interested in everything we do."

"That's probably what he's told to do in est, or wherever it is he's been," Edward tells Freddy. "In my day it was Dale Carnegie, *How to Make Friends and Influence People.*"

Sara laughs. "That could be just what Bill's been reading."

"Or he could be INS," says Freddy darkly, and seriously. "Trying to throw me out of the country on some technicality. GAY MEXICAN ACTIVIST EXPELLED. Or maybe just QUEER SPIC OUSTED."

Sara laughs, although she of course finds this alarmingly close to her own line of thought. How interesting that Bill should be almost universally perceived as a spy, is one of her thoughts.

"I imagine he's just nosy," Edward puts in. "And he's somehow got the idea that asking personal questions is attractive." He frowns. "The real problem of course is with Celeste. Just what does he want of her, or imagine that he will get?"

Freddy grins. "My dirty little mind says money," he tells them.

"That's got to have something to do with it, at least," Sara agrees. "An undemanding, elegant older woman. And Celeste's a terrific listener. Sometimes."

"Undemanding?" Edward laughs. "Our adorable martinet? Little does he know, is all I can say."

Sara too laughs, but she says, "What Celeste really demands is that people be strong and independent, I think. She wants everyone to be like her." And then she says, "I have some hunch that we won't see Bill around anymore, though. I think he got some other assignment, or something."

"Whatever do you mean?" they ask her, more or less in chorus.

"Oh, I don't know. Maybe some richer older woman somewhere else. Or gold in South America. I think he's what used to be called an adventurer."

* * *

Although she was late for dinner, Sara still finds it possible to leave early, pleading worry over Celeste—whom in fact she is quite sure to find sound asleep.

Thus she gets back to the house a little after ten. She opens the front door, and goes through the atrium to the living room. As, at just that moment, the phone begins to ring.

It is Alex—of course. Alex, very excited. "Sit down," he says. "I have something to tell you. Strong news."

Seating herself on the somewhat stiff white linen sofa, Sara almost knows what she is about to hear. And in the instant before Alex speaks she experiences an inner tremble—and a wish that she had been wrong.

But, "You were absolutely right," Alex tells her. "Your 'Bill,' Bill Jones is William Jones Priest. Who was and is CIA."

"Oh." After a pause Sara adds, "I don't ask you how you found out?"

"No. Don't. I might be tempted to tell you. Just think of it as my own Deep Throat." And he laughs a little.

Sara is fairly sure that his source is someone he knew through his father from the old, early and relatively innocent CIA days, the old forties. Someone leftover from that era and (usefully for them) still there.

She shivers, sitting in the overheated room. "I'm really scared now," she tells Alex.

"You mean that you're not sure he cropped up in your life again by accident?"

"There are no accidents." She tries to laugh. "But that's just the hell of it. I don't know."

18   Because of the weather, possibly, at first there are more
police than demonstrators, a great cordon of helmeted police, at the
plaza of the Federal Building: a rally against U.S. involvement in
Central America. The demonstrators are simply a small circle of people who have joined hands around the fountain. They have laid aside
their placards in a tidy pile; they are slowly moving around in their
circle, and they are singing. Something Spanish that Sara does not
recognize. Her practiced eye does, however, take in certain facts about
that group, to her a familiar mix of poor radicals, mostly young; and
middle-aged, middle-class "liberals," their faces lined with intelligence, anxiety and guilt, their smiles barely hopeful.

Sara and Dudley have driven up from San Sebastian, in the wet-
cotton, dark gray fog, the wind and cold. "Strictly speaking, there is
no spring in California," Dudley has explained, as though Sara might
have forgotten. Dudley's spring longings for New England are as sharp
and terrible as her pangs for love—for Sam, for being young. For
everything now irrevocably missing from her life.

They had to park some distance away, and then to walk along
grimy Polk Street, among grim-faced young lawyers, federal office
workers. Past seedy dark small stores, trashy sidewalks. They become
confused, they have to stop someone and ask, "Which way to the
Federal Building?"

They arrive a little late, then, and thus do not join the group
whose hands are joined, who are singing. They stand there isolated
in the cold, both watching: Dudley the journalist, and Sara the (perhaps former) activist.

Apart from the demonstrators and the police, standing near the cordon is a third group, who could be taken for tourists: "casual" clothes, mostly synthetics. Middle-aged, sharp-eyed men, some with cameras. Sara, who does not take them for tourists, stares fixedly in their direction. She is breathing tightly, her gaze is forced ahead. And to herself she acknowledges that she is afraid—as she used to be so often, almost always, she is terrified. And, as she has trained herself to do, she examines that fear: she looks at it in a practical way, asking herself just what could happen to her, actually.

There is nothing anyone can do to you now, she says to herself. You do not interest any given agency (probably). Anyone would have a hard time proving any wrongdoing on your part (except for harboring fugitives). You are a tall, confident woman of middle age, in dark pants, a dark red sweater. The heavy, anxiety-choked, shabby girl of twenty years back is invisible now.

Perhaps illogically, though, the revelation from Alex that "Bill" really is Priest, and is and was CIA, has scared her badly. It is as though, with that confirmation of her darkest instincts, everything else that she most fears and half believes has also been proved true. As though most of the world were indeed in the hands of criminals. Of organized crime. Drug kings. Old, quite mad deposed movie stars, from Grade B films.

At that moment, though, as if to bring cheer, and strength, there is an actual parting above of clouds and fog, and a burning white sun shows through. And, possibly even more remarkable, at that very same moment reinforcements appear: a small troop of new people with placards: NO MORE VIETNAMS, U.S. OUT OF NICARAGUA, STAY OUT OF REAGAN'S WAR. These people all cluster around the other group. Joining forces.

"Sam and I always got really dressed up for peace marches, in the sixties," Dudley tells Sara, once they have started back on the long drive to San Sebastian. "I'd wear my best skirts and shiniest boots, and Sam would actually put on a coat and tie. We thought we should look respectable. Not try to look like hippies." She laughs. "As though we could have. But it's odd how much fun those marches look like from here. In retrospect, I mean."

"I guess I was one of the hippies."

"I used to wish I were," confesses Dudley. "So many middle-aged people did wish that, you know. But at least I didn't try to look like one. And Sam . . ." She trails off, as she catches herself often doing these days, as she tries to speak of Sam.

Do not speak ill of the dead. Surely one of the strongest, earliest, never-ever-mentioned prohibitions, Dudley has recently observed to herself. Since Sam's death—his departure, as she thinks of it. She has spoken, so far, only good of him, she has presented the two of them as an only happy couple. Especially, she is aware, she has done this with Sara, whom she very much likes, with whom she would like to have an honest friendship, more honest than would be possible (she thinks) with Celeste, for example. She would like to be more "open," less New England. However, as she talks about peace marches with Sara, she wonders if there would be any point, really, in continuing with the truth: "Sam always managed to wander off somewhere, though, and show up much later, really drunk. Not just peace marches, he liked wandering off from anything, anything organized. Including me, an essentially organized, tidy person. He was crazy about bars, especially of course the Cedar. I have no idea what anyone means by love. I felt quite as much rage and even hate for Sam at times. In these last years, living out here in San Sebastian, when I could make Sam laugh I would think, Oh good, he likes me. But at least at the start of peace marches we always looked good. Successful and happy."

Naturally she says none of this aloud to Sara. Naturally not, and so the drive home, over fog-shrouded hills, past mist-concealed fields and woods, is quiet, for the most part. Not saying what is most on her mind, Dudley experiences a familiar wave of loneliness, and she wonders: Does Sara ever feel so isolated? Does she too wish, at times, to say what she does not? More likely, Dudley believes, Sara says more or less what is on her mind.

*　*　*

"Such a terrible day" is the first thing that Celeste says to Sara, as Sara comes into the living room, around teatime. Then, seeming to remember, she asks, "How was your peace march?"

"Really more of a rally than an actual march," Sara can't resist saying. "But it was okay. I was glad we went."

"I'm sure you're such a comfort to poor Dudley." Saying this, Celeste looks so very sad, so in need of comfort for herself that Sara is very moved. And worried.

And helpless. How to comfort heavily guarded, tightly controlled Celeste, with her scornful nose, her rigid, upright posture? "It's hard to tell how Dudley does feel," she attempts. "She's so, so New England."

"I suppose." But Celeste's interest has seemed to subside. Her huge black, black eyes shift their focus, and she returns to herself, her own pain.

And Sara sighs, and gives up. She feels with Celeste less a generation gap than an unbridgeable gap in concerns, Celeste's being wholly personal, narrowly "social," in some ways aesthetic. In no possible sense "political."

Celeste knows that she almost assuredly has something quite terribly wrong: well, she has the most wrong thing of all, the unmentionable horror, of which almost everyone finally dies. Daily she studies and considers her symptoms: blood.

On a very occasional more cheerful day she thinks it could be an ulcer, but from what Polly has said the color of her blood is wrong. Not an ulcer.

Death, the idea of death, is not what she so much minds, Celeste has worked out; dying will be a fairly simple matter, she believes, a losing of consciousness, quite possibly welcome, like sleep. But the stages on the way to death, the ways that the world has now worked out for people to die, there's the real horror: hospitals, surgery, anesthesia. Terrible nurses, mean doctors. Pain, indignity. Reduction of one's self to a degraded, helpless and unclean infancy.

Celeste has had certain operations—gall bladder, a hysterectomy; she knows the hospital, the surgical experience, and she cannot, cannot go through any of that again. Much less the further horrors of chemotherapy, radiation—whatever they choose for her. She cannot even go to a doctor to describe her present symptoms. She does not want to see a doctor, to be operated on. To be fixed, maybe even cured. She is too old for all that.

She would rather die.

And on her way to dying, should she arrive at a time of awful pain, there are pills one can take. One can choose to go to sleep, for good.

Celeste believes that she is making a rational choice. She knows what she is doing; it is her privilege not to have medical care if she doesn't want it. No surgery, no long painful bright sleepless hospital nights.

At times she feels quite rational about it all.

At other times, though, she inwardly rails against what is wrong with her, and especially against its location: humiliating. *Ugly.*

No wonder Bill left, she thinks. And while of course she did not breathe a word of her affliction, ever, to him, very likely he sensed something wrong with her. He smelled illness, along with her appalling age. He may even have thought her joking when she said to him (and oh! no one would ever know the courage that took), when she said, "Bill darling, I'd really like us to be married."

He laughed, of course they laughed together, seated side by side at a corner table at Vic's, over the specially ordered salads. But Celeste was serious; she would never have said such a thing as a joke, no one would, no woman. And then when he overheard her whispering at her party to her friends, though, confiding her secret, their secret—well, no wonder he ran, ran out on her.

And how could she ever even have thought of another life, with Bill? After Charles, a second chance? *How,* when beneath her clothes she is withered, dry, terrible, old? She is bleeding almost every day, she is probably dying.

If only Celeste would go to bed earlier, then Sara would not have to use the phone at such odd hours, so very late, waking Alex in New York, where it is often almost morning.

However, there is a certain sexiness to these strangely timed calls;

it is even sexy, in a way, that she, Sara, almost always makes the calls. Aggressive Sara, strong Sara, reaching out for Alex, touching him across three thousand miles. She sits curled on Celeste's white linen sofa, in her old flounced flannel nightgown, her wool robe and sheepskin slippers. She is cold, hearing the drip of fog in the night outside. Shivering, thinking of sex. Calling warm Alex, and smiling to herself at the prospect of his voice.

She even postpones, momentarily, the actual placing of her call, the light touch on the now familiar numbers, their tinny music. As she savors what seems a new sense of herself.

Years back, despite knowing this to be unhealthy, if not actually "sick," Sara used to speculate as to what, possibly, Alex could "see" in her. And none of her conclusions then were politically acceptable. Because I make love to him, she thought, and he's probably only had fairly passive, timid girls. Or because he has no idea how beautiful he is, he does not especially value himself in that way.

Now, however, Sara's overriding sense of herself is one of strength. I am an exceptionally strong woman, she thinks. I have withstood a great deal, every fact of my life proves strength. No wonder Alex, who is genuinely good (I think) and intelligent and kind but hesitant to act—no wonder Alex should be drawn to me. To strength. He sees someone who will act for as well as with him.

Smiling now at her own unwonted self-approval—is the sin of pride politically incorrect, or are you supposed to think well of yourself, these days? (she believes that you are)—Sara then pushes the telephone buttons, and leans back into the sofa to listen to the ring.

Poor Alex, she always wakes him, and always she is torn between guilt and affection, sheer fondness for his sleepy, fumbling voice.

However, tonight the phone continues to ring and ring, and no Alex, sleepy or otherwise, comes on the line.

Outrageous: how dare he not be there? Thinking that, reacting in that quick and primitive way, Sara further thinks, He's out with someone—or, rather, he's there in the apartment, he is listening to the phone and knowing who it is—with some beautiful passive blonde, who barely touches him.

And Sara also thinks, This stupid fantasy is sheer regression. I could have thought of it twenty years back.

But that hot jealous flood is not so easily halted as Sara even thinks, I could go to bed with that silly David, he's handsome enough, in his way, and I could somehow let Alex know. If we're supposed to be such honest platonic old friends.

Curiously, perhaps, these strenuous emotions have the effect at last of wearing Sara out, and she falls asleep, curled there in her bedraggled flannel gown, in the deep white linen.

Waking to blackness, still, she looks at her watch—tiny, very pretty, a recent present from Celeste. ("I never use it, my darling, and you'll have it someday anyway. Might as well now.") It is just after 4 a.m., that classic hour for insomniacs, for crazies. However, not in New York, where it is just after seven, and time to get up.

Wanting then more than anything to talk to Alex, to tell him about the march, and the new-old infiltrators there, and how frightening she finds the information that Bill indeed is Priest, is CIA—wanting so badly to tell Alex all that, which Alex alone could hear and understand, Sara still does not make the call.

She is wide awake now, and absolutely clear in her head, and she thinks, I cannot call Alex now, at seven-fifteen, and not find him in. I simply cannot take that risk.

Sara gets up from the sofa and heads off to her room, to bed, as, with the most wry of inward smiles, she mutters to herself, "Well, so much for strength."

19 "Dear really beautiful Celeste. Where has all this time gone? I can tell you, I really had some trouble getting up for writing to you. The way I cut out could really have ticked you off, I wouldn't blame you. I didn't even get to tell you how I appreciated your little 'joke,' even if I was sort of the butt, in a manner of speaking. Anyway, your party was super, some fancy blast, and I really got a big kick out of meeting all your friends. And especially that niece, or is she a niece? of yours. Was her name Sally? Give her my best regards.

"You probably wouldn't believe what I've been up to, and into these past four months. All business, unfortunately. But among other things I have been going to Berlitz (now there's an experience I could have done without, talk about a bunch of creeps) anyway, I took this crash course in Spanish, and now I can really *hablar*.

"Of course I've been crossing my fingers that something would send me back to California, but no such luck. I have to go way down south, and I don't mean Dixie. But I'll be thinking about you, Celeste, and your lovely home, and your friends and your 'niece.' "

Celeste, fastidious about the written word, as indeed she is in most areas, is fairly appalled by this letter, her first from Bill. Sent, she notes, from Washington, D.C. One of Charles's great charms for Celeste was his prose style, which she considered exemplary, of its kind: clean and clear and vigorous—even elegant, at times.

Whereas that of Bill is simply vulgar, she concludes. Is even more than a little disjointed, and in her view patently insincere. She knows that many people have trouble with the written word, one should make certain allowances, but still: this is an awful letter. He even sounds slightly crazy, Celeste decides, and she thinks, I only cared about him, to the extent that I did care, because I am actually not in the best of shape myself.

She does not show the letter to Sara (certainly *not*), nor to anyone, ever. Over breakfast she only says to Sara, that next morning, "Oh, I heard from Bill. Finally. I forgot to tell you."

"Really?"

Sara does not do well at trying to appear casual, in Celeste's opinion.

"Yes, I think he must be off to South America," Celeste throws out, herself very casual.

"Really? What country, do you know?"

"I've no idea." With some satisfaction, Celeste notes Sara's totally thwarted look, her outraged curiosity.

She observes too that Sara looks—well, "pretty" is actually the most descriptive word, odd as it may seem for bold Sara. Her face looks all smoothed out, her skin very lightly tanned, perhaps from all those walks with Dudley, in this unusual warm clear weather. Her hair too is smooth, pulled becomingly back in a way that Celeste herself suggested, and was quite startled to see that Sara in fact adopted.

"He just said South America?" Sara now pursues.

"Actually not even that. I just put things together from what he did say." Celeste purses her mouth, and is silent. And then suddenly, for no good, discernible reason, she thinks: Sara is having a love affair with that David, it must be David, there's no one else around. And she's always out.

"Well, that's very interesting," Sara comments, still going on about Bill. "Horrible, isn't it, how things fall into place?"

"They do?"

"I mean, so much turning up in South America. Bad loans, guns, coke, along with their usual earthquakes and floods and buses falling off cliffs? Have you noticed how natural disasters almost never befall the rich?"

"Sara, I do not see Bill as a natural disaster. Nor as evil as you seem to insist on believing."

"Well, maybe not." Sara looks at her watch, not the present from

Celeste but a large practical one that she boasts about having found at Walgreen's. "It's such a terrific day, I think I'll go for a walk." (As though she had no appointment! Were meeting no one.)

Once Sara is gone, precipitately out the door, Celeste begins to reflect, seated in her sunny boudoir, at the small carved desk. And one of the first things that occurs to her is Sara's singular lack of any acting ability; she has none at all, not an ounce.

And it was very wise indeed of her, Celeste, not to show Bill's letter to Sara; with Sara's very melodramatic tendencies—"paranoid" seems the fashionable word, in some circles, these days—God knows what Sara would have made of it. Recently Sara has even asked Celeste if Celeste thought their phone could be "bugged." Imagine! The Timberlake phone, Charles's phone. No doubt Sara imagines that Bill is bugging their phone, somehow.

"But why did you tell us he was gay?" is one of the things that Sara has asked Celeste, about Bill.

"Oh, that was just my little joke." Celeste laughed.

Her own reasons for that "joke" were fairly complicated, actually, and included a genuine confusion as to the sexual direction of Bill. They used to kiss a lot, he and she, but not in what Celeste considers a passionate way. They were like adolescents, but very early adolescents—these days, that would be about nine years old, from what Celeste has gleaned from various articles she has read. But the impulse to state that Bill was gay also sprang from a desire to get there first, so to speak: if anyone else should happen to take that view of Bill, Celeste would want to appear to know already.

Now, though, as she watches the creeping of sunlight into and across the polished floorboards of her bedroom, Celeste feels incredibly remote from Bill; he now seems to have come and gone in her life without leaving a trace. How difficult now even to recall all that emotion, all that tremulous waiting for phone calls, those delicately stirring kisses.

But she actually feels both remote from Bill and from everyone she knows, from even those near at hand. From Sara, from Dudley, from Edward and Freddy, who are coming over for dinner tonight.

She wonders if this is a part of getting ready to die. Could this be what the approach of death is like, this calm, this passive sadness?

Very likely so.

Celeste has to absolutely force herself to do her exercises. First the Yoga, then some mild aerobics.

Contrary to Celeste's somewhat retro-romantic view, as Sara herself might put it, Sara is certainly not "having an affair" with David, nor with anyone else. What she is doing, and what must in large part account for her look of much-improved health, of looking "pretty," is following Celeste's own prescription for strenuous exercise. Which she would not have admitted to Celeste. "Oh, Celeste, you're so right, I've been walking ten or twelve miles a day really fast, and I feel a hundred times better."

Never, never would she have said such a thing, although that statement expresses the literal, simple truth. And furthermore she would have liked to make that acknowledgment to Celeste, as a sort of present, a way of saying, "You're really great. I do what you say, sometimes." But she cannot.

But she does walk. She walks all the way to the coast, where she stands up on those bluffs, and she breathes, and contemplates. And she speaks very firmly to herself, at those moments. She says, "You don't have to be afraid anymore. You're all right now, you're much better." And she wrestles with the problem of whether or not she should tell Celeste what she actually knows about Bill. Bill the coke-head, Bill of the CIA.

In the early hours, which are Sara's chosen time for walks, the pale gray June fog banks that linger above the sea are delicate, thin veils. Wafting, ephemeral. The sea distantly shimmers. "It's all so beautiful that even I find it hard to be depressed," Sara has said to Alex, in a recent phone call. (He had called her late one night, her usual hour for ringing him: he had been down in Washington, he said, sort of poking around, and he thought she might have tried to call him. Well, no, she actually hadn't, Sara lied.)

She told Alex then about the peace rally, the old-new faces of infiltrators, informers. She said how afraid she sometimes is. "It's like running through some terrible woods and making it out, and then you stop to be afraid" is how she put it.

"That's just right, how it is." (Good, kind, responsive Alex.) "But the point is," he continues, "you are out. That's what to keep in mind."

"I'm not always sure. This fucking phone sounds bugged."

"Well, what if it is? You're Sara, and you're staying with Celeste. You went to a peace rally with Dudley. You make phone calls to me in New York. Sometimes. Big fucking deal, as we used to say."

Sara laughs. "Well, when you put it like that." And then she tells him, "I even worry about that dopey David. The waiter guy I told you about. With the beard and yellowish eyes, who was such a jerk at Celeste's big party. But he follows me around, or I think he does. I run into him a lot."

"He's probably got some kind of a crush on you. I used to follow you around."

"Oh, you never did. I would have known." Not saying, I was following you, I was the one with the crush.

"Oh, did I not. You had a class in that building with the funny name, up by the campanile. Birge. I used to sit so casually on one of those benches at the side, trying to look at the saucer magnolias, to think hard about magnolias. And sometimes you'd really mess me up, leaving by another door. And I'd have to tell myself it wasn't deliberate, you weren't avoiding me."

Inordinately pleased, Sara laughs—she is half-ashamed of such pleasure.

"You seem to think anyone who likes you is some kind of a freak. Or a spy, for God's sake."

This is so accurate, and so awful, so mentally unhealthy, as Sara knows perfectly well, that she has no answer other than her convenient old irony. "Well, maybe I'll confront this David, and see what he has in mind, since I'm so devastating that he can't possibly hurt me."

"Do that. But if something comes of it just don't tell me. I don't want to hear about it."

* * *

Alex too is certainly "much better." Sara had this thought on seeing him in New York, and she thinks this increasingly as they talk, and talk. He is more his own person, is "stronger," more defined.

Alex himself tends to attribute any changes in himself to his shrink. "She's a most unusual woman."

But he has also pointed out, "I'm really only okay by myself. It's 'relationships' I can't seem to handle."

"Except by long distance," Sara has to add.

He laughs, a little embarrassed, but then he reminds her, "It's you who won't let me come out there. And if you say you're afraid of me too, I'll know you're lying."

"No, it's not that. I'm not." I'm not quite ready to see you yet, is what Sara actually means, and is quite unable to say. For one thing, she worries about what will actually happen, what must happen, when they do see each other again. Suppose the sex is not as great as the friendship they seem to have developed?

Alex continues to talk about his Spanish studies—enthusiastically. He is now meeting every week with a group that includes a poet from Nicaragua. "In fact, it seems more or less a country of poets. I think I should have that trip pulled together in a couple of months."

On some days, turning her back on the sea, Sara heads down the overgrown, rutted path, now never used, leading past Polly's small house and eventually to the town (this being, among other things, the one road on which Sara has not run into David). She would never have simply dropped in on Polly, but she liked the idea of Polly's nearness. Sara liked Polly, though she barely knew her, always smiling as she passed that house.

The inevitable day arrived, however, when Sara's smile and her glance toward the vine-covered, stucco box encountered Polly herself, seated—or rather, sprawled—on a tattered rug, on the patchy grass. Polly apparently digging in her garden.

Sara waves, half-intending to continue, but Polly stops her. "Just stay here for one minute, which is all I've got. But I have something to say."

Coming in through the broken, slatted gate, approaching Polly, Sara is not at all surprised to hear Polly's message. Polly, with no preamble, says to Sara, "I'm more than a little worried about Celeste. You've got to get her to see a doctor. *Make* her go."

"Really? It's that bad?" Even an expected message can be very shocking, as this one is.

Near Polly's sandal-shod feet is an oblong package, newspaper-wrapped. ("It looked like money, honestly, a packet of bills she'd just dug up," Sara to Alex, later. "Talk about eccentric." Alex: "Well, the banks aren't doing too well, she may be quite right.")

"She throws a few symptoms at me from time to time," explains Polly, her pale brilliant eyes squinting up into the sun, and at Sara. "I knew what was wrong with Charles, so she overrates my diagnostic powers. He had the same thing I'd had, though, for Christ's sake. The old big pancreatic C. And Celeste may be okay, but someone other than me has to check her out."

Picking up her trowel then, returning to dirt, Polly further admonishes, "Well, you do what you can."

Thus dismissed, Sara promises, "I will," and gestures goodbye—although she would have given a good deal to stay and talk to Polly. What symptoms does Celeste now have, *how* serious are they?

The thought of a serious illness—well, cancer—and a terrible slow death for Celeste is entirely horrifying to Sara. *Horrifying,* and at the same time, along with the horror, Sara experiences a sort of rage: How could you, Celeste? I didn't come out here to watch you die, I already did that with Emma. I love you, you have to stay around. We've just begun to talk, and I need you.

Continuing down the road, that day, she does not run into anyone. She does see Victor Lozano, the heavyset, dark, quite bald repairman from the local garage. Who is pushing along a battered bicycle, one of Polly's that he must have repaired. He and Sara exchange the muted hellos of people who almost but not quite know each other, and Sara thinks, Now, there's a really sexy-looking man. That Victor is something else.

"One absolutely horrible thing, of course," says Freddy quite loudly to Edward, as in adjoining rooms they dress to go to Celeste's for dinner, "one awful thing that must affect everyone is that every god-dam cold makes you think you have it. Have AIDS."

Curiously, perhaps, this is the first explicit mention between them of the possibility of AIDS for themselves. And the implications, none of which he has not already considered, are, to Edward, staggering. He is barely able to ask, with what he believes to be a suitable lack of concern, "You're getting a cold?"

"Yes—no, I don't know. I think so. I feel terrible. Probably I'm just tired."

Edward smiles as Freddy, fully and perfectly dressed, appears. Edward says, "You don't look tired, but then you never do. Ah, youth."

Freddy in fact has never been more beautiful, in Edward's view. Once a pretty boy ("that pretty boy of Edward's"), he is now a beautiful, thoughtful, intelligent, somewhat saddened man. With his dark cat sleekness, his wry mouth and delicately pointed chin, Freddy looks simply extraordinary, Edward thinks. Even in the most conventional clothes, as tonight: black blazer, pale yellow shirt, black knit tie. "I like that blazer on you" is what Edward says.

"Yes, but do you think it's really me?" Camping it up, Freddy laughs.

"I guess. Or at least one of you." And Edward too laughs.

"Well, maybe it'll cheer Celeste up just a little. She likes having a nice clean blazer around. Old Charles was famous for blazers, wasn't he."

"True enough." Edward hesitates. "But tell me about your cold. You really have one? You took lots of C?"

"Darling Edward, don't try to infect me with your New England hypochondria. We spics are tougher than you are." He pauses. "Unless of course I do have AIDS." But then he giggles, a fake high sound. "I can't, though—it doesn't start with a cold. Edward darling, is it really true that you actually sold a house today?"

"Well, yes, actually I did. In Cupertino," Edward tells him—having entirely forgotten about this sale. "I did it in spite of myself," he rattles on. "They loved it, despite all the drawbacks I took such pains to point out. They would not take no for an answer, and they gave me an offer I really couldn't refuse."

20 Mourning must indeed take a great many different forms, has been one of Dudley's most recent conclusions; unfortunately what has emerged as her own strongest, most consistent feeling toward Sam, Sam dead, is a passionate, towering rage. She hates him now, most of the time. She wishes they had never met.

The first cause of this rage is of course the simple fact that he died, leaving her one more time. If he had not been such a drunk, and then stayed so fat, he would not have died so young—well, these days sixty-four is young.

A more legitimate source of anger, though, is the fact that he had made no recent will. Like so many people, Sam always meant to, never quite got around to it. As a result, although the house, all paid for, becomes entirely hers, the income from Sam's stock, the good IBM, bought on a whim during Sam's palmiest days, the high-riding early fifties—all that reverts to his rich, yuppie-lawyer daughters, theirs by an old (fifties) will. Not a lot of money, but enough to make a considerable difference in Dudley's life—the difference in fact between enough money to live on very pleasantly, and not quite enough. If Dudley would choose to contest this obviously unfair lapse, she would almost undoubtedly win, so her own lawyer informs her. But she does not so choose: other considerations aside, the idea of going to court against *four* lawyers is more than a little intimidating.

It is necessary, then, to change her life. Not entirely, but quite a lot: to spend about half what she did before Sam died, which is a little tricky since most of her fixed expenses will remain the same, unless they go up, which is highly probable, these days. Dudley will not buy any clothes—easy enough, she certainly needs none. Will not take small trips to San Francisco, and God knows not larger ones to New York, or Boston. She will eat more beans, less meat, or maybe no meat at all; in a theoretic way she has always believed in being a vegetarian. Which was out of the question with Sam, a meat-and-potatoes man.

The point is, she will waste absolutely nothing, Dudley decides, and she will try very, very hard not to waste more of her energy in rage at Sam. Poor Sam, he couldn't help dying, he surely did not want to. (Or, on the other hand, did he?) She knows that her rage is wasteful.

She knows too that what she is going into is hardly poverty; she is not going out on the streets—but she has to tell herself just that, from time to time.

However, she is indeed very angry, and given her own private irrevocable principles, she can say almost nothing of what she feels to anyone, which naturally makes her feel worse. She can certainly not tell Edward, perhaps least of all Edward, as New England in principles as she, albeit her oldest, possibly closest friend. Nor to Celeste, nor Polly (and Dudley is interested to note that Polly of them all seems the strongest possibility for such confidences).

At night, most nights, she sits alone in the creaking wooden ark that is her house. She sips her diet Coke, she watches (sometimes) educational TV, she tries to read. She remembers every bad time with Sam that ever happened. Contrary to the received view, which holds that after people die you remember only the good, Dudley remembers only the bad, the worst.

She has, then, these terrible nighttime lonely reveries, and during the day, or at social occasions with friends, she has to speak mournfully, even sanctimoniously, of Sam.

And in the privacy of her mind she wonders: Did Celeste ever rage at Charles? Was she ever angry at Charles after he died? Certainly she never seemed so.

Brooks Burgess has called Dudley several times in the past few months. They have had brief, rather stilted conversations, in which almost nothing is said beyond the politest, most vacant inquiries as to each other's health. Hanging up, Dudley always wonders why he called. But she also observes in herself a sort of pained affection for that deep but tentative, almost disembodied voice on the telephone. He would like to see her but he doesn't quite dare ask, has been one of her conclusions. And she acknowledges that she would miss his calls at least a little if he stopped.

One night, though, he calls somewhat later than usual, and he seems more in a mood for conversation—as Dudley fleetingly thinks, Oh dear, does he drink too?

He even asks, conversationally, "It takes some getting used to, this living alone, don't you think?"

"Indeed. But I think I may get to like it." Actually Dudley has not thought just this before; she is simply cheered by the fact of this conversation.

He laughs very briefly. "I suppose we may. And then we'll feel really guilty, right?"

This unlikely (Dudley believes) remark from Brooks has the effect of making her like him more, and she simply says, "I'd love to see you sometime, if you're ever around."

"Well—" It turns out that one of the reasons he called was that Brooks has to make a trip to Santa Cruz, he has a daughter there. And could she possibly—is there somewhere they could meet for lunch?

Dudley, one of those fated to promptness (a considerable problem with Sam, whose habits were very Southern, in that way: always late)—Dudley arrives at the appointed hour on the chosen day for their lunch. And then proceeds to wonder if she somehow got both wrong, if she wrote down twelve-thirty instead of one, or the wrong day in July, Thursday when he clearly said Tuesday.

David has seated her at the nicest window table in the diner (her choice for lunch). She sits facing the billowing green hills, with their lacing of live oaks at intervals. A peaceful sky.

David has asked Dudley if she would like some Perrier, or anything, and she has so far refused (at the same time wondering: What is it that is so very irritating about David's friendliness?).

Sitting there, trying to concentrate on filling herself with the peaceful beauty of this view, it seems to Dudley that this is crazy, what she is doing is nuts: she is waiting for someone who is driving down from Marin, all that way, and expecting him to be anywhere near on time. Anything, anything at all could happen to delay or to prevent the trip entirely.

A yuppie-looking couple (the blonde, fashionably casual young woman a reminder to Dudley of Sam's oldest, least-liked daughter) with four young children have taken the table across the room from Dudley. The children are restless and noisy, and totally indulged by their tired, ineffectual parents, a few admonitions do nothing to quiet anyone. Watching them irritably, Dudley feels that their noise, their very commotion, is somehow preventing the arrival of Brooks.

Crazy. Truly nuts.

But just then out in the parking area she sees a car pull in that must be his, and it is, and there he is: closing his door, rushing into the restaurant. Small, dapper, anxious-looking Brooks, now hurrying toward her (will they kiss?—shake hands?) smiling and saying, "Oh, you're here! How great, I was so afraid I'd got it wrong. The wrong day, and now I'm so late—"

"Oh, not really."

Without having touched her at all in greeting, Brooks sits down across from Dudley and they both laugh, out of sheer pleasure, and some mutual shyness. And they begin to talk about the weather.

It is almost always nice in the summer up in Ross, where he lives, Brooks tells Dudley, and Dudley tells him about what he must already be aware of, the usual prevalence of coastal fog down here. The un-usualness of today, with all this sunshine. They do not, however, allow themselves to make anything of this; they do not attach signif-icance to the golden weather—no assumptions of good fortune on their own parts.

Dudley, though, does not find herself disappointed by this silly exchange. They need time; she knows that they are playing for time. Neither of them, neither constitutionally nor at this particular point in their lives, could rush into anything, even assuming that there is anything to rush into. In the meantime Dudley is simply aware of liking him (or perhaps not simply at all).

Observing in herself this renewal of positive feeling toward Brooks (even his eyes look less close together today)—Brooks, whom at Celeste's last party she did not seem to like at all—Dudley thinks of an old formulation of her own, one worked out years back, which is, roughly speaking, that first impressions, first reactions (if not necessarily in any sense "correct"), are the ones to which she returns. Simply, she liked Brooks at first, and then did not, and now she does like him—again.

(But how about Sam, whom she much disliked on sight, she can still remember thinking him such a vain, handsome man, such a green-eyed charmer, with that deep-Southern softness to his voice. Oh, a terrible man, and half-drunk besides! All of which, though "correct," was quickly blurred by sheer lust, and later by "love," and then forgotten, almost, in the long complexity of their life together. However, now that Sam is dead and she has begun to think of him with such anger, could that anger be considered a return to first impressions? Well, it hardly matters, Dudley decides.)

David comes over to take their order, and possibly because he is busy, or conceivably because he has caught some less than friendly message from Dudley, he spares them his spiel of specials, and allows them both to order what they want: seafood salads and iced coffee.

Neither of them seems to know what to talk about next, though. Instead they exchange a flutter of small smiles as both begin to eat. And Dudley thinks, How adolescent we are! Teenagers on a date, but in our case we reverse the adolescent process: we began with all that wild necking, and now we're tongue-tied. And she thinks, Well, obviously it's up to me; and she braces herself for social effort.

"How do you feel about living alone these days?" she asks him. "Are you getting to like it, do you think?"

To which she gains an unusual response. "Well, I seem to have a problem that I didn't know about," Brooks tells her after just the slightest pause, after deeply furrowing his brow. "It's just, just that I really don't like men very much. I mean, I don't much like talking to them or really being with men. Doing things with other men." He looks away, momentarily (visibly) much embarrassed.

Gently Dudley laughs. "You mean you'd rather go out to lunch or have dinner with a woman."

Eagerly, "Exactly! Women are just, oh, more fun to be with. For me." But then he says, "I guess this probably makes me some kind of a, uh, queer."

Somewhat less gently Dudley laughs at him. "Well, hardly. Not liking men is not exactly a sign of that. Or I don't think it is."

At which he too laughs. "Well, I guess really not. But you see what I mean. In my situation, my new situation, it is sort of a problem. People expect—"

"They think you'll play golf with the boys, or watch sports on TV. With other men."

"Well, yes, they do seem to expect that. But the thing is, I really like just being around women. They're easier to talk to, for me. Better listeners."

What he means is, in part, that he misses his wife, Dudley understands. He misses being married, having her around. And she herself—Dudley is of course finding him more and more sympathetic. We could turn into really good friends, is what at least a part of her mind is thinking.

In another part, though, she wonders if they will ever go to bed together, and if so, just what would they do there? More teenage necking? And how could this ever come about?

Not, she imagines, in either of their houses; it would almost have to be somewhere else, some ghost-free motel. In San Francisco? Tahoe? Mendocino? And how, actually, would we ever get into bed, Dudley wonders. What would have to be first said, to establish what they were doing?

At the present moment, though, they have reached the coffee phase of their lunch, and everything between them is still quite inconclusive, if pleasantly so.

At the end of a longer than usual pause Brooks says, "I do wish I could take you along this afternoon. But maybe another time? I rather like Carmel, although I know you're not supposed to—everyone says how corny and touristy it is. How about you?"

Has he, then, been thinking along similar lines—making plans?

"Well, I do like Carmel, sort of," Dudley tells him. Actually she dislikes almost everything about that town, and possibly this was somehow revealed in her voice?

Unenthusiastically Brooks repeats, "Well, I've always liked it there a lot." (Perhaps he too really dislikes Carmel?)

They finish their coffee with no more reference to Carmel—nor certainly with the smallest reference to their own impassioned gropings and kissings at that long-ago party. Although those moments, that really incredible exchange, must have been on both their minds, lodged within some recess of memory.

They walk to their separate cars together—or, rather, to Dudley's old car, where Brooks helps her in, after the lightest, most brushing social kiss. However, "I'd like to call you very soon," he says rather anxiously. "If that's okay?"

"I'd love it," Dudley assures him. And then, taking everything into her own strong, responsible hands, she says, "Maybe sometime we could go on a tiny trip."

"Oh, yes, indeed! What an absolutely super idea. But I must confess that I too had thought— Well, *splendid*. I'll call you tonight."

"The sexual relation in my opinion is not a sufficient or perhaps one should say an appropriate cause for two people to live together. Is that not also your opinion?" Polly, in her somewhat stilted Spanish, her pure Castilian, has just made this remark to Victor as, on a Sunday morning, the last of this rare and glorious July, they lie naked and languorous across her bed.

"Indeed, it would seem to be not practical," says Victor as with one thick brown finger he traces a line down Polly's rib cage. "But what would be your solution, in an ideal situation?" he asks her.

"Oh, I don't know! I just know that the way things are now is ludicrous. People signing up for a lifetime of monogamy, not to mention all that housekeeping. All the terrible drain of dailiness. So destructive. So non-sexual."

"Not to mention the problem of children," Victor reminds her.

"Oh, I know. The kibbutz model seems the best I have heard about." She turns toward him, smiling, her pale eyes brilliant as she lightly kisses his nearest shoulder. "But shouldn't I make a picnic? Eat outside? This glorious weather can't last, you know that."

"Ah, you must allow me to produce for you my famous *tapas*." Victor grins, displaying admirable large strong white teeth. And he continues, still in their former vein, "And may I also say, my dear Polly, that it appears to me that in your own most private life you have succeeded in resolving most of the difficulties of which you speak."

"Oh, I suppose by now I have. But it took me so long to figure anything out. For all those years, I didn't really know what I was doing. I thought maybe women were supposed to get married and have children, and that I was probably wrong not to."

"You had no dialectic."

"Exactly. Just instincts, and whoever knows enough to trust their instincts much before middle life. Or long after."

"You are correct."

"In a way," Polly muses, "I have two friends, both older gay men, and they seem to have things worked out rather well. No sex any-more, all passion spent, as it were, but they're still extremely fond of each other. They rub along in what looks like an amiable way."

"How, I must ask you," Victor asks, "are you privy to such re-markably personal information?"

"Oh, the younger one talks to me all the time. He likes to tele-phone, he thinks it's fun to gossip in Spanish."

The almost pedantic formality with which Victor speaks to her in Spanish has been for Polly an interesting contrast to his very ver-nacular, most imperfect English. In Spanish he is another man. Or perhaps he simply becomes his essential self: a self-taught intellec-tual—a classic, if somewhat anachronistic anarchist. A Spaniard.

At first, with no explanations, he began to appear more and more often at Polly's door. She never asked why he could suddenly spend both Saturday nights and Sunday mornings with her, and why he would often return to her on Tuesday, say. All so unlike the rigidity of his former schedule, the Thursday nights. She was always very glad to see him—and glad too when it was time for him to go. She asked no questions; whatever was happening between Victor and his family, specifically his wife, was absolutely no business of hers, Polly felt—and was sure that he would feel the same: Victor, she thought, is a passionately private person.

But then one day very casually Victor remarked, "My wife seems very happy in Los Angeles."

"Oh?" was all that Polly permitted herself to ask.

"Yes, she has found work there, she is very happy. She has two sisters in Burbank. I am glad, I imagine that she will stay. And my mother is more happy to have the sole care of the children. Of course with my help."

And that was that, a household to which Polly does not give a great deal of thought, beyond a distant, mild benevolence.

They do, though, always talk a great deal to each other. In fact, Victor talks to Polly like a man famished for conversation, ideas. Polly understands that this possibility, with her, is one of the things that draws him. And she in turn talks to him; he is the only person in San Sebastian to whom she has recounted the true story of her time in Spain, those years of panic, occasional minor triumph. Her sense of the landscape of Spain.

So it should not have been too surprising, as it now quite violently is, when Victor says, "It has been coming to my mind that we two could make a trip to Spain. Could we not? It would not be too expensive. Is it not time?"

"Oh—" Polly, so jolted, finds it suddenly hard to breathe: closing her eyes for one instant, she sees a long straight white road lined with pine trees, round and full, and with poplars, their leaves a deep rich yellow, almost amber, glowing. On either side of this road there are broad stretching red-earthed plains.

"Well, why not?" she asks Victor.

21 Edward is later to remember the August of that year, during which he turns seventy, as one of the entirely worst times of his entire life, the achieving of that venerable age being almost the least of it, he believes.

For one thing, the weather, that year in northern California, is spectacularly bad, especially near the coast. A thick fog envelops most of the days and weeks of that endless month, invading the coastal hills, while out at sea most unseasonable winter storms gather force, arriving at last to attack the land ferociously: lashing gales, and furious sheets of rain, as heavy as glass, as dangerous, destructive. Fishing boats, three that month, are dashed against rocks, their occupants lost. Seaside houses are severely damaged, or wrecked. ("The damage is estimated at upwards of $3 million, in this week alone.")

However, far worse than old age and frightful weather for Edward is the slowly emerging, cruel, at last recognized fact that Freddy is moving back to Mexico in January, if not earlier. For good.

First, Freddy announces that he does not have AIDS. In the course of his summer cold, the month before, when he suggested that unthinkable possibility to Edward, he went at last (he was persuaded to go, by Edward) to be tested, and the test was negative.

Freddy then went into a sort of euphoric relief, during which Edward understood that Freddy had been considerably more worried than he said. But it was nothing serious, after all, just a bad cold— while Edward still was reeling from the bare mention of that possibility: Freddy, AIDS. But you might have had it, he barely restrained himself from saying. You admitted exposure, how could you? And how could you let me know? But Freddy had already begun to say that he felt like celebrating with a trip to Mexico.

And, just as Edward was considering the taking of that trip, it became slowly, gradually, painfully apparent that Freddy meant a trip alone. At what moment actually apparent? Later Edward could not remember. It was simply, he believes, what is called a "growing realization." Growing like a hideous weed, or a tumor, Edward has thought.

However, at first it was only a trip that Freddy had in mind, albeit a long one. He had a sabbatical coming up, which he could arrange to begin in January.

With a certain irony Edward has observed that never has Freddy sounded so Latin as during this infinitely prolonged statement of his intentions. Such a profusion of alternatives, such elaboration, such *politesse*.

"On the other hand, it is entirely possible that I might instead go to Italy," Edward overhears Freddy saying to Dudley one night before a supper *à trois* that Edward is preparing in the kitchen: sweet-and-sour salmon, a favorite of Freddy's. Grinding gingersnaps, the silly secret ingredient, Edward strains to listen.

"But I very much doubt that I will," he hears Freddy continue, above the now familiar sounds of rising wind, creaking boards, rattling panes. "After all, I am so very Mexican. At the significant age of fifty, I feel myself more and more so. A spic, it is myself."

Was that the moment at which Edward first consciously thought, or *knew*, that Freddy meant to go away for good? Quite possibly so. As quickly as he can, but repressing that eagerness, that appearance of haste, Edward re-enters the room, but in time to hear, instead of Freddy's plans, Dudley's: she is off to Carmel the following week, of all the very dull ideas, in Edward's view.

"Friends of mine will be there," Dudley says, with quite unnecessary vagueness (Edward's opinion).

"Well, you two are certainly full of travel plans" is what he hears himself saying—ridiculously.

Dudley and Freddy accord him only a momentary look and then seem to take up an earlier conversation, having to do with some fancied connection between of all people Sara and David. Celeste's idea.

"But I thought they didn't even like each other," Edward puts in.

This attempt to join their conversation earns from Dudley and Freddy, almost in unison, "Oh, you are behind."

They all laugh, but then Edward is unable not to say, "You must admit it's unlikely?"

Dudley answers him much more seriously than he would have chosen. "Not at all, when you consider that Sara's a very sexual young woman. And who else is around? This Alex of hers seems to keep his distance in New York."

What on earth can she mean by that, and how can she know? What do women talk about these days? Unpleasantly pondering all this, Edward next thinks (most unpleasant of all) that Dudley is just possibly speaking of herself. Can she be? Does she think of herself as a "very sexual woman"? Oh dear, *can* she?

"Celeste, though, is not exactly reliable these days," Dudley tells them. "She's so very preoccupied." And, in answer to the question on the faces of both Edward and Freddy, "I'm not at all sure with what."

Edward asks what seems to him the obvious question. "Do you think she's well?"

Dudley answers, "I'm not sure, really. The thing is, she wouldn't tell us if she weren't."

"Would she tell Sara?" asks Freddy. "Or Polly?"

Edward chooses this moment to say, "Since we're all gossiping in this way—" But then he wonders: Are we? Or is this a serious conversation? But he continues, frivolously or not. "I was walking past Polly's house last Sunday, and there she was very *tête-à-tête* with that nice bald Spanish mechanic. You know, the one who fixes things."

"Well, maybe he was fixing something. Things do break on Sundays," Freddy reminds Edward. Ridiculously. And his voice is just slightly hostile, Edward feels.

So that Edward retracts, although his impression of Polly and Victor was very clear: two people having an intimate picnic out in the sun. But, "Of course," he says to Freddy. "I was just making up stories."

If I behave wonderfully, make wonderful meals and manage to be both amusing and serious, always, and, at the same time, if everything I say is politically correct, in your new terms, will you stay with me and not move to Mexico? Will you not abandon me? Edward feels a sort of interior weeping as silently, secretly, he pleads with Freddy. And knows it to be hopeless.

In a pleased and interested way Dudley is saying, "I don't think such a connection for Polly is all that implausible, Freddy. I've always thought Polly was very sexy."

At this Edward and Freddy exchange a mild, ironic look that says: You seem to think all women are sexy. And at this intimate, familiar communication Edward's hopes rise again, as he thinks that maybe, after all—

However, he interrupts himself to get up and go back to his salmon. It is very dangerous to hope, is Edward's belief.

Nothing more is said that night about Mexico, or Freddy's travels. Conversation at dinner is focused on the weather, the strange winter storms of August. They also discuss Dudley's new thoughts about a possible job; she would like to teach, she thinks. Is getting in touch with Santa Clara, San Jose. They also speculate about Celeste: her health—she looks marvelous, but is she really okay? And whatever happened to Bill? (None of them has been told that Celeste heard from Bill.)

"She must be a little embarrassed, to say the least, all that school-girl behavior, and then the big announcement, even if she only whispered it," Dudley contributes.

"It all had to do with mourning for Charles, I think," Edward tells them as privately he wonders: If Freddy leaves, will I be crazed in that way? Will I go into permanent mourning?

"Oh, yes, oh absolutely. It was all about Charles," says Dudley.

A few days later, Freddy remarks, "It surely might be possible that I teach in American studies at the university."

He has sounded like a man talking to himself, but still Edward asks, "What university?"

"In Mexico City." Freddy does not add, "of course." But he might as well have.

And now Edward knows. He knows that by January, at the latest, Freddy will be gone for good. And that he, Edward, will have to get through the rest of his life by himself.

He finds it extremely hard, almost impossible, to concentrate on anything but this, this departure from his life by Freddy. And he finds himself prey to the most dreadful imaginings, and impulses.

For example, suppose that instead of the "clean bill of health," of which Freddy still boasts, in a silly, inflated way—suppose Freddy did have AIDS? Edward imagines Freddy horribly weakened, maybe with those ghastly lesions, Kaposi's sarcoma. And himself: dedicated, devoted, nursing Freddy here at home until the end. But dear God, does he really, possibly, even for one instant find that preferable? *God*, does he really want Freddy to die in that unspeakable way, rather than to leave?

No, the truth is that he does not—had he a choice.

He thinks at other times of the fact of their house, although paid for mostly by Edward (at the time that they bought it, Edward had some money; he made the down payment), but the house is in both their names. They are Joint Tenants. And so, if Freddy plans to leave for good, will this stop him, even for a while? Will he wait around while they try—while Edward tries to sell the house? (It would have to be sold; Edward does not believe he could live there alone, nor does he have enough money to buy Freddy out, as it were.) Will that stop Freddy, real estate?

Very likely it will not. About money, property and possessions in general Freddy is quite insouciant. He likes to walk off and leave things, to throw things away. He would most likely say, "Oh well, dear Edward, do sell it when you can. But do not trouble yourself overmuch. I am surely in no hurry."

No, neither illness nor the weight of ownership will stop Freddy or even cause him to delay, not now. And at times Edward would like to shout at him, "Well, then go! If you're leaving, don't hang around. Just seeing you every day is a torment to me now. You constantly remind me of your absence."

Celeste, who just now wants very much to see Sara, waits disconsolately for her, hearing wind and rain, aware of cold, in her supposedly weatherproof boudoir. These concrete discomforts are so minor, though, as to be almost unnoticed, so preoccupied is Celeste with the larger issues that confront her: her secret illness (daily, increasingly, she knows what it is, what it must—can only be), and an extremely upsetting talk with her lawyer, who has just told her (in his own words) that she had really better cool it, spending-wise. Or that is what it comes down to, finally. He talked in an elaborate (to Celeste, almost incomprehensible) way about interest rates, the gross national product, treasury bills, gold, futures—as Celeste understood the simple fact that she now has less money than she used to. Less than she thought she did.

For herself she does not really, honestly mind. She is not so silly as to imagine that she is poor, and, for her, money seems an abstraction, really. She would like to divest herself of everything, she sometimes thinks. She thought this just after Charles died; she would like to strip her life down to one room somewhere, a few dollars a day for food, and a library card. She does not need all this encumbering property, this weight of a house and furnishings, clothes and jewelry, silver and china, crystal. But (and this is what she does mind) she had meant to give it away herself, to leave almost everything to Sara, who needs money; Sara will need money for whatever she plans to do next, Celeste is quite sure of that. Celeste had meant to leave it all to Sara, with a few bequests to friends, mainly Dudley.

And she wanted to leave a little money to the animal shelter. Charles's allergies to both cats and dogs made having pets impossible; before Charles Celeste had always had cats. And she thought of the animals that she and Charles might have had (rather like imagining unborn children); her notion of living in the country had always included a lot of animals, even a horse, some goats. She imagined four or five lovely fat brown Burmese cats, like Polly's, and a pair of Dalmatians. And strays, shy at first, nervous and hungry, whom she, Celeste, would feed and curry and pet back into sleekness, to pleasure in life. She even felt a sort of guilt toward these imagined creatures she has not taken in, not saved. (Not having children has never bothered her at all; as she sees it, the world is a decreasingly fit place for humans, and heaven knows there are already far too many of them—of us.)

But she has very little money, it now turns out, to leave either to Sara or to the unknown animals. And since she is dying (surely) it is too late now to rectify anything: too late to take in strays, or to be of much real help to Sara.

How did I ever get to be so old, Celeste wonders, helplessly regarding her dry pale lined face in the mirror as she waits there for Sara. *How?*

She is not even entirely sure what it is that she wants to talk to Sara about. She only feels an urgency to be clear, at last, with at least one person. With Sara, whom she has chosen to love.

She does want to talk to Sara; however, before she knows it Celeste has fallen asleep.

And so it is not until the next day that she has Sara alone—by which time she has decided not to mention money to Sara at all.

The next day at breakfast (yogurt and brown rice and tuna: Celeste's prescription for a healthy start to the day) she remarks to Sara, "I do sometimes wonder if I haven't been a little harsh, after all, in my judgment of Bill." She had not meant to say this (perhaps the healthful food induced such positive thoughts?).

Sara mutters unintelligibly.

And so Celeste continues, "I do think, my dear Sara, that it's best to try to accept people more or less as they are. Not trying to make them into other people."

"Actually I'm pretty sure I was right about Bill. In fact, I'm quite sure. He was in Berkeley and he used another name."

Celeste's worst laugh is a harsh, curt sound, almost a snort. She does this now, before saying, "I think Bill just didn't want to get married, and when he heard me saying that we were he ran off. Not exactly elegant behavior. However." She sniffs conclusively, obviously wishing to have the final word.

"I know I was right about him," Sara mutters.

Just outside the windows of their small breakfast patio, the dark green leaves of some newly potted plants now drip cold rivulets from the heavy, enveloping fog. However, high in the sky are thin pale yellow patches, faint clues that later on the fog will burn off, leaving in its wake a bright, possible new day. And this promise serves to lighten and brighten, a little, the tight dark mood into which Sara and Celeste have quite suddenly fallen.

"In fact, I think I'll go and walk right now," announces Sara.

Celeste's smile is infinitely tolerant, infinitely wise and knowing, as she says to Sara, "Well, very well, my darling. Off you go."

22 After many long phone conversations during which various trips were projected, discussed, with alternatives suggested (Carmel? Tahoe? Mendocino?), Brooks Burgess and Dudley have gone to Houston, Texas—"of all places," Dudley has just managed not to say. It made a certain sense, though: Brooks had business there. ("What's left of the business in those parts," he told Dudley; "you wouldn't believe what's happened to oil.") Also, he knew of a first-rate hotel. ("It's even quite beautiful, you'll like it.") And, as neither of them did say, they were most unlikely, in Houston, to run into anyone they knew.

Somewhat to Dudley's surprise, Brooks has turned out to be quite right about the hotel. Their room is beautiful, a large, irregularly shaped space, the far end of which is all glass and faces out into some woods, all cool and green, dark boughs, ferns—as though the room itself were suspended out there, hung from trees.

Inside, it is all very underplayed, discreet, pale "natural" fabrics, "understated" furniture. Pale brown sheets on the king-sized bed, on which Dudley now lies, trying to plan what to say next to Brooks, who will be done with some sort of meeting in an hour or so. Whom she is to meet for lunch in the bar, and to whom she must (obviously) say something.

"It doesn't matter," she would like to say, but that is a patent lie: sex does matter quite a lot, everyone knows that now. And so she amends or edits to "We don't have to let this matter." However, they do have to let it matter, of course they do: their failure at love (a quite mutual failure, in Dudley's view, although poor Brooks no doubt blames himself alone, as nice men of a certain generation will)—*their* failure will profoundly affect whatever relationship exists between the two of them, if it does not end it once and for all, for good, today.

Suppose she said something to the effect that "I like you anyway"? But no, that is an impossible sentence to say, considerably worse to hear. The point is, she hardly knows Brooks Burgess, and the naked, strenuous tussles undergone by their proximate but unjoined bodies have not served to increase their intimacy.

Dudley sighs as she considers how old age becomes more and more unfair to the old, instead of less so. As if things were not always bad enough, in terms of incapacities, weakening of most of one's faculties, not to mention certain aesthetic losses, now, in addition to all that, these days one must contend with a new mythology holding that most old people—most normal old people, that is—are still sexually quite all right; they are (they are supposed to be) capable of doing everything they did before, if (possibly) a little less lively and speedy about it all.

This is not fair.

What she and Brooks will actually do, Dudley in a very quick flash perceives, is pretend it never happened. And what she can most kindly and tactfully do is aid and abet that pretense. She is sure of this; in fact she sees no other course as remotely possible.

In the meantime she gets up and gets into her shower.

Or, she thinks, under the shower, she sees no other course for people of their age and generation and general "background." If they were twenty or thirty years younger, she thinks, in the course of a very long shower (noting too that her body is really okay for sixty-five: surely scrawny is better than fat? Even visible tendons are preferable to sags?), then perhaps some sort of discussion would be in order: openness, confrontation, whatever. *Perhaps.* Dudley is actually quite unable to imagine such a conversation, nor is she convinced of the efficacy of such talk. God knows it would never have worked with Sam, with his eternal Southern politeness, his acres of reserve, his puritan depths.

But isn't there, really, still much to be said for simple tact and politeness, even for the avoidance of certain painful issues?

Dudley wonders about all this, is not at all sure what she actually thinks. In the meantime, out of her shower, she creams her face with moisturizer, deodorizes her already odorless body, and clothes herself in immaculate silks. Adds perfume, and is ready for lunch with Brooks, who is technically not her lover. Not yet.

The bar, where Brooks has as yet not arrived, is also a pleasant, airy-looking room, deceptively cool. Sipping her Perrier, then, for no reason, or no reason that she can think of, Dudley is stricken with the most acute and painful longing for Sam. Ah, if only it were he, her old Sam, who would at any moment now walk through that wide, brass-fitted door, past the hostess (pout-mouthed, blonde) and over to her, to Dudley. His wife.

What she feels at this moment is the simplest, purest and most unbearable sense of loss: no more ambivalence, mixed memories, just loss. And she thinks of her joyless striving with Brooks, in bed, and experiences an awful wave of guilt for that most terrible act of treachery to Sam—poor dead, defenseless Sam.

Unhappily, for well over half an hour Dudley is quite alone with such thoughts—and how unlike Brooks to be so late, she also thinks. Is it possible that he has simply fled, hating failure and thus hating her by association? Leaving her there in Houston, of all unlikely places?

Since Dudley has not been outside, she is used by now to the air-conditioned cool; she even wears a light sweater draped over her silk-linen shirt, her extravagant (futile!) purchase for this purposeful trip. Other people, however, those just entering the bar, show marked effects of the heat outside. In their barest clothes, their naked shoulders or rolled-up shirt-sleeves, they enter shivering, but smiling: ah! delicious cool.

Several people, Dudley has noticed, have come in as though in shock, their faces seeming to register some disaster. Or has she imagined this? Recently, especially since Sam died, she has felt so often a sort of weight of sorrow, of generalized misfortune: Ethiopian ghosts, the hungry homeless everywhere. Bomb testing. Arms. Is it her own distracted imagination, then, that she now sees reflected in these faces from outside?

So absorbed in watching, wondering, Dudley for an instant does not register the fact of Brooks, who is approaching. Unsmiling, and also with a look of catastrophe. Who hurriedly kisses her cheek (a husbandly kiss, it occurs to Dudley). Who says, "Really ghastly news. An earthquake in Mexico City. So close, really. Some people around here felt it." And he goes on to tell her: hundreds killed, buried, lost. Buildings crumbled, toppled. Looting. Fires.

As if they too were victims (and, in a sense, ultimately they are, Dudley believes), they stare at each other, in genuine fear, near panic. Dudley and Brooks Burgess.

It is Brooks who says, "You know that feeling, that inner voice that says we'll be next?"

Dudley answers him, "Very well."

One of the things that Dudley is later to remember about that moment is her very conscious thought that now Freddy will leave Edward: in a few weeks, after the aftershocks, when the scope of the disaster is plainer, the needs of its victims clearer, Freddy will simply go down there. He will find for himself some extremely useful function; he will in effect lose himself in helping. From time to time he will write to Edward, perhaps to all of them. But neither Edward nor any of them will ever see him again.

And Dudley thinks, Ah, poor poor Edward, poor old dear. Maybe he and I should move in together, somehow? Try it out? And then, at that moment, she laughs a little at herself for such a visionary, such an entirely unrealistic program—at such a moment.

She is also to remember the day of the earthquake, with a twinge of very New England guilt, as the day on which she and Brooks first successfully made love. That afternoon, as though they had been doing it all their lives, they very gently caressed, their essential parts joined and quickened. They enjoyed.

In Houston, Texas.

Polly and Celeste, having met for coffee in the diner where irritating David once worked (David having suddenly disappeared), could not have presented a greater contrast in style: Celeste in her old red Chanel, Polly in something black from either Cost Plus or Berkeley (this is Celeste's assessment). Celeste's perfect silver-white waves. Polly's semi-baldness, wrapped in an Indian-looking red-black scarf.

Wryly they take note of each other. No need for either to comment, really, the opposition in costume being too familiar. However, Polly does say, "Well, at least we've both stuck to an anarchist color scheme."

At which Celeste smiles and allows, "Appropriately enough."

It was Polly, though, who telephoned Celeste and suggested this meeting ("I've heard so much about that damn place, how about meeting me there?"), which for Polly was unusual. Clearly she has something of great importance to divulge, which Celeste quite unaccountably dreads, does not want to hear. She has even thought of manufacturing some excuse to leave—she wanted to leave almost as soon as she got there.

And Polly does look rather severe. She has on her lecturing face, which Celeste with some reason has learned to fear.

However, what Polly almost immediately says is (so like her, no preamble): "One thing I wanted to tell you, Celeste, is that I'm planning a trip to Spain."

And oh, how like Polly to make a stern lecture out of such news, to make a pronouncement of what is so pleasant, such innocent fun! Celeste thinks all this even as she is saying to Polly, "But, darling Pol, that's really wonderful, you haven't been back there forever." Not since you and Charles were lovers, she does not say. But she has the sudden and quite enormous thought that Polly knows, Polly knows that she knows—and somehow over the years they have got past all that; it no longer matters much who did what to and with whom.

"Not since 1948" is Polly's very succinct summation. "Almost forty years." She smiles a little grimly, and then continues, "The point is, dear Celeste, it's not just me going. I mean, I'm going with a friend." A tiny pause. "A man I know."

Can Polly be blushing? Quite surely she is. She looks heated, and her pale eyes are paler than ever. They *shine*.

"But, Pol, how really lovely, and how cozy you are, going out and meeting someone and getting all involved without any of us having the slightest notion." As Celeste says all this, though, a tiny, very recent memory surfaces (what they say is true; the most recent past is really the first to go): someone seeing Polly with someone, someone "inappropriate," but that memory refuses to come into focus. "You must let me have you both to dinner, a sort of little pre-farewell party for you both."

Polly begins then to laugh, her old big full helpless laugh that Celeste always wishes were happening somewhere else. "You already know him," Polly tells Celeste. "It's Victor Lozano, the man at the garage."

"Oh."

"He's Spanish," Polly adds, quite unnecessarily.

For of course Celeste knows who Victor is, everyone knows Victor, and knows him to be Spanish. As well as bald and fat and poor and married and a Catholic, probably. For an instant Celeste wonders if this could be some sort of joke of Polly's, what young people call "putting you on." If Polly simply said that she was going to Spain with Victor (of course implying considerably more, much more, that must have already taken place between them)—if Polly said that just to see what she, Celeste, would say? But she next decides that this is not so: it is simply not Polly's sort of joke.

And so it must be true. Polly and Victor. A fact. A couple.

Well. Celeste with scarcely a thought decides not to give Polly the joy of any show of shock, on her part. "I think your trip should be wonderful," says Celeste. "Divine. Going with someone who can speak the language."

In a knowing way Polly chuckles, but she only says, "I think it will be, as you say, divine. I'm very much looking forward." And then, in an entirely different voice, she says, "Now, Celeste, about your symptoms. This bleeding you've mentioned."

"Oh, that was nothing. And anyway it's almost stopped," Celeste gets out, in a rush.

"Almost?" Polly pushes.

"Well, yes. Really not at all now. And, Polly, honestly, what a thing for us to talk about."

It was you who asked me about it in the first place: Polly's pale, severe eyes say this to Celeste, no need for the spoken words. What Polly does say is "I think you're acting very foolishly. There's a doctor I want you to go to. He's young, and it'd be less embarrassing for you with someone new. Is that right?"

"Well—" Of course this is quite true: one of Celeste's large dreads has been the description of such unpleasant (disgusting!) symptoms to dear old Dr. McGillvaray, whom she has known forever, ever since she and Charles first came to California.

"He's just over in Santa Cruz. Very smart, young but not too young. John Bascomb. Here, I wrote it down for you. Please, Celeste, just go and talk to him."

To her own considerable surprise Celeste finds this idea appealing. If this doctor is young, even she, hopelessly old and old-fashioned Celeste, can talk to him "openly": isn't openness a specialty of the young, along with "sharing"? Well, she will openly share her conviction that she has cancer; she will explain that she is going to die, and he can tell her certain facts that she needs to know—how much time she has, what the last few months of her life are liable to be like. How soon, that is, she should think about taking some pills. Though of course she will not tell any doctor about that plan. "Very well, Polly, I'll go see him." Celeste laughs, to herself an unpleasantly artificial sound. "Will that make you happy?"

"Moderately." Polly smiles.

Partly to change the subject, Celeste now says, "So odd about that young man who used to work here. Did you meet him at my party? Called David. Sara took the most violent dislike to him, really on sight. Anyway, he seems to be gone. So odd."

"Ah." Polly smiles again. "It's wonderful not to be young, don't you think so, really, Celeste?"

"Well," Celeste concedes. "On some days I do."

"Do you want more coffee? There's one more thing I really want to ask you."

Whatever it is, Celeste is sure that she does not care to hear the question, nor assuredly to answer it. But she says, "Oh, yes, I'd love more—the coffee's so good here, don't you think?" she flutters.

Polly asks sternly, "Celeste, what's this about Bill's being in South America."

Oh. "Well, that's where he is, I'm pretty sure. I'm not sure doing what exactly. He's sounding rather mysterious about it all. The way Charles used to, sometimes."

"Interesting" is Polly's comment. But then, as Celeste might have known she would, she probes further, pushing in. "What I really want to know is how you feel about him these days. What was all that about, anyway? Do you know?"

"Oh, Polly, dear Polly. If I knew I'd tell you, really. I would." And Celeste sighs, almost painfully.

"You could try." Gentle but very firm, implacable Polly.

"Well." She might as well try to tell Polly, Celeste decides. There has never been the slightest point in any pretense, with her. "Well," she begins, "I simply know that it had more to do with Charles than with Bill. You know, beginning with that really uncanny resemblance."

"Yes," Polly agrees. "That was crazy. The first night I met Bill at your house—well, it was unfair. A low blow."

"Very unfair to me." Celeste laughs briefly. "I think I sort of fell in love with Bill, or got a crush on him, whatever you want to call it, but it was really all about missing Charles. Just a crazy way of expressing how much I missed him. I'm not making sense, though, am I?"

"Sure you are, but there's something missing, I think."

Feeling prodded, Celeste still makes an effort. "I think that all my life I've been falling in love with men as a kind of substitute for something else. Not that I wasn't doing other things too. But. Do you see what I mean, at all?" Celeste is highly aware of having never in her life spoken in this way, or nearly; she is not at all sure that she likes it.

"I do see," Polly tells her, Polly with her far too intelligent eyes now concentrated on Celeste. She seems then to muse for a moment, before (so unnecessarily! Celeste later thinks) she adds, "And in a way Bill was supposed to make up for everything lacking with Charles, don't you think? A second chance?"

"Polly, that is an absolutely meaningless remark. My life with Charles was absolutely perfect, as you of all people should know. Really, Polly, you forget yourself."

Very strangely (but then Polly is very strange, *very*), Polly chooses to laugh at this. "Come off it, Celeste. Don't talk like that to me. You know we're friends for life. I can say whatever I want to, and I usually do. You know that."

That much at least is true, and so Celeste too forces a laugh, and they change the subject. Polly begins to talk about her trip.

23   The room that Sara occupies in Celeste's big sprawling house faces directly south, but east and west are also included in that broad sweep: hills, a few houses, the enormous sky, and sometimes, rarely, the sea. Waking early, on some of the perfectly clear days of October, California's Indian summer, what Sara sees before the actual sun is, here and there, a small burnished blaze, as of copper: sunlight reflected in distant scattered windows. And the air at that time is a deep pure blue, washed clean, no clouds—only an occasional jetliner that noses slowly upward, crossing the sky and heading south for Mexico, or South America.

At those times, on those rarely beautiful mornings, Sara experiences such a deep, fulfilling sense of peace as to make her feel a rush of guilt, while from her bed she watches the lovely progress of the day, for the first time in her life not having to get up.

Sara believes that this is not what she is supposed to be doing— Sara, who has never been even nearly convinced that she is meant to be happy, in her life. But this room and this view of the dawn, the white flashing wings of sea gulls, all conspire to make her feel—well, *happy*, a rare contentment and tranquil joy. Which makes her at the same time very restive.

If it were not for Celeste, about whom she is seriously worried, she would leave; that is Sara's thought, or one of them. The imperative that bids her to take care of Celeste is strongest, though. And so odd, Sara thinks: Celeste is someone whom she could quite reasonably dislike. Celeste is imperious, imperialistic (probably), materialistic (certainly that, all those clothes, that jewelry), vain—a foolish romantic. Snobbish. A poor judge of men—very poor. A political illiterate.

Why then, Sara asks herself, have I appointed myself her keeper? If she is mortally ill, why do I have to be the one to stick around and take care of her? Why not Dudley, or Polly? Or Edward? She is not exactly lacking in friends. Why me?

Sara's belief that Celeste is ill (is almost dying) comes from hints, Celeste's own small spoken words, rather than from any amateur medical observation on Sara's part. Celeste, except for dry skin and a certain pallor that seems to be chronic (and is probably at least in part cosmetic), looks splendid: she stands erect; she moves, as always, with exceptional grace, with a sometimes alarming alacrity. She is hard to keep up with, for anyone.

And Celeste is even quite unsympathetic toward her more arthritic friends—namely, Dudley and Edward. Arthritis, according to Celeste, is entirely a matter of diet: she herself conquered what she felt to be incipient arthritis in herself with a regime of fresh fish and brown rice, canned tuna, and papaya (so rich in enzymes). Almost no red meat or dairy products. (There is also her curious fondness for peanut butter, to Sara an anomalous taste: elegant Celeste, eating peanut butter? Nevertheless, that is what she does, largely in her futile effort to gain a little weight—a problem for which she expects and receives no sympathy whatsoever.) She has no signs of bodily stiffness, anywhere. No visible slowing down of anything.

She does, though, make certain remarks that Sara has found alarming. For example: "Sara darling, since you don't really care for jewelry, do you? I'm just leaving it all to Dudley, you won't mind?" Or, "I suppose the best thing will be for you and Dudley to sell this house. It's so big and impractical. So lucky that you two have become such friends."

To Sara's strong remonstrances "*Please*, Celeste, I don't want your jewelry or your house. Besides you look wonderful, you could easily outlive me," Celeste smiles wanly, and with no conviction agrees. "I suppose I could. You don't take much care of yourself."

It becomes clear to Sara, then, that Celeste for whatever reasons has decided that she will die. And soon, or fairly soon.

The only reason for her dying that makes any sense to Sara, in terms of Celeste's true character, as Sara perceives it, would be Celeste's suspicion (perhaps even her certainty) of mortal illness. The unspeakable: cancer.

And sometimes what Sara thinks is, I simply cannot go through all that again. For it was Sara, of course, on whom almost the total care of her mother, Emma, fell, during those last nightmare months of Emma's illness. Sara who witnessed actively all her mother's pain and medical indignities. (Celeste's visits of mercy were helpful but very brief.) I can't do all that, can't *see* all that again, thinks Sara, even as she excoriates herself for those thoughts.

For of course she will. She knows perfectly well that she is committed to seeing Celeste through whatever happens.

Besides, at this point in her life, Sara further thinks, what more worthy project does she have? Just what is she doing of any remote importance to anyone?

Sometimes, during Emma's illness, Sara even thought, and now she cruelly remembers thinking: Well, please get on with it, please just die. And at other times, and with equal strength, she silently begged her mother not to die. Not to leave her.

Much of which she feels all over again, transferred to Celeste.

On one especially blessed-seeming morning, as Sara lies half-dreaming in her bed, she is jolted by the sound of the telephone from the living room. And as she waits for Celeste to answer, as the phone continues to ring, she recalls a part of her dream. Which was of Alex, which was vividly sexual.

Celeste does not answer, and so Sara gets up and barefoot in her flannel gown she runs for the phone, thinking that of course it will stop before she gets there, thinking too: What's wrong with Celeste, can't she hear, can she have died?

But the phone does not stop until she picks it up and answers, a breathless "Hello."

Alex (later Sara is to think, Well, of course it was Alex). "You never call early in the morning" is her somewhat accusatory greeting.

"It isn't early. But listen, I do have some news. About our Bill. Mr. Priest."

The windows of the living room face west, exposed to sunsets rather than to dawns, and thus what Sara now sees is reflected sunlight on neighboring windowpanes, on pale rocks just beginning to shine, and glitter on the sea. Perhaps it also strikes the broad light-colored horns of Dudley's tribe of goats, Sara thinks, and she wonders where they are at just this moment.

She is watching, then, the beautiful changes in the light; she is thinking rather idly of the goats—as Alex is telling her about Bill Priest, who is indeed in Nicaragua—Managua. Almost impossible to imagine.

"He's in something called ISA. Intelligence Support Activity. Quite an ominous title when you think about it," Alex tells her.

"I won't ask how you managed to find this out."

"Well, don't." Alex goes on, "The ISA is bad news. They don't just collect intelligence, they come up with arms and supplies for their chosen causes. Guess which. They've done a lot of damage in El Salvador, and they're keeping right on at it."

"If they're so high-level I'm surprised they took on our Priest."

"He's a lot more popular than he was at one time."

It is as though, at that moment, both the dawn and the sea and the invisible goats disappear from Sara's mind, and she is back in her more customary inner landscape: bloody deaths in teeming, fetid jungles; small straw villages bombed and burning; children maimed and screaming, screaming. Men and women screaming, weeping, moaning. Her own total helplessness, rage. "Jesus Christ," is what she says, thinking less of Bill Priest, an unimportant person, really, than of the others, the big-money people in New York and Washington. The power brokers, manipulators, with their cold, cold blood, their discreet paunches, withered genitals.

This is what Sara has seen and felt for what now seems forever, as though there had been no lapse, no gap between Vietnam and Nicaragua.

"You aren't listening," Alex tells her. "Still asleep?"

"No. Yes."

Alex continues, going on about the odd career of Bill Jones Priest: fag-bashing in Hollywood, in the days when this was an approved activity. (Somehow this is not much of a surprise.) The FBI in Berkeley, the IRS in San Francisco. CIA. ISA. Nicaragua.

Sara listens, her mind or part of her mind recording all that he says—but actually she is considering the dull, implacable familiarity of it all, the terrible predictability of contemporary evil. It is as though all the people you most dislike turn out to be related to each other, is one way to think of it.

Alex is saying, "You know, I'd really like to see you."

"Oh, Alex, me too. But I'm almost scared to. I don't want to risk— oh, you know." She almost says, We're getting along so well the way we are.

"Sure, I know. Or I guess I do."

As Sara hangs up, she is thinking that, really, neither of them knows anything at all about the other. "Knows" in the sense of being able to predict the behavior of. But does anyone, in that sense, ever know another person? Sara has no idea.

Sara goes back to her dream.

A long time ago when Alex and Sara made love, acid-high or stoned on grass or even straight, their two bodies seemed sometimes to become submarine aquatic plants, all wet and wavering together. No more private shapes, or parts. Even what Sara had experienced as his extreme blond beauty, as opposed to her own heavy darkness— all that was lost in their merging.

She remembers this, she thinks of it now, recalling the sensations, the very aura of sex with Alex, far more vividly than people are supposed to be able to remember sex.

And she knows that one of the reasons she puts him off is her fear that they will fail—will have tried, as of course they must, for repetition, and not made it. That now they can only come up with an ordinary sexual exchange.

And Sara lacerates herself for this fear of sexual failure. What a coward she is, after all!

Or, she also thinks, I am really worse than Celeste could possibly be. Talk about a stupid, a totally retro-romantic.

* * *

Missing Freddy, Edward is genuinely frightened by the intensity of his feelings: such a heavy, pressing vacancy within himself, such real derangement. He misses Freddy so badly, is so wholly caught up in Freddy's absence, his lack, that the smallest decisions for himself have become impossible: which tie to put on in the morning, whether to have a piece of fish or a chop for dinner. Whether to go upstairs and lie down or to read the paper in the living room.

The problem is, he really doesn't want to do anything, for nothing that he does will bring about Freddy's return.

Remembering Freddy is as constant in his life as breathing is. Thirty years of Freddy's face, his mouth, his walk. His most intimate smells. All that is as close to Edward as his own breath, as much a part of him.

Plus which, Edward is running out of money. He has done nothing with real estate (could not bring himself even to think of it) for many months, and in ways that he cannot focus on his investments have all gone bad. When he is able to think at all in that direction, Edward believes that a crash is coming, that the economic world as rich people like himself have known it is coming to an end. And he simply could not care less.

In a year or so he will probably have to sell his house, Edward thinks, and then live God knows where. Be a street person, like those he has seen all over San Francisco, these days.

And who cares? Who gives a flying fig or a doughnut hole what happens to a silly old queer, who is almost dead, who is felled by the loss of his love?

Victor says, "But, my dear, my most esteemed Polly, quite naturally everyone knew."

"But, Victor—oh, my God! How incredibly embarrassing! What a total fool I feel."

"You should not feel a fool. They all respected you deeply, and they felt most grateful for all the good that you did. So much money!

To find it carefully on one's doorstep. Your reasons for doing it as you did are your own, no single person of our town would presume to question your right to do as you did."

"Oh—"

"And everyone—most especially myself, I should tell you—appreciated the dangers in which you placed yourself on those nights."

"Oh, Victor, dear God!"

"However, my dearest, it is no longer necessary that you carry out your wishes in a fashion quite so extreme. And so dangerous to yourself. I can most easily leave an envelope or a package beneath any door or upon any steps that you should specify to me. And in such a way that what I have done will be known to no one."

"Victor, I have never in my life felt such an ass."

At this Victor looks so shocked that Polly wonders if her Spanish has been at fault. He only says, however, "We must not think of it in this way. There is no reason for shame."

Polly sighs against his naked chest. "Maybe we could just turn out the light."

"If you wish. I had wanted though to speak further of our trip. I think that from Barcelona we go by train to Zaragoza, do you agree?"

24 "I want to be sure that you understand absolutely everything," the young doctor tells Celeste, who is not listening, really, to a word he says. Not listening to the words themselves, that is, but quite clearly hearing a voice and seeing a person: Dr. John Bascomb. A small wiry man with the nervous look of a tennis player. Very crinkled (well, kinky) short red hair, darting light blue eyes. So much like Celeste's very early husband, Bix Finnerty, who must be dead by now; he could be Bix's son, and of course is not.

But it is odd, this recurrence of physical types in one's life, Celeste has thought. First Charles comes back as Bill, and now here is Bix again, or almost, as Dr. Bascomb. Who at least is trying to be considerably nicer than Bix was.

"It's not exactly a complicated procedure, Celeste," this doctor continues. "But it could make you a little uncomfortable. That's why we give you something intravenously."

"What?" asks Celeste, who in her hospital gown, back opening, is perched on the edge of the examining table. Under these conditions, and since he seems to insist on using her first name, and especially in the light of all the extremely ugly things she has told him—Celeste now sees no point in verbal formalities. "What, intravenously?" she asks.

"Ah, Valium, probably. It won't put you out, I need you to be awake so that you can follow certain directions. And any discomfort you'll share with me right away."

"I'd be delighted."

This small joke does not especially amuse either one of them;

uneasily, distrustfully they regard each other. Doctor and patient. John Bascomb and Celeste.

To regain control, perhaps, he goes on talking. "As I've tried to explain, I find nothing intrinsically alarming in your symptoms. Nine times out of ten, just an innocent polyp. Of course our President was not so lucky, but then he's done remarkably well ever since. *Remarkably.*"

"To think that I would turn out to have something in common with our President." Celeste widens her eyes in a way that would have signaled heavy irony to any of her friends, had any friend been present.

"Well, my hunch is that you don't. My educated guess is that—well, we'll just see. Of course we plan to do a biopsy on whatever we find up there—"

At his "up there" Celeste involuntarily shudders, controlling the small spasm as best she can—and quite stops listening.

She has become extremely calm, she observes of herself. The calm of death, or almost. Her true idea, though, is that this examination, which the doctor continues to describe in such detail (he must at some point have been instructed to "share" with patients, to let them in on things, not to be just an inhuman doctor), including the horrifying preparations that Celeste must begin (if she is to make them at all) tomorrow—all this will very likely kill her off right away. And this idea has served to banish her ancient fears of malignancy: it won't matter at all (to her) what it was; she will be safely dead.

". . . anything you'd like to ask?" Poor anxious Dr. Bascomb, who is visibly not enjoying this either, who never chose this role of explainer, teacher.

"Do you lose many patients in this process?"

"*Lose?*" He looks stricken. "Oh, no, never lost one yet." He has quickly recovered. "Not doing a colonoscopy. Angiograms, now, they can be a little dangerous."

"I suppose there's always a first time," Celeste tells him, unhelpfully.

In a way she was right, Celeste thinks: she is much too old and too fragile, really, to have withstood such treatment—nevertheless, withstand it she did, and the bed in which she lies is her own. Her own bed, own room, own beautiful and familiar home.

Though her entrails—everything inside her was mauled and pummeled; she feels battered and bruised. The nice bowl of consommé that Sara brought her cools on her nightstand—impossible even to sip.

However: there she is, alive. And SHE DOES NOT HAVE CANCER. There was indeed a small polyp, the source of bleeding—but BENIGN, removed then and there, biopsied. OKAY.

"Well, lady, you seem to be okay" is what Dr. Bascomb said, in the course of things looking less and less like Bix. "Very good you came in when you did, though. Those little devils can change, we never know just when. Or God knows why."

I could live forever now, is what Celeste is thinking, if only I were not so tired. However, perhaps, say, ten years more? She smiles to herself. I am fated to live, Celeste thinks.

Outside it is raining and terrible, dark November weather. Heavy unrelenting rain that could last all winter, from the sound of it. How lucky she is! Celeste almost prays as she says this to herself. How warm and safe her room and, seemingly, her life.

Sara must be off somewhere eating her own dinner, reading, waiting for Celeste to go to sleep—so that she can make one of her interminable phone calls, Celeste imagines.

Thinking for a moment then of Sara, Celeste is informed by a sudden, very sure instinct that very soon Sara will move on. Celeste has no idea where, or with whom, if with anyone. She is only certain that whatever Sara has been waiting around for, which was very possibly Celeste herself, her "health"—since all that is resolved, is all right, now Sara will go.

And how I will rattle around then, thinks Celeste, but entirely without self-pity. It could be fun! She does, though, experience a fairly large pang of guilt: the very idea of having such a very big house, all to one's self, in these times.

She does not yet think about possibly missing Sara.

She is really thinking, and it is less thought than feeling, sensing, exploring—she is "dealing with" the huge and quite overwhelming

fact of no cancer. Only a polyp, innocently bleeding and now removed. No more blood.

She is not going to die for a while.

"*His* polyp was malignant, though, Ronnie-babe's," Alex reminds
Sara, on the phone, somewhat later that night. "Remember, last summer? But of course the surgery involved is pretty much risk free. He's
going to be perfectly all right. No problem, as we keep on saying."

"He probably will be all right, the old bastard," Sara mutters.

So many of these late-night conversations, Sara thinks: how many
must we have had, by now? And just what was it that she managed
to set in motion when in that quite odd way she telephoned to Alex
when she was in New York, and saw him, though inconclusively,
there?

For one thing, there is something very sexy about their talking in
this way, both alone, and in widely separated places. Each imagining
the other. And, lacking vision, they both play tricks with their voices,
Sara has noticed. They exaggerate the male-female difference, both
of them do this: his voice deepening, hers rising. And both their
voices full of breath, depth, range. Voices, their only (at the moment)
instruments of sex.

"Well, as I've told you, I have been really worried about Celeste,"
Sara tells him. "She thought she was going to die, I know that. And
she has such a *will*, I thought she'd decided to die, and that she
would."

A pause. Silence, breath withheld, and then Alex says, "Well, now
you can leave anytime you want to."

This is jolting—going so much farther ahead of anything that Sara
has so far thought. Tight-voiced, she asks him, "You've got something in mind?"

"Yes." A small pause. "I think you should come with me to
Managua. To Nicaragua."

Sara says the first silly thing that occurs to her. "You mean, go
chasing after Bill?"

"No. Actually nothing to do with Bill. He's what you might call a
coincidence."

"He always has been."

"Right. But something's come through. What I've wanted. Some work. And I want you with me."

And then Alex begins to explain to her what they are to do.

Dear Edward looks better than he has for weeks. Celeste is so pleased to see that; it will make everything that she has in mind much, much easier, she thinks.

He has come for tea, a prolonged ceremony involving a great deal of Celeste's best and thinnest china, her silver, plus lemons and hot milk, hot water, sugar lumps and small sandwiches, tiny cakes. Not to mention the pot of tea.

Celeste attended to all that alone; the maid is off, and Sara is up in San Francisco on some errand. But Celeste enjoyed all the effort, although admitting a certain element of bribery to herself: she "wants something," as the unattractive phrase goes, of Edward.

And, as she carefully pours out for him, remembering his preferred strength, his hot milk first, his half lump, it occurs to Celeste that this is the first time of their having tea alone: no Charles, and now no Freddy. But today she finds this idea quite pleasing rather than otherwise, and she hopes that Edward does too.

As apparently he does. "Ah, dear Celeste!" he exclaims. "Such a real pleasure to be here."

"You look so well," she tells him, managing not to say "much better." And then, as casually as she can, "What do you hear from Freddy?"

And oh, Celeste thinks, if only Edward could see the change on his own face, at that question, that name! All his cells, corpuscles—whatever skin is made of—come alive, and his eyes, and his voice, as Edward says, "Quite a long recent letter, actually. He seems to be feeling considerably better about everything. Great distress—still—down there, terrible problems about housing, people in hospitals, food and shelter, all that, but he seems to have managed to make himself somehow useful, poor dear boy." And Edward smiles, expressing what he probably believes to be benevolence, avuncular concern.

The clear fact that Edward and Freddy are or have been lovers has never been specifically recognized in any way between Celeste and Edward. Which, Celeste now reflects, has been a little silly: this pretense that Freddy is simply a sort of younger roommate, a house-mate, a nice young pal. For her to say, as she now does, "It must have been hard on you, his going off" is unusual, between them.

For an instant Edward is startled; then, as quickly recovered, he tells her, "Actually it was terrible. Horrible. As though he'd died."

Very gently Celeste queries, now that they are into it, "Almost worse, in a way? His choice, I mean?"

"Quite." A strong, heartfelt syllable. And then, as though un-leashed, Edward goes on, "But there's no reason I can't go down to visit—well, maybe next spring. A long time ago I visited in Cuerna-vaca—a woman I used to know had a charming house down there, all those flowers. And you know, so close to Mexico City. And so I could, uh, could . . ." He seems to run down at that juncture. "I could take a house in Cuernavaca for a while," he unconvincingly finishes.

As Celeste thinks, But he can't. Edward can't take a house in Cuernavaca because he can't afford to. Although she has no reason for this thought, she knows nothing whatsoever about Edward's fi-nances, his economic life. She must have not so much read his mind as received a powerful feeling, communicated to her by Edward de-spite himself, despite his habitual discretion.

And this message forces Celeste to postpone the speech that she is preparing, even as she bites into a watercress sandwich. She is still working out what to say to Edward, and how to say it.

Instead she tells him, "What an especially pretty tie, dear Edward. You're always such a pleasure, visually."

"Dear Celeste, you've seen it a thousand times."

But he is obviously pleased, and somewhat bolstered by this view of himself as a visual treat. "I think there's going to be an amazing sunset" is what he says.

And there is. After a cold gray day of November fog, as thick as rain, as wet, now in late afternoon the skies have cleared, and the sun, revealed, majestically red, descends into the sea, among huge and gilded clouds.

"Edward, I have something I would really like to discuss with you," Celeste announces.

"Oh?" Edward's old blue eyes flicker toward her, sad kindly old Edward, so bald, his face so vulnerable that Celeste almost loses cour-age. She almost dares not risk offending him.

But she must say it. "Edward, I've been doing a lot of thinking, and it seems to me that you should move over here. I mean, move over for good. To live with me. Sell your house."

This speech has left her absolutely out of breath; breathlessly she stares across at Edward, as upright as she herself is, on his white linen chair, the duplicate of her white linen chair.

Whatever is written on his face is hard to read, as though he had willed instant opacity. But then he smiles, and Celeste thinks, Ah, thank God. At least I didn't offend him.

Edward says, "What an extremely interesting idea, dear Celeste. But you must agree, I would have to think about it?"

"Darling Edward, of course. I didn't mean tomorrow. But what I did think was, Sara will be off quite soon, and as you know her room has a private entrance. And so I thought— Well, you see, it might actually work out quite well."

In a gentle easy way Edward laughs at so much babble, from obviously nervous Celeste. "I am glad you have it all planned," he tells Celeste, with the mildest possible irony.

An ambiguous remark, as Celeste thinks of it over the next several weeks—weeks of hearing nothing whatsoever, in any form, from Edward.

25 This is a letter to a friend, which friend is never specified, that Dudley imagines writing, with a certain wry pleasure, but that she does not, finally, ever write.

"It's quite a lot like adolescence, very early adolescence, that is. As though Brooks were some boy at St. Paul's, say, and I was still at the Winsor School. We write a lot of notes, and make plans to see each other, a great many of which are aborted by forces beyond our control, as plans used to be by grown-ups, and teachers. Or is it we who abort them, we the grown-ups? God knows at this stage of our lives we can't blame teachers. And then when we do get together it's not quite as wonderful as it should be. We find that we don't have an awful lot to say. Mostly we neck a great deal, and sometimes we 'do it.'"

Or, it could be an article—also not to be written.

"Does old age, then, form a repetition of adolescence? The same bodily awkwardness, though for somewhat different reasons. The same unfocused but passionate energies."

This might in fact be the nucleus of something interesting, something that Dudley indeed might write: a sort of counter to the recently much-touted joys of geriatric sex, the revelations that the very old still screw like rabbits, or most of them, or some of them, sometimes.

So far, though, all this writing has existed only in Dudley's lively mind. She is thinking in this way partly in an effort to calm herself as she waits for Brooks, as she waits and feels both agitated and unfocused. She describes what will in a couple of hours be actuality, or so she believes.

The weather so far in these early days of December has been spectacular: clear, deep blue winter skies, a warmth that is indeed unseasonal. The sea is calm and flat and blue and shining. Dudley has been taking walks with Sara and also with Edward (both of whom, as she thinks of them now, have seemed unusually preoccupied). But the weather, or something, has been wonderfully beneficent for Dudley's arthritis; she has barely a pain or a creak.

When the phone rings—always such a terrible shrill sound when one is engaged in any sort of waiting—Dudley thinks, Brooks. Something's happened. And is surprised to find herself registering a certain relief.

However, it is instead Celeste, who asks, "Do you have a minute? There's something sort of odd I wanted to tell you."

Not saying, I'm waiting for Brooks and we're going out to lunch—in a welcoming way Dudley says, as she always does, "Of course. What's up?"

"It's about Edward," Celeste tells her. "I hadn't heard a thing from him for several weeks, and then in the village this morning I got the strangest news of him. Edward is *selling his house.*"

"No—" Dudley is more shocked, more deeply shaken, really, than she could have believed to be possible. Although she herself has recently, more and more often, thought of selling her own house, somehow the idea of Edward selling his is even worse, more deeply upsetting.

And she understands then, or begins to understand, the sense in which she has imagined or felt all their houses to be joined, her house (hers and Sam's); Celeste's; Polly's; Edward's. All joined as though by blood vessels, or veins, so that the loss of one house would be experienced as a wound by all the others.

"Of all places, in the grocery store," Celeste is continuing. "Where I heard it. That clerk, the one I can't stand because he always talks so much, he's so darn friendly. And Dudley, Chinese!"

"What?"

"The house. To a Chinese doctor. I just don't know—"

"My God." "Letting them in" is the phrase in Dudley's mind, as involuntarily she imagines hordes of Chinese ("horde": a racist word if she ever heard one, how *can* she?). Vietnamese, Cambodians. Boat people.

Severely she begins to castigate herself for this automatic and entirely unacceptable (to her) reaction. One Chinese doctor and his family are not hordes, she scolds herself. And even if it were, why do you—why do we deserve such expensive privacy as we have had here? Such precious privilege, when we can't even afford it anymore?

"Who knows what's in Edward's mind," Celeste continues, but in a tone of winding up their conversation.

"You don't know where he'll live?"

"I most certainly do not." Celeste sounds unaccountably severe. "For all I know he's chasing off to Mexico after Freddy."

"Such an odd way to find out anything" is Dudley's comment. "What on earth is going on with Edward?"

"I can't imagine. You tell me. Well, dear, I'll let you go." And Celeste with her customary briskness rings off.

Leaving Dudley deeply upset, and sad, and confused (and guilty: what a horrid streak of instant racism to uncover in one's self, never mind that the feeling quickly passed, yielding both to better impulses and to reason).

But it is as though their lives were almost over, she can't help thinking that.

Which of course they are.

Is this a sign that she should sell her own house? That is one of the first things that Dudley wonders. But should she, and if she did where would she go?

The phone rings again. Surely, this time, Brooks?

No. Celeste again, who very rapidly, in a queerly apologetic tone, tells Dudley, "I felt a sort of dishonesty, leaving out what I did about Edward just now. The truth is, the last time I saw him I suggested that he move in here with me. Well, it seemed a good idea at the moment. Actually I'd thought it through. But apparently he panicked. Sort of like Bill," she snorts.

"Oh, Celeste. Not necessarily."

"Well, that's how it looks to me."

"For one thing, Celeste, the grocery-store rumor could be quite wrong."

Hanging up, frowning to herself, Dudley tries to sort out reactions to this further bit of news. She is aware of vying voices within herself, all clamorous. And one of them, she is forced to admit, insists, Why not me? How come Celeste did not even suggest that I be the one to move over there? Not that in the least I'd ever want to, of course not, but it does seem odd.

And that is about all she has time to think before hurrying off to the diner, where she is to meet Brooks for lunch.

His eyes are indeed (more than most eyes) close together, which is slightly odd with his rather wide mouth; nevertheless Brooks (by most reasonable standards) is quite an attractive man. "Well preserved" is probably applicable. He is dapper and very trim, in his invariable blazers and snowy shirts, his heavy silk striped ties. Bankers' gray flannel slacks. Dudley takes all this in, and thinks of it, as in some not-far-distant recess of her mind there appears fat rumpled Sam, with his wide-apart, slant green eyes. He appears there and he stays, and stays.

As always, Brooks's manner with Dudley is ceremonious, rather for-mal. Seeing the two of them together, one would not guess at all the amorous wrestling, the frantic, messy kissing that habitually they do. In public, Brooks chastely kisses her on the left cheek, his lips barely grazing her skin.

"You'll have a glass of wine?" he asks as they settle into their booth.

"Yes. Thanks."

And David's replacement, an entirely bland, blond and plump young man, takes their order, without telling them his name.

"Well!" says Brooks. "This most beautiful fall weather. Though I suppose one should say winter, actually."

Smilingly Dudley assents. God knows it is easy enough to fall in with this sort of conversation. "I've had some wonderful walks," she tells him. "By the sea. It's really my favorite thing to do."

For some reason Brooks seems not to like this particular bit of non-information. "We're not terribly far from the sea in Ross," he tells her. "Though no one seems to think of driving over. Some people do go to Inverness, I believe, and you get some fine sea views from there." And then he says, "I do hope you'll come up to Ross quite soon."

About this visit of Dudley's to Ross, to his house, Brooks has so far been curiously coy: the plan is hinted at, remarks are made about how nice it would be to see her there, presumably among his friends—and then it is all more or less withdrawn. The projected visit simply does not happen.

This is mildly annoying to Dudley, although she does not (she is sure she does not) cherish a burning wish to visit Ross, a pleasant enough, quite pretty enclave of the mostly elderly and very rich, she believes. Brooks's people. But perversely she decides to force the issue, trivial as she believes it to be. "We must set a date for that," she tells Brooks, feigning silliness, a silly "social" manner. "Otherwise the whole idea will just get lost, what with bloody Christmas, New Year's, all that."

Brooks looks as nonplussed, as taken aback, as Dudley has ever seen him, sitting there stiffly against the back of his chair, his mouth slightly open but soundless, his eyes small and round and blank. So that at first Dudley imagines that her "bloody" was a serious mistake; no doubt Brooks has feelings about Christmas that are strong and positive—are even religious, possibly.

However, apparently not. His set expression dissolves, and he smiles, and his posture shifts. He leans forward, his hands outstretched to Dudley's hands on the table. He even laughs. "Bloody Christmas, that's good. Though I have to admit I've used considerably stronger language, myself. I personally can't stand Christmas. And my wife always—well, she liked it. I'm afraid I have to admit that more than once—"

He seems to find it hard to finish this admission, and so Dudley fills in, "You had fights? Maybe got drunk?"

"You guessed it, lady." But then Brooks seems to feel that he has said the wrong thing, or his tone has been wrong: you don't call a lady "lady," in his lexicon. And so he shifts key. "In spite of Christmas, then, I do want you to come up to Ross. As my guest. As my—" He pauses, with a look at Dudley that she later thinks she should have been able to read, but at the time was not, did not.

". . . as my fiancée," he brings out. "Would that suit you, dearest Dudley?"

So many reactions crowd upon Dudley at once, among them a desire to cry. She is so—so grateful, so—interested. In fact, it reads like a geriatric fairy story, a rescue fantasy. Also she is touched, and utterly confused. A few tears do come, and are understandably misinterpreted by Brooks.

"My poor darling," he murmurs.

No one, certainly, has ever used those words, that particular endearment to Dudley. Surely never wild bad Sam. And for a moment she yields to their charm. She sees herself as that, a poor darling. Even, a poor brave darling. Embarrassingly, more tears come. "Christ, this is awful," she mutters into her handkerchief.

Contrite Brooks is saying, "Oh, I didn't mean, I really didn't mean to be so abrupt. We don't even have to talk about it today. I can see you're upset. Here, drink your wine and we'll talk about the weather."

And that is what they proceed to do for the rest of their lunch. In a somewhat stilted way they discuss the weather: the possibilities of rain, the relative temperatures of Ross and San Sebastian, although this second topic is hurried through with some nervousness, its implications as to future plans passed over.

It has earlier been established between them that lunch is all they are to see of each other today. Brooks has a business appointment in San Jose, midafternoon. Now, however, now that he has in that somewhat curious way "proposed," Dudley finds herself wondering if that plan will change. Will Brooks call down to cancel the appointment, and stay with her? Will he go back to her house with her, for a spot of sex?

Well, of course he will, no one would "make an offer" and then just go off to a business date. (And, upsettingly, Dudley realizes that she does not look forward with much happiness to that bit of sex.)

But: precisely at two-thirty Brooks checks his watch, then summons the waiter for their bill and announces to Dudley, "My dear, if

I don't leave in a very few minutes I will be late, and we can't have that, you know." This last is somewhat self-mocking; he is laughing a little at himself, making fun of his own compulsive punctuality, in a mild and self-tolerant way. As Dudley thinks (as she may have been intended to think) how likable he is. How kind and gentle, really. Not at all as stuffy as he might seem.

During lunch, Dudley had wanted—but not wanted to ask for—another glass of wine: Brooks drinks so little, his effect on her life will be good—as Sam's was bad?

Once at home, however, and alone, she decides that a proposal of marriage is surely cause for celebration, and she pours herself a brimming glass of chardonnay, from the bottle that she and Sara did not quite finish off the week before.

She sips, and in a mildly excited, mildly pleasurable way she thinks about marrying Brooks. She sees the happy solution to most of her major problems—namely, loneliness and lack of money. If only it would also cure her arthritis, is an inadvertent, unruly additional thought.

She thinks of the large, as yet unseen house in Ross. I can invite Celeste and Sara, and Edward up for weekends, she thinks. And Polly (and Victor?).

It is at least half an hour before she understands that she can never marry Brooks. She doesn't even like him, really, and she doesn't have to marry a man she doesn't like. Things are bad with her, she admits that to herself. But not that bad. She is broke, but not desperate. And she is often lonely, but she still has good friends, quite nearby.

And as for arthritis, aspirin works as well as anything she has so far found.

Still, it is nice to have been asked, she thinks, regretting that there is no one she can tell.

26 The hotel in San Sebastián (both Polly and Victor think of this city as the *real* San Sebastian) in which they are staying is perched back from and above the winding concrete walk that borders the sea. And the beach. The building is massive, a crumbling, white-turreted turn-of-the-century birthday cake of a hotel. And their once-elegant large room, its creaking windows opened to the view, once housed royalty.

It also once before housed Polly, long ago in the forties, who then, as now, was alone and waiting—at that time for Charles Timberlake. This is one of those coincidences that seem bizarre, outlandish to anyone who is not very old. To the old such circumstances are an ordinary plague, a commonplace.

The shape of the land at that point on Spain's northern Atlantic coast, next to France, is just slightly indented, so that the hotel faces partly west, as well as north. And it is to the west, with its dying sunlight, that Polly now looks, less for aesthetic reasons than because Bilbao lies about ninety-nine kilometers west of San Sebastián, and that is where Victor is, presumably. Unless, as she hopes, he is already on his way back to her. The sunset was minor; the horizon is now shrouded with queerly bright, grayish clouds.

Their trip together so far has been very good. Polly, not given to superlatives, would not think "marvelous" or even simply "beautiful" appropriate, although both words have crossed her mind, repeatedly.

Madrid, then Barcelona: in both cities she experienced deep stirs of recognition, seeing once more remembered majesty. The *ramblas,* certain buildings. Along with a happy regreeting of timeless restaurants, eternal small dark cafés.

From Barcelona by way of Zaragoza they drove north, stopping the night before at Olite, at the great stone castle-posada there, with its hard beds, far too narrow for love. Past Olite, the dramatically beautiful (for scenery, Polly finds the word permissible), always changing shapes of land. Broad avenues becoming steep declivities, bordered by impossibly steeper pastures. And lovely globe-shaped pines, brilliant yellow-to-amber poplars. All to Polly piercingly familiar, and quite possibly to Victor also, though neither of them mentioned this sense. In fact, as they drove (Victor drove) they spoke very little, neither wanting (probably) to reveal so much emotion. Nostalgia, Polly has thought, is extremely dangerous at our age.

Below the balcony on which Polly at this moment stands is the concrete walk, and then the broad flat beach, and the calm gray dull-sheened sea. Both the walk and the beach are populated mostly by dogs; leashed dogs, of all sizes, make their promenade with their people in tow, the stately couples, or single very old women, in various states of vigor. On the sand, with what look to be considerably younger people, of all sexes and sizes, in garbs of all sorts, the free dogs run and race, and chase nonexistent waves, stray decrepit seabirds, who barely escape.

It is the same scene of almost forty years back. Same elderly and young. Same dogs. Flat water. Birds.

But as Polly turns she realizes that it is not after all the same room in which she once waited for Charles. The same hotel, yes, but since it was she who made the reservation, was this "coincidence" quite innocent? Had she truly forgotten the name, forgotten the "Hotel Londres e Inglaterra"? Not likely. However, this is not the same room; Polly firmly decides that it is not.

Waiting for Charles, back then, was a torment. If he does not come within the next minute I will die, all my nerves will explode, is how Polly might have described her feelings at that time. She even longed for that explosion, that death, for any end to such extreme, excruciating anxiety, amounting to illness.

I am extremely ill, she had begun to think, in that room—whatever room it was—at that time. And she had wondered, not quite for the first time: Is "ill" the same as "in love"? Is what I now experience "love"? If so, thought Polly—who was very young—if so, I will never go through this again.

Which is not to say that she succeeded at that moment in falling out of love with Charles. However, she began then to fight back, as it were, to work against what she had recognized as an illness.

That night, back then, as Polly watched a shadowed moon above the flat black sea, at a surge of dangerous words, a cry: If Charles doesn't come tonight, I will die. And in answer, another voice informed her that she would not die. She would simply go to sleep alone; she was not going to die over Charles.

Which she did: she went to bed and even managed a fairly good night's sleep. And the next day there was a telegram from Charles: "IMPOSSIBLY DELAYED SEE YOU PARIS ALL LOVE."

After that she continued to see Charles, when he could see her. She even continued to be in love, but with a certain difference. She had stepped back and taken a long look at what was going on between them, and she had seen something fairly trite, and unedifying: a romantic young woman and an attractive somewhat older man, both highly sexual beings, both eager to exploit the drama of their situation. She loved Charles still, for quite some time, and she literally "thrilled to his touch." But a new voice had spoken within her.

The same, sane second voice spoke to Polly again on her next great occasion for anxiety, the worst since Charles, and much worse than Charles since it was, so to speak, more real: her cancer fear. Or first the fear and then the actuality, the diagnosis: Yes, in your pancreas, yes, there is some malignancy. We'll do our best to get it all.

And at that time the voice spoke again, telling Polly: You won't die. Not of this. Not now.

How brave you are, is what all Polly's friends and even her doctors said at that time. Which is not at all how Polly saw it. What choice did I have? was her question. I either go on as I am, which is viewed as behaving well. Or I collapse into tears, moans, total helplessness. Which would obviously make me and everyone else feel much worse.

* * *

Still: Victor has gone to Bilbao to look up a cousin who is involved with Basque terrorists there—the ETA, Victor thinks. A dangerous, very Victorlike thing to do.

And if, as the phrase goes, something happens to Victor, Polly will be—well, very upset. Still.

The night before—or, rather, late afternoon, soon after their arrival, Polly and Victor went down to the bar of this hotel, in a sort of basement. An ordinary room, much plainer, less decorated than the character of the hotel itself would suggest. And the most striking aspect of this barroom was the fact that it was populated almost entirely by women.

Tired from the drive, and at the same time elated at having arrived, actually at last in the real San Sebastián, and absorbed in each other, Polly and Victor did not at first take note of this odd preponderance of women. But gradually they did, and certain other facts about the women themselves emerged.

They were clearly not there to meet men, these Spanish women. Polly explained that to Victor, who after a cursory look around had suggested that it could be the local body shop. "They aren't dressed that way," Polly told him. "Look. They're just in comfortable clothes. Mostly jeans. Young women get all gussied up when they go to pickup bars. *Still.*"

And Victor laughed at her, and agreed. "I've noticed that," he said. "In San Francisco, all these beautiful girls in fern bars."

"Beautiful and extremely uncomfortable, most of them" was Polly's observation.

"But are these women, as we now say, gay?" is Victor's question.

"I don't know, there's really no way to tell. But I don't think so. Anyway, not all of them."

What was clearest about these women, really, was how much they were enjoying their conversations. In groups of three or four or five, or two, seriously or with a lot of laughing, they all talked, and talked, and listened to each other. Interested. Involved. Having a very good time.

"Such a change," Polly remarked to Victor as they sipped at the last of their drinks, getting hungry for dinner. "Years ago, seeing women in a restaurant or anywhere by themselves, almost automatically you'd feel sorry for them. And now, now you really don't."

"About these particular women you are surely right," agreed Victor. "Not even a bad macho Spaniard such as I could look upon them and pronounce that what they need is some men."

Polly and Victor laughed companionably at this familiar small joke, the truth being that Victor is by no means a macho Spaniard. His regard for women, generally, is full of a sort of affectionate respect. Women have a much harder time of it than men do, has been Victor's observation. They survive. They are obviously stronger than men are.

In the hotel restaurant, to which next they repaired for dinner, Victor asked their waiter about the bar. "So many women there, I wondered. Is there a convention of some sort that goes on just now, in your San Sebastián?"

And the waiter, with a narrow, unhappy smile, informed them that there was no convention at the moment, his look implying certainly not a convention of women.

"Our bar is simply known in the town of San Sebastián and in all its vicinity as a place where unaccompanied women are welcome." A set speech, delivered with maximum disapproval.

Now, waiting for Victor, it occurs to Polly that she could simply go downstairs to that bar. Right now. She could even fall in with a group of women at the bar itself, even at her age and despite her scarves and her obvious nationality. They could talk about almost anything: feminism in Spain, Spain after Franco, the ETA, terrorism.

And though she makes no move to leave the room just now, she continues to imagine those conversations.

She even imagines telling them about her five cats, which, back in the other San Sebastian, Celeste is looking after.

The night before, after dinner, as they lay against each other in the regally broad and very lumpy bed, Polly thought about the extreme affections of the flesh, her skin against Victor's warm skin as Victor began to snore. (Victor, like all the men of Polly's experience, always fell asleep first.) Polly imagined their skins pulsing separately, their bodies entirely joined. Not violently, as in sex, but absolutely. Wedded flesh.

And it would be this, this simple—but not simple: infinitely complex—this warmth of the skin that she would badly miss if Victor should not come back.

I'm not ready for that lack. I can stand it, but please don't make me, Polly prays. To no one.

As, at that most unlikely moment, in the corridor she hears first the lively footsteps, unmistakable, and then the voice of Victor. His knock. "Let me quickly come in, I have much to tell you."

27 Midnight in Managua. In the pitch-black, crowded, fetid, deathly still air, Sara, between coarse damp sheets, can hardly breathe, much less think or even possibly sleep. The night is filled with traffic, fumes. And animals. Indistinguishable machines emit strange lights, at intervals. Something, someone shrieks: birds, or cats? Dogs? Humans?

Sara believes that she will be awake for the rest of her life.

Somewhere near her, Alex breathes, too hot to touch, his shoulder a ghost-white shrouded hump. In the corner of the room are shapes of furniture, what could be chairs, a table, a dresser. Or anything: guards with guns. Dead tigers.

Whatever we are doing here I don't want to do it, Sara thinks. I'll be killed. Tortured. Before this, always the worst thing in my mind has been the Mexican jail. This is worse. Much worse.

I don't want to go north. Or anywhere. I'm too afraid.

The most immediate smell in the room is that of sex, the once-familiar sea-bog scent, slightly stale. And at first, at this post-midnight, pre-dawn time of pure horrors, Sara thinks, Oh, disgusting. Dirty sheets. Until she remembers that it was she and Alex who made love here. Incredibly, after those hours of excruciating travel. In this awful hotel, this room, this bed. This murderous, murdered city. She and Alex, now perhaps three hours ago, maybe only two, fell upon each other like high-school kids. Tearing at clothes. Ravenous, devouring. Until they lay apart, more like disaster victims than fallen lovers.

And now the terrifying day lies ahead of them. In wait for them, a jungle of hours, impenetrable, alien. A sleeping assassin.

*　*　*

The day that appears now to have lasted forever began for Sara in San Sebastian, in total darkness, but with for her a curious lightness of the heart, as though she were only meeting Alex in Mexico City for vacationing. For some tropical touring, in this dark December weather. In innocent southern climes.

She had slept well, enough sleep despite the punishing early hour, after a happily casual dinner with Celeste. Both Edward and Dudley had been invited, but Dudley was off dining with her beau, as Celeste liked to put it, and Edward was nursing a very bad cold.

Was Celeste glad to get rid of her? That thought occurred to Sara, first to be dismissed, and then rephrased: she may simply feel that we have spent enough time together, is what Sara came up with. Celeste is eminently a realist, and our being together has served its purposes for us both. I am rested and much less frightened, ready now to make some other life. And Celeste is apparently recovered from whatever fears were plaguing her. And from Bill, the Bill Priest episode.

Celeste even has said, "If you see Bill in Nicaragua, say hello. Or on second thought, don't."

"It's a fairly large country," Sara told her.

"But it does seem awfully far for you to go." Celeste allowed herself a small frown. "You won't mind if I worry just a little?"

An early dinner, sound sleep. As she prepared and then gulped down some coffee, closed her suitcase and went outside to wait for the airport van, Sara was surprised to find herself feeling so well. So almost carefree, only anticipating a trip full of interest. With Alex. And possibly—well, probably, love. Sex. Surely it has been in both their minds, during all those long sexy late-night conversations?

The air trip became very beautiful just a few hours out of Los Angeles: dipping blue views of the sea, with strange green shapes of land, and then range after range of great bare wrinkled mountains.

She was going to an interesting place, was what Sara thought then. Traveling with an old friend, an old lover who is himself very— well, interesting. And we may do some good. "Think of us as investigators," Alex had put it to her. "I've managed to find out quite a lot here and in Washington. The point is, there's a lot of other aid getting through to the contras. Private funds that the CIA may or may not know about."

"But why me? Or even why us?"

"Because of what I already know. I can tell you more about it on the plane."

"Okay."

"And because—well, it's something for me to do. An important action. And something to do with you, if you want the whole truth. I want us to be together."

This line of reasoning carried Sara all the way to Mexico City. To Alex, whom she wants to be with.

They were going to have an adventure with a purpose, then. Together. They were going to the new Vietnam. To Nicaragua.

Alex, as planned, got to Mexico City before Sara did. Wrestling her way off the plane with her bulging backpack, then pushing through the surging crowd, Sara without much trouble spotted Alex. Taller and fairer than anyone in that enormous room, it was easy to see his light tangled hair.

Tired Alex, who came toward her, grasped her, and kissed her mouth.

"Oh—"

"Well—"

"Here!"

They breathed excited syllables at each other, they laughed, and turned in the direction of the main terminal.

How conspicuous we must be, Sara thought, aware of her own height, and her very North American style: short uncurled hair, unmade-up face, her dark shetland sweater, her jeans and running shoes. And taller, thinner, blond Alex, also in jeans, shetland sweater, old tweed jacket. Their sixties uniforms. Few in those gigantic, human-packed dirty spaces were dressed as they were. No others were as tall and confident, nor, quite possibly, as loony.

After some confusion it turns out that their plane does not leave for over two hours. They have all that dead time to kill. And with almost as much trouble as it took to find the proper airline windows, they locate a big bar-restaurant, and then a small corner table at which to settle, or try to, for that time.

The room is crammed with travelers, mostly Americans, with all their varieties of luggage piled near their feet: tennis rackets, diving equipment, or—alternately, black embroidered sombreros, confetti-covered donkeys. *Piñatas.* The spoils of travel.

They order beer and American sandwiches.

"We could just go off to some Mexican beach instead," Sara says. She is aware as she speaks that this is just what she longs to do, if only for a week or so. And then, if they had to, they could continue to Nicaragua. They could, among other things, get used to each other again. She realizes that Alex is making her slightly uneasy. Not speaking, he is giving off messages of such intensity, he is possessed of such an urgent sense of mission.

"Maybe afterwards" is his response to Sara's half-idle suggestion, although he does just barely smile.

And at that moment Sara understands an odd fact, which is that she herself has made no plans for what comes after this trip. I guess I'll go back to New York and look for work, she tells herself, as though she had known all along that this would be her course. She understands too that she has committed herself in some final way to Alex. To Alex in New York.

Out of nerves, at least partly, she begins to tell him about Celeste. "It's amazing in a way how fond of her I was—I mean, I am. I could so easily not be. All those years when Emma went on and on about how great Celeste was, I couldn't see it. She just made me impatient. All those clothes."

"Do I ever get to meet her?"

"Well, sure. Of course."

But when? And how remote San Sebastian already seems to Sara, and how curiously familiar the Mexico City airport. For a moment she has the fantasy that she and Alex and all the other stray, tired, mostly unhappy-looking humans in this room have been together forever. They will always be together. This is eternity.

The sandwiches are dry and terrible, tasteless. "At least the beer's good," Alex remarks between bites. And then, "Were we here before, do you think, on our way to Mexico that time?"

"I doubt it, don't you? We were such political puritans in those days. So correct. I don't think we would have killed time in a bar."

During those several hours of waiting, in Mexico City, they only talk to each other in that scattered way. They do not discuss or elaborate on their purpose, possibly because they are already so committed to it, simply by being there.

After eating, and prolonging a second beer, the sheer weight of all the people and heavy objects in that room begins to press upon them, and so much smoke, and noise. They pay up and leave, and they then begin in an idle way to wander through the huge, crowded, filthy-floored terminal, stopping occasionally to relieve the weight of their bags, Sara's torn backpack, Alex's somewhat newer model. Or to look at something, some especially garish display of jewelry, for example, or some gaudy paintings executed on black velvet.

Thus, it is in front of an open stall whose shelves hold lines of pink pottery dogs, all sizes, all grime and fly-speckled, quite monstrous, really, that Sara and Alex have their only conversation having to do with their mutual project.

"It's a small town north of Managua," Alex tells her as Sara notices for the first time how gray his hair has got, the blond now streaked with lines of white. "A village, really," says Alex. "Near a place called Sébaco. But the thing is, I've met Max Gómez in Washington, and we sort of got along." He grins. "I saw to it that we did. So now he'll almost have to talk to me. To us."

"My Spanish isn't so great," Sara reminds him.

"Gómez was CIA."

"Oh."

"We spend the night in Managua and then pick up the chopper as early as we can the next day. I've talked to the pilot."

"Good." However, why should the fact that Alex has talked to the pilot be reassuring? "I'm still not crazy about the idea of a helicopter," Sara tells him.

Alex smiles down at her. "It'll be okay. Trust me."

At that moment, despite gray hair and devious political intentions, Alex presents a face of such innocence, such innocent goodness, that Sara is deeply moved by him, and she understands then that this is why she is going along with him. At the same time, she realizes that she is very scared. We are not cut out for this. Neither one of us is.

* * *

Back at the airline counter, they find that their plane has been delayed again. It now leaves at four-ten, giving them another hour to get rid of, somehow.

Although they agree that they are both still a little hungry, going back to the bar where they were seems out of the question. And so after some walking about (inquiries are felt to be useless) they find another public room: darkened, with a bar and small tables, at one of which they sit down, depositing their luggage on yet another dirty floor.

No food is served in this place, and so they order margaritas. This seems both correct and celebratory—for what celebration they are not entirely sure. "These are so good!" they say to each other. And, "We almost never drink margaritas, delicious!"

They each have two, and by the time they finally board the plane they are both a little high.

"There's a lot to be said for flying drunk, I think," says Sara as the plane at last zooms upward, through the noxious gray cloud cover, the fuming waste of Mexico City. Bumpily upward to the pure clear sparkling blue sky.

"Oh, right!" says Alex.

Sara is at a window, Alex next to her on the aisle, and since the plane is half-empty they share great privacy. "Oh, this feels royal!" Sara says as they climb above fleecy gilt-edged cloud banks, as somewhere below them the sun begins its descent into the sea.

Alex pushes back the armrest between them, once the seat-belt sign goes off. Quite naturally they hold hands, and begin to kiss.

It is after an especially prolonged and passionate kiss that Alex, slightly breathless, says, "You'll come and live with me after this, Sara, won't you? Please. I don't want to be without you anymore."

"Yes, of course I will. I want to too."

They begin to kiss again, as Sara with a part of her mind understands that this is all along what she intended. I have always loved Alex, she thinks. We can really make a good life, probably. Maybe even have a child together? Would that be crazy for me, at forty? Lots of women do, these days. "Alex, I do love you truly" is what she says to him. As she wonders, But *is* it too late?

"Me too," he tells her.

Below them before too long are the rich green shadowed hills of jungle, endless growth. Mysterious depths of forest, hiding animals, villages. Impenetrable.

As they sail on through the sky.

"We should try to get some sleep," says Sara, too late: they are beginning their descent. Down to Nicaragua.

Sara thinks, Oh dear, I've drunk so much. I'll never get to sleep tonight.

28 In January rain arrives, a savage, continuous deluge, ravaging the coast and flooding rivers, and a terrible cold sets in, so that Celeste and Dudley and Edward are not able to take what they have spoken of as their New Year's walk (Dudley and Edward, recalling the year before, have initiated this phrase) until the middle of the month. And at that time, suddenly for a few days the weather shifts, the storms are all blown out to sea and they are treated to dazzling clear blue skies. Healing weather for three elderly people in need of balm, though this is a judgment that none of the three would dare to make, self-pity being for them a known and dangerous enemy. But they have been severely battered, these three, indeed as though by storms, by dreadful and most unanticipated blows.

Of them all, it is Celeste whose loss has been most severe. Sara was killed (along with Alex and the pilot) in a helicopter crash, the day after she arrived in Nicaragua, and for Celeste her death has been close to unbearable. For such a very young person to be uselessly killed seems particularly horrible: Sara at forty was on the threshold of her life. And Celeste deeply loved Sara. Sara would have been a friend for the rest of my life, is how she puts it to herself, by which she means, in part, that it should have been Sara who would live on to absorb the blow of Celeste's own death. Of the two of them, it was surely Celeste who was slated to go first.

Edward's anguish has been over Freddy, who a month ago (dear Lord, it was on a Christmas note) sent the following: "I do in fact have

AIDS, as I thought last spring that I did. Please do not come here. I love you, I will love you wherever I go, eternal. But I am not now any more your pretty boy, and I do not wish you to see me. Also you must go and take the test."

As though he too were mortally ill, Edward stayed in bed for four or five days (he later cannot remember this time clearly, this blur of pain), pretending to his friends that he was down with the flu. He could not read; his only activity was the occasional opening and heating of a can of soup. And writing to Freddy, the first of the letters that were to become his chief—and at times his only—occupation.

He knew that he should go and take the blood test for AIDS, but he knew too that it would be negative. After all, he and Freddy had not—not done anything of that nature (even to himself Edward has trouble with the words), not for years. Nor anyone else (he is somehow sure that the boy at Celeste's crazy yellow party didn't count).

And he is right. He takes the test: negative. Which, horribly, seems almost a further rejection by Freddy, in the sense that at worst Edward almost wishes that he were carrying the virus. Perhaps he instead of Freddy? After a time, though, he recognizes the sheer insanity of that line of thought: If that is how I feel, I might as well get on with suicide, he says to himself. Which he quite simply decides not to do.

The alternative that suggests itself, after a couple of weeks, is what his mother would have called "something constructive." He gets in touch with the Shanti Project in San Francisco, and learns that in many cases just visiting would be much appreciated. Somewhat hesitantly he tells them, "I could read aloud. I'm rather good at that, if anyone would like it."

And that is what Edward has begun to do. On Monday, Wednesday and Thursday afternoons he drives to certain addresses, mostly in his own area, in Gilroy and Cupertino, Salinas, Watsonville. He knocks at doors, he is shown to certain rooms, sickrooms, and there, sometimes in the presence of another person—a mother, a lover, once a wife—but more often alone, he talks to and often reads to the frail, dying man who is the inhabitant of that room. The stand-in for Freddy.

"I have never agreed with the sentiments of Mr. Eliot. That business about the last temptation being the greatest treason, doing the right deed for the wrong reason. Poor Thomas Becket, remember? Even if you do something mildly useful for a silly or crazy or even a quite crass reason, it's still something mildly useful that you've done." Edward said all that to Dudley, as a sort of postscript to telling her what he was doing. "Scratch an old New Englander and you find an obnoxious do-gooder," he added, as if in apology.

"Not me, I don't think," Dudley told him. "But, Edward, what you're doing is really good."

The rumor that Edward had sold his house to a Chinese doctor turned out to be inaccurate, the truth being that Edward, as realtor, sold a house in Aptos to such a person, a scholar-doctor whose avocation is translating medieval French poetry. In the course of property negotiations he and Edward became quite friendly. Edward also likes the doctor's wife, a painter, a very pretty young woman, in Edward's view. Dr. and Mrs. Thomas Tan.

Also, the house involved was expensive, thus Edward's commission was sizable. Making him for the moment relatively solvent.

As gently as he could, he told Celeste that he simply did not believe their living together would work out well. But maybe in a year or so they should consider it again.

He gathers that Celeste has had more or less the same conversations with Dudley, who, like himself, seems to prefer living alone. Still. For the moment.

Dudley herself has not undergone severe personal tragedy since the death of Sam—as though that were not enough, she has said to herself. But in quite a different way she also cared enormously for Sara, who was just becoming an important, even a necessary friend. And she cares about Freddy, whom she has known for so many years, whom she loves.

So awful that you can't use the word "gay" anymore, Dudley thinks; Freddy was—well, he *is* genuinely gay. Warmhearted. Fun. A generous, good person. And so attractive. And of course she also feels Edward's pain, as well as Celeste's.

She still sees Brooks Burgess, though less. Christmas came and went, and she did not go up to Ross, surely not as Brooks's fiancée, nor as his "friend." And Dudley has come to understand that Brooks is actually quite content with things as they are between the two of them. He does not really want to be married again, any more than Dudley does, really. He simply wants the appearance of wanting to be married. He likes the idea of himself as a suitor, laying siege. And so it is only necessary for Dudley to tell him from time to time, very gently, that she doesn't think she wants to marry again. She misses Sam.

She is still negotiating the trip to Ireland with her magazine, along with a couple of more practical, more immediate articles. And sometimes she considers asking Brooks to come along to Ireland; at other times she thinks she will ask Celeste. I really have more fun with Celeste, she thinks. And maybe Edward too? Well, why not?

Walking along, that January day, the three of them form a rather straggling line. Celeste, much the smallest of the three, walks fastest, in the lead. Then comes Dudley, whose arthritis has recently afflicted one knee, so that she limps a little. And then Edward, who has the least breath, who huffs and puffs along.

It is finally Edward who says, "Ladies! Shouldn't we have a short rest?"

Halted, Celeste breathes hard, unable for several moments to speak, and Edward too is literally out of breath.

Dudley, though, seems quite all right, in terms of breath, and so it is she who first speaks. "Edward, you remember this time last year? Oh, it seems so long ago, but it's gone like, like nothing."

"We went for a walk?" Edward frowns, not quite remembering.

"Of course we did, and we talked about—well, we were talking about you, dear Celeste."

Still breathing hard, Celeste smiles up at her friends. "I can quite imagine that you were. That was my crazy period. Bill."

"Well, you were giving that party. None of us had met him yet," admits Dudley.

Celeste's great brown-black eyes can be seen to fill. "Nor poor Sara."

Dudley's eyes tear too as she simply says, "No, she wasn't here yet."

But Celeste is programmatically opposed to even small moments of mourning: such a waste, such expenditure of spirit. Very briskly she tells them, "He's back in the CIA, Bill is. Or still there. Living in McLean."

Digesting the terribleness of these facts: Bill returned from Nicaragua safe and sound, and Sara dead and buried there (Celeste: "No, I am not going to have that poor child dug up and 're-interred.' I am not interested in bodies")—taking in as best they can that dreadful, preposterous unfairness, the three of them are quiet for a time, all breathing hard. However, they are all of an age to have witnessed worse instances of injustice. Life itself is very unfair, they all know that.

"But look, what an incredible day this is," exclaims Celeste, and she points toward the hazily golden west, where soon the sun will set. Now, in late afternoon, the blue air has begun to chill, though still perfectly clear. From where they stand, on their green hill, they can see all their houses.

And they can see much of the town. San Sebastian, their town. Only, it isn't our town at all, Dudley is thinking. We've quite consciously kept ourselves out of it, back from it (all of us except Polly, that is). Dudley finds this frightening, not in any specific way: she does not imagine that those particular townspeople will rise against them, three relatively innocuous elderly people—but rather in a general way that those long ignored, those dealt with most unfairly, if dealt with at all, must eventually challenge the ruling complacency. *Terrifying.* She imagines cataclysms.

"Well," Celeste announces. "My house for tea. It's time. But I have to stop off on the way to feed Polly's cats."

"I'll just stop by my house to check the mail," Edward tells them. "I'll be there in a jiff."

In his mailbox Edward finds exactly what he would have most hoped for, a card from Freddy—and Freddy on a trip to Oaxaca, where his sister lives. (Edward remembers this fact about Freddy instantly, as he remembers everything connected to Freddy.) The picture is from the Tamayo Museum, a green pottery jar of exceptional beauty, to Edward's greedy eyes. "This week I am visiting here," Freddy writes. "A place that I love. We have perfect weather. I wish that you could be here too. All love from Freddy."

Edward seizes on these words, which he will continue for days to ponder. Famished, he scrutinizes constructions, he searches out possible signals.

The first and most obvious meaning is that Freddy is feeling better, he was able to make this small trip—although Edward knows that the reprieve may be temporary. But: "I wish that you could be here too." Well, of course Edward could be there, in a flash. In less than a day. But is that what, literally, it means?

In any case, something to think about. Happily. By the time he gets to Celeste's, his face is out of control, Edward feels. He can't not smile.

Celeste and Dudley too have a card to show him. From Polly, in Barcelona. "My favorite city," Polly writes. "I'll hate to leave. But back Jan. 25. See you then. Love, Polly." On the other side is a picture of the Maritime Museum, a great vaulted interior of glass and stone, in the foreground the bare wooden ribs of a ship. And the picture has a caption, a motto: *Navegar es necesario. Vivir no es necesario.*

" 'It is not necessary to live.' How very Spanish, and how very like Polly, don't you think?" Edward, who is still smiling, asks them this.

They agree.

"The twenty-fifth is next week, though," Celeste exclaims, in some alarm.

"Well, isn't that all right? You sound as if Polly isn't supposed to come home so soon," Dudley gently chides.

"No, of course that's not what I mean. I just meant, what do we do now? About, uh, them?"

"You mean, the fact that they are together?" Dudley teases. "Polly and, uh, Victor?"

"I suppose I do mean that. But you must admit, it is odd? We haven't exactly known him before."

"Do you mean, do we have a dinner for them?" asks Edward. And he adds, "Why not?"

"I think so too," agrees Dudley. "It's what we always do, isn't it? Someone coming back from a trip?"

"Well, fine then. But who else will we have?" asks Celeste. And then she answers herself, "Maybe, just ourselves? In fact, I think that will be perfect. A little celebration."

A NOTE ON THE TYPE

The text of this book was set in a digitized version of Electra, a typeface designed by W. A. Dwiggins for the Mergenthaler Linotype company and first made available in 1935. Electra cannot be classified as either "modern" or "old-style." It is not based on any historical model, and hence does not echo any particular period or style of type design. It avoids the extreme contrast between thick and thin elements that marks most modern faces, and is without eccentricities that interfere with reading. In general, Electra is a simple, readable typeface that attempts to give a feeling of fluidity, power, and speed.

Composed by Creative Graphics, Inc.,
Allentown, Pennsylvania

Printed and bound by The Haddon Craftsmen, Inc.,
Scranton, Pennsylvania

Typography and binding design by
Dorothy Schmiderer Baker